W9-CBD-694

CAN'T LOOK AWAY

Also by Carola Lovering

Tell Me Lies

Too Good to Be True

CAN'T LOOK AWAY

*

Carola Lovering

ST. MARTIN'S PRESS
New York

First published in the United States by St. Martin's Press, an imprint of St. Martin's Publishing Group

CAN'T LOOK AWAY. Copyright © 2022 by Carola Lovering. All rights reserved. Printed in the United States of America. For information, address St. Martin's Publishing Group, 120 Broadway, New York, NY 10271.

www.stmartins.com

Designed by Donna Sinisgalli Noetzel

Library of Congress Cataloging-in-Publication Data

Names: Lovering, Carola, author.
Title: Can't look away / Carola Lovering.
Description: First Edition. | New York : St. Martin's Press, 2022.
Identifiers: LCCN 2022003368 | ISBN 9781250271396 (hardcover) |
    ISBN 9781250271402 (ebook)
Classification: LCC PS3612.O855 C36 2022 |
    DDC 892.8—dc23/eng/20220131
LC record available at https://lccn.loc.gov/2022003368

Our books may be purchased in bulk for promotional, educational, or business use. Please contact your local bookseller or the Macmillan Corporate and Premium Sales Department at 1-800-221-7945, extension 5442, or by email at MacmillanSpecialMarkets@macmillan.com.

First Edition: 2022

10 9 8 7 6 5 4 3 2 1

For Rob and James Crane, loves of my life

I'll never know and neither will you of the life you don't choose. We'll only know that whatever that sister life was, it was important and beautiful and not ours. It was the ghost ship that didn't carry us. There's nothing to do but salute it from the shore.

—CHERYL STRAYED

CAN'T LOOK AWAY

Chapter One

Molly

2013

Molly never would have gone to the concert in East Williamsburg if Nina hadn't dragged her there.

It wasn't actually a *concert*—not really—but one of those bars with a grungy back room where desperately-trying-to-make-it-bands played for free on the weekends.

Nina offered to buy Molly's drinks if she came with, because Cash was going to be there, and Nina was dying to sleep with Cash for the third time. And if Molly was being honest with herself—which she almost always was—she knew she had nothing better to do, and that if she didn't join Nina she'd sit at home in sweatpants and reheat Thursday's pad Thai, twisting her fork into the limp noodles with the festering knowledge that, on this perfectly good and possibility-filled Saturday night—the first one of the new year—she should be somewhere else.

At the bar, Nina ordered two tequila sodas and pretended not to notice Cash at the other end, drinking Bud Heavies with his cohorts, their laughs open-mouthed and dramatized and, in Molly's opinion, obnoxious.

"He texted, 'Come hang tonight,'" Nina whispered anxiously, glancing toward Cash's corner of the room. "And he texted me the address, but is it dumb that I showed, Moll? Is it desperate? Do I look okay?"

Nina's chocolate hair fell in loose waves around her bare, bronzed-even-in-January shoulders—Molly would be forever jealous of her friend's perfect Colombian skin. Dewy makeup smudged the apples of her cheekbones, and mascara lengthened her already-thick lashes. In a crimson silk top and dark jeans, Nina—as always—looked like a knockout.

"You look amazing," Molly answered, ignoring her best friend's first two questions.

The bar was filling up and getting louder, a rising drone of voices saturating the space and clouding Molly's eardrums. She thought of the empty two-bedroom on Withers Street that she shared with Liz— they'd been roommates since sophomore year of college—and the pad Thai chilling in the fridge, and the twenty-five hundred words she hadn't yet written that were due on Tuesday. Molly wasn't into going out these days, not the way Nina, Liz, and Everly were. They'd all met at their small liberal arts college in Vermont, after which they'd migrated to New York together, the party vibe still very much their calling card.

Tonight, Liz and Everly were at some girl's birthday thing in SoHo, and Molly hated to leave Nina without a wing woman when she knew her friend really, *really* liked Cash, even though Cash was, in her opinion, immature and uninteresting and not remotely good enough for Nina. And besides, Molly possessed the self-awareness to admit that she *had* been in a bit of a rut, and she needed to make herself go out more, if only because "out" was the place where life happened, where inspiration and possibility had the opportunity to strike.

Nina ordered another round and closed her tab, and the bartender watched her as she signed her bill—the way so many men shamelessly stared at Nina—and winked.

Nina handed Molly the full tumbler of ice and tequila—no soda this time, just lime—and Molly felt the first sip of the second drink spread through her limbs, dense and pleasant, anchoring her more decisively into the night.

"I always forget how much I like tequila." One side of Molly's mouth curled effortlessly as she sank back onto the barstool.

Nina tilted her chin forward and smiled. "You're drunk off *one* drink?"

"I'm not drunk." Molly twisted a lock of her wheat-blond hair, drawing in a breath. "I'm sorry I've been lame lately. I've been so in my head. With the writing stuff. I'm glad you dragged me out."

"I'm glad I dragged you out so you could witness Cash ignoring me at the dirtiest bar in Bed-Stuy." Nina drummed her freshly manicured nails—a shiny eggplant color—against the bar top.

"We're not in Bed-Stuy, Neens."

"This far from the river, we might as well be."

Molly rolled her eyes as—suddenly—Cash appeared behind Nina. He slung one of his long, brawny arms around her delicate neck.

"Hey, girls." Cash smiled widely. Nina beamed, her eyes blooming with delight as if she were five years old and meeting Mickey Mouse at Disney World.

"You remember Molly? You met at Everly's apartment a couple of weeks ago."

"I think so?" Cash's thick eyebrows knitted together. "You're the writer?"

The question caught Molly off guard. "No, I'm just—I'm getting my MFA."

"In creative writing," Nina chimed. She knocked back the rest of her tequila.

Cash pursed his lips, confused.

"I'm just not sure what I want to do with my degree," Molly added quickly. "Maybe teach."

"This girl is my smartest friend," Nina crowed drunkenly, wrapping her arms around Molly's shoulders.

"What do you do again?" Molly asked Cash.

He opened his mouth to speak, just as the bar lights dimmed. Someone cleared their throat into the microphone.

"Ladies and gentlemen," a male voice bellowed theatrically from the stage. "It is my *absolute* honor to welcome my dear friends—friends who are more like brothers—the extraordinarily talented Danner Lane to the stage!"

The crowd cheered, the bar quickly emptying as dozens of twenty- and thirtysomething Brooklynites pushed their way toward the back room, toward the stage.

"There are a lot of people here," Nina observed.

Cash pushed his thick brown hair back from his forehead. "Have you heard Danner Lane's stuff? Jeb, one of the owners here, the guy who just announced them, is old friends with the Lane brothers. But they're honestly sick—they're on iTunes *and* Spotify now."

Three guys—all of whom appeared to be in their midtwenties— stepped onto the stage. One sank down behind a massive drum set, and the other two held guitars, positioning themselves in front of the drums.

"Let's move closer," Cash suggested. His friends were still at the bar, but he led the way toward the front, worming through the tightly packed crowd, Molly and an enchanted Nina in tow.

"They're brothers?" Molly asked loudly, glancing up at Cash.

"Those two are brothers." Cash stabbed his middle and index fingers in the direction of the stage. "Drums and bass guitar. The other one is Jake Danner. He's guitar and vocals. They all grew up together."

The Lane brothers looked similar, with wispy auburn hair and pale complexions, their frames lanky. But Jake was the one Molly couldn't take her eyes off of.

He was the color of honey—honey skin, golden curls that fell in front of his eyes as his fingers expertly plucked the strings of his guitar. When he looked up, Molly saw that his eyes were pale blue, and clipped right to hers, and she suddenly felt glad to be twenty-three and single, living in the greatest city in the world. Her mind—which had felt a bit dark and crowded lately—cleared.

Jake smiled broadly, and Molly felt a drop-kick in her gut. Keeping his eyes fixed to hers, he spoke into the microphone.

"Hey, East Williamsburg." His voice was clear and perfect in pitch, edged with the slightest twinge of a Southern drawl. "It's Saturday night, and we're Danner Lane, and we're gonna play some music."

When the same thing would happen years later at Madison Square Garden—when Jake would find and hold Molly's gaze in the crowd, this time of thousands instead of seventy-five—it would be habitual for them. Danner Lane would be opening for Arcade Fire, and they would be rising in the ranks—soaring, making it—but Jake would still need Molly, his Molly, the one who tethered him to the ground.

In East Williamsburg, he opened his mouth to sing, the melody of a famous Elton John song filling the room, followed by the most exquisite voice Molly had ever heard.

And now I know
Spanish Harlem are not just pretty words to say

Her life, Molly sensed in some deep, subconscious crevice of her heart, as Jake's eyes pierced hers, would never be the same.

Chapter Two

Molly

Meredith Duffy shoves a glass of champagne into Molly's right hand, so forcefully that the golden liquid sloshes over the rim.

". . . and Whitney lets Liam *sleep* in the DockATot," Meredith is saying, her voice hushed. "It's *so* irresponsible. I don't know what business she has bringing two more kids into the world."

Molly stares into her champagne flute, watching tiny bubbles race to the surface.

"I mean, you would never have let Stella sleep in a lounger, would you?" Meredith presses. She leans in toward Molly, so close that Molly can see the shrunken pores on Meredith's unblemished nose.

"I didn't have a DockATot with Stella," Molly answers truthfully. "They weren't really a thing back then."

Meredith nods carefully, absorbing this, and Molly is, as usual, tired of these conversations. Like so many young mothers in Flynn Cove, Meredith seems to take great pleasure in backhandedly lambasting her friends' parenting styles. The gossip makes her voice speed up and her pupils dilate with glee, like a narcotic. Molly doesn't want to know what Meredith says about her behind her back, but she's sure it's something suitably passive-aggressive.

"Well, cheers to raising our babies right." Meredith gives a thin laugh, then clinks her glass against Molly's and tips the champagne back into her throat.

Molly sighs, counting down the minutes until she can leave. She gazes toward the living room, visible from the kitchen through the open floor plan, where Whitney Cooper has plopped herself onto an upholstered slipper chair in front of a pile of presents. Her belly is swollen and enormous underneath a pale-yellow empire waist dress—twins due next month—and despite this being her second baby shower, there is no shortage of gifts at her feet.

"Are you not drinking?" Meredith's question is infused with mild panic as she studies Molly's untouched champagne.

"Can't." Molly shakes her head, forces a smile. "I teach on Sunday afternoons."

"Oh, that's *right*." Meredith exhales. "I've got to get to your class one of these days. Well, I'll give yours to Betsy, then. God knows that woman is always ready for a top-off." She plucks the flute from Molly's fingers and is already halfway across the room, heading in the direction of a Pucci-clad Betsy Worthington, before Molly can respond.

With Meredith gone, Molly feels her shoulders relax. She counts her lucky stars that she really does teach Vinyasa flow at three, and she wasn't forced to admit to Meredith that the real reason she's not drinking is that she did her embryo transfer on Thursday and is under strict orders from Dr. Ricci to avoid alcohol as if she were pregnant.

And maybe she is pregnant, Molly lets herself imagine, in the middle of Meredith Duffy's newly renovated kitchen, the chatter of female voices around her fading as the dream blooms in her mind. A baby brother or sister for Stella, finally. Molly pictures her daughter's blond head bent over a bassinet, and a warmth spreads through her lower abdomen. Eight more days and she'll know for sure.

The sound of a fork scratching across a plate pulls Molly out of her head, and she swallows the hope down like it's something sharp. She stares across the room at Whitney's giant belly and reminds herself that she probably isn't pregnant, that she and Hunter have been through this too many times already, that they've set themselves up for one too many disappointments, all the while draining Stella's college fund to try to give her a sibling. She's lucky to just have Stella, Molly tells herself for the thousandth time. She has one healthy, beautiful child, and that's something that millions of women struggling with infertility would kill for.

Molly takes a pink macaron from a white tray and drifts into the living room to watch Whitney open her presents. She looks at her watch, which reads five of two. *Twenty more minutes,* she tells herself, biting into the gooey cookie.

She makes small talk with Edie Kirkpatrick, who tells Molly much more than she cares to know about the various golf tournaments her husband is competing in across the East Coast this summer.

At two fifteen, Molly thanks Meredith for hosting such a lovely after-noon, then sneaks out the back door. It's a ten-minute drive to the studio where Molly teaches, and technically, she doesn't have to be there until fifteen minutes before class starts, but the thought of spending another second with all those women is more than Molly can bear.

She feels low as she drives across town, missing Nina and Everly so much that a lump forms in the back of her throat.

She thinks about what Hunter would say—what Hunter *will* say, when she tells him the shower was a drag. *You don't have to go to those things, Moll. Why bother if they make you so unhappy?*

Because I actually do like Whitney, Molly will say. *Whitney is one of the ones I could actually see myself being close with, and I wanted to show my support.*

And then there's the piece of it she won't tell Hunter: that Meredith and Betsy and Edie and that whole group of women are the social scene in Flynn Cove and that the occasional bits of connection she feels when she's with them are better than nothing. It's better to have some form of female companionship in her day-to-day life—unfulfilling as it may be—than none at all. Right?

In the parking lot of Yoga Tree, Molly takes out her phone and crafts a text to Whitney.

Whit-so sorry I didn't say goodbye, had to rush out early to teach. That was a beautiful shower and you are just glowing! Let me know if you're up for a walk sometime in the next couple weeks, assuming the babes don't come early! Xo

Molly rereads the text three times, chewing her bottom lip and won-dering if her tone is overeager, or if it's awkward or assumptive to call her friend "Whit." *God,* she thinks. *I didn't used to be so insecure. I didn't used to be so fucking neurotic.*

Molly hits Send before she can agonize over it a second longer. She's about to put her phone away when she sees a notification for a new voicemail, a call she must've missed during the baby shower. She doesn't recognize the number, but it's a 917 area code. New York. She hits Play.

Molly, hi, it's Bella. Sorry to bother you on the weekend. I'm calling because . . . well, I sent you an email, did you see it? I know it's

*been forever—legitimately years—but the other day I walked by
that place on Bleecker, the little French bistro where we met for
lunch when I first signed you. Remember it was the middle of a
snowstorm, and we drank all that red wine? Well, I thought of that,
and it made me smile. Anyway, I'd really love to catch up so, just
call me? When you can? We should talk.*

Molly blinks, chews her bottom lip. She pictures Bella in one of her
crisp, starchy button-downs, horn-rimmed glasses, raven hair piled on
top of her head. She did get Bella's email, two weeks ago, and never responded. Molly feels a twinge of guilt, but not enough to do anything
about it. Certainly not enough to actually consider calling her back. She
chucks her phone into her bag, tries to forget the voicemail and the person who left it. Molly can't think of Bella without thinking of Jake, and
she can't handle that, especially not when she has a class to teach.

There are only six students signed up for Vinyasa flow, which isn't too
surprising. Sundays at Yoga Tree are never particularly busy, especially
when the weather is nice like today.

Three of the students are Molly's regulars, two are drop-ins who look
familiar, and the sixth is a woman she doesn't recognize. The woman is
slender and tanned, lying on her mat in black Lululemons and an olive-
green sports bra. She looks to be in her late twenties or maybe early
thirties, Molly thinks, observing her silver belly button ring, which rises
and falls on the woman's flat stomach as she breathes. Something about
her reminds Molly of Nina—her coloring, maybe, her slightly edgy style.
Molly doesn't love teaching yoga—certainly not the way she used to,
and she often complains to Hunter about how tired it makes her—but
today, suddenly, she is glad to be there. She's grateful for the thing that
dragged her away from Meredith Duffy's house and for the warm, cozy
skylit studio with its patchouli scent and attentive, willing practitioners.

The new woman has risen to a seated position, watching Molly, her
spine perfectly stacked and straight. Molly looks at her midsection again
and thinks that her own stomach used to look like that, before she had a
baby. It's never quite gotten back to what it was, even though Stella is five
now. But Molly doesn't feel bitter or judgmental, and the woman grins at
her with full, wide lips.

Molly begins the practice without much effort. Teaching comes easily
to her at this point; the sequence she has chosen to teach that day—

hamstrings and hips—spills out from memory. She's always very present when she teaches yoga—she has to be; she can't miss a beat—and she doesn't let her mind turn to other thoughts until her students are lying like corpses in Savasana. Sometimes, at the end of class, she presses each student's shoulders and pulls their necks up to straighten their spines, massaging their temples with essential oils. But today she's not in the mood to touch anyone; she sits and breathes on her own before cuing them out of Savasana to end the practice.

"Namaste," she says calmly. During her yoga teacher training in Brooklyn years earlier, Molly learned the meaning of *namaste* in Sanskrit: *I bow to the depth of your soul.* She remembers being so affected by this when she was a twenty-three-year-old teacher in training, convinced it was the most honorable utterance in existence. She'd even been close to getting the Sanskrit translation tattooed below her collarbone—thank *God* Nina had talked her out of that one. Now, the word feels meaningless most of the time she hears herself say it. This thought makes her feel cynical and old.

After class, Molly perches herself behind the front desk as her students gather their belongings and leave the studio. She chats briefly with her regulars—Meg's hips have been tight and she loved the sequence; David, a friend of Hunter's, asks how Stella is doing and what their plans are for Memorial Day weekend. The woman with the belly button ring lingers, carefully zipping her yoga mat back into its case, then checking her phone.

"That was a really great class," she says suddenly, catching Molly off guard. She approaches the desk, and Molly sees up close how beautiful she is, though she doesn't actually look like Nina. The apples of her cheeks are flushed from the workout, and her eyes are a striking green. She pulls her dark, glossy hair into a ponytail and smiles, revealing straight white teeth. Molly notices the fine lines on her forehead and around her eye creases, and decides she must be at least thirty.

There are things she doesn't love about teaching, but she loves this—being in the teacher's seat, the confidence it brings her, the confidence that reminds her of her old self. "I'm Molly. You have a great practice."

"Thanks for class, Molly." The woman slings her yoga bag over one shoulder, and Molly notices the cartilage piercing in her left ear, the same tiny, thin gold hoop that Molly used to sport herself. She removed it on her wedding day—it didn't feel very bridal—and never put it back in.

The earring isn't glaring, but it's still the kind of mildly edgy accessory that would provoke hours of gossip between women like Meredith Duffy and Edie Kirkpatrick.

"I'll definitely be back." She adds, "My husband and I are newlyweds who just moved here. I've been looking for a good studio."

Molly smiles warmly. "I'd love to have you again."

The woman's eyes linger on Molly's in a way that feels slightly unnerving, but mostly intriguing. "Have a nice rest of your weekend," she says brightly, and Molly watches her walk out the door, hoping, genuinely, that she does come back.

Chapter Three

Sabrina

You are even more radiant in person than you are in pictures. I know, I know: I shouldn't be surprised.

I spent much of class watching your ankle bones from ground level, their delicate structure, and the way your heels form a near perfect ninety-degree angle with the soles of your feet.

I know what you're thinking, and no, I don't have a foot fetish, not even close. What I do have is a preoccupation with you. It isn't sexual; I suppose you could call it emotional, if you're the kind of person who needs everything *explained*, but that wouldn't be quite right, either.

So where were we? At the feet. Let's keep working our way up, then.

Your calves are slender—you have the kind of naturally skinny legs that stay that way even when you put on weight. I've seen you pregnant—you don't know that, of course, but we'll get to it later—and even then, your legs were stems. Your belly has seen better days; even underneath your loose-fitting top, I can see the belt of flab that forms when you fold forward. But your body is good, there's no doubt about that, especially given the fact that you had a baby. Five years ago now, but still. My mother held on to an extra fifteen pounds after she had me. Never lost it. I give you credit.

Moving up. Your rib cage is slight, and your breasts are barely there; because of this, you are the kind of woman who looks good in clothes. This makes me jealous. I'm a 34C, and there are so many shirts and dresses I can't get away with. Your shoulders and arms are toned but not excessively, and your wrists are twiggy. Your fingers are long. You're tall, Molly. You're taller than I thought you'd be.

You have a graceful, sloping neck and a heart-shaped face. Pale, clear skin—I'd love to know your skin-care routine—and wide hazel eyes. And your hair—your hair is your pièce de résistance, it has to be. Big, messy waves of golden blond, and I bet you haven't colored it a day in your life. That beautiful heap twirled on the crown of your head is complex and layered and untamed—like you, maybe. I'm the opposite. My own hair is dark and sleek and dries pin straight in the sun. I am one-dimensional; I know what I want and I know how to get it. And I won't stop until I do.

I meant what I said, Molly; you taught a great class. I can tell teaching yoga isn't your passion, but you're talented. Or maybe you're just well versed; maybe you've spent years spitting out the same sequences using the same inflection in your voice during the appropriate moments. Maybe it's a recording inside your head and all you have to do is press Play.

Either way, your class was a solid one, and like I said, I will be back. But I'll see you again before then. We've got a lot of ground to cover, you and I.

Chapter Four

Molly

2013

On Monday, two days after her night out with Nina in East Williamsburg, Molly's phone rang as she walked home from Angelina's, the café on Berry Street where she worked as a barista four shifts a week. An unfamiliar number filled the screen. Molly hesitated before answering, securing her headphones into her ears the way she always did when she walked and talked.

"Hello?"

"Hi, is this Molly Diamond?" The voice was male—low and confident, but friendly.

"Yes. Who's this?"

"This is Jake Danner. You were at my show on Saturday night. At the Broken Mule."

Molly's stomach pitched. The guy with the honey curls and light blue eyes? She remembered him in vivid detail, and she now realized why his voice—the one that brought tears to her eyes during a cover of "Mona Lisas and Mad Hatters"—sounded familiar.

"Anyway, sorry to be calling you out of the blue like this," Jake continued. "I asked my friend Jeb—the owner of the bar—if he knew you, and he doesn't, but he got your number from his buddy—err—Calvin? The guy your friend was with."

"Cash?" Molly cracked a smile, then wondered how Cash would've known her number. Had *Nina* given it to him? And if so, why hadn't Nina mentioned any of this to Molly?

"Cash! That's it." Jake paused. "Look, I don't normally track down girls I see in the crowd at my shows. I've never done this before, actually, I just . . . I saw you on Saturday and . . . would you by chance like to have dinner with me this week?"

Molly crossed Havemeyer Street, a gust of cold wind whipping her cheek. She hadn't been on a date since November—her New Year's resolution was to spend more time focusing on writing and less time dating, since the men she picked either turned out to be shitty, or didn't interest her at all. Besides, she didn't believe Jake "had never done this before." He was hot—classically, incontestably hot—and the lead singer of what appeared to be a very up-and-coming band. He probably slept with a different girl every weekend.

"This week is . . ." Molly started, her voice trailing. She couldn't stop seeing Jake's face, the way he seemed to light up as he stepped close to the microphone, the way his eyes locked hers as he gripped his guitar, and she knew, with clear conviction, that she couldn't turn him down. She couldn't help thinking of Liz, either. If Liz knew she was being asked out by a hot guitarist and was considering saying no, she'd bang Molly over the head with a cast-iron pan.

"Molly?" Jake's voice—that hint of a Southern drawl—sent a hot shiver down her spine. It was a bad idea, it had to be, but she felt herself nodding into the phone.

"I have a big assignment due for school tomorrow, but I'm free later in the week."

"Great. How's Thursday? And I didn't realize you were in school."

"I'm getting my MFA at NYU."

"That's amazing. I can't wait to hear more about it. Thursday works?"

"Yeah." Molly couldn't help the smile that spread across her face, ducking her head to block the wind. She pulled her hat down lower over her ears.

"Cool. What neighborhood are you in? I'll make a reservation."

"I'm in Williamsburg, but away from the water, toward East Williamsburg."

"Across the BQE?"

"Exactly."

"I'm not far. Roebling and North Tenth. We're neighbors." There was a flirtatious confidence to Jake's tone, and she could picture him grinning on the other end of the call. "See you Thursday, Molly. Good luck with your homework."

Molly knew Jake could've been teasing her, but she had the feeling he was being genuine. After they hung up, she immediately called Nina.

"Did you give Cash my number to give to Jake Danner?" Molly exhaled into the phone the second Nina answered. "Because he just called me and asked me out."

"Oh! Yes!" Nina sounded surprised at having answered the question. "Hang on one second."

Molly heard the sound of the TV in the background, then a door slam shut.

"Sorry, Moll. Oh my *god.* I'm at Cash's."

"Right now?"

"*Yes.* I haven't left since Saturday! That was the best night *ever.*" Nina's voice lowered to a whisper. "And I was here all day yesterday, and then Cash convinced me to play hooky with him today."

"Wow, Neens, that's grea—"

"Anyway, sorry I didn't text you, I just haven't had a second alone . . . but *yes,* I guess Jake texted Jeb, who texted Cash, asking for your number for Jake. Wait, he *called* you? That's so romantic."

"Is it?"

"Absolutely. I can't believe he asked you out. I mean, I can believe it, but still. Danner Lane is, like, hot shit. Cash said they have a record deal. You have to go on the date. You're gonna go, right?"

"Well, I wasn't sure, but—"

"*Molly.*"

"*Relax,* Nina. I said yes. We're going out Thursday."

"Yes! That's so great. If you guys hit it off, then maybe we can double date. Oh my *god,* I need to chill. Cash is probably gonna toss me to the curb, like, tomorrow."

"No, he won't, Nina. You have to have more confidence."

"And *you* have to stop believing that just because you spark with a guy it means he's dangerous."

Molly said nothing. She thought of Darby, of Cameron. She knew Nina wasn't wrong.

"I'd better go." Nina sighed. "I'm literally closed off in Cash's bathroom, he probably thinks I'm pooping or something. I'll call you tomorrow, okay?"

"Okay." Molly laughed, hooking a right onto Withers Street, her apartment finally in sight. "You'd better go *cash* in. Love you, Neens."

"Good one, Moll. Love you, too."

Upstairs in their third-floor apartment, Liz was cooking a Thai curry that made the whole kitchen smell like coconut and turmeric.

"Yum." Molly let her backpack slide off one shoulder and onto the floor. She peered over Liz's shoulder into the pot simmering on the stove.

"It'll be ready in five," Liz said as she stirred. She wore black leggings and a trendy mesh workout top—a recent purchase from Lululemon, Molly guessed, based on the giant shopping bag she'd spotted next to Liz's bed. Her short brown hair was pulled back, her face flushed from forty minutes on the treadmill. Liz worked as an executive assistant at a hedge fund; she had to be at the office at the crack of dawn but never stayed a minute after five, and had usually already gone to the gym and started dinner by the time Molly got home from her shift at Angelina's.

Liz made good money at the hedge fund—over six figures when you factored in her yearly bonus—but it wasn't enough to fund her outrageously expensive taste. Luckily, Liz's father had made a killing in private equity, and she still had access to his Amex. It was technically for "emergencies," but none of her purchases at Intermix, Saks, or Barneys were ever questioned.

Some rich girls annoyed Molly, but not Liz. Perhaps because she was so generous of spirit, letting Molly borrow from her endless supply of designer clothes, jewelry, and brand-name makeup whenever she wanted. Liz never allowed Molly to pay for a single cab or grocery store run. She was conscious of the fact that her roommate's financial situation looked nothing like her own, that Molly lived very much paycheck to paycheck, always picking up extra shifts at Angelina's and battling to stay on top of her student loans. Plus, Liz was honest and self-deprecating in a way that made it impossible to dislike her. She constantly called herself things like *spoiled* and *materialistic,* and while it may have been true, Molly didn't actually think of her that way. On the contrary, Liz was grounded, and refreshingly real, and nothing if not disciplined.

"*Friends*?" Liz suggested. "I'm craving season three. The episode where Joey puts on all of Chandler's clothes."

Molly smiled longingly. Dinner on the couch in front of *Friends* was their ritual. "I wish, Lizzie, but I can't. I have fifteen hundred more words to write before the workshop tomorrow."

"Ah. I forgot."

"So I'm taking half that Adderall you gave me and locking myself in my room for the rest of the night."

"Sounds like a party."

"By the way, did you know Nina has been at Cash's since *Saturday*? They played hooky together today."

"Really?" Liz turned away from the stove, raised an eyebrow. "How do people get away with playing hooky from work?"

Molly shrugged. Nina was an assistant at a public relations firm in the Flatiron District. Her job was serious, but it seemed to be less demanding than Liz's and Everly's.

"God, Cash is such a moron." Liz scoffed. "Why does Nina pick these lax-bro duds?"

"I was with them on Saturday. He's not so bad."

Liz rolled her wide brown eyes. She opened the cabinet and reached for two white ceramic bowls. "Are you gonna eat in your room, or has that Addy already kicked in?"

"I'll have a little in my room. Thanks. Hey, guess what, Lizzie?"

"What, Moll?" Liz scooped brown rice into the two bowls, topping each with a ladleful of curry.

"This guy . . . from the band that was playing at the bar on Saturday . . . he just called me. When I was walking home."

"Really?" Liz plucked two forks from the silverware drawer. "Did you hook up with him on Saturday or something?"

"No. I just saw him, from the crowd. We made eye contact."

"Eye contact. Steamy."

Molly punched her playfully in the arm. "But it's weird, right? I didn't even talk to him on Saturday."

Liz's brow creased. "What do you mean, you didn't talk to him? You didn't give him your number?"

"No." Molly shook her head. "He got it from a friend who knows Cash, who got it from Nina. Do you think that's strange?"

Liz shrugged. "Nah. It's proactive, which I like. Is he good looking?"

"Very. And he just had this . . . *presence*. Onstage, I mean. A certain je ne sais quoi. Though I'm not sure he's my type."

"What does that even mean?" Liz rolled her eyes again. "Clearly you're attracted to him."

Molly raised an eyebrow.

"Not everything is doomed," Liz said, reading her. "Not everyone is going to turn out to be a disappointment."

"You sound just like Nina."

Liz swallowed a bite of curry. "Maybe I'm turning into an optimist."

"You?" Now it was Molly's turn to roll her eyes. "Never."

"Just suck it up and go on a date with the sexy musician. Get out of this rut you're in."

"It's not a rut." Molly sighed, flashing Liz a reluctant grin. "We're having dinner on Thursday."

"Good girl. Now, go and write, with that brilliant brain of yours." She handed Molly her bowl of curry, whispers of steam rising from the top.

"Hey, Liz?"

"Yeah?"

"For this date, I'm going to need you to find me something to wear."

Chapter Five
Molly

May 2022

Molly drops Stella at Becky's before her early appointment with Dr. Ricci. As far as mothers-in-law go, Molly knows she lucked out with Becky O'Neil. When she pulls her car—a black Audi SUV—into the driveway, she sees Becky crouched in the garden, tending to her roses.

"My girls!" Becky hops up when she hears the car, wiping dirt on her sun-bleached jeans. She wears a wide-brim straw hat and the same Wayfarers she's owned since Molly met her. Stella leaps out of the car and wraps her arms around Becky's waist, her little blond ponytail swinging.

"Grammie!"

"Bye, Stell!" Molly calls, blowing her a kiss. "I'll pick you up from school."

But Stella is already halfway across the front lawn skipping toward Bodie, Becky's Australian shepherd.

Becky walks toward the car, and Molly rolls the window all the way down.

"Today's the test?" She removes her sunglasses and hooks them in the crevasse of her green-and-white-striped oxford. Her straight, snow-white hair—which she stopped dying when Hunter was in college—falls just above her shoulders.

"Yeah." Molly nods. "Cross your fingers."

"They're always crossed, Moll. You know that. Is Hunter meeting you there?"

"No. He's at a conference in the city."

"You're going alone?" Becky's face falls. "Goddamn it, Hunter. Wouldn't hurt him to miss one lousy conference." She says this, but they both know it's not true. Hunter is a VP in marketing at Octagon, the sports and entertainment agency headquartered in Stamford, just twenty

minutes south of Flynn Cove. His work-life balance isn't terrible—
nothing compared to the finance guys'—but still, Hunter's job is big,
important. It requires a lot of him.

"It's been on his schedule for months," Molly emphasizes. "Some
huge thing with Mastercard. It's okay, Beck, it's just another blood test.
It's not realistic for Hunt to come to every single one."

Becky nods slowly, pressing her lips together. "I'll be thinking of you."
Her almond-brown eyes rest on Molly's, deliberate and kind, just like
Hunter's. Crow's-feet crack the skin around their edges.

"Thanks, Beck." Molly puts the car in reverse. "And thanks for getting
Stella to school."

The O'Neils' white-shingled colonial fades in the rearview mirror as
Molly hooks a right out of the driveway, making her way toward Dr.
Ricci's on the west side of town. Dr. Ricci is one of the best fertility spe-
cialists in the country; miraculously, her group has an office right in the
small town of Flynn Cove.

Molly's nerves are jangled as she drives, and she fiddles with the radio.
She thinks about Hunter. This is their third round of IVF—their fifth
embryo transfer—and she needs it to work. She still doesn't understand
why it was so easy with Stella the first time and why it's so impossible
now. After their first transfer, several years ago now, Molly did get pregnant, but she lost the baby almost right away. A "silent miscarriage," as
Dr. Ricci referred to it. The blood test showed adequate HCG levels, but
then there was no heartbeat at the ultrasound. And Molly hasn't been
able to get pregnant since. She doesn't think she can bear the news of
another negative test or miscarriage, or the look on Hunter's face when
she informs him of yet another failed attempt.

Molly lands on SiriusXM's Coffee House station playing a George
Ezra song; she can't remember its name, but it's one she's used often in
her yoga playlists, and the beat steadies her. She inhales through the
nose and exhales out the mouth, the way she teaches her students. The
song ends too quickly, and another begins. In an instant she knows it,
the catchy, too-familiar rhythm of the intro—she would know it in her
sleep, in her death, probably. But it's different from the original—raw,
unaltered by synthesizers. An acoustic version, from the sounds of it, one
she hasn't heard before. And there it is, flashing across the media screen
above the center console: "Molly's Song (Acoustic)."

She feels a sharp stab of annoyance.

"How are people *still* playing that fucking song?" she says—almost yells—aloud to no one.

She wants to switch the station, but her arm is frozen on the steering wheel. She lets herself listen, surrenders to the nostalgia that squeezes her heart like a fist at the sound of his voice.

Five days ago I didn't know
The feelings in me now

It's not even a good song, she thinks as she speeds through a yellow light, all the while knowing that, on the contrary, it *is* a good song. It's a great song, the best song Danner Lane ever released and the only one— five years after the band split—that still gets played on the radio.

The gentle plucking of the guitar slows as the song fades out. Molly isn't prepared for what comes next, as the radio show host's voice fills the car.

"That was Jake Danner, everyone, with his recently recorded acoustic version of the old favorite, 'Molly's Song.' Beautiful, isn't it? I'm lucky enough to be here with Jake this afternoon, who's kindly agreed to say a few words to our listeners. Jake, great to have you on today. How's it going?"

Molly turns numb, her heart in her throat. She pulls into the parking lot of Dr. Ricci's office and slows the car to a stop, her whole body prickling and hot. And then Jake is speaking, the sound filling the Audi.

"Thanks, Aaron, thanks for having me on the Coffee House. I'm doing well. Just happy to be here talking about music."

"You know how much we all loved 'Molly's Song' when it came out in—god, was it 2014? Anyway, it's a real treat to hear you perform it again, and this acoustic version is so raw. Now, I've heard some rumors, but can you tell us if a solo album might be in the works?"

Jake laughs softly, passively, and Molly imagines him brushing a hand through his hair. She wonders if he still wears it long or if he succumbed to a crew cut. "Oh, I don't know about that, Aaron," he demurs. "I suppose time will tell, won't it?"

Molly kills the engine and bolts out of the car, unable to stomach the familiar pitch of Jake's voice a second longer. The sound of him is an invasion, an assault on the years she's spent pushing the past as far back as she can.

As usual, Dr. Ricci's waiting room is packed. Molly finds the only open seat, wedging herself between two women flipping through glossy magazines. She fiddles with her wedding ring, agitated, the lyrics of "Molly's Song" on repeat in her mind.

Your beautiful mind, your secret smile
Change me, won't you change me

Molly glances around the room at all the tired, stressed-looking women—many of whom appear older than she does—and tries to shift her anxiety toward gratitude. So many of these women would kill for a daughter of their own, and how lucky is she to have Stella? Only one of her fellow patients sits straight and alert, and she is staring in Molly's direction. It takes a moment to place her—perfect posture, bright green eyes. Yes, it's the woman who took Molly's yoga class two Sundays before.

"Sabrina," a voice says as though the universe is reading her mind, and suddenly, the woman has plopped down in the newly vacant seat beside her. "I was in your yoga class the other weekend. I'm not sure I actually introduced myself. You're Molly, right?"

Molly nods slowly, caught off guard. "Yes. Of course I remember. Hi." She keeps her voice low; Dr. Ricci's waiting room is not exactly a chatty environment.

Sabrina smiles, and Molly notes, once again, how attractive she is. Her dark, glossy hair falls long and loose around her shoulders, and she wears one of those thick, knotted headbands that seem to be trendy lately. Molly tried one on in a store the other day and decided she couldn't pull it off—her head seemed to be the wrong shape; it looked like some sort of embarrassing want-to-be crown.

"Sorry I haven't made it back to your class yet." Sabrina's voice is genuine. "Things have been so busy. I've been in the city nonstop, dealing with a work crisis."

"No worries," Molly says, surprised and slightly intimidated. None of the women she knows in Flynn Cove have serious careers—or even work at all.

"I was in fashion merchandising for years," Sabrina continues. "Now I consult for a few brands. There's been this huge disaster with the fall line at Dolce and Gabban—" She pauses. "Well, I shouldn't go into details. But you get it. You're a working woman."

Barely, Molly thinks, insecurity piercing her stomach. But it isn't the time or place to explain to Sabrina that teaching yoga isn't a career for her, that it never has been, never will be. She thinks of Bella's voicemail and feels sick with something she can't define. A kind of nostalgia for a life she didn't choose.

Molly swallows, eager to change the subject. "You're new to town, aren't you?"

Sabrina nods. "This is my first appointment here, though I was seeing another fertility specialist in the city, before we moved. My husband and I have been trying for over a year." She blinks, her emerald eyes clear and calm, and Molly wonders how a relative stranger can be so forthcoming on a topic that's so private and painful.

"Are you seeing Dr. Ricci?" Molly asks.

"Yes. I've heard excellent things."

"She's the best. You'll be in good hands." Molly manages a smile, and something about the expression on Sabrina's face—so expectant, so open—makes her want to say more. "It's . . . not easy. I get it. Believe me."

The woman to Molly's left glances up from *Good Housekeeping* and shoots them a pointed look, a silent order to please shut the hell up.

Just use your words, Molly thinks of the woman, observing yet again how no one in this town ever says what they mean—it's all fluff and in-sincerity and passive aggression.

Sabrina presses her lips together and lowers her voice to a whisper. "Maybe we could . . . get together sometime? I don't know many people in Flynn Cove. I don't know anyone, really." She looks at Molly hopefully, and Molly is struck again by her candor, a quality that reminds her of Nina and Everly, one that feels glaringly absent in the Meredith Duffys and Edie Kirkpatricks of Flynn Cove.

The door at the far end of the waiting room swings open, and a nurse steps through, squinting at her clipboard. "Molly O'Neil."

"I'd love that," Molly says impulsively, gathering her jacket and MZ Wallace tote. "Let me give you my number real quick."

She taps her cell into Sabrina's phone and stands, her insides twisting as she remembers what's about to happen. "Good to see you again. And good luck today."

"You, too," Sabrina replies, and her smile reveals those sparkling white teeth. "I'll text you, and we'll get something on the calendar."

The blood test is routine and quick; a needle prick on the inside of

Molly's elbow. Five minutes later, she is told she can leave and that Dr. Ricci will call her with the results in a few hours. Molly wonders if she'll see Sabrina again in the waiting room, but she is already gone.

At home, she sits on the couch and waits for her phone to ring. Hunter has sent a bouquet of white roses—Molly's favorite—which she's placed in a glass vase on one of the side tables. She looks around the living room and admires it, her favorite room in the house. She loves the high ceilings, the stained wood beams that Hunter sanded himself before they moved in. There are huge windows that fill two opposite walls, drenching the space in constant light.

Molly is grateful that Stella is at school; she loves her daughter with her whole heart, but she couldn't wait for the news with her here, bouncing around the house and asking her endearing but endless questions.

Mommy, how can fish breathe underwater?

Mommy, what did I do when I was in your tummy? Wasn't I bored?

Mommy, what does "several" mean?

Molly crosses her legs and looks at her watch—it's been over an hour now—and runs through a mental list of people she could call to pass the time. Nina. Everly. Her mother. Hunter. They're all at work but will pick up if she calls, she knows. But she doesn't really *want* to talk to anybody. She wants these minutes to herself, to wallow in the thin, shrinking space between hope and despair. IVF has failed so many times. Thousands and thousands of dollars down the drain; so much money she'll lose her mind if she really thinks about it. But this is how it goes for some, she's heard, she's read. It fails and fails, until finally it doesn't. This is the time it will work. *This* is the time it will work.

Molly leans back into the couch pillows and visualizes the space below her belly button, concentrates to see if she can sense a fledgling life there. Could she sense it with Stella this early on? She can't remember. In all honesty, it feels like a lifetime ago.

The golden light is strong streaming through the windows, almost too bright. Molly doesn't know how long she sits there, or how much time passes before her phone rings. But there it is, buzzing on the coffee table that Hunter built from a beautiful piece of black walnut, and Molly's fingers are sweaty as she swipes to answer it, her gut roiling.

"Hi, Molly." Dr. Ricci's voice is neutral and betrays nothing. "I have your results from this morning's bloodwork." Deep breath in. "I'm so sorry . . ."

But Molly doesn't hear the rest. She feels the phone slip in her hand; she feels her body freeze with shock; she feels the promise of all the tears she'll cry for the rest of the day and night, wrenching sobs that'll keep her from sleep. Another crack splits through her heart, deeper this time.

Chapter Six

Sabrina

You seem sad walking into Dr. Ricci's office. I've watched several other women enter the building before you, and they've all got a bit of hope in their stride. Not you.

Your blond hair is parted in the middle and runs in long, loose waves down your back. You've never taken the plunge and cut it short, have you? It might look good that way. Something fresh. A welcome change. But maybe there's a part of you that's stuck in the past. How could there not be?

You're hunched slightly; your head is bowed so it's hard to get a glimpse of your face. You're a woman who's lost something. It's not detectable to everyone, but I see it. Believe me, I am someone who knows sorrow, too. I am someone who knows loss.

Your expression changes when I approach you inside the waiting room. Your eyebrows jump and your jaw drops slightly, and I can tell you don't remember me. I remind you, and the corners of your mouth lift. I wonder if you're being polite or if you're genuinely glad to see me again—if I had to guess, I'd say the latter. We hit it off at Yoga Tree; it wasn't an illusion.

You're dressed nicely for the doctor. A sage-green cotton dress, gold hoops swinging from your ears, leather sandals that look like they could be from some Grecian market. You're not as conservative as most of the women in this town. You march to the beat of your own drum, as far as I can tell. Ironically, your style is not unlike my own.

Today, you've even put on a little mascara, and your cheeks have that natural pink flush I've always observed in pictures. You really are pretty, Molly.

We briefly acknowledge our fertility struggles—an experience that binds us, no doubt. You keep your voice hushed, and I sense this is a topic you're self-conscious about at the root, but you clearly crave the kind of connection I'm offering. There aren't a lot of women like me in Flynn Cove, that's for sure.

So you and I will get together soon, and that will be splendid. I'm looking forward to spending some quality time with you, something beyond the passing pleasantries of thanking you for yoga or the five brief minutes in Dr. Ricci's packed waiting room.

I'm looking forward to meeting your husband at some point, too. You didn't tell me Hunter's name, but I know it, obviously. I know a lot about you, Molly. Much more than you realize. Obtaining all this information hasn't been easy—after all these years, you *still* haven't caved and gotten Instagram. What's that about, anyway? Are you trying to prove something? Or trying to hide something?

Nevertheless, I have my ways. Your friend Liz was helpful in pointing me in the right direction for a good long while. Once I learned your married name, that gave me a window into so much more.

Still, it doesn't feel fair how unbalanced our relationship is, Molly. I know so very much about you, while you hardly know a thing about me. But don't worry. That will change soon enough.

Chapter Seven

Jake

2013

On Thursday, Jake was proud of himself for getting to the restaurant before Molly. He had a habit of running late, but tonight—even with the snow coming down—he arrived right on time.

It was a nice place, Italian, and much fancier than the spots where Jake usually ate dinner. Between the white tablecloths, candlelight, and the sounds of hushed conversations and classical music, the feel was intimate, cozy. The hostess led him to a table in the back, against a wall of tastefully exposed brick.

Jake's memory of Molly Diamond was hazy, diluted; it was more a *feeling* he recalled than her physical appearance. But when the front door swung open and she breezed through, he remembered why he'd chased Jeb's friend down for her phone number with an urgency that felt excessive, especially for him.

The current of Jake's blood quickened as he drank in the sight of her: sandy-blond hair falling in loose waves around her shoulders, a warm smile breaking across her face as she waved, striding toward him. She shimmied off her wool coat, which was damp with melting snowflakes, and draped it over the back of the chair across from his.

"Sorry I'm late," she said, pulling off her hat and taking a seat.

Words momentarily escaped him as their eyes met, the blurred memory of his gaze locked on hers from the makeshift stage at the Broken Mule sharpening into a focused reality.

"Hey there," he said, continuing to study her—the sharp structure of her flushed cheekbones, the scooped cut of her top. A pair of bulky earrings—the kind girls seemed to be wearing these days—swung from her ears. They were a jade color that brought out the green flecks in her hazel irises.

"It's really snowing out there, and I wore these dumb shoes." She gestured down to her feet, a pair of leather boots with spiky heels.

"You're hardly late." Jake smiled, suddenly a little nervous. There was something about this girl, and he felt relieved that his instinct from Saturday had been right—particularly since that wasn't always the case. "I was just on time for once in my life."

They ordered a bottle of Chianti, and as the wine settled in Jake's stomach, his nerves began to dissipate, replaced with something solid and pleasant that hummed just under his skin. He listened to Molly talk about NYU, where she was pursuing her MFA in creative writing.

"So you graduate in the spring, and then what?" he asked.

Molly twirled a fork into her plate of carbonara and shook her head. "I don't know. I should know, but I don't."

"Hmm." Jake spun the stem of his wineglass with his thumb and forefinger. "You want to write?"

She hesitated. "Yes. But I never say that out loud."

"I get it. It's a lot of pressure."

"It isn't just that." Molly blinked, her lips slightly parted. "Not everyone who wants to write gets the luxury of being able to do so."

Jake swallowed a bite of pasta. He said nothing, studying her.

"I have student loans to pay, you know?" She brushed a loose strand of hair off her collarbone. "I need to think about a steady income."

Jake nodded. "I get it. I still have loans to pay off, too."

"Really?" Molly looked genuinely surprised. "Sorry, it's just . . . most of my friends don't relate to that."

"Neither do mine, actually." Jake thought of Sam and Hale, of the college fund Mr. and Mrs. Lane had started for them when they were babies. "My parents never saved any money."

The waiter came by and refilled both their wineglasses. Jake took a generous sip, his head buzzy and light. They were on their second bottle of Chianti.

He watched Molly, admiring the graceful curve of her neck as she tilted her head back, tipping the wine down her throat. "What do you want to write?" he asked. "A novel?"

Her expression brightened. "Well, I have this collection of short stories I'm working on for my thesis. And I've always thought . . . they're kind of linked, see. The stories. So I thought I might be able to turn them into a novel." She paused, shaking her head. "I can't believe I just said that."

Jake's eyebrows knitted together. "Said what?"

"That I'm writing something that I think could be a novel." She reached for her wine again.

"Yeah. Wow. That's the craziest thing I've ever heard. Especially from a creative writing student." He eyed her playfully.

Molly laughed, but there was a self-consciousness there. Something that didn't quite fit with her otherwise assured demeanor. "It's just . . . it's a dream I've never voiced to anyone," she told him. "Barely even to myself. I'm not sure why, because you're right. Most of the students in my program are there because they want to write fiction, or poetry, or whatever. It's kind of the point of an MFA."

Jake considered this. "Maybe you haven't voiced it because actually making it happen feels like a pipe dream," he offered. "And the commitment it requires means acknowledging that you could fail. That you might be faced with a reality where it doesn't work out, and you're left wondering how you could've been as dumb as every other aspiring creative who wastes their time trying."

"Yeah." Molly's hazel eyes scorched his. "Exactly."

"But you know what?" Jake peered at her with genuine empathy, because he got it. He understood, possibly more than anyone. He used two fingers to tap the side of his head. "All that is just chatter in here. Ignore it. Because sometimes, it does work out. And that's what you need to focus on."

"Easy for you to say." She grinned, lifting an eyebrow. "My friend Nina told me about your record deal. That's . . . incredible, Jake. Truly."

"Thanks." He rested his forearms on the edge of the table. "Look, can I give you a piece of advice?"

"Of course."

"Danner Lane still has a long way to go, so it's not like I have it all figured out. But one thing I know for sure? *Talent* is overrated. It only gets you so far. If you really want to do something—if you want to *be* something—you have to put in the work. The physical, grueling hours. And no one wants to admit this, but it sucks a lot of the time. But if you work really, really hard? You can make things happen."

Molly glanced over Jake's shoulder, a dreamy sheen glazing her eyes.

"I know it's hard not to think about the money," he went on. "But you can't. Do what you need to do to pay the bills—a day job, whatever it is. The money will come later."

Molly looked back at him, a smile playing at the edges of her mouth. "I really, really needed to hear all that, Jake." Her gaze was vivid, honest, and he liked that about her—that she wasn't putting on a show. She wasn't trying to be somebody who had it all figured out; she wasn't tripping over herself to impress him, the way girls so often did.

When the waiter dropped the check, Jake snatched it up before Molly could get a glimpse of the total: $196—expensive, but Sam had warned him when he'd suggested this place. Jake dug out his wallet and slipped his Visa inside the bill. It was certainly a splurge—six months ago, the number would've put a pit in his stomach—but things were different from how they had been. He could afford it. Danner Lane was making money, real money, and for the first time in Jake's life, there was a cushion in his bank account.

Outside the restaurant, the snow had stopped, and the air was still and cool. Jake exhaled, his breath a white puff of air between them. He rubbed the back of his neck.

"That was fun. Sorry if that place was kind of stuffy. Was it stuffy?" He blinked, suddenly anxious again, which caught him off guard. He wasn't used to these kinds of nerves around the opposite sex. "Sorry, I'm rambling. I didn't think you'd say yes to dinner." This wasn't completely true, but it felt like the right thing to say. Jake was only moderately aware of his habit of doing this—of relaying to women the flattering remarks he knew they liked to hear.

"It wasn't stuffy. It was delicious." Molly stepped closer, and the details of her face—the sweeping line of her lashes, the small scar above her left eyebrow—mesmerized him. Jake inhaled the scent of her, heady notes of vanilla and sandalwood. "I just normally don't go to places like that because I'm a poor student," she said.

Jake nodded in agreement. "I can't really afford restaurants like that, either. For the rest of the week it'll be ramen, ramen, and ramen. All thanks to *you*."

Molly grinned. "Why didn't you think I'd say yes?"

Jake shrugged, struck with the sudden certainty that he didn't want to bullshit this girl. There was a quality to her that captivated him—he'd felt it the moment he'd spotted her in the crowd at the Broken Mule. It wasn't just that she was beautiful—there were thousands of beautiful girls in New York, and he'd come across women that were more striking. It was the way she'd looked so firmly rooted, he decided, utterly present and expectant, ready for something to happen. On the phone, when he'd told Molly he'd never tracked down a girl from one of his shows, he hadn't been lying.

"Well, first I thought you might have a boyfriend," he told her. "And then, when I called you, I thought there was a good chance you'd be creeped out. I meant what I said on the phone, though—I've never done that before."

"*Sure.*" She tipped her head teasingly. They hadn't finished the second bottle of wine; still, they were both a little drunk.

"I swear!" Jake reached forward and took both of Molly's hands in his, squeezing gently.

"Do you date a lot?" she asked, blinking up at him.

"Nah." He shrugged, uncomfortable. "Things have really been picking up with the band . . ." He paused, propelled by the urge to share more, to be honest in a way that didn't always come naturally. "Truthfully, I'm—" He stalled. Her gloveless hands were warm despite the cold. "I'm in the middle of a breakup."

"Oh." The playful expression on Molly's face dropped, the air between them shifting as she drew her hands away.

"It's over, it really is." Jake studied her hopefully, hating himself for ruining the moment, and even more for dodging the truth until now. He thought of Sisi, of their drawn-out eighteen months together. He wasn't in love with her, and being around Molly made him all the more certain that he never would be.

Jake sighed. "Sisi wanted to move in together, and I guess . . . I guess I didn't love her as much as she loved me. And I started to feel guilty about that." He wrapped his arms across his chest, rubbing his shoulders. "I should've ended it months ago. I just kept putting it off—I'm not good with confrontation—but I've been over it for—" He paused, latching his gaze to Molly's. "For a while now."

Molly pulled her red hat lower over her ears. "Are you fucking with me?"

Jake shook his head. "I promise I'm not."

She blinked. Her nose and cheeks were pink, her blond hair a halo around her face, and Jake thought how pretty she looked, on this frigid January night, underneath the glow of the streetlight on Driggs. Around them, snow had begun to fall again, little white flakes dancing down from the inky sky.

"I promise," he repeated, stepping toward her. He lifted his hand to her face, tracing his fingers along the scar above her left eyebrow. "What is this from?"

"I fell out of an apple tree when I was seven," she explained, her voice breathy, electricity whirring in the space between them.

"I'm a little drunk," Jake admitted, one side of his mouth curling. "And it's cold. Walk you home? Or . . . do you want to come over and listen to music?"

Molly rolled her eyes. "You just told me you're more or less in a relationship, and you want me to come over?"

"I'm *not* in a relationship," Jake insisted. "Not anymore. Besides, no funny business. Just music."

She gave a small smile. "*Your* music?"

"God no. I'm not that kind of narcissistic artist. I was thinking more like . . . Blink-182?"

"Blink-182? Random."

"Not random. Blink-182 is my favorite ever. They're all I listened to as a kid. They have some great fucking songs. They're probably the reason I wanted to start making music."

"Danner Lane sounds nothing like them. No offense."

"None taken. Punk rock was a nineties thing, and it should stay that way. But it's iconic. Come on." Jake reached for one of Molly's hands, and she let him hold it as they walked. "I'm only four blocks away. One song and you can leave. And Sam and Hale won't be there to bother you."

"Sam and Hale being . . . your roommates?"

"Yeah. And my bandmates. They're brothers. So it's the three of us. We grew up on the same street in North Carolina. We started dicking around with music in the Lanes' garage when we were—God, it must've been elementary school? Maybe Sam was in middle school by then. He's a year older than Hale and me."

"North Carolina." Molly nodded. "I had a feeling you were from the South."

"Why, 'cause of my accent? It's pretty faded."

"Oh, it's definitely there. But I like it." Molly grinned.

When they reached his walk-up on Roebling, Jake was relieved to find the apartment relatively clean. He sensed Molly absorbing the boyish details of his place—the cheaply framed Led Zeppelin poster on the wall above the navy sectional, Hale's PlayStation controllers tangled on the floor in front of the sixty-inch flat-screen.

Molly sank down on the couch, and Jake handed her a glass of whiskey over ice. He took a sip from his own tumbler, let the Johnnie Walker burn the back of his throat. He crouched beside a box of vinyl records in the corner that he'd never bothered to organize, digging out the album he needed. Then he placed the record on his beloved Crosley turntable—the one he'd found for five dollars at a neighbor's estate sale in high school—and lowered the arm. The sound of a familiar song filled the room, blaring through a pair of old-school speakers framing the television.

I took her out, it was a Friday night
I wore cologne, to get the feeling right

The song brought a heavy nostalgia that permeated the room, and Jake watched Molly's mouth work its way into a knowing smile.

She turned to him. "Oh my god. I can't believe you have this on vinyl."

He sat beside her on the couch—not too close—and they sang the words together, the volume of their voices amplifying at the line: *Nobody likes you when you're TWENTY-THREE!*

Molly sank back into the cushions and laughed deeply, the sound coming straight from her heart. "You were right, Jake. This is a great fucking song. Especially because I'm twenty-three."

"Me, too," he said with a smile. "But only for another month."

When it ended, she asked if they could hear the song again. And he said yes, they could hear it as many more times as she wanted. And then he brushed a strand of wheat-blond hair off her face and told her she was beautiful, especially when she laughed, and it was the first and only time in Jake's life when he loved someone like that—so suddenly and assuredly, without needing time to tell, without questioning it at all.

Chapter Eight

Molly

May 2022

The last weekend in May is gorgeous in Flynn Cove. The trees are full and lush with blossoms, late spring in full force. Molly has always loved this time of year, and she's glad when Sabrina texts her to ask if she'll be at the Memorial Day parade. When Molly says that she will—Stella has been talking about the parade's bicycle decorating contest since last year—Sabrina suggests they meet there.

The village of Flynn Cove spans just three blocks, but there's a lot packed into those streets: the post office, the fire department and police station, an old-fashioned deli, a hair salon, a movie theater, two restaurants, an Episcopal church, a gourmet market and café called Gwen's, a high-end kitchenware store, and two retail shops—Southern Tide and an overpriced boutique that sells three-hundred-dollar sweaters and monogrammed baby gifts.

Today, the main roads in town are blocked off for the parade, which is crowded with families and at least a hundred decorated bikes. Molly likes the parade. It's one of the only annual events in Flynn Cove that doesn't seem to revolve around the country club, where she and Hunter—to the shock of people like Meredith Duffy and Betsy Worthington—are not members. Sometimes Molly thinks they should just bite the bullet and join, but it's outrageously expensive, and Hunter doesn't golf much, and so what's the point, really, other than to prove something? To shell out thousands of dollars to prove that she—literally—can belong?

"Mom." Stella tugs Molly's arm, pulling her out of her thoughts. "What do you think?"

Molly glances down at her daughter's bicycle. Red, white, and blue streamers weave through the spokes of each wheel and wrap the entire frame of the bike, covering the normally purple part. Hunter has fastened a giant blue pinwheel to the front basket and two shiny red cheerleading poms to either end of the handlebars.

He wipes his hands on his Carhartt shorts and grins. "Pretty good, huh?"

Molly crouches next to Stella on the street, smoothing her pigtails. "This looks like first place to me," she praises, despite the dozens of identically adorned bicycles in the street around them.

Then a voice calls her name, and Molly turns to see Sabrina striding toward them. Sabrina waves in greeting, flashes her megawatt smile. Straight white teeth.

"Hey!" Molly stands, genuinely glad to see her. She introduces Sabrina to Hunter and Stella, enduring a stab of annoyance when Hunter's eyes linger on Sabrina's slim, bronzed legs stemming out of white cutoffs. Molly could never get away with wearing shorts that short—not in this town.

But she isn't worried—not actually. Hunter is a good man, as faithful as they come, and he swings his arm around Molly's shoulder in what she knows is an apology for accidentally admiring another woman's figure. "Great to meet you," he says cheerfully.

"Likewise." Sabrina tips her head back, gazing up at the sun. "God, it's nice out. Summer finally decided to show up."

"Your husband couldn't make it?" Molly asks.

Sabrina rolls her eyes, then slides a pair of tortoise-shell sunglasses down from the crown of her head. She adjusts them on the bridge of her small, straight nose. "He had a work thing come up last minute."

"On a holiday?" Stella chirps, and Molly can't help but smile at her daughter, whose incredible five-year-old mind is constantly impressing her.

"On a holiday." Sabrina nods, lifting her shoulders and flipping her palms up. "Crazy, I know." She turns to Molly. "But I wanted to come, anyway. From what I gather, this parade is a pretty big spectacle."

"It's fun," Molly admits, shifting her weight to one hip. "It's definitely a big Flynn Cove event. And a blast for the kids." She pauses, cringing internally at how old she sounds. *And a blast for the kids.*

"She's beyond adorable." Sabrina glances at Stella, who has turned her attention to her best friend, Jade Patel, near a cluster of bikes beside them. Hunter has started chatting with Jade's father. "She has your coloring."

"Stella's an awesome kid." Molly smiles. "*Very* curious. Nonstop questions."

"That's so fun." There's a trace of sadness in Sabrina's voice.

"You'll have your own, very soon I'm sure." Molly twists her hair back into a low bun, securing it with a clip.

"*Sabrina!*"

Molly recognizes the voice. It's Meredith Duffy, who has stood fifteen feet from Molly and Hunter all morning, but avoided eye contact until now. Her stomach flips. She hadn't realized Sabrina knew Meredith. She isn't sure why this makes her feel so insecure.

Meredith approaches them, hooked arm in arm with Edie Kirkpatrick—a gesture that reminds Molly of high school, the way she and her best friend, Rachel, used to link elbows on their way to class.

"And, Molly, *hello.*" Meredith's and Edie's smiles are matching, saccharine sweet. Their foreheads are shiny and lineless, and they each hold giant iced teas from Gwen's. If they're judging the length of Sabrina's short shorts, it isn't obvious.

"Don't the kids' bikes look sensational?" Meredith glances in the direction of her daughter, Emma, who's in Stella's class at Flynn Cove Elementary. Emma's bike is more bedecked than Stella's, an enormous cluster of red, white, and blue balloons fastened to the seat, swaying majestically in the breeze.

Edie's son Walker is a year older, but many of the kindergarten and first-grade mothers seem to flock together. Molly met them this way, through their children, when she and Hunter moved to Flynn Cove in time for Stella to start preschool. That was almost three years ago now, but Molly is still cognizant of her role as a somewhat outsider. It isn't just that they don't belong to the country club, though she's sure that's a piece of it. Molly was only twenty-six when she had Stella—it happened before she and Hunter were ready, honestly—and her younger age is something she feels in the presence of women like Meredith and Edie and Betsy, who are all pushing forty and well onto their second and third children. They've never seemed to *get* Molly, who arrived in Flynn Cove at age twenty-nine, wearing worn Converse and mala beads, her hair untamed, a three-year-old on her hip. As the years passed and Molly never conformed to their bright, preppy clothing and enthusiasm for things like the garden club, their confusion seemed to morph into a kind of mild distaste, even resentment.

"And how do *you all* know each other?" Meredith glances between Molly and Sabrina, her curiosity clearly piqued.

"Molly and I met when I took her amazing yoga class earlier this month," Sabrina gushes.

"Ah! How lovely. I've simply *got* to get to your class one of these days, Molly." Meredith gives a forced grin, and Molly has to stop herself from rolling her eyes. Meredith says the same thing nearly every time they see each other, and Molly knows the words are empty. She'll never actually show up at class.

"I love your shoes, Sabrina." Edie gestures toward Sabrina's sandals, which are a toffee color, with thin leather straps wrapping up the length of her ankles.

"Me, *too*." Meredith nods emphatically in agreement.

"Thanks." Sabrina smiles casually, flips her hair. "Confession? I totally copied Molly. She was wearing a similar pair the other day. I'm obsessed with her style."

Meredith and Edie purse their lips, looking as perplexed as Molly feels. Molly does own similar gladiator sandals. Was she wearing them the other day when she ran into Sabrina at Dr. Ricci's? She must've been.

Molly gives Sabrina a grateful smile. "Thanks. That's sweet of you to say."

Edie swallows a sip of iced tea, checking her phone. "All right, Mer, it's almost ten. We should make sure the kids are ready to go."

"Have a good one, ladies," Meredith calls with a wave. "See you at the club, Sabrina. Molly, you know, if you'd like Colin and me to sponsor you for next year, all you have to do is say the word. Happy to get you in the door!"

Molly says nothing, smiling stiffly as Meredith and Edie disappear into the crowd of patriotic colors. If she were braver, bolder, she'd say the words gathering in her mind: *No, Meredith, Hunter and I are not considering joining the Flynn Cove Country Club. We have a mortgage and tens of thousands of dollars of outstanding IVF bills and aren't in a position to drop a hundred grand on the FCCC's initiation fee. And neither of us even like golf.*

Her insides twist into a hard knot at the new knowledge that Sabrina and her husband belong to the club. They've barely been in Flynn Cove five minutes, and already they've joined? Molly doesn't want to feel disappointed, but she can't help it.

At eleven on the dot, the parade begins. There's the high school marching band followed by police officers and veterans in uniform waving, floats from local businesses like Gwen's Café and Waterside Car Wash that toss out handfuls of candy, then the shiny red fire trucks, their sirens blaring. The bicycles are last, more than a hundred children pedaling through the streets, balloons and streamers fluttering in their wake.

Emma Duffy's bike wins second prize. Stella doesn't win a prize at all, but her face is steady as results are announced through the megaphone. Molly is proud of her daughter, who isn't always so even-keeled in the face of disappointment, and grateful that they seem to have evaded a meltdown.

Hunter offers to take Stella home. "If you two wanted to grab an iced tea or something?" he adds, glancing from Molly to Sabrina.

Molly sees the effort in his face. He's relieved his wife has a new friend, and he desperately wants them to hit it off.

"Or a drink?" One half of Sabrina's pink mouth slides into a grin. "There's a bottle of Whispering Angel in my car."

"Even better." Molly smiles. "Skipping Beach is only a few blocks away. We can drink it there? It's so nice out."

"I *love* Skipping Beach!" Stella chirps, wrapping her arms around Molly's thigh. "Can I come? *Please*, Mommy?"

Molly glances at Sabrina, who winks at Stella. "The more the merrier."

Fifteen minutes later, the women spread two yellow-and-white-striped towels over the sand. Skipping Beach isn't yet crowded—most of Flynn Cove is still finishing up at the parade.

"Not too close to the water, Stell!" Molly calls to her daughter, who is already chasing a particularly large seagull toward the surf.

Sabrina pours the rosé into two plastic cups, the pale pink liquid *clunk clunk clunking* through the nose of the bottle.

She hands one of the cups to Molly. "I just thought . . . wine beats iced tea, especially on a holiday weekend, right?"

"Obviously." Molly grins. "I haven't met many women around here who would day drink. Everyone is so . . . by the book."

"Ha. Connecticut is fucking boring." Sabrina flashes Molly an apologetic look. "No offense."

"None taken. You live here, too, now."

"Touché." Sabrina laughs. "So tell me honestly, do you think I'm a total snoot for belonging to that stupid club? My grandparents used to live in Flynn Cove, and I grew up visiting them here. They were very involved at the FCCC, so I felt like we *had* to join. But it's kind of dumb. My husband doesn't even golf."

"Neither does Hunter, really." Molly feels like Sabrina is reading her mind. "But no, if you have family ties, of course it makes sense. Hunter grew up here, and his parents were never FCCC members. His is a big boating family, they belong to the yacht club, over on Harbor Street? It's smaller, there's tennis, no pool, but it's nice—Stella sails there, and she's crazy about it. Hunter taught me to sail, too, so it's become a big family activity."

"That sounds so great." Sabrina stretches her legs long on the towel, leans back on her elbows. "And really, who needs a pool? The FCCC pool is overrated. I'd take this beautiful public beach over that tub of chlorine any day."

"Oh, same. I'm a total beach girl." Molly sips her wine. It's a little warm from sitting in Sabrina's car, but it's making her limbs feel pleasantly loose, her head light.

"So you guys have been here for a few years?"

Molly nods. "We were in Brooklyn before. Hunter loved growing up here—his family is, like, fourth-generation Flynn Cove or something, and the town is such a part of him. He lost his father when he was just out of college, and he always thought he'd come back and settle down near his mom." Molly adjusts her Ray-Bans on the bridge of her nose, gazes out at the ocean. "I resisted for a while—all my friends are still in the city, and I loved it there—but the schools here can't be beat. So when Stella turned three, it just felt like the right time to make moves."

Molly omits the part of the story that involves Jake—the weekend morning she spotted him from a distance at the farmers' market in McCarren Park. His head was bent over a carton of strawberries; she could only see the side of his face, but it was a profile she'd recognize anywhere. Stella was in the stroller, and Hunter was busy inspecting fistfuls of swiss chard, and Molly had beelined for the park's exit so quickly she'd nearly plowed down an older couple browsing artisan cheeses. Later, back at their apartment, she told Hunter to call the Realtor in Flynn Cove, the one he'd been mentioning since Stella's first birthday. He was so happy that he didn't question her abrupt change of tune. But Molly knew she couldn't stay in a place where running into Jake would never stop being a risk.

"That makes sense." Sabrina nods, pouring them more rosé. She peels off her white tank top, revealing a black bra that could double as a bathing suit, and her perfectly taut stomach. "I hope you don't mind," she says. "My body hasn't seen the sun since last summer."

"Of course not." Molly pauses. "Can I ask you a question?" She turns to face Sabrina, fueled by the wine, by her own curiosity and the desire to talk about something real, for once. It feels like every conversation she's ever had with women in Flynn Cove is about house renovations and wallpaper or what the kids are up to and where everyone is vacationing in August.

"Duh." Sabrina flips onto her belly, swinging her heels.

"I don't mean to pry, but I was thinking the other day, after I ran into you at Dr. Ricci's . . ." Molly draws in a breath. "When we first met at Yoga Tree, you told me you and your husband were newlyweds. So you can't have been trying to conceive for *that* long, right?"

Sabrina swallows. "We got married in January but started trying awhile before that, actually."

Molly is caught off guard. "Oh?"

Sabrina drops her chin. "I had a bad eating disorder for much of high school and college. I lost my period for a while. I had a strong hunch that conceiving would be difficult, given what I'd put my body through, and my OB had always suggested the same. So we actually started trying last fall. We figured if I got pregnant right away, it would still be early enough that I could hide it at the wedding. But I didn't, of course. So now it's been . . . eight months. I know that isn't *that* long, and I'm thirty-one—relatively young—but still. If there's a problem, I'd rather know sooner."

"Oh, Sabrina." Molly feels a pull of empathy. "I'm sure everything is fine, but I understand. Every month feels like an eternity when you're trying. And it's smart to be proactive."

Sabrina nods. "If I'm not pregnant by the end of the summer, we'll do IUI. Ricci says we'll need to before insurance will cover IVF."

"The insurance stuff is such a pain in the ass," Molly commiserates. "Ours doesn't have infertility benefits at all. It's been . . . a huge investment."

"It will be worth it in the end, I'm sure."

Molly isn't so certain. "You'll be in good hands with Ricci," she says instead. "Her practice has such a high success rate." Over 70 percent, in fact—one of the highest in the country—yet Molly remains in the minority of patients whose body just refuses to work the way it should. This time, at least.

"But Stella . . ." Sabrina hesitates. "Stella you conceived naturally?"

"Yeah." Molly watches her daughter, her small body crouched as she plays in the sand. Stella's imagination is wild and enormous; she can play by herself for hours on end. Rocks and sticks and leaves and shells all quickly become her friends, part of a magical world that is Stella's alone. "I didn't even have to think about it the first time—that's the craziest part. I was just pregnant, like that." Molly snaps her fingers. "So I thought trying for a second baby would be the same." She exhales. "The day I saw you at Dr. Ricci's a couple of weeks ago, I was in for my blood test. For the results from our latest embryo transfer. It was our fifth transfer, and it didn't work."

"Oh, Molly."

"We've been trying for almost four years. I did have a miscarriage, during our first round of IVF, which gives me hope that at least . . ." Molly pauses. "That at least it almost worked once. Maybe it will work again."

Something dark flashes across Sabrina's face, but just for a moment. "You're right to be hopeful. I'm hopeful for you."

"Thanks." Molly takes another sip of rosé. "It's just nice to have someone to talk to about all this crap."

"Seriously." Sabrina turns onto her back again, sitting up. She digs a bottle of sunscreen from her bag. "And yeah, it's like all these women in Flynn Cove just pop out perfect baby after perfect baby, and if anyone is struggling, no one ever talks about it."

"That's what I always say to Hunter." Molly feels a bit drunk—the wine is going straight to her head—but she feels like she can tell Sabrina anything and it won't be an overshare. "Hunt keeps saying that if I really can't stand it here, we can move. I think he's sick of hearing me complain all the time." Molly unbuttons her linen top, tosses it to the side. She has on a nursing bra—an old nude one she still wears all the time because it's comfortable—but she isn't embarrassed. Her body looks good, not *so* different from Sabrina's, she thinks with a jolt of confidence.

"Where would you move?" Sabrina rubs sunscreen into her arms, which already look tan. Around them, the beach is beginning to fill with families, but luckily no one Molly recognizes. She doesn't want this moment interrupted.

"That's the thing, we wouldn't move." Molly shakes her head. "I know that Flynn Cove is the right place for Stella to grow up. The schools are better than basically anywhere, and she loves her friends and sailing, and having Hunter's mom right around the corner is huge. Becky's great—she takes Stella horseback riding, babysits all the time. It just . . . it works for us to be here, if I'm really honest with myself." She smiles at Sabrina. "Besides, not *everyone* is so terrible."

"Meredith is kind of terrible," Sabrina demurs, and they both crack up.

"The fucking worst, right?"

When their laughter subsides, Sabrina taps her cup against Molly's. "To new and lasting friendships."

"To new and lasting friendships," Molly repeats. She closes her eyes, inhales the smell of salt and brine rolling off Long Island Sound. The warm sun beats down on her skin, and it's hotter than she realized.

"Stella!" she calls, flipping her eyes open. "Come here, baby. Time for sunscreen." She turns to Sabrina, gesturing to the bottle of Coppertone on her towel. "Mind if I borrow that?"

"'Course not."

Stella skips over. "Are you wearing bras?" she asks, her little raspy voice sending a stitch of affection through Molly's heart.

"Yes, sweetie. Sometimes it's okay to wear bras on the beach because they look like bathing suits." Molly tries not to laugh.

"You guys look like my Barbie dolls," Stella observes, hands on her hips.

Sabrina grins. "Your mom certainly does, but I don't know about me. Barbie has blond hair."

"Teresa has black hair." Stella holds out a broken scallop shell. "Mommy, look what I found. I think there was a crab living in it before."

"I don't know if crabs live in those kinds of shells, baby." Molly places her cup in the sand and picks up the sunscreen. Stella's skin isn't as pale as Molly's; by the end of the summer, she'll be brown as a berry, but she still burns easily if Molly isn't careful. "Here, let me do your face. The sun is strong today."

Stella plops down on the towel. She's wearing red shorts and a blue-and-white-striped T-shirt, looking perfectly patriotic. "But I think . . ." She pauses, pushing loose strands of white-blond hair off her face. "Mom, I think some crabs *do* live in those kinds of shells."

"You think? Maybe you're right." Molly gives Sabrina a knowing smile.

"We can look it up on the computer when we get home," Stella decides.

"That sounds like a good plan." Molly rubs sunblock into her daughter's face and arms, then has her stand so she can do her legs and the tops of her feet. Stella throws her head back in feigned exasperation, and Molly has to smile—it reminds her of Hunter's melodramatic body language when she asks him for help with something mundane, like taking out the recycling.

"Can we go swimming, Mommy?"

"Not today, Stell. We didn't bring your bathing suit. Next time."

"'Kay." Stella studies Sabrina. "Are you coming swimming next time?"

"I don't know that Sabrina wants to swim in Long Island Sound, baby."

"Why, Mom?"

"Some people don't like to swim in it. It's a little dirty."

"It's *dirty*?" Stella's jaw drops.

Sabrina laughs. "Well, it still beats the club pool."

"*That's* for sure." Molly nods, appreciating their new in-joke.

"I like pools," Stella offers, sinking back down onto Molly's towel. "Grammie has one."

Molly pulls her daughter between her legs so that she's resting on her stomach. "Grammie's pool is cold, though, right?"

"*Freezing.* And it has frogs in it."

"Basically, it needs to be heated and cleaned," Molly explains to Sabrina. "Becky's more invested in her garden."

"Where's your pool?" Stella asks Sabrina.

"Well, it's not *my* pool. It's the pool at the country club in town."

"Oh yeah. I went there with my friend Harper. We had chicken nuggets and vanilla milkshakes."

"That's right. You and Harper had fun that day." Molly hands Sabrina the Coppertone. "Thanks."

"Anytime. This has been such a great morning."

"It really has. I love Skipping Beach when it's not overcrowded. We'll have to come back."

"Count me in." Sabrina grins.

There's something so likable about her, Molly thinks. She's comfortable in her own skin. Happy-go-lucky in a way that reminds Molly more of her old self.

Molly feels almost giddy as she gazes out over the lapping waves, wine slackening her limbs, her daughter snuggled against her chest. And a new friend by her side. Molly has a strong, heartening feeling that Sabrina will be in her life for a long time.

Chapter Nine
Sabrina

Jake Danner. The name—if written, if read, if heard, if spoken—sends an electric shiver up my spine. Those three syllables are ground into my subconscious, a permanent footprint on my heart.

I can only imagine how confusing this will be for you to learn, Molly. That I, your new gal pal in the suburbs, am well acquainted with your ex. And not just any old ex: the one who got away.

But here's the thing: Jake was mine before he was ever yours.

Let me start at the beginning. The beginning of Jake and me, anyway, which is the only beginning that really matters in my life.

I was a twenty-one-year-old student at the Fashion Institute of Technology in Manhattan when Jake Danner walked into my life. You know when you make a batch of chocolate chip cookies and there's one that comes out that's just absolutely perfect? Crispy at the edges, doughy in the middle, with the chocolate chips spread evenly throughout? That was Jake. Mr. Fucking Perfect, if I'd ever seen him.

We met at a bar in the East Village—near my apartment, and around the corner from the studio space he rented with his bandmates. He had tan skin and blue eyes and a disarming smile, and when he looked at me, I instantly felt lit up from within. It was summer, and the mood in the city was light and happy; he bought me a vodka soda and we sat on the back terrace under rows of string lights, talking and drinking for hours, long after the friends we'd come with had gone home. His voice matched him perfectly—genuine and cool, shot through with a slight Southern drawl that puddled my heart. He'd just graduated from college in North Carolina and had moved to New York to try to make it as a musician, he explained. He told me I reminded him of Mila Kunis; I said he looked like the epitome of an up-and-coming rock star, because he did.

And that was all it took, really. We fell in love quickly and easily. It was a perfect year—my last at FIT, his first in the city. Jake lived in Williamsburg but worked most nights busing tables at an upscale Greek restaurant in Nolita. He hated it, but the tips were good, and there wasn't yet money coming in from the band. After his shifts, he'd walk the ten quick blocks to my apartment on East Fifth Street, slipping in the door past midnight. I always waited up for him, sliding my hands underneath the waistband of his boxers the second he crawled into bed beside me. On those nights, he smelled of garlic and grilled meat, but I didn't mind. Everything about him intoxicated me.

That year, I was busy interviewing for jobs in fashion merchandising, while Jake and the Lane brothers focused on finding representation and putting together a debut album, playing for free at Arlene's Grocery and whatever other local bars would have them. In the spring, a guy named Jerry Ruffalo signed on to be Danner Lane's manager. It was the same week I got a job offer from Marc Jacobs, which would start after graduation. I was top of my class at FIT, Molly. I'm no slouch.

Jake and I went out to celebrate our good news. We shared a pitcher of strong margaritas, and when Jake told the bartender about my job offer, he brought us a round of tequila shots. Doubles. We were drunk when we left the bar, too giddy to be hungry. It was hot out, one of those wonderfully humid nights when the city just cloaks you in heat, and Jake and I walked out to the East River path to catch a little breeze.

"My Sisi." Jake looked at me, and a slow smile spread across my face. I wasn't crazy about the fact that people still called me Sisi—my old childhood nickname—but coming from Jake's lips, the moniker always sounded endearing. "Will your parents be at graduation next week?" he asked.

A hard block formed behind my collarbone, the way it did when I'd been drinking and thought about my parents. "Yeah, right." The wind blew strands of hair into my face, and I brushed them away. "They didn't even come to my high school graduation."

Jake studied me, his eyes softening in surprise. "Neither did mine."

"Really?"

He nodded somberly. "You would think, especially with us both being only children . . . that they'd want to be there."

I swallowed hard. "I know."

Jake gazed out over the dark, glossy river. "Sometimes I think my parents wish they hadn't had me at all."

"I'm sure that's not true," I said, though I knew it was possible. I often had the same thought about my parents. I knew what people were capable of.

"No, like—" Jake paused. "I heard them once. My mom said it."

"What do you mean?"

He was quiet for a few moments. Then, his eyes found mine. "I was in fifth grade. I'd been at the Lanes', practicing in their garage like we did most days after school. I walked in the back door just before dinner and overheard my parents talking from the mudroom—they hadn't heard me come in. My dad said, 'He's always next door with those gingers and their liberal folks, it's almost like he's part of their goddamn family and not ours.' And then my mom said—verbatim, 'cause I'll never forget—'I know. Some days, I think we'd all be better off if that's the way it was.'"

Jake's anecdote silenced me. I stared at him, at the pain that contoured the edges of his face. I almost couldn't believe that we shared the same wound, the one that never really healed.

He gave a sad smile. "I've never told anyone that before."

I reached for his hand, running my thumb over his callused fingers. Something rich and warm—honor, maybe—blossomed around my heart. "Not even the Lanes?"

Jake shook his head. "As much as Sam and Hale are my chosen brothers, there's a distance between us when it comes to . . . family stuff. They'd never be able to understand what it's like to go through life without that kind of unconditional love. What it feels like to just sort of float along, untethered."

I stepped closer to him, resting my cheek against his chest as the hot wind whipped off the river against us. "Well, *I* understand. I know that untethered feeling exactly."

"You do?"

"Yes. My parents don't give a shit about me, either." My voice caught a little. The tequila had me feeling raw, emotional. I knew I'd lose it if I went into the details. "So to answer your question, they won't be at my graduation next week. Believe me."

"Screw them, then." Jake moved his hands up my back and neck, tilting my face to look at his. "Because I'll be there." When he leaned down to kiss me, my whole body rang.

Together, the two of us were unshakable, a power couple. I treasured having him on my arm at parties and events; I saw the way other women ogled him whenever we were out on the town, the envious stares they'd shoot me. My friend Debbie referred to him as "a snack and a half," and it was easy to see why. Jake wasn't oblivious to his good looks, but he didn't seem to know just how handsome he was, either. At least not back then. He wasn't arrogant or assuming; when girls were flirtatious, his response was friendly, but he didn't flirt back. It was part of why I loved him so insanely. And why I trusted him, too.

I went to as many of Jake's shows as work allowed, always finding my way to the front of the crowds, which became more and more packed as Danner Lane's following grew. Onstage, Jake was committed, radiant, *alive*. He said it grounded him to know I was there, but he rarely acknowledged me—he was too in the zone. I loved seeing him play, loved watching his fingers brush the steel strings of his guitar and knowing what those same hands would do to me later. I treasured that of all the enraptured girls in the audience, only I got to have him.

I started looking for two-bedroom apartments over the summer, with the idea that we'd move in together when my lease was up in the fall. We never *really* talked about it—it just seemed like a logical, unspoken next step. We were spending every night in the same bed; we were ambitious; we were in love, tethered only to each other. Our future was bright.

"Let's make Jake-and-Sisi babies," he whispered one night in July, when we'd been dating a year.

"You want to have babies, now?" I laughed. We were lying in bed; he was playing with my hair.

"Not *now*. Just, someday. Think about it—how awesome would our kids be?"

And I did think about it. In truth, I'd been thinking about it for weeks, since that night on the East River path: the dream of our life together taking hold in my mind, rooting there, blooming. I would be a loving, adoring mother—the opposite of my own, who spent her days numbed out on Oxy and chardonnay, almost as oblivious to my existence as my father.

With Jake by my side, we'd be an invincible team. We'd fill the void of unconditional love in each other and funnel it down to our children. We'd create the family neither of us had ever had.

The sounds of a lively summer night in the city drifted in through the open window—girls clicking along the sidewalk in heels, cackling with drunken laughter as they headed to meet their friends or crushes at whatever bar or club was calling them. It was fun out there, no question—I'd been a party girl in college and knew just how extraordinary such nights could be. But in that moment, nothing could've lured me from the solace of Jake's warm body, his heart beating steadily against my chest, loving me.

I felt it then, as he ran his fingers through my hair: the certainty that our lives were bound together forever, that this perfect man who held me safely in his arms would be the father of my babies. Besides, he'd just said so himself.

But that October, when I crafted an email with a carefully curated list of StreetEasy links and sent it to Jake, something shifted. He didn't respond. And for a few torturous days after that, he was distant. He blamed his preoccupation on drama with the band, but I knew something was seriously wrong when he didn't come over after his shifts at the restaurant three nights in a row. He finally called, said we should meet in Tompkins Square Park when I got off work.

"I don't want to move in together, Sisi," he confessed that evening, shifting uncomfortably on the park bench beside me. I'll never forget the way it felt to hear Jake say those words.

My heart dropped into my stomach. "Jake, I know those apartments I sent are on the pricier side, but you know we can make it work with my trust fund; you wouldn't need to pay more than you already—"

"This isn't about money, Sisi."

I felt my throat dry up and tighten, like it was fighting to swallow sand. "Maybe it's too soon," I managed.

"Yeah," he mumbled, staring at the ground, the dead grass curling below our rickety bench. He reached for my hand, and the relief in my body was so immense I wanted to cry. He wasn't breaking up with me.

For the rest of the fall, Jake and I fell back into a routine. The passion had cooled, but I knew we would find it again. We were just busy. Danner Lane's momentum was continuing to build—they were playing more local shows than ever and were finally on the brink of signing a record deal. And I was swamped at work, up for a big promotion. I re-signed my lease at East Fifth Street for another year. We were still so young, I had to remind myself. What was the rush to move in together, anyway? I didn't mention the idea to Jake again.

The week before Christmas, I got really sick. I threw up in the trash bin under my desk at the office because I couldn't make it to the bathroom in time. When it happened again the next day, my work friend Kim placed a pregnancy test next to my keyboard.

"I just have a feeling," she said.

I went home that night and peed on the stick. The test was positive. I froze, staring at the two pink lines in disbelief. I ran out to Duane Reade in my pajamas and bought half a dozen more tests—every brand the store sold. They were all positive.

My heart pounded behind my rib cage. How had this happened? I was on the Pill; we were careful. Had I been sloppy and forgotten a day or two the previous month, with the chaos of work and the stress of Jake's cooling detachment? It was possible.

I didn't call Jake. He was already back in North Carolina for Christmas and hadn't invited me to go with him, even though he knew my parents hadn't spoken a word to me about joining them for the holidays. I'd only received a rushed, poorly crafted email from my mother, stating that they'd flown to Barbados and hoped I'd have a nice holiday in New York with "the boyfriend."

Part of me was still too pissed at Jake for leaving me alone at Christmas to call; another part worried about his reaction to the news. Pregnancy was quite a bomb to drop.

But as I lay in bed that night and imagined the growing cluster of cells inside my body—half me, half Jake—I remembered his words from the summer, which were never far from the center of my mind. *Let's make Jake-and-Sisi babies. How awesome would our kids be?*

Jake wanted this; he'd *said* it. There was nothing more miraculous than a baby, a new life, and perhaps that was what we needed to solidify our love, to get back to the place we'd been before.

I woke up the next morning with a fresh perspective, ready to share the news. But when I called Jake, he didn't answer, and the automated greeting said his mailbox was full. I waited all day for him to try me back, but the only person who called was Kim, and I lied when she asked me if the test had been positive.

Jake didn't call the next day, or that weekend, or on Christmas. Sleepless nights passed, my body shaking with nausea, my mind churning, my heart sick with desperation. Where was the father of my baby? Why was he ignoring me? Ignoring *us*?

Jake was already back in the city when he finally called two days after Christmas, claiming he'd forgotten to pack his phone charger and hadn't been able to find one at home.

I wasn't stupid. By that point, I'd understood that Jake was in no way ready to be a father. Not yet. This child wasn't going to save us. On the contrary, telling him about the baby would rip us right down the middle.

I realized this first in my gut, then my heart, and luckily the rest of my body wasn't far behind. It was a Saturday night, and Jake was out playing a show in East Williamsburg. I'd told him I was coming down with something, too sick to go, but he didn't seem to care. I still remember the blood, the way it ran down my thighs onto the floor, how it smeared the seat of the toilet. I let it sit there till the morning before I bothered wiping it up. That blood was all I had left of the most precious thing I'd ever known.

January was a frigid month in the city, but not as cold as Jake. He'd withdrawn again, dodging my calls and blaming the band for the lack of free time that was turning him into a shitty partner.

One Sunday morning, he finally mustered the balls to dump me, but not before I saw him with you, Molly. I was a shell of myself by then, empty and hollow as a tin can, never not thinking of the blood, the sight of it swirling down the toilet. But I hadn't lost my common sense.

I spent the Saturday before he left me in Tompkins Square Park, which was kitty-corner from his studio. He'd told me he'd be there all weekend, practicing with the Lanes. The day was blustery, below freezing, but I was too immobilized by pain to feel the icy cold. I waited to see him leave the building, my eyes peeled for the sight of his distinct hair, the familiar of the line of his shoulders.

When Jake finally emerged from the swinging doors, he wasn't alone. You were with him, hand in hand, both of you bundled in winter coats. I remember you were wearing a gray wool jacket and a red hat with a pom-pom, your wheat-blond waves long and loose—I'll never forget that very first sight of you. From my post in the park, I watched the two of you walk south on Avenue A. While you waited for the crosswalk to change, he leaned over and kissed your cheek, and it took every fiber of restraint not to run over and claw at your face. I waited until the two of you were out of sight before walking the six blocks back to my apartment, bitter wind whipping my face. I turned on the shower as hot as it would go, stepped under the water, and screamed.

Chapter Ten
Molly

2013

Molly fell for Jake quickly, easily. She'd known she loved him since that first night, though she waited two more dates to sleep with him—Nina said she absolutely could *not* do so sooner than the third date, not if she wanted their connection to become something real.

And the magic of it was, Molly felt sure Jake was falling for her, too. One February afternoon, over Presidents' Day weekend, they were working in Jake's apartment. Molly was editing a short story for her thesis, and Jake was writing a new song for the album. Snow fell heavily outside the windows, piling high on the sidewalks and emptying the streets. Sam and Hale were back in North Carolina for the long weekend, and the apartment was cozy and warm, filled with the sound of Pachelbel. Classical music helped Jake focus.

From the other end of the couch, Jake nudged his socked foot against Molly's. She glanced up from her laptop. He smiled at her, his eyes gleaming blue, and she was filled with an almost unbearable blend of affection and awe. He was hers. How was it possible? She often thought of Jake's ex, of the girl who'd tried and failed to make him stay. She couldn't imagine the pain of loving someone like Jake and having him not love her back.

"You know what the song I'm writing is called?" he asked.

Molly shook her head, mirroring his smile.

"'January Girl.'"

Molly said nothing, a clamp over her heart. She was tempted to make a joke—*Who's February Girl, then?*—but she didn't. The moment was real, and she didn't want to trivialize it.

Her heart felt like a balloon, inflating inside her chest. It could've carried her to the sky. She'd never experienced this before—the feeling that her own exhilaration was safe. Molly was certain they loved each

other—she knew musicians didn't write songs about girls just because—
even though it would've been crazy to say it after only six weeks.

Nina had always told Molly it would happen this way, that when she
met the right person, it wouldn't be complicated. She'd just *know*. And
Molly did know. She knew Jake was the light that touched her darkest
corners. She knew that because of him, her deepest dreams felt conquer-
able. She knew that his touch sent waves of electricity through her body,
that being physically near him—even just in the same room—made her
feel more alive than anything or anyone else ever had.

Walking home from a shift at Angelina's a few weeks later, Molly
realized that something big was finally happening to her in New York.
It was Jake Danner.

The way he consumed her was like her senses had been woken up
after a long hibernation. The intoxicating smell of his skin, raw cedar
mixed with bar soap; his clear, unadorned voice; the protected, treasured
way he made her feel. Images of him, conversations that replayed in her
head, took up every square inch of Molly's mind.

She wasn't completely naive; she realized that what she felt stretched
beyond healthy love. Some days, it felt closer to obsession, and this worried Molly. But Jake wasn't a fantasy, she had to remind herself. He wasn't
some toxic, wishy-washy fuckboy, like she'd worried he might be in the
beginning. He could have picked any girl out of any bar, but he had
picked her. He adored her. He'd written a *song* about her.

"This is the honeymoon phase," Liz explained over Chinese takeout
with Nina and Ev. "Lots of sex, lots of long, lazy days inhaling each other's
scent. Just enjoy it, Moll. It ends eventually."

"The honeymoon phase, she means," Nina cut in, chewing a spring
roll. "Not the relationship."

Liz shrugged as if to say: *Not necessarily.* Molly flashed her a glare,
she couldn't help it. Lately, she had an odd feeling that Liz wasn't entirely
happy for her.

Everly scooped more fried rice onto her plate. "Moll, you're just
freaking out because you never had this with Kevin or Darby. And definitely not with that Cameron guy."

Molly looked at her best friends. Sometimes she truly believed the
three of them knew her better than she knew herself.

Thus far in her life, Molly had dated only a few men. In high school,
there'd been a short-term boyfriend, Kevin, who'd lasted only half of her

junior year. Molly hadn't been a particularly great girlfriend to him—in retrospect, she knew she hadn't felt enough of what you're supposed to feel when you commit to someone. In college, there was her relationship with Darby, a tumultuous year and a half that began her freshman fall, his senior, and ended when he called to tell her he'd met someone else, the real estate broker who'd found his rent-controlled apartment on Beacon Hill.

These last eighteen months in New York postcollege had been Molly's first real exposure to the world of "dating." And though nothing particularly satisfying had come of it yet—there was only Cameron, the Ph.D. student she'd fallen hard for who'd turned out to be a (self-proclaimed) emotionally unavailable recluse—on her more optimistic days, Molly carried the feeling that, when it came to love, something big was bound to happen to her in this city.

She didn't think of herself as picky, but her friends told her she was. Everly pointed out that she liked only smart guys, which was true, but Molly thought that was a reasonable attribute to seek. Nina didn't always seem to care about intelligence in the men she dated, but Everly's girlfriend—a graphic designer named Sage, whom she'd met online—was sharp as a tack. And Liz; well, Liz was in another category altogether, because she'd never been single, not for more than a minute. She'd jumped straight from her long-term high school boyfriend to her college—and current—boyfriend, Zander, whom she'd been with for five years now. According to Liz, they'd be married by the time she was twenty-eight. At twenty-three, that still felt a lifetime away.

Molly's actual problem, she knew, was her fragile trust in men. She'd been eight the day her father tossed his bags into the back of the station wagon and drove away, a memory she carried with her, the defining image of her childhood. The dreary March afternoon that Darby called and told her there was another girl in the picture, Molly felt a range of crushing emotions, but shock wasn't one of them. At the same time tears dripped down her face, Molly had wanted to laugh at the strange realization that she wasn't surprised. Men were going to leave her. The darkness in her had been waiting for this.

"You really don't think I've had a relationship like this before?" Molly probed her friends.

"Sorry, but no." Nina shrugged.

"Even with Darby?"

"Ugh, especially with Darby." Liz scrunched her nose. "I know he broke your heart, but he was such a worm."

"What we mean," Nina said, giving Liz a pointed look, "is that all those guys—except for Kevin, I guess—made you feel bad more often than they made you feel good. *That's* why this thing with Jake feels different."

Molly was falling in love, that much was clear. So hard and fast it would've been easy to lose control. But the irony was, with Jake at her side, Molly now felt more in control of her life than she ever had before. Her productivity and motivation had reached an all-time high.

Jake inspired her writing more than any professor at NYU, more than any of the authors she worshipped and reread most fervently. Molly was in awe of Jake's work ethic and commitment to his craft; it impressed and attracted her on a deep, subliminal level that manifested as influence. Working late into the night in Jake's apartment on North Tenth Street, Molly liked to imagine them as an artsy couple from the sixties or seventies—Patti Smith and Robert Mapplethorpe, perhaps.

By April, Molly had finished her thesis and was already working on fusing the individual stories into a novel. Jake had a connection to a literary agent—a woman he knew through the Lanes—who'd told him she'd be happy to take a look at Molly's book when it was ready.

Molly's book, as Jake was always referring to it. The idea of publishing a legitimate novel had once felt like a pipe dream, but because Jake believed it was possible, Molly had begun to believe it could be, too. "Molly's book is incredible," he gushed to her friends over drinks at Skinny Dennis. They were out with their significant others, celebrating Nina's birthday. Molly felt a warm glow spread through her chest at the realization that, for the first time ever, all four of them were in relationships. Good relationships, too.

"Molly's book?" Liz raised an eyebrow. "If my roommate were writing a book, I think I'd know about it."

Jake said nothing, and suddenly, the air was charged with a sense of challenge, the way it often seemed to be when Jake and Liz were in the same room. Molly didn't understand what it was about him that seemed to get under Liz's skin. Couldn't her friend just be happy for her? Molly had always supported Liz and Zander.

"I'm connecting the short stories from my thesis to become a novel, hopefully," Molly explained, swiveling her beer glass. She felt uncomfortable, a twinge of guilt that she'd never shared this with her friends before.

Though the majority of her classmates at NYU were aspiring writers, Molly didn't like to admit she was among them. She'd lied about it on more than one occasion, explaining to her professors and classmates that she'd likely use her degree to teach or pursue a career in publishing, rather than write professionally.

Until Jake, her dream of a life spent creating fiction remained private, a deep-rooted ambition from childhood she'd kept hidden in a tiny corner of her heart. It was Molly's father who'd fueled her love of reading and literature at a young age. He'd stocked her bookshelves with classics like *The Wind in the Willows, Charlotte's Web, Alice's Adventures in Wonderland,* and *The Lion, the Witch and the Wardrobe.* At night, he was a writer himself, closed off in the office downstairs long after Molly's mother had gone to bed. By day, he worked as a car salesman at the Saab dealership in Denville, the suburban New Jersey town where Molly was born and raised.

After her mother kicked her father out, Molly tore apart the office for bits of writing he might've left behind. She had a feeling she'd never see him again, and she desperately wanted whatever scraps of him remained. But she'd found nothing. He'd taken all of it with him, to wherever the wind had blown him next.

What her father did leave behind were books. Boxes and boxes of books, the bulk of his collection. James Baldwin, Joyce Carol Oates, Toni Morrison, Jay McInerney, Cormac McCarthy, Joan Didion, Tom Wolfe. The names of her father's most cherished literary idols.

There was a note taped to one of the boxes, his familiar scribble: *Never stop reading. Read everything you can get your hands on.*

That was it. Those were his parting words. No "I love you," and nothing at all for her brother, Andrew. The truth was, Molly had never blamed her mother for making him go. Her father intrigued and enchanted her, but by the age of eight, Molly had understood that he wasn't a reliable man. She'd seen what he'd put her mother through, and no woman deserved that.

Nonetheless, his message stuck. Molly never stopped reading. And the reading made her want to write. She suspected that's the way it had gone for her father, too.

"Are you seriously writing a book?" Liz's eyes were glued to Molly.

"It's a new idea, but something Jake has been helping me with. Or encouraging me to do, I should say."

"It's really, *really* good." Jake slung his arm around Molly, and she couldn't help the smile that spread across her face. "This girl is a seriously gifted writer."

A month later, Molly graduated from NYU with her MFA, high honors on her thesis. Her mom and Andrew came to graduation along with Jake, and afterward, the four of them trudged uptown to J. G. Melon, her mother's favorite restaurant in the city.

Molly loved her family—her mother's strong spirit and contagious enthusiasm, her brother Andrew's self-deprecating humor and deep intelligence. Andrew was three years younger than Molly and had just finished his junior year of college. He was a political science major who planned on going to law school, and even though he and Jake had next to nothing in common, they still hit it off.

After lunch, her mom and Andrew caught the train back to Denville, where her mother still lived and worked.

Before they hopped into their taxi bound for Penn Station, her mother shrouded Molly in a cloud of her signature Lancôme, squeezing her on the street outside Melon's.

"I'm so proud of you, Moo," she whispered, using the nickname she'd had for her daughter since she was a baby. Originally, it was *Molly Moo*, but only the *Moo* part had stuck.

Molly leaned her head on Jake's shoulder on the subway back to Brooklyn—exhausted but happy.

"Your mom and brother are great," he said as the train roared underground, cutting across the river.

"They're the best." She nodded against him, quiet for a moment. "You never talk about your parents."

He made a sound—not a laugh but a scoff. "There's not much to say."

"Well, what're they like?"

"They're not like anything."

"Come on." Molly nudged him. "You're really not going to tell me?"

A few beats of silence passed. "My parents are nothing like your mom, Moll." Jake squeezed her hand. "That was a really sweet present she got you."

Molly sighed. He clearly wanted to change the subject. "I know," she said. "I'm still shocked. I wasn't expecting that."

For graduation, her mother had gifted her a yoga teacher training program at Bhakti, the Williamsburg studio where she practiced. Molly had mentioned her interest in the program to her mother earlier in the spring. She loved the idea of teaching yoga; it seemed like an ideal, flexible way to bring in extra cash—much more appealing than continuing on at Angelina's and coming home in the evenings to run her espresso-stained uniform under hot water and wash the stale-bread smell from her hair. The most popular instructors at Bhakti made a hundred dollars per class, just for an hour of work. That was what Molly brought in over the course of two whole shifts at Angelina's, tips included.

Besides, she went to Bhakti so often she basically knew the sequences by heart. She could see herself making playlists and creating themes around her classes. She'd wear bright-colored leggings and a signature Bhakti tank, grabbing matcha with the other teachers between classes and discussing things like headstands and chakras. She'd come home centered and grounded and ready to write.

But the program was expensive—two thousand dollars—and she never would've asked her mother to pay for something like that. Her mom worked a solid job—she'd been a labor and delivery nurse at the hospital in Denville for almost thirty years—but she'd raised two kids with one income and was extra careful with money, especially after the reckless way her father had abused their finances. The Diamonds had always had enough to get by, but there was never much left over.

Molly had been hesitant to accept such a generous gift, but her mother had insisted. Molly suspected it had something to do with the heart-to-heart conversation they'd shared a month earlier, when she'd been home for the weekend and had confessed to her mom that she wanted to use her degree to give writing a real shot.

"I just don't want you to think I'm trying to follow in Dad's footsteps," Molly had admitted, nestled beside her mother on the couch.

"All I care about is that you chase your dreams," her mother had replied, smoothing Molly's hair. "It doesn't matter what your father did. Besides, you're a much better writer than he ever was. Trust me. And he didn't have a shred of your discipline."

Jake grabbed Molly's hand as the subway slowed to a stop at Bedford Avenue. They ran up the stairs and out of the station, back into the light.

On the corner of North Seventh, he looped his arms around her neck. "You're going to be the sexiest yoga teacher in New York."

She laughed. "Will you come to my classes?"

"*Yes.*" Jake pressed his forehead against hers. "As long as you give me

Savasana massages at the end." He grinned, leaning in to kiss her. Molly parted her lips to let him. She could've kissed him forever. It was surreal, still, that he belonged to her.

Later, Danner Lane was opening at Brooklyn Bowl. Molly hardly ever missed Jake's shows, but that night she had plans with her friends. Since they hadn't been able to attend her daytime graduation, Everly insisted they all get together at Radegast for celebratory drinks.

It was only 7:30 when Molly left Radegast, tipsy off a full pint of cider after no real dinner. It was still light out, the sky a deep blue streaked with pink clouds. Molly didn't think there was anything better than a late May night in the city, the summer stretched ahead like a promise.

The evening had been cut shorter than Molly anticipated when her friends scattered off in various directions: Nina to a work event, Everly to dinner with Sage, Liz to a party with Zander. Molly hadn't planned on going to Jake's show, but Brooklyn Bowl was only nine blocks away. She could get there just in time to catch the opening act.

At the entrance, Molly flashed her ID to the bouncer, who nodded with disinterest before letting her inside. Molly glanced at her phone—it was quarter of eight. Danner Lane was on in fifteen minutes; she still had time to find Jake and surprise him.

She peered around inside the venue, which was busy but not yet packed, and scanned the room for Jake. Maybe he was already backstage.

Molly pushed through a group of men in office clothes—crisp tailored shirts, loosened ties—and one of them bumped her with his elbow.

"Sorry," he said, glancing over his shoulder. His right hand clutched a drink, his left lifted in apology. Their eyes met, and the man tilted his head, as though he recognized her. He was handsome in a classic, textbook way—dark, floppy hair, square jaw. Did she know him? Molly didn't think so, and she didn't have time to figure it out. She wanted to find Jake before he went onstage.

And then, all too suddenly, her head turned, and there he was. Standing by the bar, and not alone. A woman's arms were wrapped around his neck, her body and lips pressed to his. And not just any woman—it was Maxine. His manager's assistant, the skanky girl who constantly flirted with Jake and was always calling him nicknames.

Molly felt her body go rigid, her cells freezing with shock. Her heart thrashed so hard against her chest she could hear the blood pumping in her ears. This wasn't real. Was she having a nightmare? Some kind of lucid dream? She wanted to cry out, to scream, but she couldn't move. She couldn't make a sound.

Then Jake pulled back, his eyes flickering over Maxine's shoulder. They landed directly on Molly's. For a split second, he looked confused. Then, as if in slow motion, his face morphed into an expression of white-hot panic. In a flash, he disentangled himself from Maxine. He bolted toward Molly, but she sped for the exit. The venue was filling quickly.

Molly felt the tears spill over, streaming down her face, and out of the corner of her eye, she saw the dark-haired guy again, the one wearing a dress shirt and tie. He was still staring straight at her, ignoring his friends, his lips parted in concern as though he'd just watched the entire scene play out. Molly rushed by him, the crowds swarming around her as she swung open the double doors and stumbled out onto the street, not the same person she'd been ten minutes before.

Chapter Eleven
Jake

2013

Jake left Molly's apartment at quarter of six, just as she was heading out to meet Nina, Liz, and Everly at Radegast biergarten.

He had to swing by Brooklyn Bowl for sound check, which only took thirty minutes. Then, he headed back to his place to shower and shave. He threw on a fresh pair of jeans and a white T-shirt with a picture of Bob Dylan smoking a joint on the front—one of his favorites to wear during a show. Sam and Hale had already been dressed and ready before sound check. As usual, Jake was the one running behind.

When he arrived back at the venue, his crew was by the bar. There was an open case of Brooklyn Lager—the bartender Damian always let them drink for free when they played the Bowl.

Sam pursed his lips at the sight of Jake, as if to say, *Cutting it close.*

In response, Jake rolled his eyes, as if to say, *Stop always being so anal about timing. We're not on for an hour.*

They could communicate like this, without words. Hale, too. Jake had known the Lanes forever—since he was in diapers—and they were the closest thing he had to brothers.

Hale tossed Jake a beer. Their manager, Jerry, was there, too, and his assistant, Maxine.

"Where's alt-J?" Jake asked. alt-J was the band they were opening for. Jake was a huge fan and had been excited to play this show for months.

"You just missed them." Jerry rubbed his dark beard. "They ran across the street to grab a quick bite at Reynard."

Jake nodded, cracking open the beer and taking a thirsty sip. "I really want to meet those guys."

"There's always the after-party," Maxine said coyly, her eyes landing

on Jake. She handed him the bottle of Jack Daniel's they'd all been passing around.

Jake took a swig, averting his gaze. He and Maxine had hooked up
a few times the previous fall, when he and Sisi were on the rocks. On
the rocks in Jake's eyes, at least. Sisi had seemed to think nothing was
wrong in their relationship, though he'd tried to tell her several times his
feelings had changed. But communication had never been Jake's strong
suit, so perhaps his attempt to slowly and easily let Sisi down—instead
of ripping off the Band-Aid—had missed its mark.

He shouldn't have resorted to cheating—Jake knew this. But sometimes he knew what was right and did the opposite, anyway. He couldn't
articulate the reason behind this behavior, but he knew it wasn't calculated. He hadn't wanted to hurt Sisi—not at all. He'd just grown tired of
how entitled she was, tired of sitting across from her at restaurants and
listening to the rude, snarky way she treated the waitstaff. Sisi worked
hard, but she was spoiled, constantly throwing her trust fund in his face
like a weapon whenever they argued. Worst of all, she lacked any self-
awareness; she was unwilling to acknowledge the parts of herself that
had begun to turn Jake off, and he knew she was never going to change.

He'd slept with Maxine only three times. She'd made it easy for him,
honestly. She attended every show with Jerry, behind the scenes, ensur-
ing it all ran smoothly. She could be a little desperate, but she was good
at her job, and she'd never failed to make it clear to Jake that she would
fuck him, if that's what he wanted. Maxine was a few years older—late
twenties, probably—with jet-black hair and an impish look about her,
plus one of the best bodies Jake had ever seen. Curvy hips, tiny waist,
perky breasts. She was smoking hot.

Jake never told Sisi he'd cheated. What was the point? Emotionally,
he was over their relationship, and he was *going* to break up with her—
he'd just been too swamped with the band to deal with it.

With Maxine, it had been casual; she didn't seem to want more than
sex, which was ideal. When Molly entered the picture in January, Maxine
hadn't acted jealous. She'd only ruffled Jake's hair one night, after a show,
and said, "You sure move through them quickly, Jakey." She was always
calling him *Jakey*, which he hated.

Jake finished his beer, then two more. The bottle of Jack went around
the bar a few more times, dulling the edges the way Jake liked. He felt

light and buzzy. When Maxine passed him the whiskey again, Jerry intercepted.

"That's enough for Danner." He grabbed the neck of the bottle and took another pull for himself. "You guys are on in twenty. Backstage in ten, Jake." Jerry wandered off, and Jake realized that he and Maxine were alone at the bar. Well, not *alone*—people had begun to funnel in for the show—but Sam and Hale had disappeared. Had they gone backstage already?

Jake stood. He felt dizzy, shaky on his feet, and regretted the last couple of whiskey pulls. With those, on top of the Brooklyn Lagers, plus the IPA he'd chugged getting ready at home, Jake was on his way to being drunk.

Maxine moved toward him, lifting her chin so that it brushed his chest. Her bee-stung lips curled into a grin. "Jakey."

He drew in a breath, shaking his head. "I can't, Maxine," he told her. "It's different with Molly. You know that."

Maxine placed a hand on the side of his neck, the pads of her fingers gripping his skin. She stepped closer, blinking up at him. Her shirt was tight and low-cut, revealing a generous sliver of cleavage. He hated that he was turned on. It was just biology. It almost made him angry, the physical way his body responded when his heart was somewhere else. Alcohol made the resistance feel even more impossible. Maxine's pillowy lips brushed his. Jake closed his eyes and let the haze of his mind take over.

When he looked up, when he blinked over Maxine's shoulder to find Molly staring directly at him, Jake thought he had to be dreaming. He held her hazel gaze for a passing moment, disoriented. But then the realization hit him, a dropkick in the gut: he wasn't dreaming. He was there, at the Bowl's crowded bar, much drunker than he was supposed to be, Maxine's arms coiled around his neck.

Jake shook Maxine off him, panic rising in his chest. A primal, blinding fear locked each of his senses. No. *No.*

Molly vanished into the crowd as he fought his way toward her, pushing between throngs of concertgoers, some of whom recognized him, who called out his name. He ignored the fans, but by the time he reached the exit, Molly was gone. Then a hand yanked his shoulder, jerking him around.

"*Jesus*, Danner, where the fuck have you been?" Sam looked furious, his face beet red, and he was out of breath. "It's ten past eight, we're supposed to be onstage right now. Let's *go*."

The performance was Jake's worst to date—sloppy and half-hearted—and as a result, the worst show in Danner Lane's short history. Afterward, Sam and Hale wouldn't look at him. They left Brooklyn Bowl with Jerry and Maxine without saying goodbye, leaving Jake alone in a prison of his own self-loathing.

He stumbled down Wythe, calling Molly again and again. But she didn't pick up, and finally her phone stopped ringing at all, so Jake went home and crawled into bed. He fell into fitful bursts of slumber, and at 6:00 a.m. when it was clear good sleep was out of the question, he got up and left the apartment.

A girl was just buzzing into Molly's building when Jake arrived. She balanced a cardboard tray of coffees, and Jake held the door for her, then followed her inside. He practically sprinted up the three flights of stairs.

Molly opened her door almost right away when he knocked, which told him she'd been up, that she hadn't slept, either.

At the sight of her—bleary-eyed, tangled blond hair—Jake's eyes filled. He wasn't used to crying in response to his emotions, but he was too panicked to be unsettled by his own vulnerability, the way he normally might've been. He loved her. He'd suspected it for a while, but now—in this terrible moment—he knew for sure. He loved her in a way he'd never loved another human being before in his life.

"Nothing happened," he said breathlessly. "Maxine—she came on to me." It was the truth, and Jake needed her to know it. "There was all this whiskey—" He paused, the pain of the memory lodged in his throat. "She kissed me, Moll. She kissed me for half a second, and I pushed her off of me. I *swear.*"

Molly reached behind Jake to close the front door, which felt like a positive sign. She wasn't kicking him out. At least not yet.

She rubbed her eyes and walked into the living room off the kitchen, sinking down onto the couch. He loved the way she looked in her over-size NYU T-shirt, her long legs tucked underneath her. He wanted to crawl into her lap and stay there forever.

Jake lowered himself to sit beside her, slowly, carefully—testing her limits.

"I'm in love with you, Moll," he said helplessly. "I know it's the absolute worst time to say that for the first time, but I can't not tell you. It's all

I thought about all night. That I love you and if I lose you, if I fuck this up, I'll never forgive myself."

Molly looked at him, her eyes shiny and wide. He touched the faded scar above her left eyebrow, tracing it with his finger.

"Do you promise, Jake?" She blinked back tears. "Do you promise that's all that happened with Maxine?"

"I promise." He wrapped his arms around her neck, pulling her close. He inhaled the vanilla and sandalwood scent of her, as precious to him as his own heartbeat. "I promise." He whispered it again and again, his face buried in her hair.

Years later, when the acoustic version of "Molly's Song" would release and a shot at a solo career would finally begin to feel possible for Jake, he'd think back to this night, to how close he had come to losing Molly. Of course, he did lose her, eventually. And he would wonder, not for the first time since he started writing music again, where in the world Molly was, right at that moment. He'd wonder if her hair was still long and wild, the way it had been when they were together. If she still ate cinnamon raisin toast with peanut butter for breakfast every morning. If the scar above her left eyebrow was the same, or if the years had faded it further.

Three lines would drift into his mind then, without much effort. He'd grab his pencil, catch the words before they escaped him.

Wild hair
Wild heart
Take me back to our wild start

Chapter Twelve
Sabrina

Obsession has always interested me. The best artists, the most brilliant innovators, they've all been driven by it. It straddles the line between passion and insanity; it instigates creativity and genius despite the darkness in which it lingers. To be obsessed with someone or something is to adopt a single-minded drive that reduces the rest of the world to sheer insignificance.

That's how it was for me, with Jake. I couldn't shake him from my system, though I will admit: I didn't try very hard. Fixating on Jake was an itch I took pains to scratch. I fed it like my own precious beast. I thought of the blood constantly, disappearing down the toilet, and wondered where it had gone. The remnants of our baby. A life that would never be.

My closest friends from FIT, Debbie and Elena, didn't know about the miscarriage, but still, they were worried about me. They tried to set me up on blind dates with "catches" named Chad and Owen and Derek. But I didn't want Chad or Owen or Derek; I wanted *Jake*. Jake, whose callused fingers plucked the strings of his guitar the same expert way they plucked all the right strings inside my body.

He had been mine for eighteen perfect, euphoric months, and now he belonged to someone else. He belonged to you. It wasn't right.

In the midst of my grief, I'd lost weight, and stupid Debbie went so far as to call my *mother* in Palm Beach when she saw how much. I suppose fifteen pounds is a lot for a petite gal whose BMI is already on the verge of low. But Debbie didn't understand that my mom lived most of her waking minutes in a reclined position in front of Bravo or by the pool, desensitized on painkillers. When she did muster the energy to leave her couch or chaise, she played golf with other rich housewives and nibbled lettuce under the clubhouse terrace.

Still, Mom did bother to text me one evening in March. It was the first time I'd heard from her in months.

Debbie says ur not eating. U have to eat little shrinking Sisi!!!

I decided right then and there that I was done being called *Sisi*. It was a name that made me feel like a child, and I'd started going by *Sabrina* at Marc Jacobs, anyway.

Nobody at work seemed to notice or care about my diminishing waistline—all girls in fashion are twigs; disordered eating is par for the course. I still loved my job—I'd gotten a big promotion in the fall—and was grateful for the escape work provided. But when I left the office each evening, my thoughts had nowhere to go. I'd get back to the privacy of my apartment, pour myself a generous glass of chilled white wine, and think of nothing but Jake.

And you, Molly. Over the years, I've spent a great deal of time focused on you.

Jake started posting more on Instagram that first year you were together. His photos were often of the band, informational posts regarding Danner Lane's past and upcoming shows. But there were also plenty of you.

A square shot of you sitting outside at a restaurant drinking a Bloody Mary, your aviators slipping down the bridge of your nose. #mygirl

A photo of you standing on the street in a cap and gown, tall and long-limbed, a wide smile spread across your face as you wave your diploma in the air. #mygraduate

A picture of you with a rolled-up yoga mat tucked under your arm, flashing the peace sign in front of Bhakti Yoga. #myyogateacherintraining

An artsy shot of you at the beach: a close-up of the back of your shoulder and tangerine bikini strap, strands of your wheat-blond hair caught whimsically in the wind. #mymuse

A rarer photo of the two of you together, sitting side by side on the front stoop of an ambiguous building, your head on his shoulder, a set of keys dangling from his pointer finger. #myroommate

The guy who hadn't wanted to move in with me after more than a year together was shacking up with a new girl after six fucking months.

The night I saw that Instagram post, I texted Chad—one of the dull finance guys Debbie and Elena had forced me to go on a date with several months earlier—and asked if he could meet for a drink. It was a week-night; I think it was past ten. We went to the Penny Farthing and did a series of Fireball shots before I dragged him back to my apartment, where we screwed on the living room floor. I closed my eyes and tried to drown out thoughts of you and Jake in your new apartment while fibers of the sisal rug chafed my back, Chad thrusting mightily.

It wasn't the first time I'd brought a near stranger into my bed with the hope of extinguishing Jake from my mind. It never worked, though, and after Chad left, I curled into a ball on the couch and cried myself to sleep.

I hated you, Molly. I really, really hated you. And perhaps this hate was exacerbated by the fact that I didn't—and couldn't—know a thing about you. Not even your last name. Jake sometimes referenced you as "Molly" in his posts, but he never tagged you.

You remained a mystery to me and to all the girls who ogled Jake from afar as the hype behind Danner Lane skyrocketed. To be honest, I've never been able to understand what it is about you that had him so smitten. You're pretty, yes, but you're not the most beautiful girl in the room. If you wore sexier clothes and more makeup, I might be able to see it, but you let your features remain muted, ordinary. But I, on the other hand—I turn heads. Admitting this doesn't make me conceited, just honest.

That winter, a year after Jake left me, Danner Lane embarked on a twelve-city tour following the successful release of their debut album. I didn't have to be stalking Jake to get this information—everyone knew. The dates and venues were listed all over social media and the band's website, and ads for the tour appeared across the city.

There was one stop that caught my eye. Saturday, January 25, West Palm Beach, Danner Lane opening for the Black Keys.

I wasted no time booking a round-trip ticket to Florida. I emailed my parents and told them I'd be coming home that weekend, knowing they would never bother to ask why. Then I texted Martelle, my closest friend from childhood, who still lived in Palm Beach.

Coming home the weekend of 1/25, save the date, I have concert tix!

Martelle replied immediately, with two smiley faces and about a hundred exclamation points.

I banked on the fact that Jake would be traveling alone—I knew there was a chance you'd be there, following him around on tour, but my instincts told me you wouldn't be. You just seemed more independent than that.

After the show, Martelle and I would find a way to get backstage and say hi. I'd explain that I'd been home for the weekend, that Martelle and I had tickets to the Black Keys and hadn't realized Danner Lane was the opener. What a coincidence. What a small, small world.

Chapter Thirteen

Molly

2013–2014

The irony of that terrible night at Brooklyn Bowl was that it sealed Molly and Jake's relationship; coming so close to losing each other brought them to a new level, one where they were openly in love. After months of privately knowing that she loved him, Molly was finally able to say it, finally convinced that he felt the same way, that he had from the beginning. Aside from the Maxine hiccup—Molly had become more and more convinced that the moment she'd witnessed was the extent of it; nothing had actually *happened*—her life with Jake felt close to perfect.

At the end of June, Liz announced that she was moving in with Zander in Greenwich Village when her and Molly's lease ended in August. Molly felt a stab of hurt and nostalgia—she and Liz had been roommates for five years—but she wasn't fully surprised. Liz was eager to move in with Zander, and Molly had known it would happen sooner rather than later. But she hadn't expected such short notice. It was nearly July; she only had a month to find a new roommate.

Molly vented to Jake about the situation that night while he cooked them spaghetti and meatballs, Frank Sinatra playing in the background. Jake loved Sinatra.

"Move in with me," he said plainly, when she'd finished speaking.

"What?" Molly held a full glass of Malbec and placed it down on the counter. Her jaw lowered. "Jake, it's barely been six months. We can't move in together."

"Why not?"

"Because—because that's so *fast*. We're still so young."

"We're in love, Moll."

Jake had a way of taking such complex, monumental decisions and boiling them down to the simplest answers.

"Think about it," he continued, stirring the tomato sauce. "Liz left you hanging. Would you rather scramble to find some random person to live with, or move in with the guy who cooks for you every night? Who writes songs about you? Who loves you to pieces?" He raised a wooden spoonful of sauce to his lips.

"You don't cook for me every night." Molly grinned, nerves and excitement building in her stomach. "Be serious, Jake."

"I am being serious, Molly." His light blue eyes rested on hers. "Sam and Hale were just saying the other day that their buddy is moving to the city and needs a spot. I could give him my room, and we could find our own place. You and me. Why does it have to be complicated?"

"The Best Is Yet to Come" blared in the background—an omen, it seemed—the notes of Sinatra dipping and rising, and Molly stared at Jake's face. His handsome, golden face. The sweet smell of simmering tomatoes filled her nostrils.

"You never say what you're thinking." He paused. "Is this about Maxine?"

"*No,* Jake. You know that's behind us."

"Then what is it?" he pressed. "Just say it."

"Fine." Molly sighed, brushing a wisp of hair off her face. "If I'm being honest, I've always sort of had this pact with myself . . . I've always told myself that I would never move in with someone unless . . ." Her voice trailed.

"Unless what?"

"Unless I was sure we're going to end up together." She watched the words land, the indiscernible expression appeared on Jake's face. "I know that sounds old-fashioned. I didn't mean—I just meant that we're young. And I'm sure you don't want that kind of pressure on you."

"Moll." Jake set the spoon down. His expression grew serious. "I *do* think we're going to end up together. Don't you?"

Molly smiled. The answer was so easy; she didn't even have to think about it. Maybe it was the naivete of being twenty-three, the freedom of being able to choose with your heart over your head, of not being trapped by implications or inevitabilities. Or maybe it was Jake; maybe the two of them *were*—plain and simple—meant to be.

"I do," she said truthfully. For a moment, she let her mind wander back to six months earlier, a life without Jake. An enjoyable life, too: one with friends and family and books and yoga and vacations. But a stubborn darkness had persisted inside her, a crushing form of self-doubt that dissipated when she met Jake. He made everything so much better; he took her world and brightened it, like the filter on her phone that made images sharpen and colors pop. She'd never been this happy.

Jake put the lid on the skillet and let the sauce continue to simmer. He walked around the counter to where Molly stood. He tucked her long, blond waves behind her ears and kissed her deeply.

"Then let's do it. Let's live together. Just say yes," he said, but Molly was already nodding.

They moved into a one-bedroom on Driggs Avenue, just around the corner from the subway. The apartment was small, nothing fancy, but it was theirs. It was a fifth-floor walk-up, but the selling point had been the wide, east-facing windows in both the bedroom and living room that flooded the mornings with light. That first summer together, they fell into an easy, intuitive routine.

Jake spent part of most days at the studio with Sam and Hale. When it came time to record the album, their producer, Ron Dixon from Dixon Entertainment, flew in from LA. Jerry oversaw the recording, too, but fortunately, Maxine only worked events. The band's debut album—titled *The Narrows* after the beach in North Carolina where Jake and the Lanes had frequented as adolescents—was set to release in December. Danner Lane was being pitched as Mumford & Sons meets Kings of Leon, though Molly thought there was another comp there, too—something slightly more cheerful and pop-infused. Maroon 5, perhaps, though Molly didn't think Jake would be thrilled with that comparison. Crosby, Stills, Nash & Young, he'd like better.

When Jake got back from the studio in the afternoons, he often spent several hours writing new songs. He liked to work on the floor, with his notebooks splayed out on the coffee table. Molly was normally home by then, unless she was subbing; she'd finished her yoga teacher training at Bhakti in August and had been assigned five weekly classes, all of them morning. And though she wasn't yet making nearly enough to support herself—new teachers at Bhakti brought in just forty dollars per class—Jake still convinced her to give up her afternoon shifts at Angelina's.

"Otherwise, you won't have any time to write," he'd argued when she'd objected. "I can afford to pay more of our rent right now, so what does it matter?"

"But it's not just about rent, Jake. I have loan payments to make every month."

He'd nodded, contemplating. "I can pay your loans, Moll."

"Jake, I can't ask you to do that."

"You didn't ask. You know I have a bunch in my savings from the record deal—I can swing it right now, so why not? We're a team. When you get your big, hot book deal, or start getting paid more at Bhakti, we can reevaluate."

Molly didn't like the idea of her life being subsidized, not by Jake or anyone. But he was right—if her schedule stayed this packed, she'd never have time to finish the book.

And so, she'd conceded. Every day, when she was finished at Bhakti midmorning, Molly went home, made a quick lunch, then spent the rest of the day writing. The only problem was the lack of space. Their apartment was small, and with Jake at the coffee table, there wasn't an ideal spot for Molly to work.

One morning in late September, she came home from Bhakti to find Jake was still there.

"You're not at the studio?" Molly's backpack slid off her shoulder, dropping to the floor.

"I got distracted on my way to the subway." Jake stepped to the side, extending both hands in presentation. "Look what I got you."

In the corner of the living room was a small wooden desk. Molly's laptop was perched on its surface, along with a blue ceramic lamp and an Obama mug filled with an array of pens and pencils.

"Jake, where did you—"

"That secondhand store on Bedford. You know the one right before the L train? I've been meaning to pop in there. A writer needs a place to write. You never had a desk when you lived with Liz, did you?"

Molly shook her head, her lips parted in surprise, in pure appreciation. "You carried it up here yourself?"

"It wasn't too heavy." Jake looped his arms around her neck, leaning down to kiss the side of her face. "The wood's a little grubby. I was thinking I'd paint it white. You like it?"

Molly looked up at him, deep into his bottomless blue eyes. "It's perfect."

From that point on, they fell into a new rhythm—Jake on the floor, Molly at her desk—feeding off each other's energies. They could be alone together, wholly immersed in their own creative worlds while just several feet apart. At seven or eight in the evening, they'd come up for air, one of them wandering over to the other and nuzzling in, signaling a stopping point. They'd open a bottle of wine and make an easy dinner, or order in, or sometimes head out to meet friends for drinks and a bite.

Afterward—more nights than not that first year—they had sex. Consuming, fierce, unhurried sex, their eyes locked, their bodies fixed in a steady rhythm that grew more familiar and mutually beneficial each time. In the middle of working on her book—the demanding but purposeful task of connecting and editing and rewriting the contents of her thesis—Molly found her mind drifting to her sessions in bed with Jake, replaying moments that were often specific and mechanical. She was sure she thought about it too often, but she'd never experienced sex like theirs before—not even close.

That fall, Danner Lane had fewer gigs in order to increase demand for shows around *The Narrows'* release. To build buzz around the album, Ron had arranged for a single to come out in advance of the launch, and so "Salt River" dropped mid-October. Molly came to every concert the band did play—Jake said he needed her there, but she would've gone regardless. Liz liked to say it was because Molly felt threatened by Maxine, but this wasn't true. Molly had become more and more tempted to tell Liz to go fuck herself.

At Jake's shows, Molly stood near the front but always off to the side. She never failed to be entranced by the expert way he handled the guitar while singing his heart out. His talent was extraordinary, but it was his stage presence that truly made him shine. That je ne sais quoi she'd seen from the start.

What became obvious, as time passed, was that of the three of them, Jake was the one who captured the audience. He was Danner Lane's clear front man, and not just because he was lead vocalist. Sam's and Hale's lanky frames and pale, freckled skin only magnified Jake's movie star looks.

The first week in November, a month before *The Narrows* released, Molly emailed her finished manuscript to Bella, the literary agent Jake knew. As promised, he'd introduced them over email, and Bella seemed excited to read Molly's book. Molly's body prickled with nerves as she sent the file into cyberspace—her heart and soul and two and a half years of work boiled down to a single Word document. Molly had never felt so vulnerable in her life.

The novel's heroine was a bookish, fatherless girl named Grace navigating her twenties in Brooklyn while falling for a tortured artist named Sebastian. Grace's experiences were not unlike Molly's—Sebastian not *not* reminiscent of Jake—but wasn't it Mark Twain who said, "Write what you know"? *Needs* was her working title, and she was pitching it as literary fiction, though that felt a bit presumptuous.

But now, it was out of her hands. And all she could do was hope that Bella—or some other agent, if not Bella—would fall in love with her writing, and the rest would stem from there.

When *The Narrows* dropped on December 12, it made a big splash, largely thanks to the attention "Salt River" had garnered in the prior two months. *Variety* and *Billboard* both profiled the band that first week, and iTunes sales soared. "Salt River" was still the clear favorite, followed closely by "Give It Love, Give It Time" and, to Molly's delight, "January Girl."

Over Christmas, Molly went home to Denville, and Jake went back to North Carolina. This meant ten days away from each other, the longest they'd been apart since meeting. Molly knew space was healthy, but it still felt like an eternity. She assured herself the time would fly. After the holiday, Jake would meet her down in Florida—Molly's family always spent the week between Christmas and New Year's visiting her grandmother in Naples.

The evening before her morning flight, Molly was tossing sundresses and sandals into her suitcase and daydreaming about seeing Jake's face the following day, when her phone began to ring. The "What's My Age Again" ringtone told her Jake was the caller.

"Hey, love. I'm packing."

"Hey, Moll." Something in his voice was hesitant, off.

"You okay?"

He sighed deeply. "Yeah, actually, I'm pretty excited. But I also have some not-so-great news."

Molly's stomach pitched.

"Jerry just called. He heard from Ron, and they're adding *eight* more stops to our tour. Eight more cities! Can you believe it?"

"Wow, Jake. What's the bad news, then?" Molly asked, though she already knew.

Jake's voice grew less animated. "They want us in Boston on Friday to play a New Year's Eve show, to be one of the openers for Vampire Weekend. It's last minute, I know."

"Wow," she repeated, her voice small. Molly loved Vampire Weekend, and she knew this was a huge coup for them, but she wasn't in the mood to gush.

"And from there we head up to Portland, then fly to Chicago . . ." He paused. "I'll send you the updated tour schedule. But yeah, basically they have us starting the tour now, instead of mid-January. So I can't make Naples. I'm so sorry."

Molly felt tears behind her eyes—the burning, welling sensation, the tightness in her throat. She knew she was being ridiculous—this was a huge deal for Danner Lane. But she was devastated; she couldn't help it. All week, she'd dreamed of being in Naples with him—swimming in the ocean together and drinking Goombay Smashes in front of the sunset and watching him get to know her mom and Andrew and her grandmother. Molly squeezed her eyes shut, let the images swirl down the drain.

"Moll?"

She nodded into the phone. "Yeah. Okay. That'll be really big for you guys. It's just late notice, is all."

"I know." Jake sighed, and even though half of Molly was pissed at him, she wished she could jump through the phone and into his arms. "I'm sorry. It's out of my control. But maybe you can come out and meet us on the road after Florida? We're opening for the Black Keys in West Palm Beach at the end of January . . ." He paused, and she heard the drumming of his fingers. "I guess the timing doesn't line up well, but maybe there's another show that would work? I'll be gone till the first week of February. Then they want us back in New York to do some local shows."

"This is all . . . it's so exciting." Molly hoped she sounded more enthused than she felt. She sat down on the edge of the duvet and looked around her childhood bedroom. Everything was still the same—pale pink paint on the walls; pink-and-white herringbone carpet. Even her old dollhouse was still perched in the corner, taking up a mountain of space. It was ridiculous. "But I don't know if I can meet you on tour, Jake."

"Why not?"

"I have a job, for one. I have to teach."

"Can't you get a sub?"

"Not really. I need the money. It's my only source of income at the moment. And it's not like I have extra cash for plane tickets."

Jake was quiet for several long beats. "Let me see if Dixon would pay for your flight. Okay?"

"Do you really think they'd do that?"

"Maybe. It doesn't hurt to ask."

"Okay." Molly sank back into the pillows. The thought of not seeing Jake for more than a month made her unbearably anxious.

Jake sighed. "Hey, I'm so sorry about this. I really love you. I hope you know that."

Fresh tears pooled in Molly's eyes, gliding down her cheeks. "I love you, too," she managed, trying to hide the emotion in her voice. "And I'm really proud of you. I'm just bummed because I miss you. But this is big, Jake. You deserve it."

"Thanks, Moll. I miss you, too. It hurts, the way I miss you. But it's only a month—okay, a little more—and it'll fly. You'll be teaching, and writing, and I'll be back before you know it."

"I'm not really writing at the moment," Molly said, stifling a sniffle. "I'm sort of in limbo, still waiting to hear back from your friend."

"What friend?"

"Bella. Your agent friend. The one you know through Sam and Hale."

"Oh. Right."

"It's been almost two months, and I haven't heard anything. And I followed up. Do you think that's a bad sign?"

"Nah. You know how busy people get around the holidays." Jake paused. "But I can check in with her, if you want? Though I don't want to annoy her."

"What do you mean?" Molly asked. "I thought you knew her?"

"Well, yeah, but she's not exactly a *friend*, Moll. She's Sam's god-mother's daughter. I met her a bunch when we were younger, when she and her family would visit the Lanes. She's, like, five years older than us or something."

"Okay." Now Molly was annoyed. It had been Jake's idea to connect them in the first place; he'd made it sound like an easy ask.

"You know what, never mind. I'll just reach out and be casual—I'll mention that you said you pitched your manuscript, and see what she says. Okay?"

"That would be great, if only for my peace of mind. Thanks."

"Cheer up, Moll. Tomorrow you'll be swimming in the ocean."

"Yeah."

"Life is good."

For you, Molly thought, but she didn't let herself say it. She hated the way spite made her feel—bitter and small—and besides, she *was* proud of Jake. Nothing had been handed to him; he'd worked tirelessly to get to where he was. He and Sam and Hale had worked odd jobs all throughout college and their first years in the city, pooling their money to pay for rented studio space. It was only just last summer that Jake could finally afford to stop busing tables at the Greek restaurant where he'd worked since arriving in New York. Danner Lane was the product of years of practice and dedication and hustle and sacrifice. Molly, of all people, had to understand that.

The following week, as she sat on the beach in Naples with her family, Molly barely heard from Jake. He didn't let her know if Dixon would consider covering the cost of her flight or if he'd followed up with Bella. As she lay on her chaise and anxiously thumbed through the most recent *New Yorker,* Molly could only assume he hadn't. The pit in her stomach deepened as the days passed.

Her mother rubbed sunscreen on her back—this always made Molly feel like a little girl, but it was the part she couldn't reach—and asked how Jake's tour was going.

"Fine," Molly lied, unable to tell her mother the truth—that she didn't actually know.

He'd called only twice that week, both times late, hours after Molly had fallen asleep. His voicemails were quick and breathless. *Sorry, Moll. What a crazy day. The show was amazing—we killed it, we really killed it—and then went out after. Too late, probably, I'm so fucking tired. And drunk. I miss you so much. Let's try to talk tomorrow, okay? I love you.*

But when Molly would call him back the next day, it would go straight to voicemail. She knew Jake well enough by then to understand how he operated; she knew he'd probably passed out and forgotten to charge his phone overnight. She didn't let herself think about Maxine being on the tour, because she just couldn't go there. Molly trusted Jake—she had to. Trust was relationship oxygen. Without it, she and Jake wouldn't survive.

She had a text from him when her plane touched down in New York.

Lost my charger for forty-eight hours—just found! Can you talk?

The next month went on like that. Jake on the road, partying, missed calls, drunk texts, crappy communication. During the first substantial conversation they'd had since Jake left—a couple of days after Molly got back to Brooklyn—she asked if there was any news about Dixon paying for her to come meet him on tour or if he'd heard from Bella. Jake had sighed audibly, and she'd imagined him sitting on the edge of the bed in his hotel room, rubbing the back of his neck the way he did when he was agitated or hungover, or both.

"Fuck. No. I need to check in with Ron. I'll do that today."

"What about Bella?"

"Bella?"

"*Bella.*" Molly could no longer mask the aggravation in her voice. Pent-up frustration bubbled to the surface. "Are you serious, Jake? The literary agent you know. The one who's had my manuscript since November."

"Right. Shit." Jake's voice was gravelly and pained. "I'm so sorry—no. I'll email her this afternoon, I promise. We're going to a lunch now with some friends of Jerry's. I'll do it after that."

But Jake hadn't done it after that; he didn't do it at all. Molly had never been overly brash or confrontational, so she seethed silently, in the privacy of her own mind. It was something Liz had always told her she needed to work on. Throughout the rest of January, she taught her morning classes at Bhakti, miserable as she braved the cold during the walk back and forth from the apartment, her mind spinning between missing Jake and resenting Jake, the feelings clashing and clawing at each other inside her heart, an ever-present gnawing in her stomach. The Jake she'd fallen in love with had her best interests at heart; to say he'd always gone the extra mile for her was an understatement. Molly wondered if she'd been fooled, duped, but then her love for him would bubble up and she'd be hit with a paralyzing mixture of fear and longing.

Her breaking point came the afternoon of January 26. It had been the longest month of Molly's life, the Jake-less days trickling by—languid, interminable. As agonized as she'd been over their relationship, she still counted the minutes until he was back in New York, back in her arms. Their long-distance dynamic had been terrible—unacceptable, she knew—but once he was back, they would fix it. The old Jake—the adoring, reliable Jake, the one who buoyed her—was still in there, and he'd be home in less than a week.

It was a Sunday, and Molly was catching up on some emails when a new message from lenore.smith@gmail.com appeared in her inbox. Molly didn't recognize the address, and she didn't know anyone named Lenore Smith.

There was no text accompanying the email, just a single photo attachment, which Molly double-clicked. The image came to life, filling her computer screen.

Molly's breath stopped in her throat; she felt the color drain from her face as an overwhelming déjà vu took hold. The photo showed Jake kissing a girl—a girl who wasn't Molly. She couldn't make out the details of her face, but she wore a fitted magenta minidress, and her arms were wrapped around Jake's neck, pulling him close, their lips pressed together in the middle of what looked like the dance floor of a grimy club. The girl's hair was so blond it appeared almost white, a detail that told Molly it couldn't be Maxine. A strange part of her expected to feel a shred of relief over this, but the horror was too all-encompassing.

Molly's heart dropped into her gut. She felt too sick to move. Her hands trembled as she slapped her laptop shut and stared at the wall in front of her, her eyes fixed to the space beside Jake's Led Zeppelin poster. She didn't know how much time went by before she made her way into the bathroom and threw up.

Liz told her to dump him; Nina told her to talk to him before she jumped to any conclusions; Everly came over with a bottle of Tito's and held Molly while she sobbed on the couch.

Molly waited until Jake got home to confront him. Nina said it was important to see the look in his eyes when she did.

When he walked in the door the following Saturday, he carried a bouquet of creamy white roses. Molly's favorite. The last she'd heard from him was a five-minute phone call three nights before. The look on his face was oblivious, and it ripped through Molly's heart. She hated what a relief it was to see him, at the same time white-hot rage pumped through her veins. Standing in front of him, taking in the familiar sight of his olive skin and pale blue gaze, she almost couldn't believe how much had changed in her own mind. She felt the weight of all those nights and days without him, the countless phone checks and stomach flips and the worry that wrapped itself around her like a cobra, suffocating. And finally, the photo. The photo that was a million knives spearing her heart, *more* incontrovertible proof that Jake was a cheater.

Now she had to know if he was a liar, too.

"Did you cheat on me?" Molly locked on Jake's eyes as she spoke; she watched his smile drop. Tears dripped down her face, and suddenly, she couldn't support her own legs.

She felt her body crumple in the weight of Jake's arms; she inhaled the smell of the roses against his jacket as the sobs escaped from her body, giant and racking.

Jake lowered her onto the couch, collapsing beside her.

"No." His voice was far away in between her sobs. "But a random fucking girl walked up to me and kissed me at a club, out of nowhere. She literally just came up to me and started kissing me. I pushed her off, it was two seconds, I barely even got a good look at her. I was so angry, Molly. Then she just disappeared, and I never saw her again. It was last weekend—I'm so sorry I didn't tell you. I should have, but it was honestly nothing, and I didn't want to freak you out."

Molly stopped crying. Her brows knitted together. She sat up slowly, leaning back against the couch. She hadn't mentioned the photograph to Jake, and he knew exactly what she was referring to. Did this mean he was being honest? Or did he somehow know about the photograph and was attempting to *sound* like he was being honest?

She grabbed her laptop, flung it open. The photo attachment from lenore.smith@gmail.com appeared on the screen.

"Someone sent me this picture."

Molly made sure to watch Jake's reaction closely. The expression on his face was one of sheer, indisputable shock.

"Are you fucking kidding me?" He stared at the picture for what seemed like ages, his eyes narrowing in horror as he took in the details. "I can't believe . . . Molly." He turned toward her, his breath choppy. "This is exactly what I was just telling you about. This is the random girl who came up to me in the club and kissed me for two seconds. This is her." He stabbed his finger at the screen. "Where . . . Where did you get this?"

"Some random person sent it to me. I told you." She pointed to the email address.

"Molly." His voice had grown raspy and panicked. He shook his head in disbelief. "Someone must've set me up. Oh god. Oh god." Jake dropped his face into his hands. Several moments passed in silence. When he looked up, a lone tear snaked down his cheek. It was the first time Molly had ever seen him cry. "I . . . I think this girl was a crazy fan. She must've had a friend take the picture or something. She must know I have a girlfriend—I mean, anyone who wanted to know could find that out. But I don't know how she got your email address. I know that sounds insane, Molly, but that has to be it. It's the only thing that makes remote sense."

Molly studied Jake's face, the way it was twitching in agitation and terror. She exhaled, flooded with confusing relief. The anxiety had dropped from her body like a second skin, but what was left was boiling anger. Because while the past several days had consumed her with the horrifying reality that Jake had been unfaithful, it wasn't the whole picture. That wasn't the reason she'd been a wreck for the entire month. She'd banked on her own forgiveness; she hadn't expected the anger that rose inside her, unyielding and lucid.

Molly and Jake fought all night, the next few hours a blur. She let the emotions tumble out of her subconscious like lava—every last one—escaping the stale, stuffy place they'd been brewing for weeks. He apologized; he owned his distant and aloof behavior—his absence from every element of her life—with genuine, ashamed admission.

At one in the morning, she stuffed a canvas tote with clothes and toiletries. She didn't fully want to, but she couldn't stop remembering the way her mother had looked at her in Naples, that mixture of worry and foreboding, an image she couldn't shake.

"Never put up with a man who puts you second," her mother had said on New Year's Eve, after Molly had been particularly quiet at dinner. Molly's mother was the strongest person she knew—she always had been. She was the type of beautiful, successful, steadfast woman who'd never let a man walk all over her. Molly had never doubted her mother when she kicked her father out, told him to never come back.

She was only in third grade then. When she got a bit older and would ask for details on why Dad had left, her mother's answer was simple and pragmatic: he was selfish, he strayed, he was careless with money.

Molly had always been grateful to have a mother like hers as a role model. As she and Jake argued, the words played on repeat inside her head: *Never put up with a man who puts you second.* It was a piece of advice that made all of this so refreshingly simple.

"I'm going to stay at Everly's for a bit," Molly said.

Jake sat on the couch and rubbed his eyes, which were red around the rims. "Please don't." He stood, his tall, strong body a magnet threatening Molly's stance. "I fucked up, but I didn't cheat. You have to believe me."

"I told you, Jake, it's more than that."

"I know, I just . . . I don't know what happened. I got sucked into this . . . other *world* when I was on tour, but it didn't mean for a second that I stopped loving you. My love for you is everything. It's my baseline, my reason for getting up in the morning. You have to know that."

"It doesn't fucking *matter*, Jake!" Molly was sick of yelling, her throat raw. "It doesn't matter if you love me if you can't actually show up for me. My dad loved my mom, and he was a piece of shit!" She closed her eyes, which were swollen from crying. *He was selfish, he strayed, he was careless with money.* So far, Jake was two out of three.

She heaved the canvas bag over her shoulder—a shoulder that had become bonier in the last several weeks—and blinked.

"So, what, I'm a piece of shit, then?" Jake stared at her, shaking his head in disbelief. He looked as destroyed as she felt. "I'm not your father, Molly."

She swallowed. She was so thirsty, suddenly. "I love you, but the past month has been hell for me, and I can't just . . ." Molly sighed, heavy with exhaustion. "I can't just pretend it didn't happen. I need to go."

Molly left the apartment before she could change her mind, stepping over the bouquet of roses that now lay on the floor, the brown paper crinkled, the snow-colored petals littering the entryway.

It was cold outside, but the air felt fresh in her lungs. Molly had almost forgotten it was a Saturday night; despite the late hour, Driggs swarmed with barhopping twentysomethings, loud and drunk and oblivious to her pain. That was the thing Molly loved most about New York—the city never let you get too caught up in your own problems; it was always reminding you that there was something more, something bigger than yourself.

A vacant taxi cruised down Driggs, and Molly stuck out her arm. She gave the cabbie Everly's address.

Chapter Fourteen
Molly

June 2022

The last week of June, Sabrina invites Molly and Hunter over for dinner. Molly had been with Sabrina earlier that day—they'd gotten mani-pedis then lunch on the back patio at Gwen's—and Sabrina had suggested it. *I think we're free Friday, if you are,* she'd said. *Let me double-check with hubby and I'll text you.*

Hunter is lounging on the couch watching ESPN, and Molly looks up from her phone. "Dinner at Sabrina's on Friday, okay?"

"This Friday?" He takes a sip of his beer, eyes glued to the television. "As in, the day after tomorrow?"

"Yes."

"My brother and Tara are coming down this weekend."

"So? They live an hour away. They come down all the time."

"So they'll want to have dinner."

"Well, you didn't mention that until now. Can't we just see them on Saturday?"

"Moll." Hunter places his glass on the coffee table. He wraps his arms around her hips and pulls her down on the couch. "Why are you so worked up about this?"

"I'm *not* worked up." She fidgets in his grasp. She hates when he tells her she's worked up, even when he's sort of right.

"Okay, but why the urgency about Friday? You've seen Sabrina practically every other day since the two of you met."

Molly sighs. She *has* seen lots of Sabrina lately—they go for coffee, and walks, and Sabrina comes to nearly every Sunday yoga class—but an invitation to dinner at her house feels different. More formal. Plus, Molly has been curious about Sabrina's husband, a workaholic who hardly comes up for air. She explains as much to Hunter.

"Okay, okay," he concedes, working his thumbs into the tight spot below her neck. She relaxes into his grip, drops her head forward in relief. "I'll tell Clark and Tara we'll see them on Saturday."

"Thank you, Hunt." Molly nuzzles her face into the crook of his neck, inhaling the scent of him—beer and aftershave. "Best husband ever," she says, and she means it. She doesn't know how she got so lucky with him.

Friday evening, Molly riffles through her closet, contemplating an outfit. White pants and a nice top are what she'd *normally* choose for an intimate dinner party in Flynn Cove, but something about Sabrina makes her reach for a blue-and-white-striped linen sundress she hasn't worn in years—a more boho piece she bought with Nina at a boutique they loved in Williamsburg.

Molly's phone pings from her dresser. A text from Sabrina.

Excited for tonight! One thing—do me a favor, and don't mention our run-in at Dr. Ricci's to my hubby. He's extra sensitive about our fertility issues right now, and I'd rather not open that can of worms . . . best to just say we met at your yoga class and leave it there, if that's all right. Anyway, it's the truth ;)

Molly reads the text and smiles knowingly. She understands. Hunter doesn't like talking about the fertility stuff in public, either.

He lies on their king-size bed reading to Stella, who's clean from her bath and wearing her favorite unicorn pajamas. Even though her daughter is five—almost six—Molly can't help but think of her as a baby, especially after bath time when her fine blond hair is combed and her sweet-smelling skin is damp. She's nestled against Hunter's chest while he reads *The Runaway Bunny*, and the sight of them melts Molly's heart.

"Daddy, read that page again." Stella kicks her little foot, and Molly can almost acutely remember the magical feeling of that same foot kicking inside her belly.

"Mommy, why are you wearing that dress? Is it new?"

"It's old, actually." Molly smooths the skirt. "I wanted to wear something nice because Daddy and I are going out to dinner. That's why Bridget is coming to babysit you. She'll be here in fifteen minutes, actually." Molly looks at Hunter as she says the last part, telepathically ushering him to get out of his gym clothes and into the shower.

Stella's blue eyes widen, morphing into that trancelike stare that tells Molly her daughter is deep in thought. "So why is it an *old* dress?"

"I got it with Aunt Nina in New York City, eight or nine years ago, probably."

"Eight or nine years? I wasn't born then."

"You weren't born then, no."

"Doesn't Mommy look beautiful?" Hunter asks Stella, gazing at his wife, the way the dress hugs her body. Her hair is pulled up, a few pieces sprinkling out of the loose knot. A smile spreads across his face as he admires the long, graceful slope of her neck.

"Yeah." Stella giggles, pulling her little knees into her chest. "Like Elsa." She starts humming the theme song from *Frozen*, the movie that has more or less played on repeat in their house for the past three years.

Molly grins. "Okay, Stell. Daddy's gonna finish *The Runaway Bunny*, and then he needs to get dressed. Bridget can read you another story when she gets here."

"*Rainbow Fish?*" Stella's expression brightens. "That's the one Bridget always reads me."

"That sounds fine." Molly disappears into the bathroom to finish her makeup. She never wears much, but something about tonight feels special, and she has the desire to look good.

Half an hour later, when Hunter has finally showered and dressed and seventeen-year-old Bridget is reading to Stella in her room, they leave the house.

Sabrina and her husband live ten minutes away, farther from town, in the most inland part of Flynn Cove where the properties have more acreage. Their place is big—at least twice the size of Molly and Hunter's simple saltbox—and set back from the road. It's white painted brick, with those gorgeous cedar roof shingles that Molly is constantly admiring. She and Hunter have enough money, just not as much as most people in Flynn Cove. Certainly not so much that they can justify spending 50 percent more on a cedarwood roof.

Hunter's Volkswagen crunches over the gravel driveway. He puts the car in park and raises his eyebrows. "Nice place."

Molly nods in agreement. She didn't look up the house on Zillow when Sabrina sent her the address, but now she's tempted. It has to be worth at least a few million. She's caught off guard—she hadn't realized Sabrina was rich. But then, *most* people in Flynn Cove are rich, so Molly isn't sure why she's surprised. It's one of the things she dislikes most about living in this town, the fact that she constantly feels like some kind of pauper just because she and Hunter don't have the "nice" roof or belong to a stupidly expensive country club. It screws with her gratitude. She and Hunter are insanely lucky to have as much as they do.

Molly unbuckles her seat belt. "Feels European, almost."

"Hey." Hunter places a hand on her arm, gives it a gentle squeeze. "I know it's been a tough few weeks."

She looks into his wide brown eyes. Even when things between them are hard—even when they're bickering or stressed or residually exhausted—his eyes are her harbor. Her safe place. Her home.

"It has," she replies, thinking of the failed embryo transfer, knowing that's what he means. Molly has been devastated since they got the news—of course she has—but what she doesn't tell Hunter is that her budding friendship with Sabrina has been a welcome distraction. "Well, we still have one more embryo from this round. We'll try again, right?"

"Of course." He smiles gently, but she can see the pain in the contours of his face. Sometimes she thinks this is the hardest part—how heartbroken he is, too.

"I know it's expensive, Hunt . . ."

"You know my mom is helping, and she's glad to be."

"I know, but I just think . . ." Molly pauses, hesitant. "If this next transfer fails . . . what then? How many times can we do this? We've already spent a good chunk of our savings, and we can't bankrupt your mother."

"We won't. You know we won't. We just . . . let's not get ahead of ourselves. Let's take this one day at a time. That's what Dr. Ricci always says."

Molly nods, smoothing the dark flop of hair away from his brow. She loves the way he looks just after he shaves—his jawline sharp and clean, that signature crooked smile playing at the edges of his lips.

"Besides, it worked before. It will work again. This is going to happen for us. I know it, Moll."

She nods, squeezing his hand, then glances toward the house. "We should go in."

They walk across the Belgian block–lined driveway and up the broad slate steps, while Hunter comments on the exquisite masonry. The front door is painted a dark, glossy blue. Molly rings the bell, buzzy with anticipation.

Sabrina answers the door moments later. She wears a long white caftan and cradles a glass of rosé in her palm—ice cold from the looks of it—the delicate stem extending below her fingers. Her green eyes are coated in eyeliner and a heavy dose of mascara, and her dark hair falls loose around her shoulders.

"Hi!" Sabrina smiles broadly, her teeth gleaming white. "Hunter, it's *so* nice to see you again. And, Molly, you look incredible." She wraps her free arm around Molly, who inhales a whiff of spicy perfume. "Come in, come in."

Molly and Hunter step inside the house, just as a male hand cracks the door open wider.

And then, she sees his face. Lightly tanned skin, honey curls, blazing blue eyes. A face she knows by heart. A face she held in her mind's eye for longer than she likes to remember. A face she's tried and failed to forget, its imprint lingering stubbornly on her soul.

Her heart turns to stone. And she is back in Brooklyn. And she is twenty-three and twenty-four and twenty-five and twenty-six.

"Molly, Hunter." Sabrina's voice is sweet and welcoming, her smile explosive. "This is my husband, Jake."

Chapter Fifteen
Sabrina

"What a coincidence," Jake says, a little awestruck. You and Hunter just left our house, and he's staring at the front door, which just clicked closed behind you, a dreamy sheen in his ocean-blue eyes.

Yeah, total coincidence, babe. You and I—both very much city people— just happened to move to the same small Connecticut suburb as your ex and her husband.

But that's exactly why we're here—it's time for you and my husband to *finally* resolve some things, Molly. For his sake and for the sake of our marriage. It's time for him to know who you really are, so he can stop looking over his shoulder for the one who got away. Jake and I love each other, and we deserve a shot at real, lasting happiness. The kind you thought you'd found with him—at least until he went on tour.

I bet you didn't know I was on that tour, Molly. As Jake would say— *What a coincidence.*

I flew to West Palm Beach after work on that Friday in late January, and Martelle and I met up Saturday morning for a boozy brunch at Buccan. I love Martelle—she's the kind of friend who's always down for anything, though I can't say she has much ambition. At the time, she'd just started dating her now husband, Perry, a real estate mogul whose bank account meant she'd never have to work. Not surprisingly, they've never left Palm Beach.

I was never like Martelle—I'd always wanted to get out of Florida. It felt like a bubble; the weather was consistently pleasant, and as much as I enjoyed the sunshine, it could also be stifling, and I'd always been a bit skeptical of the lack of seasons. Before my father retired and moved us south to an oceanfront villa in Palm Beach, I'd spent the first nine years of my life in New York. I had fond memories of how Manhattan would change with the weather: the early buds of spring outside the windows of our apartment on tree-lined East Seventy-sixth Street; steamy summer nights when the air felt like velvet coating my skin; crisp fall afternoons in Central Park with my nanny, Rebecca; the eager, bustling crowds that swarmed FAO Schwarz at Christmastime. I'd always known that I would make it back to New York someday.

After brunch, Martelle and I did mani-pedis and blowouts before heading back to my parents' place to get ready for the concert. My father wasn't home, and my mother may as well not have been—she'd locked herself in the den with a bottle of Chard; I hadn't had more than a two-minute conversation with her since I'd been back.

Anyway, I wanted to look my absolute best for Jake. After scrounging through my closet, I decided on a black leather miniskirt with a white crop top and combat boots. Hey, it was 2013, and I was twenty-fucking-three—I could pull it off. I let Martelle do my eyeliner—she's the best at liquid. If she *had* wanted a career, I think she would've made a phenomenal makeup artist.

"Oh my god," I said when we picked up our tickets at will call, feigning shock. "You're not gonna believe this, Marty. Danner Lane is the opening act."

"No!" Martelle's jaw dropped. "What are the *chances*, Sees?"

Love her to pieces, but Martelle really is the most gullible person on the planet.

We only caught the last half of their performance—Martelle had insisted on doing an unnecessarily long photo shoot outside the venue— and by the time we found out seats, Danner Lane was in the middle of "Salt River," one of my favorite songs on the album.

When they finished, the packed audience erupted in applause, and Jake raised a hand in appreciation. Just the sight of his tall, familiar frame sent a rush of adrenaline through my body, filling every cell to the brim with intoxicating lust.

"Jeez, I forgot how hot he is. And he's *so* talented." Martelle sipped her vodka lemonade and gazed at Jake. They'd met once, when she'd come to visit me in the city the year before. She knew we'd broken up, but I hadn't told her about the positive pregnancy test or the blood. I hadn't told anyone.

"Yeah," I agreed, watching as Jake stepped toward the microphone, the guitar strap snug around his shoulders. "It's true. When he's onstage, you really can't look away."

He cleared his throat. "This next song is very special to me. It's about a girl I love very much, who unfortunately couldn't be here tonight."

Martelle gave me a pouty look that said, *Ouch, sorry.* I knew what was coming, my heart sinking in my chest as the band began the familiar, torturous tune of "January Girl."

But at least Jake's little speech confirmed what I'd hoped: *you* weren't there.

After Danner Lane finished their act, and after drinking our way through two hours of loud electric guitar spasms from the Black Keys—"You like these guys?" Martelle asked more than once during their performance—we made our way backstage.

"I have to at least say hi," I reasoned, and Martelle nodded in drunken solidarity.

"I'm an old friend of Jake Danner's," I told a security guard, who traced the length of my body with dubious eyes.

"Okay. Name?"

"Sabrina Randolph; this is my friend Martelle."

The guard sighed. "Wait right here."

A few minutes later, he reappeared, motioning for us to follow him. He led us to a room behind the stage, where Jake, Sam, and Hale were gathered with several other men I didn't recognize. They were all drinking longnecks and cracking up over something, their laughter stopping abruptly when they noticed Martelle and me in the doorway.

Jake's mouth spread into a genuine smile as he moved toward us. "Sisi! What a surprise. What on earth are you doing here?"

He was even handsomer than I'd remembered, and being so close to him got me instantly high, like he was a drug binding itself to my synapses. His eyes were such a pure, crystalline blue, and they were drinking in the sight of me. Behind him, Sam and Hale watched us, tipping their beers forward in some semblance of a greeting. Next to me, Martelle smacked her gum.

"You remember Martelle."

"Of course." Jake grinned politely in her direction.

"Anyway, what a small world. I was home in Palm Beach for the weekend, and Martelle and I had these tickets to the Black Keys. I had zero idea you guys were opening until we got here."

"Small world, indeed," he replied, dropping his gaze to my bare midriff. Exhilaration prickled my skin. I couldn't believe I was standing right in front of him—my *Jake*—after so many months away from him, dreaming of a moment just like this. We'd made a baby together. Not a day went by that I didn't think of this; being near him again, it flooded me.

"Well, you ladies coming out with us or what?" Hale stood from the chair where he'd been sitting, rubbing his auburn beard. "We're headed to Roxy's."

"Sisi's only home for the weekend," Jake inserted, well-mannered as always. "I'm sure she has to get ba—"

"Don't be ridiculous, Jake. A night out on the town with Danner Lane?" I winked. "Count us in."

Martelle whined about going out—she wanted to get home to Perry— but I dragged her along. This was an important night for me, and a girl needs her wing woman.

There wasn't room in Danner Lane's car, so Martelle and I took a separate cab. At Roxy's, I scanned the crowded room for Jake, finally spotting him at the bar.

"I'll get us drinks," I told Martelle, who was busy texting Perry.

I wormed my way through the packs of sweaty, inebriated people and sidled up next to Jake, pressing my shoulder against his.

"Two vodka sodas!" I called to the bartender, flashing my credit card.

"Drink order hasn't changed, I see." One side of Jake's mouth slid into a grin. He looked so fucking good, especially after I'd watched him kill it onstage hours earlier. In the year we'd been apart, he'd become a real live rock star with a knockout debut album, just like he'd always dreamed. I was so proud of him. I told him as much.

"I feel lucky," he answered modestly. "Lucky to have Jerry. Lucky to have Sam and Hale. Lucky Ron took a chance on us."

"Cheers to luck." I gazed up at him, tilting my chin. "How about a shot to celebrate your hard-earned success?"

"I don't know, Sisi. . . ." He laughed lightly, raking a hand through his hair.

"No one really calls me *Sisi* anymore. I go by Sabrina now." The bartender placed my drink down on the counter, and I ordered two shots of Fireball.

"Are you trying to get me drunk, *Sabrina*?" There was a flirtatious edge to his voice that sent my confidence skyrocketing. I waved the bartender back and ordered two more shots—tequila this time.

"Now I am, Jake."

His lips parted slightly, his blue eyes brightening in surprise. A thin layer of sandy stubble coated his face.

"Really, what are the chances?" He studied me intently. "Of all the shows we've played, of all the weekends . . . I didn't even know you liked the Black Keys."

"Martelle is crazy about them," I lied, shrugging. "I'm along for the ride."

The bartender lined up our shots—two each—along with my receipt. A Katy Perry song blared from the speakers, thumping in my ears.

"Bottoms up." I lifted the Fireball to my lips, waiting as Jake did the same.

After we'd knocked both of them back, I glanced around for Martelle, but she was nowhere in sight. I chugged the rest of my vodka soda and started working on hers. Jake led me to the dance floor, where Sam, Hale, and another guy—maybe their producer or one of the guys from the Black Keys—were practically gyrating to a Bruno Mars remix.

"Thanks, Danner," Hale said when Jake handed him a beer. He plugged a nostril with his pointer finger and inhaled through the other. "You want?"

Jake shook his head, his voice blunted by the music. "I'm good."

I was tempted to tell Hale that *I* wanted coke, but was hesitant to leave Jake's side. By that point, all of the alcohol—the countless drinks I'd consumed since brunch with Martelle that morning—had worked its way into my system, and I was unquestionably drunk. Drunk and ecstatic to be with Jake, to be close enough to smell the warm, woody scent of his skin. But I needed to get closer.

I grabbed his hand and pulled him deeper into the dance floor. Neon lights rained down on us from the ceiling, the music loud and thumping.

"Where's your friend?" he called over the noise.

"Who knows." I clasped my hands around the back of Jake's neck, pinning my chest against his. God, I wanted him. I'd never wanted anything so badly in my life.

I ran my fingers through his hair, relishing the feeling of our bodies being pressed together again. Joy struck through me.

"I miss you," I said, knowing with every ounce of my heart that he missed me, too. I moved my hands down the length of his torso, stopping at his belt, grasping it lightly. I felt good; I knew I looked good. I tipped my chin forward, ready for him to lean down and kiss me in the expert way that only Jake Danner can kiss.

But then, horribly, I felt him retreat. He placed his hands on my shoulders cautiously, stepping back.

"Sisi." His eyes grew serious, almost offended. "I'm with someone else now. I'm happy."

My stomach plummeted, churning. I was too drunk to feel the pain, but I sensed it looming, waiting eagerly on the other side of the alcohol. The pain would obliterate me. It would kill me, I was sure.

"Jake, can we . . . what happened, Jake? Can we just talk?" I was nearly choking out the words; I hated myself for being unable to veil the desperation in my voice. "Just for a minute? Outside?"

"No, Sisi." Jake turned his head to the side, his discomfort palpable. The music continued to blare; Bruno Mars morphed into something hammering and awful from Swedish House Mafia. "You're drunk," he said. "Let me call you a cab."

"Fuck you," I spat. "I'm not drunk. Why *her*? Tell me why her."

Jake closed his eyes, exasperated.

"Go home, Sisi," he said. And then he disappeared into the crowd, under the flashing lights, gone from me again.

But I didn't go home. Instead, I wandered up to the second floor of the club, devastated, enraged. I stood near the edge of the balcony and looked for Martelle, but she was nowhere in sight. From above, I noticed Jake had wandered back to one corner of the dance floor with Sam, Hale, and the rest of their group.

I didn't think too hard about what happened next; I only knew *something* had to be done, and the opportunity was now. Now or never.

The two girls next to me were college-aged, wearing glittery eye makeup and drinking Amstel Lights. I could tell by the way they were dressed—tacky polyester getups, probably from the bargain bin at Forever 21—that they could use the cash.

I moved closer to them, lingering at the perimeter of their conversation for a few moments before I pounced. "You want to make a grand to-night? Each?"

They glanced at me, their eyes narrowing in confusion. The trashier one—a short, curly-haired platinum blonde—scowled. "We're not hookers."

"I know that. See that guy over there?" I pointed at Jake, down on the dance floor. "The tall one with the dirty-blond curls? Navy T-shirt?"

"Uh, yeah."

"If you walk right up to him and start kissing him . . ." I looked at the blonde, then turned to her friend, a pudgy redhead. "And *you* take a picture of it—a *clear,* relatively close-up picture—and then text me the picture, and never tell a *soul* about any of this, I'll wire a grand into each of your bank accounts tonight."

Big Red looked at me like I was some kind of mental patient, which, in the throes of my obsession, perhaps I was.

The blonde nudged her. "That's, like, two months' rent, Sally."

Big Red placed her hands on her hips. "How do we know you're not full of shit?"

"You don't," I said, crossing my arms. "But see this Cartier love brace-let on my left wrist? That cost six g's, and I have the matching ring at home. The diamonds in my ears are real, and I have a trust fund so deep, I can buy whatever I want. You can choose to believe me; if not, no big deal—I'll find a couple of girls in this club who do."

I began to pivot on my heels, turning forty-five degrees before Big Red placed her meaty hand on my arm. "We'll do it."

And that, Molly, is how you ended up with the photo in your email inbox, the photo of Jake kissing a random blonde at a sweaty club in West Palm Beach.

It was easy to get your email address—all I had to do was call Bhakti Yoga and pretend to be a student who *adored* a teacher named Molly, who was dying to write her to thank her for such a life-changing class.

It hurt to see that picture, I'm sure. I can imagine the sting. But like I told you before, Jake belonged to me first. I was well within my rights to do everything in my power to get him back.

Chapter Sixteen

Jake

2014

The fourth morning Jake woke up without Molly beside him—without her warm body inches from his fingertips or the sight of her messy blond hair strewn across the pillow—he climbed out of bed with a fire in the pit of his stomach. He put on a pot of coffee and grabbed his notebook and sat down on the floor in front of the table where he liked to do his writing.

And all day, Jake wrote. And rewrote. And crossed out sections and crumpled up pages and strummed lightly on the guitar in between, until he was sure the new song was nothing short of perfect. Then he called Sam.

"You okay, Danner?" Sam sounded concerned. "We haven't heard from you. We have a show tomorrow, remember."

Jake rubbed the nape of his neck, realizing he hadn't bothered to brush his teeth all day, or change out of his sweats. He hadn't eaten anything except a couple of pieces of toast around noon.

"Molly left," he told his oldest friend. "We had a fight the night we got back from tour. She left and hasn't answered my calls since. I've sent texts, emails . . . but nothing."

"Oh, Danner." Sam's voice was heavy, empathetic. He was in a long-term relationship with a girl named Caroline. Jake knew that Sam, more than Hale, would be able to understand. "What happened?"

Jake sighed, considering the question. He thought of Molly's words the night she left—*This is about more than just the picture, Jake. It's not what you did, it's what you didn't do.*

It shouldn't have taken Jake until now to realize what she meant—he knew that he was emotionally stunted in this way—but the truth was, he'd needed a few days to process, to let it all land. Jake had never loved a girl the way he loved Molly. Sisi was his only other serious relationship, but what he'd had with her didn't compare. He'd had an especially weird taste in his mouth regarding Sisi ever since she turned up at the show in West Palm Beach and came on to him at the club. He couldn't shake his vague suspicion that Sisi had had something to do with the photograph Molly received in her email—the one of him being aggressively kissed by that random girl. But that was insane, Jake told the more rational half of his mind. Sisi might've been drunk that night, but she wasn't *crazy*. At least not that crazy.

And even if a subliminal part of Jake suspected her involvement, it was best to keep that theory to himself, he reasoned. The last thing he wanted to do was make Molly think there was a jealous ex in the picture—let alone a jealous ex who lived in New York.

If Molly ever spoke to him again, that was. If he'd fucked it up for good, he knew he'd never forgive himself.

"I was just . . . I was a total dick to her when we were away," Jake told Sam. He decided not to mention the photograph. "And I didn't even re- alize it. I was just thinking about myself and the band and getting caught up in the allure of it all. I stopped prioritizing her. I didn't call her when I said I would—I fell off the face of the earth. I made and then broke all these promises. And I don't know why. There's something wrong with me, Sam."

His friend was quiet for a moment, and Jake sensed that Sam knew exactly what he was thinking. *What if I'm turning into my father?* Jake also knew that Sam would never treat Caroline this way, and he suddenly felt so acutely awful—a sharp, intense pang of self-loathing—that he al- most couldn't bear it.

"Well, tour was a shit show," Sam said eventually. "We drank too much. I don't think any of us knew it would be like that."

"That's not an excuse."

"It's not like you cheated on her. And that crazy chick who tried to rape you on the dance floor in West Palm does *not* count."

"It's not about that." Jake picked up the bottle of beer he was drinking—his third of the afternoon—and tipped what was left down his throat. "Was Caroline mad at you?"

"No, but I'm a better communicator than you are. You're shit with your phone."

"I know."

"So if you know, you have to be aware of it, and you have to try to be better about it. It's not that hard."

"Don't make me feel worse, Sam," Jake said, though part of the reason he'd called Sam, not Hale, was for precisely this reason. Sam's morals were solid, and he liked it that way. He liked playing the role of big brother to Jake and Hale—he always had, ever since they were kids. Jake needed that right now.

"Do you know where she is?" Sam asked.

"Still staying with one of her girlfriends, I assume."

"Well, what are you gonna do about it?"

Jake glanced toward the east-facing windows. The light outside had grown dim and gray; he couldn't believe it was already past six. He looked down at his notebook splayed open on the coffee table, felt his heart pick up speed, the fire burning inside.

"I need you and Hale to meet me at the studio."

"Now?"

"Yes. Please."

"I'm exhausted, Danner. And we have back-to-back shows starting tomorrow. I need one more night off."

"I wouldn't ask if I weren't desperate, Sam." Jake spun the empty beer bottle around in his fingers.

"What is it?"

"I wrote a song today. I think it might be the best one yet. I want us to play it out."

"Tonight?"

"I have this momentum going. Just trust me."

"It's a song about Molly, isn't it?" Sam sighed. "All right. I'll tell Hale. We'll meet you in an hour."

"Molly's Song" was released as a single in March. It might've been too soon after the release of *The Narrows,* from a tactical standpoint, but Jerry and Ron didn't care—they knew from the very first listen it was going to be a hit.

The same month, Danner Lane was slated to open for Arcade Fire at Madison Square Garden. It was a monstrously huge deal—it would be the band's greatest exposure yet, without a doubt—and Jerry wanted them to kick off the set with "Molly's Song."

In the meantime, Danner Lane continued to gain traction. Their shows at top venues around the city—Bowery Ballroom, Music Hall of Williamsburg, Glasslands—were consistently sold out, and "Molly's Song" became their most purchased song on iTunes, tripling "Salt River" in downloads.

Jake didn't know if Molly had heard it yet, but he could only assume she had—everyone had. In the two weeks since the song had been out in the world, Jerry had already been approached by the producers of *Shameless,* a new Showtime series, requesting the use of "Molly's Song" in the season finale.

A few days before the Madison Square Garden show, Jake sent Molly an email with an invitation to attend.

Moll,

We're opening at MSG on Saturday. It won't mean anything unless you're there. I put your name on the guest list with two VIP passes, which you can pick up at will call. Please come. I miss you and love you so fucking much. I'll never stop being sorry.

Jake

PS: I heard from Bella the other day. She said you guys had a great lunch meeting, and that she's obsessed with your writing and that she's offering you representation for Needs. *I'm so proud of you, Moll. You earned this. You deserve it.*

Jake hadn't heard from Molly by the time Saturday rolled around. He couldn't shake the nerves in the pit of his stomach. He was anxious about the show—playing MSG was by far their most monumental opportunity yet, and one he couldn't fuck up—but it was more than that. Jake knew in his gut that if Molly didn't come that night, they were over. If he didn't see her face in the crowd—her big hazel eyes, her high, reddened cheekbones—the face that was perfect to him in every way—he'd probably never see it again.

Backstage, Hale swung his arm around Jake's and clinked their beers. With his free hand, he gestured out toward the stage and the twenty thousand people in the audience beyond.

"This is it, my friend. We're fucking *making* it."

"We've dreamed about a moment like this for a long time, huh?" Jake tipped the neck of his bottle back and swallowed.

"Since middle school, probably." Hale nodded. "Dicking around in the garage, me on the drums, you and Sammy on guitar. Hey, don't sound so depressed, Danner. Maybe she's out there. And if she's not, you can have any girl you want tonight. You're the hotshot pretty boy on lead vocals. You're the one they all want." Hale's tone was strange; it was unclear how serious he was being.

"We built this band together," Jake said. "The three of us are equals."

"Ha." Hale stepped back, tossing his empty bottle into the trash. "That's not true anymore, and you of all people know it."

"Hey," Jerry called from behind them. "It's a packed house out there. Ron said he can't remember the last time he's seen this many show up for an opening act at the Garden. Get rid of that drink, Danner. You guys are on in five."

Walking out onto the stage of Madison Square Garden and seeing the crowd—the chock-full, seemingly endless sea of people cheering and screaming, the thousands of tiny lights that glowed from their phones— was unlike anything Jake had ever experienced.

It was like stepping into a dream, Jake thought as he took it all in. He saw himself at eleven years old, strumming his old steel-stringed dreadnought, the one he'd snagged for ten bucks at a neighbor's estate sale. Next to him was Sam on the bass he'd gotten for Christmas that year, with Hale behind them, ripping away on his five-piece drum set. They were in the Lanes' garage—Jake could still smell the distinct, musty aroma of mothballs and gasoline. They were practicing their cover of "Sweet Home Alabama," high on adrenaline and unobstructed optimism, anchored in a state of bliss you can only know in childhood, when there's no weight on your shoulders and nothing's at stake and time is a vacuum where you feel like you'll be a kid forever.

And then Mrs. Lane was opening the garage door and calling them in for dinner, and Jake noticed that his stomach was grumbling and thought how much he liked staying there for dinner, that it was so much better than going halfway down the block to his own house, where his father would be drunk on the couch and his mother would direct him to "find something" in the fridge when he said he was hungry.

When Jake was playing music with Sam and Hale, all that not-so-great stuff about life fell away, and there was only the guitar and the steady beat and the way that it made his heart feel to sing. Neither Sam nor Hale liked the singing part—that was always left for Jake—and besides, it wasn't Jake's fault that he'd grown up to be better looking than they had.

Fuck Hale, Jake thought, dismissing his friend's words from earlier. He brushed his fingertips to the strings of his guitar—a gesture that always made him feel a bit more rooted to the earth—and the arena exploded. Jake's eyes swept the front of the crowd that was the VIP section, and maybe it was because he wanted it so ferociously that he willed it to be true, but there she was, right there in front of him, the only person in the ocean of people that he existed for. Her wide, even smile, that tumble of blond hair. Jake felt his breath catch in his throat.

He inhaled slowly, clipping his eyes to hers. "Hey, New York City. It's Saturday night, and we're Danner Lane, and we're gonna play some music." Cheers erupted, lights twinkled and flashed. Molly held on to his gaze and nodded, something like forgiveness flickering in her eyes. Peace washed over Jake's heart.

"We've got a new song for you guys, though some of you might've heard it already." The crowd roared, which told Jake that they knew what was coming, that it was the reason many of them were there. "This one is for my Molly."

The air in the Garden was still, humming with anticipation. Hale began to pick up on the snare drum, Sam threading the bass with expert hands. Jake leaned in toward the microphone and began to sing.

Five days ago I didn't know
The feelings in me now
Your beautiful mind, your secret smile
Change me, won't you change me

Chapter Seventeen

Molly

June 2022

Molly's jaw drops—it actually *drops*—but she's too paralyzed with shock to close it.

"*Molly?*" Jake speaks, and it's like she's looking at a real-life ghost. It's too much. Is she dreaming? She blinks hard.

She feels Hunter's hand on her elbow, steadying her. *Good,* she thinks from somewhere far above. *Because I'm currently detached from my own body.*

"I'm sorry . . . ," Sabrina starts, glancing from Jake to Molly to Hunter, then back to Jake. "Do you all know each other?"

"Yes," Jake says. His eyes are glued to Molly's, and she feels woozy, like she might faint or throw up or possibly both at the same time. "Molly and I . . . we knew each other in the city. Years ago." Jake exhales. "Small world." His gaze drifts to Sabrina, and for a moment, he seems to peer at her strangely. But then his mouth breaks into a grin, the classic Jake Danner smile. Apparently, he's recovered from shock much faster than Molly.

"No!" Sabrina lets out an excited laugh. "What are the *chances*?" She pulls the door all the way open. "Come on in. What can I get you two to drink?"

Hunter says nothing, his mouth gaping. The color has drained from his face, and he hasn't stopped staring at Jake.

Molly opens her mouth to speak, but her heart jumps into her throat. She can't get her voice to leave her lips. How is this possible? She's been friends with Sabrina for nearly a month now, and all this time, Sabrina has been married to *Jake*?

"Wine," Molly manages, her voice hoarse. She feels Jake watching her. "Whatever wine you have open. Thanks."

"Um, scotch and soda?" Hunter finally peels his gaze away from Jake and looks at Sabrina. "Thank you."

Sabrina leads them through the foyer and to the bar off the immaculate chef's kitchen. "This really *is* a small world," she says, oblivious to any awkwardness. She pours Molly a glass of rosé while Jake fixes Hunter's scotch. "Let's sit out on the terrace. It's such a nice night."

The backyard is green and spacious—two acres, at least—with a patio overlooking a turquoise lap pool. Molly sinks down onto the cushion of an expensive-looking teak love seat. Hunter sits beside her, a protective hand on her leg, and Sabrina chooses a matching chair across from them. Molly watches as she lights two glass hurricanes on the white resin table.

Jake remains standing, looking more uncomfortable than he did in the doorway, as if it's all starting to sink in. He wears a blue oxford that matches his eyes, the top two buttons undone, with khaki shorts and loafers. It's an outfit he wouldn't have been caught dead in when Molly knew him, one he would've deemed "preppy yuppie" with a tone of pure snark. Back then, Jake had been all jeans and frayed T-shirts, tattered Vans, and his beloved hoodies.

Molly sips her wine and watches him as discreetly as she can manage. He looks older, undoubtedly—the skin on his face less supple, slightly roughened—but still so beautiful. A beautiful man. Molly felt it the first time she saw him, and she feels it now, her insides turned to putty. But how—*how*—has he wound up here? Jake Danner, married and living in the suburbs, in a gorgeous house that looks like something straight out of a Pinterest board? It's literally the last thing Molly ever would've expected of him.

Molly's knowledge of what Jake has been up to over the years is almost nonexistent, and she's liked it that way. She knew Danner Lane had split long ago—she'd read about it in the tabloids but had also heard the news in an email from Jake himself nearly a year after their own breakup, an email to which she'd never responded. But after that, nothing, and neither of them had ever been big social media users. Much to her friends' chagrin, Molly never got an Instagram, and she almost never updates Facebook.

When people ask her why she's not on social media—and so many people ask—she claims it just isn't for her. She doesn't feel the need to be so connected, to post publicly about her life. But the secret truth Molly keeps locked in her heart is that she doesn't want to be found. More than that, she doesn't want to *find*. She's seen Nina spiral into countless Instagram black holes, digging up photos of Cash and his fiancée, Olivia, making herself miserable. Molly doesn't want that. She doesn't want to know.

Hunter has asked Sabrina a question about pool maintenance, and Jake slides into the chair adjacent to Molly's. She observes his bare knee, jiggling slightly, the pale blond hairs that coat his golden skin. She has so many questions for him and no idea where to start, so she says nothing. She sips her wine, feels the cold, tart liquid run down the back of her throat, warming her gut. She and Jake both pretend to listen to Sabrina and Hunter discuss pool heating systems.

"I remember that dress," he says finally, so quiet it's almost a whisper.

Molly runs her hand along the linen fabric of the skirt. "Funnily enough, I haven't worn it in years until tonight."

"You used to wear it all the time." Jake's eyes land on Molly's, and there's a fire low in her belly, and she knows they are both probably thinking of all the times he tore that dress over her head. She pictures it, a blue-and-white-striped puddle on the floor next to their bed in Williamsburg.

Molly inhales and exhales slowly; she needs to stay present. "I can't believe you live in Flynn Cove," she says. "When did you move here?" She feels like this is a detail she knows—Sabrina must have told her?—but Molly can't remember. Her mind is suddenly pure fog.

"We moved in March." Sabrina answers the question for Jake; she's finished talking pool mechanics with Hunter. "We left the city so Jake could get a change of scene, some peace and quiet. He's working on something—a side project." Sabrina glances at Molly and Hunter. "Jake used to be a musician, and he's trying to get back into it."

"They know that, Sisi." Jake smiles stiffly.

Sisi. Why does that name sound so familiar?

"Oh, duh." Sabrina laughs, waving her hand. "Well, anyway. My grandparents used to live in Flynn Cove—I think I told you that, Moll—and I have such fond memories visiting them as a child. When this place came on the market, we fell in love."

"I can see why," Molly says. "It's gorgeous." She can palpably feel Hunter's discomfort next to her. He's barely said a word since they arrived.

"Thank you." Sabrina smiles. "I can't believe I'm only just having you over."

"When did you two get married?" Hunter asks, breaking his silence. Molly notices the empty tumbler in his hand—he's already drained his scotch.

"Earlier this year. January." Jake's eyes flicker to his wife. "The wedding was in Miami. Sisi's from Palm Beach."

"Guilty. I'm a Sunshine State girl." Sabrina grins and spreads her thin, toned arms across the back of the chair. In her short-sleeved white caftan, her dark hair falling over her shoulders in two glossy plaits, she looks like a petite Grecian goddess.

And then the memory shakes loose from the deep-seated roots of Molly's past. She hears Jake's voice on their very first date, words she replayed countless times in her head during their first few months together, weighing their significance: *Sisi wanted to move in together, and I guess . . . I guess I didn't love her as much as she loved me.*

Sisi was Jake's ex-girlfriend Sisi, the one he'd dated before he and Molly met. He hadn't mentioned her often during their time together, but the name was still permanently implanted in some crevice of Molly's mind. Sisi was Sabrina?

"Molly's grandmother used to have a place in Naples," Hunter tells Sabrina. "She passed away last summer, but before that, we used to go down there after Christmas every year."

"I'm so sorry to hear that." Sabrina's face falls. "Naples is beautiful."

Molly's mind is still back in 2013, remembering *Sisi,* and it takes her a moment to register that she needs to respond. "It *is.*" She smiles tightly. "And thank you, but it's okay. My grandmother lived a long life. I do miss going to Florida, though."

Sabrina nods. She picks up the bottle of rosé from the ice bucket and refills Molly's glass. "Okay, I'm sorry, maybe I had a *little* too much wine before you guys got here, but I'm just putting two and two together . . ." She glances from Jake to Molly, her emerald eyes shiny. "You and Jake know each other from way back when, and your name is Molly. You're not . . . *Molly* Molly, are you? Like, 'Molly's Song' Molly?"

Molly is momentarily stunned; it doesn't seem normal that Sabrina is asking this question in front of Jake. Then again, isn't this what drew her to Sabrina in the first place, her willingness to cut through bullshit and say something *real*? She glances at Hunter, who stares into his empty glass. She's grateful for the wine dulling the edges of this excruciating moment.

She opens her mouth to speak, but Jake answers the question first.

"Yes." His voice is even and cool, and he's looking at Sabrina strangely again. "Molly and I haven't seen each other in—god, I don't know how many years. Not since the height of my Danner Lane days."

Molly wishes she could climb out of her own skin. More than anything, she is desperate to know what is running through Hunter's head beside her. She wants to crawl into his lap and melt away.

"Wow." Sabrina's expression is indecipherable. "Crazy."

"Crazy," Jake repeats.

"Well, no need for this to be awkward." Sabrina's mouth lifts into a hopeful smile. "You're both married now! And Molly and Hunter have a gorgeous daughter. Perhaps I'm jumping the gun, but I see the four of us being great, great friends." She winks at Molly. "Moll and I already are."

"A daughter?" Jake's sandy eyebrows jump as he turns toward Molly. "I didn't know you had kids."

"Stella," Hunter declares proudly, placing his tumbler down on the teak table a bit too hard. "She's the best."

"Stella." Jake works through both syllables slowly. His eyes land on Molly's again, and she feels for a sharp, fleeting moment as if they're alone, as if it's only the two of them in the entire universe, as if it always has been. He smiles. "What a great name."

"She's a doll," Sabrina says brightly. "She's almost six, right?"

"Yep. I can't believe it." Molly stares into the bowl of her wineglass, which is somehow empty again.

"Is she a summer birthday?" Sabrina asks.

Molly nods. "August."

Sabrina stands, smooths the front of her caftan. "I'm going to pop the salmon in the oven. We can eat in fifteen."

Dinner is served in the dining room, another pristinely decorated space that leaves Molly even more curious about the source of Sabrina and Jake's—or the Danners', she supposes she should call them—finances. She knows nothing about Jake's current income, but can't imagine the profits of a few years of way-back-when rock band stardom would've extended so far as to get them a house like this in Flynn Cove.

"Jake, what do you do for work now?" Hunter asks, and Molly thinks perhaps spousal telepathy is real. "Sabrina mentioned the new music venture, but is there anything aside from that?"

Molly shifts uncomfortably at the way Hunter phrases the question.

Jake swallows a piece of sourdough, and Molly watches the rise and fall of his Adam's apple. She still can't actually grasp that he's here, right in front of her. She is sitting in *Jake's* grass cloth–wallpapered dining room. She is eating roasted salmon off *Jake's* Mottahedeh china. The Jake she knew didn't own matching socks.

"Sisi—sorry, Sabrina—her dad started an insurance company, and the Manhattan office was kind enough to bring me on a few years back." A slightly rueful expression passes across his face. Working a corporate job is the last thing Molly ever expected of Jake. Even after Danner Lane's split, she'd always assumed he'd found a career that kept him involved in music—or at least something creative.

"To be frank, I inherited a pretty sizable trust when my dad sold Randolph Group," Sabrina adds candidly. "Which is how we bought this place. I'm consulting for a few brands right now, but no longer full-time. It was just too much to keep commuting into the city once we moved out here. Freelancing is more convenient."

Hunter nods politely, but Molly knows he's surprised. Most young couples they're acquainted with in Flynn Cove wouldn't be so up-front about their lavish lifestyles being subsidized by rich parents. Sabrina's honesty is, at least, refreshing. Molly can also sense that she and Hunter are sharing the same thought. They've both heard of Randolph Group—everyone has. It's a giant company. Sabrina must be absolutely loaded.

"And what about you, Molly?" Jake asks. "Still writing, I hope?"

She sips her wine, thinking of Bella's voicemail sitting in her inbox. She should just delete it.

"Wait, you're a *writer*?" Sabrina perks up at this. "You never told me that, Moll."

"I'm not," Molly says quickly. She gives a strained smile. "Back in the day, I wrote a bit. Not anymore." She blinks, hating the way it feels to admit this to Jake, how lost she sounds in this moment, the lack of confidence in her voice. "But I'm still teaching yoga."

"I told you that's where we met, babe. At Yoga Tree." Sabrina squeezes Jake's arm, and Molly feels herself flinch. Out of habit, maybe. Old, ingrained jealousy. "Molly is an *incredible* teacher."

"Always has been." Jake smiles gently in Molly's direction, and his eyes are so blue and disarming, and she wishes he would stop *looking* at her like that, like he's trying to pass her a silent reminder that he's seen her naked a thousand times. Or maybe he's being friendly and normal, and she's just being hyperneurotic as usual, ramped up on fertility hormones that distort and dramatize the way she sees the world.

Molly glances at Sabrina, paranoid that she, too, can sense an edge of flirtation in Jake's voice. But Sabrina just sits there with a mollified expression glued to her face, nursing her rosé. Because why *would* her new friend be worried that something is amiss? Molly and Jake dated in their early twenties, when they were practically children. They're both married to other people now; Molly has a child of her own.

So what, really, *is* the problem? Molly isn't sure; she only knows that at this stage in her life, having come as far as she has from the girl she was at twenty-six, living in the same small town as Jake Danner feels impossible. Unbearable.

The problem is: she really likes his wife. Sabrina is the first woman Molly has met in her three years in Flynn Cove whom she's clicked with—well, besides Whitney, but sometimes Molly wonders if she's ever *actually* clicked with Whitney, or if she's just tried to convince herself she has. And okay, clearly Sabrina is privileged, but she's not gaudy or entitled like Meredith and Betsy and Edie. She doesn't wear flashy jewelry or dress like a Stepford wife; she doesn't believe that the sun rises and sets on the Flynn Cove Country Club.

Sabrina is refreshingly open. Molly appreciates that she was candid about her parents' money. She knows for a fact that Meredith's husband has a trust fund—*that's* how the Duffys pay for the upkeep of their waterfront mansion and additional homes in Southampton and Aspen—but Meredith would never acknowledge this. She just waves her black Amex around town, acting like she's earned the diamond tennis bracelet on her wrist, and the bimonthly visits to Dr. Jeffers that keep her face line-free, and every other material comfort that's simply fallen into her lap.

Sabrina isn't trying to be someone she's not. She has a cartilage piercing on her upper ear and frown lines between her eyebrows and a devout yoga regimen. She possesses humility and self-awareness and a grounded sense of perspective. Sabrina seems serious about her career in fashion, but her interests extend beyond designer clothing lines. She often brings up politics and current events; she sends Molly great podcast recommendations and op-eds from the Sunday Review. Molly smiles at her with genuine appreciation and remarks that the meal is delicious.

"You think so?" Sabrina looks touched. "I never used to cook in the city, but I figure now that we have this big old kitchen, I ought to give it some use."

Molly takes another sip of wine, feels it settle warmly below her collarbone. Sabrina is right—this doesn't have to be awkward. Molly can ignore whatever strange thing is going on with her heart, and remember that she and Jake are older now, and happily married to other people, and yes, despite this surreal coincidence, maybe the four of them really will be great, great friends.

Chapter Eighteen
Sabrina

You must know by now, Molly, that my sleuthing skills are quite advanced. Once I knew your last name (thanks to Bhakti Yoga), I found you on Facebook. Most of your settings seemed set to private, but your profile photo was of you and a girl with short, dark hair neatly brushing her shoulders. You're standing on the beach wearing cover-ups and aviators; she's smiling at the camera, and your face is turned in profile, your mouth open wide in laughter. Crucially, the girl in the picture was tagged. *Liz Esposito.*

As it so happened, the hedge fund where Elizabeth Esposito worked—thanks, LinkedIn—was located three blocks south of my own office in midtown.

One February evening, I followed her. I waited in the lobby of her building until she came down, recognizing her instantly in the silver Moncler puffer she sported in several of her Instagrams. I trailed her for four blocks, watching closely as she fiddled with her Spotify and checked her texts and eventually brushed through the revolving doors of the Equinox on East Forty-third Street. I watched through the big glass windows as she used her key card to sign it at the front desk, proceeding through the turnstile when the light flashed green.

An hour later, I became the newest member of Equinox. I already belonged to a gym downtown, near my apartment, but it didn't matter. The need to find out if you and Jake were still together was primal and urgent, and Liz Esposito was my ticket to this golden nugget of information—I felt it in my bones.

The next evening, I didn't bother waiting in the lobby of Liz's office building. Instead, I perched on a chair in the spa-like locker room of Equinox and bided my time. I could just tell, from Liz's small, sculpted legs and snappy stride, that she was the type of gym bunny who went every day.

I scrolled through Instagram and work emails until Liz arrived at quarter past five. I waited for her to change into gym clothes, and when she made her way upstairs toward the long row of treadmills overlooking Fifth Avenue, I followed her. Equinox was crowded, and Liz's eyes had been glued to her phone since the moment she walked in—it's not like she'd noticed me. It's not like she thought anything at all when I hopped on the treadmill next to hers. She didn't so much as glance my way.

We ran side by side, our legs in tandem on the speeding belts. *Swoosh swoosh swoosh.* Liz stared straight ahead, clearly in the zone as she maintained her seven-minute mile, a pace I was inspired to match. I suppose I was trying to tire myself out to make what happened next appear more natural. My legs did ache—I wasn't used to running this fast. And when I let them give out—when I let myself pause just long enough so that I flew back, my feet skidding off the end of the treadmill, my ass smacking the floor with a thud—it was even more natural than I'd imagined. With my open Poland Spring bottle in one hand, I'd "accidentally" flung water on Liz. She noticed my fall immediately. She stopped her machine.

"Oh my god!" she exclaimed. She crouched beside me, and I took in the details of her small, fox-like face. Her chest glistened with sweat, but she smelled clean, like deodorant. "Are you okay?"

I nodded, wincing in semi-faux pain. Perfectly, I'd arranged for my headphones to rip from my phone during the crash. "January Girl" by Danner Lane blared from the shitty iPhone speaker.

"I'm an idiot," I said, sitting up. "I was trying to keep a seven-minute mile, and I'm just not there yet. *So* sorry for spilling on you."

"It's just water." Liz shrugged passively. "I'm a seven-minute mile, but only after years of training. I ran track in college."

"Wow. Impressive."

"Hey." She gestured to my phone. "You like that band."

"Love them."

"Ha." Liz scrunched her nose. "You'll never believe this, but that song is about one of my good friends—my old roommate. She used to date Jake Danner."

"Stop it." *Used to date. Jackpot.*

"Seriously. 'January Girl,' because they met in January." She rolled her eyes. "Kinda lame."

We stood. Liz's blasé, possibly snarky attitude toward your relationship with Jake had my curiosity extra piqued. But I couldn't act *too* interested, not right off the bat. I could tell immediately that Liz was cool and detached, yet perceptive. You know what I'm talking about, Molly. With someone like her, you have to play your cards right.

"That's crazy." I wrapped my headphones into a neat circle around my fingers. "I'll let you get back to your run. But hey, I just joined here this week. Are there any classes you recommend?"

Liz placed a hand to her hip. "Like yoga?"

"I'm more of a Pilates girl."

She nodded. "More my speed, too. Um, yeah. Check out Erin's class. Mondays and Wednesdays at six."

"Cool. Thanks. Have a good one. I'm Caitlin, by the way."

"Liz."

She waved goodbye. I took note of her nail polish, glossy and black.

There was an edge to Liz that captivated me, Molly. Mostly I just liked that she didn't seem particularly enamored of you—I got the sense that the two of you had drifted apart. I wanted to know more, and I knew that would happen—Liz and I would become friends around the gym, I'd make sure of it. But in the meantime, she'd already given me the critical piece of information I needed: confirmation that you and Jake were no longer a couple, no doubt thanks to my handiwork.

Danner Lane had a big show coming up—they were slated to open for Arcade Fire at Madison Square Garden in March. I knew this was huge for Jake; the Garden had always been his holy grail of venues, and even though they weren't the main act, it was still a big fucking deal.

I bought two tickets to the concert—floor, center stage. I debated bringing Debbie or Elena along, but ultimately decided to make it a date night. I needed to make Jake jealous. So I called up a guy named Warren, a good-looking advertising executive I'd had casual sex with around the holidays. I'd ditched him the moment he'd made it clear he wanted more; he was too straitlaced, too Banana Republic. Most of all, he just wasn't Jake.

But Warren *was* the most attractive man I'd slept with since Jake, and I decided he'd have to do. He accepted my invitation to the concert pathetically quickly, volunteering that he was more than willing to bail on a friend's birthday dinner to attend. What a loser.

Warren wanted to get drinks before the show at some "cool" cocktail

lounge he knew of in Chelsea, but I was adamant about seeing the opening act. My plan was straightforward: stay through the whole show, then
pop backstage to congratulate Jake. Similar to my plan in West Palm
Beach, but this time would be different. For starters, I had Warren on my
arm—that would show Jake what he was missing—and, more important,
I had confirmation that *you* were out of the picture. Officially.

The Garden was packed; there was hardly an open seat in the house.
Warren was overeager, and I needed to be drunk, so we were already two
and a half cocktails deep by the time Jake and the band stepped onto the
stage. The crowd went wild; *The Narrows* had been an outrageous success
since its release, and I had a feeling I wasn't the only one in the audience
more interested in Danner Lane than Arcade Fire.

"Ohhh, *these* guys," Warren slurred, already tipsy. "Now I see why
you wanted to be here early." He slung his arm around me, and I fought
the urge to fling it away. "They're everywhere. They have that new song
everyone's obsessed with."

I took a sip of my drink—some sweet, lemony vodka thing. "'Salt
River'?"

"Nah, not that one. Uh, let me think . . . my roommate's girlfriend,
like, plays it on repeat. It's about some chick. 'Molly's Song,' that's what
it's called."

"Excuse me?" I spun toward Warren, so quickly my drink splattered
across the floor.

Warren shrugged. "Haven't you heard it? It's all over iTunes."

I flashed my gaze back to the stage, where Jake looked utterly perfect
in dark jeans and a worn tee. A little bit rock and roll, a little bit country. Tim McGraw meets Kurt Cobain. I felt my limbs turn to butter. I
watched his hands grip the microphone, the same way they'd gripped
the back of my head when he kissed me.

"Hey, New York City." The smooth, distinctive sound of his voice
sent a delicious ripple through my body. "It's Saturday night, and we're
Danner Lane, and we're gonna play some music."

Quickly, discreetly, I pulled up the iTunes Store on my phone and
searched *Danner Lane*. Sure enough, "Molly's Song" was listed as their
top track. It had just been released as a single the week before. I couldn't
believe it. *How* had I missed this? Work had been insane since Fashion
Week, but still. How did I let myself get so cocky that I stopped keeping
close tabs on Jake? Even *Warren* knew about "Molly's Song," for fuck's sake.

"We've got a new song for you guys, though some of you might've heard it already." Jake's clear voice boomed through the mike, that slight Southern drawl pulling the edges of his words. "This one is for my Molly."

The crowd exploded. My insides twisted violently; the taste of bile and lemony liquor burned the back of my throat. I knew I would be sick. *My* Molly. I had to get out of there.

"Bathroom," I mouthed to Warren, who was already bouncing his knees in tune to the music. He flashed me a stupid, goofy grin and a double thumbs-up.

I grabbed my purse and shimmied my way through the row of mesmerized people. I bolted for the exit, not stopping until I was all the way down the escalators and outside the arena, safely on the street.

Liz had been wrong. She'd been so, so, so wrong. I hailed a cab home, ignoring the series of texts that had come in from Warren, asking if I was okay. I put in my earbuds and played "Molly's Song" on repeat, letting every excruciating lyric sink into my consciousness.

When I got back to my apartment, I marched straight into the bedroom. I threw my purse on the floor and opened the top drawer of my nightstand, digging out the framed photograph of Jake and me that I'd kept beside my bed when we were together. It was my favorite picture of us, a selfie taken on the High Line that first summer we spent as a couple. We look stupid happy, our smiles reaching our ears, a slice of the Hudson River visible in the backdrop.

I studied the photo, my hands trembling as I recalled the details of that perfect Saturday. We'd gotten Mexican food at Tacombi after the High Line, then walked over to the Lower East Side for a gig Danner Lane had at some dive bar. I don't remember the name of it, but I remember the way Jake played that night, the way no one in the crowd could take their eyes off him while he sang into the microphone. I remember how he pushed me up against the bar after the show and kissed me, long and hard, in front of all the girls who wanted him to be theirs. But he was mine.

I couldn't bear to look at the picture for another second. I flipped the frame around and smashed it against the side of the nightstand. I smashed it over and over again, until shards of glass littered the floor and the bed. When I looked down at my hands, they were covered in blood.

Chapter Nineteen

Molly

That spring, a month after Molly moved back in with Jake, *The Narrows* peaked at number two on the Billboard 200 album chart. "Molly's Song" was in its eighth consecutive week at number one on the Billboard Adult Pop Songs chart.

Meanwhile, Danner Lane had started preliminary work on its second album, which Dixon wanted wrapped up by the end of the year. And Molly was deep in the trenches editing *Needs,* passing revisions back and forth with her new agent, Bella Wright.

"I don't understand why Bella is *this* heavily involved in the editing process," Molly told Jake one Sunday afternoon, when they were working in the living room. "She's an agent. I thought editors were supposed to do the editing."

"Well, what does Bella say?" Jake glanced up from the coffee table, where he was scribbling notes on a new song.

Molly stretched her neck to the left and yawned. "I try not to ask her too many questions. I'm just lucky she signed me."

"You're not *just* lucky. You're an exceptional writer, that's what you are."

A smile crept across Molly's face. "Well, *luckily,*" she started, twisting around in her desk chair, "Bella thinks this is our last revision before she starts sending the manuscript out to editors."

"That's so exciting, Moll. Think about it—you could have a real book deal, practically any day now. It's amazing." Jake smiled.

"It is kind of amazing, isn't it?" Molly gazed at him dreamily. "But I don't want to get my hopes up." She closed her laptop, standing. "I'm going to rinse off."

In the shower, Molly lathered her hair with Garnier Fructis—Jake's signature shampoo—and inhaled its sharp, citrusy scent. She'd been using his shampoo ever since she moved back in; it was her way of luxuriating in the small things about him she'd so desperately missed.

Staying at Everly's had been fine, given the circumstances. Everly lived in a true one-bedroom in Dumbo, walking distance from the digital agency where she worked as a junior strategist. Between work and staying at Sage's, she was almost never home, which meant that Molly mostly had the apartment to herself.

She'd kept as busy as she could. She subbed extra yoga classes and scheduled drinks with friends she hadn't seen in ages and cooked new recipes in Everly's kitchen. When Bella finally called, apologizing profusely for the delay and eagerly offering her representation for *Needs*—which she'd devoured—Molly was so happy she almost forgot she was miserable. Still, the way she missed Jake was a hole in her heart, and not being able to share her good news with him seemed to only make her pain worse.

She knew about "Molly's Song"—everyone did. One night, a week after it released, she was out with Nina and Liz and Ev, and noticed friends of friends of friends whispering and pointing in her direction. She knew what they were saying. *That's Molly—like* the *Molly—from "Molly's Song."*

It was a good piece of music, and she knew it was making Danner Lane even more famous, but she didn't care. It wasn't enough. If she let herself remember the way she felt when Jake was on tour—the sudden and silent way he disappeared from her life—the anger in her heart grew so overwhelming she thought she might implode.

It was Nina who convinced her to go to the concert, when Molly told her about Jake's email and the VIP passes.

"Your ex-boyfriend, who you still clearly love, who's so in love with you that he wrote a song about you that is currently *the* actual most-played song in the universe, is performing at Madison Square Garden, and he wants to serenade you there in front of thousands of people. This is an astronomical life moment, Molly. You're going. And I'm going with you."

The day before the show, Molly was still on the fence. She was packing up after subbing back-to-back classes at Bhakti when her boss approached her behind the front desk. Veronica was Bhakti's studio manager and possessed the most quintessential yoga body Molly had ever seen.

"You've been getting so much great feedback lately." Veronica squeezed Molly's shoulder.

"Have I?" Molly forced a smile, her mind elsewhere.

"Absolutely. I hear it from students all the time. Plus, there was that girl who called here raving about your class. She sent you an email, right?"

"Huh?" Molly cocked her head. "What girl was that?"

"Oh, I can't remember her name . . ." Veronica pursed her lips in thought. "It was about a month ago, maybe six weeks? This girl called the studio asking for your email address. She said she loved your class and wanted to write to you. You never heard from her?"

Molly shook her head. She cared a lot about her teaching; she would have remembered if a student had emailed her. But six weeks ago was when she received the email from lenore.smith@gmail.com. She knew exactly when it was because the image of Jake kissing the platinum blonde had been living rent-free in her mind ever since. If someone had called the studio asking for her email address, it lined up with Jake's story. It was plausible that the perpetrator *was* a crazy fan who knew about Molly, who'd somehow figured out that she taught at Bhakti. Hadn't Jake tagged the studio in a photo of her on her mat last fall? The thought gave Molly the heebie-jeebies even as it flooded her with welcome relief. She'd suspected Jake had been telling the truth, and now she felt herself moving closer to this conviction. By the time she got back to Everly's apartment, she felt certain of his honesty. Still, it didn't negate the rest of his behavior on the tour. And she couldn't forget how much his disregard had hurt her.

The next night, Molly put on her favorite pair of jeans and a lilac crop top. She'd let Nina do her makeup, and they'd headed to Madison Square Garden. And when Jake walked out onto the stage, when his bright blue eyes found hers in the midst of tens of thousands of concertgoers in the biggest arena in New York City, it felt exactly like it had that very first night she saw him play at the Broken Mule—like they were the only two people there. And something in Molly shifted. She felt the anger that she'd been holding on to so tightly dissipate. She felt the power of *them*— the magic of what they had been and still had the potential to be. And she finally saw, with the lightning bolt of clarity she'd been yearning for, that refusing to forgive Jake wasn't going to keep her heart safe.

She knew that she wouldn't spend another night in Everly's apartment. The war inside her was over; her head finally agreed with her heart.

The shower door opened, pulling Molly out of the memory and snapping her back to the present. The wonderful, miraculous present. She felt Jake's hands slip around her midsection as he stepped under the water stream behind her, pressing his mouth against the back of her neck. It was chemical, their sex, and she'd missed it just as much—if not more—than all the other parts of them.

"I'm glad you followed me in there," Molly said as they lay on the bed afterward, their clean, damp limbs tangled. Afternoon light the color of lemons flooded through the sheer blinds.

Jake kissed her forehead, which he almost always did after they had sex. "I love you," he whispered.

"I love you, too."

"Hey, Moll?"

"Yeah?"

"Let's have a really, really good summer."

And they did. A dozen of their friends went in on a share house in Amagansett, and Molly and Jake went out there whenever Danner Lane didn't have a weekend show. It was a summer filled with beach days, barbecues, sunset cocktails on the deck, nights out in Montauk, Saturday morning trips to the farmers' market, and good friends.

Jake brought Hale, Sam, and Caroline out when there was space, and on those weekends, the nights always ended with the boys playing music around the fire, Jake and Sam strumming their acoustics and Hale making drums out of upside-down Tupperware.

"A private Danner Lane concert in my own backyard!" Cash would declare, drunk and gleeful, cracking open his millionth beer of the day and night. Nina would wrap her arms around his neck and roll her eyes. They were adorable, Nina and Cash, and even though they'd been together awhile—just as long as Molly and Jake—it still made Molly smile to see her best friend so deliriously happy.

All summer, girls ogled Jake wherever they went. They stared shamelessly, asking for autographs and pictures.

"That would annoy the shit out of me," Liz remarked one afternoon at the Surf Lodge, when a flock of blondes in bikini tops and shorts swarmed Jake, begging for a group photo.

But it didn't bother Molly. Despite all they'd been through, she trusted him, and in her gut, she knew their love was strong—hadn't it already been tested? Besides, Jake made it clear to the world that he was taken; he said so in interviews, he posted about it on social media, he kissed her in public. She was Molly of "Molly's Song," and she knew from the shameless way they studied her that the fangirls were jealous.

Labor Day weekend, the Amagansett house was full and Danner Lane didn't have any shows, so Molly and Jake took a road trip. Their first stop was New Jersey to see Molly's mother and Andrew. Molly was a bit nervous about how her mom would react—she was still dubious of Jake after what they'd been through the previous winter—but the visit went better than expected. Molly showed Jake around Denville—her favorite breakfast spot, the pool where she'd spent three summers as a lifeguard, the park where she and Rachel and their crew got drunk in high school. Molly wished she could introduce Jake to Rachel, but her old best friend had moved to Colorado for college and still lived out west, and they'd done a surprisingly terrible job of keeping in touch. It made Molly sad to think about this. Rachel was someone she'd always assumed she'd be friends with forever.

At night, Molly and Jake slept in the twin beds in her pink childhood room. Her mother grilled swordfish and fresh summer corn and asked Jake all about life as a famous musician.

After dinner, Jake and Andrew went into the den to watch tennis, and Molly helped her mom with the dishes.

"He seems devoted to you, Moo."

"Thank you for saying that, Mom. He is."

"Just don't get ahead of yourself, okay?"

"What do you mean?" Molly placed a handful of silverware in the sink.

"It's only been a year and a half, with a rocky patch in the middle." She handed her daughter a pot to dry. "Just keep your wits about you. People change, especially when they're young and have dreams." Her mother blinked, and Molly noticed a new batch of lines around the corners of her caramel eyes, and the thick gray roots that had yet to be dyed blond. At fifty, her mother was still an attractive woman—she always had been—but Molly hadn't noticed these signs of aging until recently.

Molly could only assume her mother was insinuating something about her father—when she made comments like that, she almost always was. And Molly's father had been young when he left—only thirty-three. The older she'd gotten, the more Molly realized that she barely knew anything about her father, except that he'd been a writer at heart and that his dreams had been thwarted.

The next morning, Jake and Molly packed up the car and headed farther south, toward North Carolina. It had been Molly's idea to visit Jake's hometown, and she'd pressed when he'd resisted.

"We've been living together for over a year, and I *still* haven't met your parents," she'd challenged.

"You don't want to meet my parents, Moll." Jake had sighed. "My mom is . . . she's very conservative. She doesn't really have a lot to say. And my dad, well . . . I'm surprised he's still around, to be honest."

"Well, he *is* around. And that's more than I can say about mine."

The Danner home was roughly what Molly expected from the outside—a one-story ranch slightly smaller than her mother's own average suburban house, but not by much. The neighborhood was green and lush and a ten-minute drive from the ocean.

Mrs. Danner greeted them in the front hall. She was a petite woman with a silver bob and dark eyes. She wore a pale yellow button-down and boxy khakis that Molly's mother would've called "old lady pants"; the outfit combined with her lack of a dye job made her appear older than she probably was. She set them up in separate bedrooms—*I told you she was conservative,* Jake muttered under his breath—and said they should wash up for dinner.

Though it wasn't big, there was a coldness to the house that Molly couldn't ignore. There was little variation in color—mainly beiges and taupes—and hardly anything on the walls. It lacked the busy, lived-in feeling her own home had always evoked, despite the fact that it had only been her, her mom, and Andrew there.

After she showered, Molly put on a green sundress, combed out her hair, and swiped a coat of mascara on her lashes. By the time she made her way into the kitchen for dinner, Mr. Danner was there—he'd been napping when they arrived. He sat at the table in front of a full pint glass, and Molly was so shocked by his appearance she couldn't speak. Even though his curls had gone gray and he was notably disheveled—red-rimmed blue eyes, unshaven, slumped posture—he was the spitting image of Jake, and Molly could see that he had once been as radiantly handsome as his son.

"Well, aren't you a sight for sore eyes." Mr. Danner spoke in a thick Southern accent, circling the glass in his fingers. "Jake never said how pretty you were. Not that he says much to his folks at all, these days. He didn't even say y'all were coming until . . . what was it, Lorna? Friday?"

Mrs. Danner said nothing as she tossed the salad. She'd put on a different shirt and some pink lipstick, but still wore the old lady khakis.

"Easy, Pop." Jake stepped into the room, and Molly felt her shoulders relax. "Can I help you, Mom?"

Mrs. Danner shook her head. "Fix yourselves a drink, if you'd like." Her voice was quiet. She seemed timid as a mouse.

Dinner was a shrimp casserole cooked in cream, and it felt so heavy in Molly's stomach that she had to force the bites down. They ate at the kitchen table—which overlooked a small patch of backyard—with the overhead light blazing and no music in the background. Conversation was minimal, too. It was mostly Jake asking his mother questions, which she answered quickly and without enthusiasm. Mr. Danner refilled his pint glass more times than Molly could count, keeping one eye glued to the small television perched on the counter. Neither of his parents asked Jake about the band.

When they'd finished eating, Mr. Danner switched to bourbon and disappeared into the den.

"He'll be passed out in an hour," Jake whispered to Molly as they cleared the plates. His mother had gone to take the trash out. "I think we should leave in the morning."

Molly nodded, unable to object. Being in this sterile, eerie house around Jake's dysfunctional parents, she understood why he hadn't wanted to come back here.

"But I'll take you to the beach, tonight, if you want." His eyes were desolate, and Molly squeezed his hand. Her heart was overwhelmed with love for him.

"Yes, please."

Jake was quiet on the drive out to the Narrows. Molly stared out the window, watching the last of the sunset between the trees as it slipped below the horizon, a tangerine line scorching the earth. She felt somber and strange, eager to shake the hours with Jake's family from her memory. Until that moment, she'd always believed she and Jake shared the experience of coming from broken homes. But her home wasn't broken, not like Jake's. Yes, her father had left their family—or had been pushed out by her mother, Molly had never been fully sure which description was most accurate—but her family was still a family. Her mother and Andrew would do anything for her, and vice versa—it was an unconditional love that she carried in her heart and never questioned. Jake, she understood for the first time, had never had that. Molly couldn't remember the last time she'd felt so profoundly sad.

Their rental car didn't have four-wheel drive, so they parked it on the side of the dirt road and walked hand in hand toward the water.

"I know this is more of a bay than the true ocean," Jake said, breaking the silence. "But it's my favorite spot on the coast. Sam, Hale, and I . . . we spent so much time here." He sat down on the sand, placed his elbows on his knees.

"It's beautiful." Molly slid off her sandals and slumped down beside him. She watched the moonlight float on the bay, squished the sand between her toes. The sound of the gentle waves crashing was like a tonic, and the tension dropped from her body. "I'm so sorry." She didn't know how to verbalize what she was apologizing for, only that Jake would understand.

"Don't be." Jake glanced at Molly. "It wasn't all bad, growing up here. It might've been, if I hadn't had the Lanes." He tipped his head back, gazing up at the inky-blue sky. "They were my family, really. I spent every waking hour there that I could."

"We should go see them. Mr. and Mrs. Lane, I mean."

Jake shook his head, his curls ruffling in the warm breeze. "They moved to Charlotte. John—Mr. Lane—is a professor. He started teaching at the university there a few years back."

"Oh." Molly shifted closer to Jake, resting her arm against his. "Can I ask . . . was your mom always like this?"

"Lobotomized, you mean?" Jake shrugged. "More or less. It's gotten worse, that's for sure. My dad has worn her down over the years. I used to try to help her . . . I tried so many times . . . to tell her to get help, to leave him. But she always refused, so I stopped."

"Is he abusive?"

"Not physically. That's probably the reason she pretends nothing's the matter. He's just an awful, selfish drunk. He went to jail for a bit when I was a kid."

"He did?"

Jake nodded. "For a year and change when I was in elementary school. It was his third DUI. I was in the car when they arrested him."

"Jesus, Jake. Why didn't you tell me before?"

He sighed, pushing his heel through the sand. "I hate thinking about it. I was six. All I really remember is being in the back seat—the awful, sour smell of his truck—and then flashing red and blue lights in the rear-view mirror. I waited in the police station for hours till my mother came and got me." He glanced up at Molly. "I'm sorry. I should've told you."

"It's okay." A seam split through her heart as she reached for Jake's hand, pressing her thumb to his palm. "For the record, I think *both* your parents are selfish. I couldn't believe that neither of them asked you a single question about Danner Lane."

"They don't care about Danner Lane. They thought I should grow up and be a doctor or a lawyer, something useful like that. They always said our music was a silly way to pass the time."

Molly felt tears in her throat. She squeezed his hand tighter. "Hey. I'm sorry I made you come here."

"Don't be. You were all excited to see where I grew up, and I thought there was a chance . . . I thought maybe something could be different, this time. But it never is. He's always a little bit worse. Sometimes I feel . . ." Jake's voice trailed.

"Like what?"

"Never mind."

"No, tell me."

Jake sighed, dropping his head. "Sometimes I feel like I don't know how to be a good man. No one ever showed me, you know? And that scares me."

"Oh, Jake." Molly pressed her cheek against his shoulder. "You *are* a good man."

"I don't know."

"Stop. We just need to get out of here. We'll leave tomorrow, crack of dawn. Yeah?"

Jake nodded. He wrapped an arm around her, pulling her in close. "Can you promise me something, Moll?"

"Anything." She studied his face. In the moonlight, she could see the tiny spray of freckles by his right cheekbone.

"Promise we'll never end up miserable like that, okay? Like my folks, I mean. Promise me."

Molly inhaled the smell of salt and brine. Summer was ending, the

Amagansett share house was over, and she realized this could be their last time at the ocean for months.

"I promise," she told Jake, leaning in to seal the moment with a kiss. Then they stood and brushed the sand off the backs of their legs, leaving the Narrows the way they had come.

Chapter Twenty

Molly

July 2022

The day after the dinner at the Danners'—Jesus, the *Danners'*—Molly calls Sabrina to thank her. She could text, but she wants to hear her voice. She's hoping Sabrina won't sound as strange as Molly feels in the wake of the news that Jake—*her* Jake—is Sabrina's husband. How is it possible, she thinks for the umpteenth time. How is the world *that* small?

It's not yet five, but Molly takes another sip of the wine she's poured, lets it dull the edges as she waits for Sabrina to answer the phone. She tries not to imagine her ex-boyfriend's hands running along the length of her friend's toned body.

"Hi!" Sabrina sounds cheerful, per usual. They exchange pleasantries, catch up on the events of the day. Stella got first place in a sailing race at camp; Sabrina was crushed with work.

"Anyway," Molly starts, after she's thanked her for hosting on Friday. "I have to admit, I sort of freaked when I realized Jake was your husband. I just . . . I hadn't seen him in a really long time, and I couldn't believe it. And on the Yoga Tree sign-up, it always says Sabrina Randolph—"

"Does it?" Sabrina gives a soft laugh. "Maybe it's connected to the name on my credit card or something, because I did take Jake's name. I'm Sabrina Danner now."

"Oh." Molly is caught off guard. "Well, anyway, I was upset because I thought it might make things awkward or weird between you and me. But the more I think about it, I realize it doesn't need to be awkward. It *isn't* awkward, is what I'm trying to say." Molly isn't fully sure that she means this, but she wants to.

"I completely agree," Sabrina says. "It's a crazy coincidence, that's for sure, but isn't life full of them? Besides, you and Jake dated when you were what, twenty-three? It's not like it was super serious, from what I gather."

There's a pang in Molly's gut as she grasps Sabrina's words. Is that what Jake had told her? That he and Molly hadn't been serious? Was he *kidding*? They'd dated for years, most of which they'd lived together. They'd talked about marriage, they'd declared their eternal love for each other more times than Molly could remember. Jake had called Molly his muse—there were interviews in *Rolling Stone* and *Variety* that quoted this. The most successful song of his career was named after her, for crying out loud.

Frustration seizes Molly; it expands in her chest. But it's not Sabrina's fault, she thinks. And why the hell should she *care* if Jake downplays their relationship to his wife? He's only doing it out of kindness, no doubt; he doesn't want Sabrina to feel threatened. And Sabrina *isn't* threatened. Molly is happily married to Hunter—very happily married and has been for years. Until she came face-to-face with him last week, Molly hardly thinks of Jake anymore. Except for long car rides and dull mornings cleaning the kitchen and when that *stupid song* comes on the radio, he's barely popped into her head at all. His golden skin and cerulean eyes and warm, piney smell have been nothing but faded memories, so irrelevant to Molly's present-day life they may as well not be real at all.

"Molly?" Sabrina's voice snaps her back to the moment. "Sorry, maybe I'm wrong, I didn't mean—"

"No, you're right. What Jake and I had was . . . fleeting." Molly says this kindly, trying to imagine how she'd feel if it were the reverse situation and Sabrina were Hunter's old flame. She wouldn't want a reason to worry, either. "There's something I remember, though," she continues, suddenly nervous but unsure exactly why. "Something I wanted to ask you."

"Of course."

Molly slides onto one of the island stools in the kitchen, pressing her forearms onto the marble counter. Hunter is picking Stella up from a playdate—she has the house to herself. "So, the other night, Jake called you *Sisi*. And I . . . I have this distinct memory of him, when we were together, talking about a girl named Sisi. A girl he'd dated just before me. Was that you?"

There are several long beats of silence. It's a bit odd, Molly thinks, how long Sabrina waits to speak. She hears her breathing on the other end of the phone.

"Yes," Sabrina says eventually. "I suppose I didn't realize our time-lines were so close. But yes, Jake and I dated for a year or so when he first moved to New York. I was finishing up at FIT. We were young and immature—it fizzled, then. We didn't reconnect until later in our twenties."

"Got it," Molly says, though she's immediately certain that Sabrina isn't sharing the full truth. Jake's words echo inside her head: *Sisi wanted to move in together, and I guess . . . I guess I didn't love her as much as she loved me.*

During moments of doubt in her relationship with Jake, Molly used to think back on these words, comforted by them. Jake *had* loved her enough to move in together. Their love was reciprocal, not the way it had been with this Sisi girl.

But people change, Molly reminds herself, resenting the egotistical part of herself that feels she still deserves to reign over some small corner of Jake's heart. Obviously, Jake's feelings for Sabrina evolved the second time around.

"And yeah, I used to go by *Sisi.*" Sabrina laughs. "A dumb nickname from way back when. No one really calls me that anymore. Except for a few friends and Jake." She pauses. "Listen. What're you guys doing for the Fourth of July? Why don't you come to the club? I know it's kind of a scene, but there are supposedly great fireworks. Could be fun for Stella? And we can just get drunk."

Molly considers this. They usually spend the Fourth with Becky, watching the town fireworks from her Boston Whaler. But Molly *has* heard the FCCC fireworks are supposed to be incredible—a true spectacle—and she knows Stella will go crazy over them. And maybe Whitney Cooper will be there; maybe Molly can introduce Sabrina to Whitney—they'd probably like each other—and she could display what small bit of clout she has after nearly three years in this town.

"That sounds really fun," she says. "Thank you. Count us in."

After they hang up, Molly pours herself another glass of wine. She takes a sip—the Sancerre is cold and crisp. And she knows it's wrong, she knows her mind is playing tricks on her, but still, she closes her eyes and savors the fact that in less than a week, she'll see Jake again.

On the Fourth of July, Molly, Hunter, and Stella leave the house at six to meet the Danners at the club.

The early evening boasts clear skies—perfect conditions for fire-works, Molly explains to Stella, who is wearing a red-and-white-striped dress, her butter-blond hair in two neat braids.

Jake and Sabrina meet them in the lobby of the clubhouse, which feels more formal to Molly than inviting. The floors are a dark, polished ceramic, and plaques naming the annual golf and tennis tournament winners climb the walls in high stacks.

"O'Neils!" Sabrina raises her hands from the other end of the lobby, striding toward them with her megawatt smile. She's wearing an ivory sheath dress and espadrilles, her long, dark hair pulled back into a low, sleek pony. Gold statement earrings are pinned to either ear, bringing out the flecks in her perfectly made-up eyes.

Jake appears behind her, a small, ambiguous smile playing over his mouth. For a moment, Molly is knocked off center by that familiar, throbbing longing. Her bones feel heavy and hot. Something tugs at her from below. She watches him shake Hunter's hand—the two men she has loved most in her life. They are similarly tall, but different almost every-where else. Jake's curls are as unruly as they always have been; Hunter's thick black hair is neatly combed.

Suddenly, Jake is leaning in to kiss her on the cheek, and his distinct, familiar scent—something woody and warm and wholly unique to Jake—almost paralyzes her with nostalgia. Like every other man in the clubhouse, he wears slacks and a navy sport coat, and Molly can't get used to him in such conservative, preppy apparel. She remembers seeing him in a jacket and tie only once when they were together, at her cousin's wedding in Maine.

Before she can fully process what is happening, Jake's gaze moves to Stella, and then he's crouching in front of her, and this is a moment for which Molly is fully unprepared.

"You must be Stella," he says, his smile growing wider.

"Who are you?" Stella asked bluntly. Everybody laughs.

"I'm your mom's friend Jake." He extends a hand, and Molly feels numb and shaky on her legs as she watched Stella's small palm fit inside Jake's. He tilts his head. "How old are you?"

"Five and three-quarters."

"Five and three-quarters," Jake repeats, smiling warmly. "That's a great age."

"My friend Harper said they have a cotton candy machine here."

Jake nods and points to the door. "I saw it outside by the putting green."

Stella's cornflower eyes widen, and she places her hands on her hips. "Cotton candy is my favorite food."

"Really? Mine, too." Jake grins, standing.

"Boiled sugar really covers all the main food groups," Molly jokes. Next to her, Hunter is silent, and she squeezes his hand.

"You two need some drinks." Sabrina stabs her middle and pointer fingers in Molly and Hunter's direction. "Southsides are the signature here." She gestures toward her own beverage, a lime-green concoction garnished with mint leaves. "Let's hit the bar, and then we'll get Stella— and maybe Jake—some cotton candy?"

"Yes, please," Stella chimes.

"Cotton candy *after* dinner, Stell," Molly corrects.

"Oops, that's right." Sabrina flashes Molly an apologetic smile. "Dinner before dessert, duh."

Dinner is an extensive buffet of hot dogs, burgers, wings, potato salad, baked beans, corn on the cob, and a variety of other holiday-appropriate options. There's also a separate sushi station and a fantastic salad bar. Molly has heard the food at the club is exceptional, and it certainly lives up to its hype, she decides as she douses a piece of yellowtail sashimi in soy sauce.

The five of them sit at a round table under the giant covered terrace overlooking the pristine golf course, immaculately maintained rolling slopes of shamrock green. The sun is beginning to drop, settling behind the trees and casting a warm, golden glow across the grass. *There are probably two hundred people here,* Molly thinks, glancing around at the packed tables of families and realizing, with a jolt of irony, how alike they all appear. Husbands in pastel pants, wives in expensive cocktail dresses, adorable children clad in smocked gingham. The parents enjoy a steady stream of drinks, Southsides and Dark 'n' Stormys with rum floaters that elevate the volume on the terrace, dozens of boisterous conversations mixed in with rich pockets of laughter. And though it all feels slightly affected, Molly can't deny that it's *nice* sitting here, sipping strong, sweet cocktails and watching the sun set over a beautiful golf course with her family, the heart of the summer before them.

Molly smiles and waves at a few familiar faces—the mother of Stella's classmate, one of her regulars at Yoga Tree, Whitney Cooper's husband,

George. *Is Whitney here?* Molly mouths to George. He shakes his head, then uses his arms to mime rocking a baby. Molly nods, realizing then that of course Whitney wouldn't be there—her twins are barely two weeks old. She's surprised George has even come.

At the next table over, Molly spots Betsy Worthington wearing the same red dress she herself has on, a Faithfull the Brand number from last year—sweetheart neckline, blouson sleeves, little white flowers printed into the cherry fabric. Betsy is staring at Molly, her eyes narrowing in competition. She doesn't wave, just frowns before turning back to her toddler, who is dragging chicken fingers through a puddle of ketchup.

"Molly O'Neil!" a female voice sings, and suddenly Meredith Duffy is approaching their table. She wears a navy dress with white piping and a giant coral red necklace, her infant son propped on one hip. "And Hunter," she crows, her platinum bob shaking lightly as she bounces the baby, who wears a seersucker onesie with an American flag smocked to the front. "Oh! And Sabrina and Jake!"

"Meredith! Bryce!" Sabrina's eyes brighten, and she gives the baby's leg a gentle squeeze. "Don't you two look festive."

"How do you all know each other again?" Meredith glances from Sabrina to Molly. "Oh, *wait.* I remember. Yoga Tree, plus *you two* have some history, from what I understand." She uses her free hand to point between Molly and Jake.

Molly feels her jaw slacken. How the hell does *Meredith* know about her history with Jake?

"That's right. These two had a little fling back in the day. *Such* a small world, right?" Sabrina laughs, and Molly is surprised by how much she suddenly sounds like Meredith.

"The smallest!" Meredith adjusts baby Bryce on her hip. "That is too cute."

Molly can't help it. She draws her gaze across the table to Jake's, and he is watching her, his expression forlorn, the opposite of amused. It wasn't a fling, and it isn't cute—*fling* and *cute* are two of the last words either of them would use to describe something as sacred and meaningful as what they had together—but correcting Meredith and Sabrina is obviously out of the question.

"So does this mean you two are thinking of joining or what?" Meredith raises an eyebrow.

"Probably not anytime soon," Hunter says, swooping in to save Molly.

"There's lots going on at the yacht club—Stella's very into the sailing—so we're covered."

"But there's no golf course there!" Meredith exclaims. "And no pool."

"My grammie has a pool," Stella chirps. "And an Australian shepherd named Bodie."

Molly wants to hug her child at the same time she wishes she could smack Meredith for being so obnoxiously inconsiderate. Does she simply want Molly to state the obvious? Admit that they can't afford the insane six-figure initiation fee on top of the annual membership? Would hearing her say it out loud give Meredith the twisted satisfaction she so glaringly craves in her plastic, arrogant heart?

Meredith looks down at Stella and smiles coyly. "But if you belonged to *this* pool, you and Emma could be on the swim team together. *And* they have milkshakes at the snack bar—really tasty ones. The yacht club doesn't have milkshakes, from what I'm told. I'd be happy to put a good word in for your family so you can come here whenever you want. All your parents have to do is say yes."

Stella looks at her mother with wide, hopeful eyes, and Molly feels the blood pounding in her temples. She grips the end of the table to stop her hands from shaking. That's it. Involving Stella in this—*baiting* her—is beyond what Molly will tolerate. Her boiling point has been reached.

"Meredith," she starts, craning her neck to meet Meredith's beady gaze. She isn't even an attractive woman, Molly thinks, and yet somehow, she's deemed herself queen bee of Flynn Cove.

Hunter clears his throat, placing a protective hand over Molly's knee underneath the table.

"That's enough, Meredith," he says sharply. "It's a big financial commitment to join this place, as you very well know, and like I said before, it's not something we're considering at the moment. There are a lot of ways to spend that kind of money." He lowers his voice, his eyes narrowing. "And I don't appreciate you roping Stella into this conversation. It's completely inappropriate."

Meredith's jaw is practically hanging on the ground, and she doesn't seem to notice baby Bryce's drool dripping down the front of her silk dress. Molly knows this will be the front-running topic for Meredith's gossip for the rest of the summer—how *rude* Hunter O'Neil was to her at the club fireworks—but Molly doesn't care. This is why she loves Hunter. For knowing when to step in and save Molly from her own fragile anger, for standing up to self-important pot-stirrers like Meredith Duffy, for marching to the beat of his own drummer in a town that makes it next to impossible to do so.

Meredith looks expectantly at Sabrina and Jake, waiting for one of them to jump to her defense, but they both sip their drinks and ride out the awkwardness of the moment in silence. Finally, Meredith scowls and stomps away, red-faced and covered in spittle. *Sorry,* Molly mouths across the table. Sabrina rolls her eyes and flicks her wrist, as if to say, *Fuck it.* Jake's eyebrows inch up toward his hairline, and he flashes Hunter a thumbs-up. The anger inside Molly has reduced to a simmer; gratitude blooms inside her chest for the others at the table. Especially Hunter.

Stella turns to Molly, tilting her chin. "Mommy, can I get cotton candy now?"

"I think now is the perfect time for cotton candy, Stell."

"Does he want to come?" Stella looks at Jake. "Cotton candy is his favorite food, too."

Jake laughs—a deep belly laugh that jostles a collection of memories loose from Molly's subconscious.

"I'd love to, Stella," he tells her. "Thank you."

"That Meredith woman is a real twat," Jake says five minutes later, shoving a massive section of cotton candy into his mouth.

"Shh." Molly gestures down at Stella, but her daughter is fully invested in her dessert and not paying them much attention. She glances back at Jake. "How did she even know we had . . . history?"

Jake swallows. "Maybe Sisi mentioned it at some point?"

"I didn't realize they were close friends." Molly feels vulnerable and strange, like she's back in middle school.

He shrugs. "Those women are always gossiping by the pool. Sometimes Sisi sits with them."

"Really? I didn't think Sabrina spent much time at the club pool." Molly's stomach flips. She feels ridiculous—she's thirty-two years old. Why does she care who Sabrina is friends with? And why in God's name is she talking to *Jake* about this?

"I'm not sure." He shrugs again. "I've been working every weekend."

Molly tucks a loose piece of hair behind her ear. This is the first time, she realizes, that they are somewhat close to being alone. They've drifted away from the cotton candy cart, away from the crowds. "Right. The new album." She smiles. "That's wonderful, Jake. That you're making music again."

"Yeah." He nods. "It is, Moll." She at once resents and cherishes the fact that it's so easy for him to call her *Moll,* as if no time has passed since their carefree, lovebird days on Driggs.

"She's got spunk," he says, nodding his head in Stella's direction. "Just like her mom."

They glance at Stella, who is plopped down on the grass, elatedly dissecting her massive pillow of pink-and-blue puffed sugar.

"I don't know if I have as much spunk as I used to, Jake."

"And why's that, Moll?"

Her shoulders drop. "Life, I guess."

"You look the same, you know."

Molly laughs. "That's something a woman in her thirties will always appreciate hearing. But you seem the same, too, mostly," she adds. "Except your Southern accent is hardly there at all anymore. And the preppy garb is new. The Jake I remember lived in sweats and unwashed tees."

"I was pretty grubby, wasn't I? My tortured artist days. Sisi's had a big influence on my . . . attire. Though you know I could wear a paper bag and be happy."

"A paper bag? Not here at *the club*?" One side of Molly's mouth curls.

"I would do it in a heartbeat if I could spare Sisi the embarrassment. Give these folks something to talk about." Jake swallows his last bite of cotton candy. Behind them, the sun is a stripe of neon slipping behind the horizon. Dusk is falling, a slight chill in the air now. "It's ironic, isn't it? That we both ended up in a fancy suburb, married to rich people. Who woulda thought?"

"Hunter isn't rich, Jake." Molly shoots him a look. "Not like Sabrina, anyway. I mean, his mom has some money—she helps us, sometimes. But mostly we're trying to save, for college and stuff."

Jake shakes his head contritely. "I'm sorry. That was presumptuous of me."

"It's all right. Truthfully, Flynn Cove has changed since Hunter grew up here. From the way he describes it, the town used to be more laid-back—nice, but definitely not as ritzy."

Jake nods. "I guess that makes sense, with all the hedge funds out here now."

Molly can't help but smile. "I'm surprised you know where the hedge funds are, Jake."

He gives a goofy grin. "I'm very corporate these days." A few beats of silence pass. Jake blinks. "There are so many things I want to ask you," he says. "I don't even know where to start."

Goose bumps prickle Molly's skin all over. She glances down at the ground, at the short, evenly mowed grass. Finally, she looks up. She finds Jake's eyes. "What would be your top three?"

He juts out his bottom lip, considering. "One, are you happy here? Two, why did you stop writing? And three . . ." He pauses, locking her gaze. "Why did you leave without saying goodbye?"

Molly's eyes fill with tears; she blinks them back. Jake steps toward her, so close that the edge of his hand brushes hers, her skin burning all over from the single spot of his touch. Just then, the first firework sounds in the distance. An explosive pop. Around them everyone oohs and aahs and shuffles to make their way toward the first hole, where families are setting up Crazy Creek chairs and picnic blankets to watch the show.

Stella springs to her feet, discarding her half-eaten stick of cotton candy. She grabs hold of her mother's leg with sticky fingers as Molly backs away from Jake, the intensity of the moment between them dissipating as quickly as it arrived.

"Mom!" Stella points to the sky, her gaze wide-eyed with wonder. "Fireworks!"

"I need to take her to wash her hands." Molly turns away from Jake. Has he seen her cry? God, she hopes not. But she feels him watching her, his eyes full of concern.

"We'll meet you over there," he says. "Sisi—Sabrina, I mean—she's got a big, checkered picnic blanket. Look for that."

Molly doesn't realize how fast her heart is beating until she and Stella reach the quiet of the women's locker room. It's peaceful in here, smelling of lavender and baby powder. She checks the mirror; her mascara is smudged below her eyes. She dabs at it with a tissue.

"Why are you crying, Mommy?" Stella rinses her hands in the sink, her little knuckles still dimpled with baby fat.

"Jake—my friend who likes cotton candy—was telling me a sad story." Molly hands her a paper towel.

"What's the story?"

"I'll tell you later, okay? We don't want to miss the fireworks. But I'm all better now."

"Good." Stella takes her mother's hand as they leave the locker room, and Molly is in awe of her daughter's sweetness, her pure-hearted compassion. "Hey, Mommy?"

"Yeah?"

"I like Jake."

Molly smiles, her throat full of tears again. "Me, too, baby." She squeezes Stella's hand. "Me, too."

Chapter Twenty-one

Sabrina

It was a nice evening we had on the Fourth of July, don't you think? I can tell you were genuinely worried about your history with Jake getting in the way of our friendship. That's sweet, Molly, it really is. I'm touched you've grown so fond of me.

I'm sorry about downplaying your relationship with Jake—I saw the way your face fell when Meredith called it a "fling"—but really, your ego could use a good check. It's a bit presumptuous to walk around assuming you're the love of everyone's life.

Anyway, I'm glad you and Hunter were able to join us. It is a bit snobbish, the whole country club thing, isn't it? My grandparents never belonged to the FCCC, by the way. They didn't even live in Flynn Cove, or Connecticut for that matter. I never actually *met* my grandparents—all four were already dead by the time I was born. The closest thing I had to a grandmother was my great-aunt Lenore, my maternal grandfather's sister. She was a gem. She lived an hour from us in Miami, but she used to pick me up on the weekends and take me to South Beach for lunch, or to play mini golf—activities that never would have crossed either of my parents' minds. For my tenth birthday, Lenore took me to the aquarium, and we went swimming with dolphins. Her house was much smaller than ours, but it was cheery and cozy and smelled like beeswax candles. Lenore smelled like beeswax, too. Her hands were always warm. She died of a stroke when I was thirteen.

Anyway, I only lied about my grandparents belonging to the club so you wouldn't think I was as pretentious as those women like Meredith Duffy and Betsy Worthington, who you can't seem to stand.

The truth is, I did want to join the FCCC. And not because I care about status—I don't, not actually. What I *do* care about is family. Children.

The memory of the blood in the toilet, of the violent river running down my legs, is forever imprinted in my mind and heart, a loss I've never really gotten over.

So yes, you and Jake had a bit more than a fling. I'll admit that you inspired his music more than I ever did, fine. But Jake and I created a *baby* together, for fuck's sake, and that's more than you can say, Molly. And I know that we are meant to create more; I feel this in my gut, in my bones. It's our destiny to build a family together, a real family, the kind neither of us were born into. Most people don't know the loneliness of not being loved by their own parents. But Jake and I—we do. It's part of our pull on each other the way we fill a mutual void you will never understand.

I've lied to you about plenty of things, Molly, but one area where I've actually been honest is in my struggle to have a child. This is a struggle that you and I share, a haunting desire that binds us. The only difference is that my hurdle is not biological—at least not that I know of. *My* hurdle is psychological. My hurdle is Jake.

It wasn't always this way, obviously. *Let's make Jake-and-Sisi babies,* he said once upon a time, his eyes lighting up with excitement, filling my heart with possibility.

But now, he's hesitant. There's something holding him back, something that was never there before.

Later, he says.

Soon.

I'm not ready.

I'm still not ready.

Stop pushing, Sisi.

I know that once it happens—once we do conceive, once he holds our little baby in his arms—his fears will melt away. In the meantime, I'm doing what I can. The FCCC is a family-oriented place—about as family-oriented as it gets. Chubby babies floating with their mothers in the turquoise pool, tots in tennis whites with miniature rackets, neatly dressed children sipping Shirley Temples in the clubhouse while their parents mingle. Camp, swim team, junior golf.

Jake and I are practically the only members without children, which means *everyone* is constantly chivvying: *When are we going to see a little Danner around here?*

It's the perfect excuse to take the conversation home to Jake. Like I do tonight.

We're lying in bed. Clean sheets, freshly ironed by our cleaning lady, Priscilla. She comes twice a week.

I'm ovulating, according to the app on my phone. Jake doesn't know. He's propped up on a pile of pillows, scribbling in his notebook. I lean over to his side of our king bed, slip my hand under the waistband of his boxers.

"Sees. I'm working."

I ignore this. I take the notebook from his hands and drop it to the floor, hooking my thighs over his hips. I push his boxers all the way down, press my lips to his stomach, work my way south.

"Sisi. Not now."

I don't listen. I take him in my mouth, and he's growing hard. Progress. I slide my lips all the way down till he rams the back of my throat. He usually goes crazy when I do this.

"*Sisi.*" He pushes me away, off of him, yanks his boxers back up.

"Jesus, Jake. What?"

"I just think we should be careful."

"*Careful?*"

"You know I'm not ready. You got your period two weeks ago. I know what that means."

I say nothing, waiting, testing him.

"Now is your . . ." He pauses. "Fertile window."

"Calm down. I'm on the Pill."

"You never remember to take it."

He isn't wrong, but I'm surprised he knows this. Jake is secretly very perceptive, though he probably doesn't realize I "forget" to take my birth control on purpose.

I sit up, irritation rising in my chest. "Why don't you want to have a baby?" I'm not yelling, but almost.

"That's not what I said." He sighs, interlacing his hands across his chest.

"Everyone keeps asking when we're going to have one."

"Who's 'everyone'?"

"I don't know. People at the club."

I watch Jake resist the urge to roll his eyes. "We're both still young," he reasons. "Your mom was almost forty when she had you."

"That was a completely different situation, and you know it." I scowl. My parents' choice to have me was a *now-or-never* sort of verdict, a decision they came to as my mom got past the point of "advanced maternal age." In retrospect, having me is something they likely regret. Or at least look back on with indifference.

"I'm not like my mother," I press. "I *want* a baby. And I don't want to be fifty when my child is in grade school."

"Look, I've been busy with work and the solo album." Jake swallows, his Adam's apple dipping. "I need the summer to focus."

"Fine. So we'll start trying in the fall." I don't give him the luxury of posing it as a question.

He fiddles with the edge of the top sheet. French blue scalloped embroidery. He stares at his fingers, lost in thought. Finally, he looks up. "Did you know my ex lived in Flynn Cove?" The question is so out of nowhere, it spears me. It cuts right into my center.

"What?"

"Molly." He locks my gaze, a flash of blue. "I mean . . . I'm sorry—it's just . . ." He sighs, runs a hand through his unkempt hair. "What are the chances we both end up living in the same tiny town?"

"Um, I don't fucking know." I will the panic out of my voice, edging my stance toward anger. I need to play my cards right here. "What does that have to do with anything we're talking about? Sounds like a question you should be asking a therapist, if you care so much." I glare at him. I can't stand it, Molly, the degree to which you're under his skin. "She's my friend," I add, because that seems relevant to mention.

"I know. I'm sorry, Sees." His face falls. "Come here."

"No." I scoot off the bed, though I want nothing more than to go to him. To wrap my limbs around his body and bury my face in the crook of his warm neck and exist there forever.

"Sisi." His voice is pleading.

But in this moment, I have leverage, and I'd be stupid not to use it. I storm into the bathroom and lean against the vanity. I don't realize I've been crying till I look up at the mirror, my eyes shiny and red around the rims. I turn on the tap. I double cleanse my face and do my whole routine—toner, vitamin C, half a dozen expensive serums that probably don't even work. I brush my teeth.

When I reappear in the bedroom, I'm calmer. Jake looks genuinely sorry, watching me ruefully, his notebook still discarded on the floor.

"You've been crying," he says.

I want to tell him then, the thing I've never told him before. The blood. Our baby. I open my mouth to speak, to say the words, but I can't. What good would they do? Jake would only wonder why I lied to him all this time, and the last thing he needs is another liar in his life. He has you for that.

I came here to show Jake who you truly are, what you're capable of, and time is ticking. I'd assumed that you'd be too guilt-ridden not to reveal yourself, but perhaps I underestimated you, Molly. Perhaps I'll need to encourage your honesty in a different, more forceful kind of way.

I think of our baby, a heavy mix of longing and hope weighing in my body. I think of you, just a few miles away across town, sick with the same yearning.

Eventually, sleep pulls me under.

Chapter Twenty-two

Jake

2014

One Sunday evening in late October, after Molly left the apartment to get dinner with a friend—Liz, he was pretty sure—Jake headed to the studio to meet Sam and Hale. They were behind on the second album, and Ron wanted the song list finalized by the end of the year.

Jake loved Brooklyn in the fall; the crisp quality of the air and the way the leaves on the trees lining Driggs seemed to catch fire for a few precious weeks, bright flames of gold and amber lighting up his city. He didn't mind that the season preceded winter, the way Molly did.

It was a pleasant evening—not too cool, the sun dropped low in clear skies—and Jake would've walked across the bridge to the East Village if he hadn't been running late. He was in a good mood—he had been for a while now. He didn't think he'd ever take it for granted again, having Molly back in his life. Sometimes, he couldn't believe how lucky he was that she loved him the way she did. Every now and then, he felt a flash of guilt, like he would never actually be deserving of that kind of love, and Molly would never truly understand why. The month without her was a period of murky darkness he didn't like to remember, and so he did his best not to think of it. This was how Jake Danner lived his life—by pushing the hardest parts into the past and keeping them there.

That wasn't to say he hadn't learned from his mistakes. He had, this time. Molly made him want to change—made him want to be better—in a way that no one else had before. He felt a wave of love just thinking of her: the way she sat at the little desk in their apartment in her favorite blue-and-white-striped dress, her legs crossed underneath her, her pale hair pulled back into a loose knot that piled around the nape of her neck.

Jake had also been in especially high spirits since Danner Lane's sold-out show at Terminal 5 several nights before. On top of that, he felt great about the song he'd finished that afternoon and was eager to show it to Sam and Hale. They were already at the studio when he arrived, perched on the grubby leather couch, drinking Heinekens.

Sam rubbed his trimmed beard. "You're late."

"Am I?" Jake glanced at his phone, which told him it was quarter of seven. "Only fifteen minutes."

"You're always late, Danner," Hale said, annoyed. He yawned, raking a hand through his tousled hair, which was the same auburn color as Sam's. "Let's get this over with. I'm tired."

"Big weekend?"

He shrugged. "Couple of parties."

"Did you meet a nice lady friend? Did she keep you up late?"

"Let's see what you wrote," Hale said, ignoring him.

Jake unzipped his backpack and removed his notebook, handing it to Sam. Jake may have been their lyricist, but Sam was the one who handled the instrumentation. He turned lyrics into pieces of music.

"'Our Summer'?" Sam jutted his bottom lip out, the way he did when he was on the brink of reproach. "Is this another song about Molly?"

Jake opened his mouth to speak, but closed it. Sam looked up when he'd finished reading, his wheat-blond brows knitted together. He said nothing.

"*Every* song in this fucking album can't be about your girlfriend, Jake." Hale rolled his eyes. "'Our Summer'? That's too fucking pop-y."

"So we'll change the title. Why don't you read the damn lyrics before slamming it?" Jake glared at Hale. His high spirits were quickly dissipating. He could tell Hale was in one of his feisty, combative moods, coming off a long bender of a weekend that had probably started on Thursday after the Terminal 5 show, and he didn't feel like bearing the brunt of his friend's hangover.

Hale grabbed the notebook from Sam and started reading out loud.

Your blond hair on my pillow
Like silk across the sheets
An easy morning kinda love
The girl of all my dreams

Hale's face twisted. "What is this shit, Danner? We can't play this."

Jake's heart picked up speed, heat filling his chest. "Why don't you write something, then, Hale? Instead of drinking and snorting your way through the weekend while I sit at home doing all the work for this fucking band."

"Guys, cool it." Sam snatched the notebook from his brother, his gaze growing stern. It was the same dynamic that had existed between the three of them since they were kids—Sam, the eldest, the most level-headed of the trio, breaking up Hale and Jake's squabbles. "Danner, what I think Hale is trying to say is that the new album is starting to feel a bit . . . for lack of a better word . . . well, yes, pop-y. Off-brand. We're a Southern group at our core. We don't want to trade that stroke of country for . . . well, something inauthentic."

Jake rubbed the back of his neck. "We can be a little country and a little pop at the same time. That isn't inauthentic. Look at Zac Brown Band."

"*This*"—Hale stabbed his finger at the notebook—"is so far from Zac Brown Band. You just want to be a fucking pop star, Danner. You want to be Adam fucking Levine. Nick fucking Carter, maybe."

Jake glared at Hale, suspecting he'd had more to drink than just the Heineken. Whenever Hale got really wasted, pent-up resentment inside of him tipped over the edge, and he was more hot-tempered than usual. Jake wondered how long these feelings had been brewing.

Sam's gaze flickered to his brother. "Don't be a dick, Hale." He turned to Jake, his light brown eyes softening. "Look, I think part of the reason *The Narrows* worked so well is because it's a true reflection of us, of who we are. It's about North Carolina, growing up, crabbing in the bay, moving to New York. There are a couple of love songs, yeah, but it's more substantial than that. And this new album is just feeling like . . . a bunch of songs about trying to get the girl back. 'Molly's Song' works, obviously, but we can't have a dozen renditions of 'Molly's Song' that aren't half as playable."

The air in the studio felt suddenly stuffy and stale, and Jake desperately wanted to leave. He knew Molly wouldn't be home yet, but he wished he were there, anyway, sitting on the couch with a glass of whiskey by the open window, waiting for her to walk in the door. "I don't know what to say. We're already more than halfway done with the album."

"We haven't officially started recording."

"Why don't you see what Jerry and Ron think before you tell me we need to start over."

"I already have, Danner." Sam's mouth was a thin line.

"You've talked to Jerry and Ron about this?" Jake's stomach seesawed. He felt like he had in the third grade, the day he and Hale got sent to the principal's office for stealing Richie McNell's lunch money from his cubby during recess. It had been Hale's idea.

"They've seen the lyrics, Danner. They've heard the recordings of the songs we have so far, and they agree we're starting to sound like a boy band."

"Is this why you wanted to meet tonight?" Jake shook his head, exasperated. "To give me some kind of warning?"

"It's not a warning, Danner." Sam sighed. "We're just looping you in."

"Well, gee, Sammy, thanks for looping me in on your secret meetings with *our* manager and producer." Jake felt the fire building inside him. "I'm only the fucking *front man* of this band!" He regretted the words the second they left his lips. He watched them land on Sam's and Hale's faces, their expressions turning shocked, then sour with disgust. "I didn't mean—"

"Can't believe you finally admitted it." Hale scoffed, twisting the cap off a fresh beer. "Fifteen years we've been playing together and it's always been the elephant in the room—the fact that you think you're better than us because you have a pretty face. I just never thought we'd hear you say it out loud."

"What? I don't think I'm better than you, and I don't have—" Jake took a deep breath, leveling himself. "Hale, I'm the one who writes the songs. Do you have any idea how much work that is?"

"Uh, yeah, I do, because the three of us used to write the songs *together,* Danner. Remember? And then you went and wrote every song in *The Narrows* behind our backs, and Jerry ate the album up, and now you've made yourself the contracted songwriter without ever actually talking to Sam or me. And in case you don't know, this is how you operate. Jake Danner does whatever Jake Danner wants to do because it's Jake Danner's fucking world and we're just lucky to be living in it!"

Hale's words echoed around the studio. This was uncharted territory. There was a palpable shift in the air between the three of them, one that had never occurred before, not in the two decades Jake had known the Lanes and called them his family. Blood pounded in his ears.

"That's not how it went down, and you know it, Hale." Jake tried to sound assertive, but he felt weak. "And you guys could've at least asked me to be part of your conversation with Jerry and Ron."

"Seriously?" Sam turned to him, bristling. "We discussed this with Jerry and Ron on Tuesday, when they called for a dinner meeting. Ron was in from LA. They invited you. You told them you had other plans."

Jake closed his eyes, his mind winding back to Tuesday. Yes, Jerry had called him in the early afternoon—something about a last-minute dinner with Ron being in town. But Jake had already promised Molly they would try that hip new Indian place on Bedford with Nina and Cash, and he wasn't going to cancel. Molly had made a reservation; they'd had the date on the calendar for weeks. He was done letting her down. So he'd told Jerry he couldn't make it.

"Yeah. I remember now." Jake nodded slowly, rubbing his neck again. "Look, guys, I'm sorry. I don't know what to say. You could've told me sooner."

"I didn't want to bring it up before Terminal 5."

"I see."

"I think we should call it a night." Sam's voice was thin, detached. "Cool off a bit. We'll meet later this week. In the meantime, let's work on changing direction. Ron expects a delay, given the circumstances, but he wants to see an album by the end of February, which gives us a little over four months. Doable, yeah?" Sam's inquiry was pointed at Jake, who nodded helplessly.

"Hale, if you want to help me write . . ."

"You mean, help you fix the album while you rake in the bulk of the songwriting royalties? No thanks."

Jake shook his head. "This band was never supposed to be about money."

"Everything is about money, Danner. Whether or not we like to admit it." Hale gave a harsh, derisive laugh.

Jake could feel their anger—not just Hale's but Sam's, too. It was a heavy, unsettling presence that made him want to escape, to shrink down into nothing.

"I'm sorry," Jake repeated as he left the studio, not sure at all that he meant it. He thought back to writing the early songs on *The Narrows*, the way they'd poured out of him, the most cathartic experience of his life. He'd explained this to the Lanes afterward, and at the time, they'd seemed excited, not bothered in the least. The three of them had been elated when Jerry went crazy over the tracks Jake had written and when that first batch of songs went on to help seal them a record deal. When

Jake had been contracted as the writer, neither of the Lanes had objected. Of the three of them, Jake was the one with the knack for lyrics and chord progressions, while Sam nailed the arrangements and Hale killed it on the drums in a way that often shadowed the guitars. They all understood their roles; they had for years. So why was Hale fighting Jake on his now? And why hadn't Sam jumped in to defend him?

With the demand for new music, the weight of Danner Lane rested on Jake's shoulders, and he wasn't even allowed to say it. Despite Hale's claim, the Lanes weren't aware of the time Jake put into perfecting each and every verse and chorus, the late nights he pulled reading the songs out loud to Molly, revising the melodies again and again until the words flowed flawlessly.

It was months of his hard work down the drain, and Sam and Hale didn't care. Frustration swallowed Jake whole as he made his way back to Brooklyn underground, the L train sucking him below the East River, a giant worm tunneling through the earth. He sensed a stormy anger hovering, but felt too sad to access it. Instead, he was overcome with the terrible, lucid realization that everyone he'd ever loved had, at some point in his life, told him he was selfish. It didn't matter that Jake tried to be a good man; clearly, he was hardwired to hurt, to disappoint, to miss the moral mark. It ran in his fucking blood.

Chapter Twenty-three
Molly

2015

Molly stayed out late with Liz. She hadn't seen much of her recently, not since the Amagansett share house over the summer. And even on those weekends, Liz had seemed distant and vaguely disappointed in Molly for being back with Jake. She hadn't said so explicitly, but Molly knew her friend well enough to sense it. What Molly had begun to realize was that Liz didn't like it when Molly got too happy—it knocked her off balance. *Liz* was supposed to be the one with the serious live-in boyfriend and steady career; Molly was the struggling writer who fell for duds like Darby and Cameron. Liz relished her role as advice-giver, high up on her perch. She was competitive and calculated at heart, and threatened by Molly's sudden escalation to her same "place" in life. Liz had followed a certain trajectory and cared deeply about her position on it. She'd invested years in her relationship with Zander before he'd agreed to move in together; Molly and Jake had needed only six months to be ready. Molly finally understood: to Liz, this was a threat.

Jake had picked up on Liz's MO from the beginning. He didn't know why Molly put up with her, and frankly, Molly was starting to understand his outlook. But in her heart, she loved Liz and missed her desperately. She missed their nights together, cooking and drinking too much wine, howling with laughter and watching *Friends* until they couldn't keep their eyes open. Liz had been Molly's most devoted friend—her best friend, for a while—and Molly couldn't just forget the intricacies of their recent, sisterlike closeness. So when Liz had texted asking to meet up, Molly was hesitant, but ultimately eager to see her.

When Molly got back to the apartment, drunk off sangria from Liz's favorite tapas spot, Jake was already asleep. She sat down on the edge of bed and brushed a lock of hair off his forehead.

"Jake?" she whispered. She wanted him to wake up; she wanted to curl into his body and tell him about her night, but he'd been so exhausted lately, working on the new album, and she knew she should let him sleep.

He was up early the next morning, drinking coffee and writing, when Molly wandered into the living room, a hangover tugging at the back of her brain.

"Hey," she said, placing a hand on the exposed patch of skin above his shoulder. "Want pancakes?"

He mumbled a reply, something short and incoherent that told Molly he was grouchy, preoccupied.

"What's wrong?"

"Nothing." His eyes stayed glued to his notebook.

"Don't you want to hear about dinner with Liz?"

"Right." Jake didn't look up from the coffee table. "I do, Moll, but later. I'm swamped right now."

Jake stayed in a bleak mood all day and the day after that. For the rest of the fall and through the winter, a dark cloud seemed to accompany his presence. A glaze coated his eyes that Molly could only partially penetrate, but she'd seen it before and knew what it signaled: the one-track mind of a tortured artist consumed wholly with his craft.

Things weren't *bad* between Molly and Jake—their love was solid after all it had been through—but his sudden, almost ferocious preoccupation with rewriting the new album caused a shift in their dynamic, plucking them out of the dreamy, besotted daze in which they'd been since the summer.

After that they moseyed along hazily and erratically, some days better and others mundane, a fiery fight here and there. A cheerful, cozy fall morphed into a long, desolate winter. Jake was increasingly moody and discouraged, while Molly remained frustrated by the continual lack of movement with her manuscript. Bella had sent *Needs* out to more than a dozen editors, and while a couple of them had loved it, they'd taken their sweet time to ultimately tell her: not quite enough. She and Bella were back to the drawing board.

"Why don't you work on your portfolio in the meantime?" Bella suggested over lunch.

"My portfolio?"

"You know, a professional collection of your work. Do some freelance writing for magazines or lit journals. It's a good way to build up your platform, and the money isn't always terrible. You must have a few decent contacts."

Molly didn't know anyone who worked in magazines except for Nell, an old classmate from undergrad who was in editorial at *Cosmopolitan*. They'd both been English majors and still saw each other every now and then through their loosely intertwined social circles in the city.

Molly felt as if she'd stripped down naked when she sent the email to Nell explaining that she was working on a novel and looking to do some freelance articles while she revised it. Was *Cosmo* seeking writers?

That's how Molly ended up with her byline underneath headlines like "Eight Totally Random Things That Make Men Horny" and "Five Songs You Need to Add to Your Sex Playlist Tonight."

Jake peered over her shoulder one afternoon while she was working.

"We don't have a sex playlist." He frowned.

"I know." Molly closed her laptop. She didn't like it when Jake read her stuff before it was finished.

"So why are you writing about sex playlists?"

"They're all assignments, Jake. I don't choose the topics." Molly felt tense, edgy. At the root of it, she was embarrassed to be writing articles about vibrators and sex positions, but *Cosmo* paid well—fifty cents a word—and she needed the money. She'd pitched ideas for pieces she actually wanted to write to outlets like *Vogue* and *Slate* and *The New Yorker,* but never heard back from any of them. She'd submitted her favorite chapter of *Needs* as a short story to a number of literary journals. Crickets.

One evening in late January, Molly trekked to the Upper West Side for the launch party of a novel written by her friend Anya from NYU. The book was a literary thriller that had already been optioned for television and lauded by *The New York Times*. Refilling her wine at the makeshift bar, Molly heard a female voice speak her name.

". . . and have you *seen* the stuff Molly Diamond is writing for *Cosmo*? Complete trash—makes me cringe! Apparently, she's working on a novel. Bet it's total junk, too. Weird that she never told any of us she was trying to publish. It's like she thinks she's better than everyone because she dates that famous singer now. You know, the hot one. He has to be cheating on her."

Cheap Merlot sloshed over the rim of Molly's plastic cup. She turned around to see Shannon Jennings—a girl from her workshop at NYU—gossiping with another classmate she recognized. Shannon's face froze, except for her jaw, which fell to the floor.

"Excuse me, Shannon." Molly rushed by her. It didn't matter how much she willed back the tears—they were tight in her throat, moments away.

"Molly, sorry, I didn't recognize you with your hair pulled—"

But Molly didn't hear the rest. She set her wine down on the nearest table and beelined for the exit. She wished she could've retorted with something cool—the kind of biting remark Liz or Everly would've made—but Molly had never been great with quips or confrontation.

She felt a stab of guilt for leaving without saying goodbye to Anya or the handful of others she'd kept in touch with from grad school, but she was already wiping her eyes by the time she made it out onto the street. Shannon's words played in her head on the long subway ride back to Brooklyn. Molly didn't know how to stop them from hitting her rawest nerve, the one that cracked her wide open. The only place she could think to recover was in the manuscript, and so that's where she went when she finally reached her apartment. Jake wasn't home. She didn't know where he was or what time to expect him back—he'd left for the studio in the morning, and they hadn't spoken all day.

Molly opened her computer and stared at the document that had consumed so much of her life—years, at that point. Her heart and soul poured into ninety-seven thousand words. This was it. Shannon's voice echoed in her mind again: *Bet it's total junk, too.*

Molly laughed out loud to no one, a hollow sound bouncing around her rib cage. *Needs* probably was total junk. Jake probably was cheating on her. Her father probably was flourishing wherever he'd landed, his life rich and whole without her. Molly poured herself a glass of wine and sat in this sad, cynical moment, almost basking in the pain of it. She drank half the bottle in bed, and when Jake got home, she pretended to be asleep. She knew he'd be stressed and eager to vent, and she was tired of being his punching bag.

That's why, on a particularly dismal Tuesday in February when Molly was working at her favorite coffee shop on Grand Street, pointlessly dissecting *Needs* for the trillionth time, she didn't mind it when a tall, good-looking man in slacks and a navy overcoat approached her table. His thick hair was dark and neatly combed, his complexion pale—the physical opposite of Jake, she noted, except for his height. The café was packed; he gestured to the seat across from hers and asked if it was taken. Molly shook her head.

He sat down and unpacked his briefcase, but not before extending a strong, sturdy hand, chilled from the cold outside.

"I'm Hunter," he said, his voice kind. His brown eyes were disarming, and strangely familiar.

Chapter Twenty-four
Molly

July 2022

Molly's phone vibrates on the counter, teetering across the kitchen island like a beetle on its back. She's busy scrambling eggs for Stella and lets the call go to voicemail.

"But do you really think we can get an Elsa cake *and* an Elsa piñata, Mommy?"

Stella has been asking questions about her upcoming *Frozen*-themed birthday party for weeks. No, months.

"I think anything is possible, Stell." Molly touches the end of her daughter's button nose. "You'll just have to wait and see."

Stella drops her chin into her hand, a wistful sheen blooming in her eyes. She's such a little dreamer. Molly hopes that will never change.

She slides the plate of eggs and buttered toast in front of Stella and picks up her phone.

One missed call from a number she recognizes instantly, and not just because of the North Carolina area code. She memorized Jake's number years ago. Molly's heart bounces in her chest. Did he know hers by heart, too? Or did he still have it saved in his phone? Or get it from Sabrina? There's no voicemail. Why did he just call her?

Hunter trots down the stairs, and Molly flips her phone facedown on the counter. He gives her a quick kiss, and she inhales the familiar menthol smell of his aftershave. His eyes move over her with concern.

"How are you feeling?" he whispers so Stella doesn't hear. It's the day after Molly and Hunter's latest embryo transfer, their sixth to date. The last embryo left from this round.

"Fine. Nervous. A little tired."

"Just take it easy today, okay?" He gives her shoulder a gentle squeeze and turns to Stella. "Ready to go, squirt?"

Molly adjusts his tie. "She needs to have a few more bites."

"I need to have a few more bites," Stella repeats.

"Eat up, then. Dad's gonna be late for his meeting."

After they leave—Hunter always drops Stella at camp on his way to work—Molly stares at her phone for an indeterminate amount of time. She doesn't think she can bring herself to call Jake back, so she puts in her AirPods—the noise-canceling ones Hunter got her last Christmas—and blasts Laura Branigan while she cleans the kitchen. She brushes crumbs into the sink and sponges down the pans and Windexes the marble counters until they sparkle.

Gloria, you're always on the run now.

Her mother loves Laura Branigan. She used to blast the cassette on road trips and sing every word at the top of her lungs, Molly and Andrew in the back seat. The music reminds Molly of being young and free. Not a care in the world.

When the kitchen is gleaming, Molly returns to her phone. She pauses Spotify and calls Nina, who picks up on the second ring.

"Sorry, I know you're at work."

"It's fine. I have my own office since I got promoted, remember?"

"*Right.* Nina Vasquez, director of publicity."

"That's me."

"Proud of you."

"Thanks, babe. So what's up?" The sound of her best friend's voice is like a tonic. Molly pictures Nina sitting behind her desk at the PR firm where she works, her long, chocolate hair swept back while she sips her coffee.

"Jake just called me." Molly sinks down onto one of the rattan counter stools, the ones from Serena & Lily that Hunter hates. He says they're overpriced and unoriginal, very keeping-up-with-the-Joneses. He isn't exactly wrong.

"He *called* you?" Her friend's shock is affirming. Molly has already filled in Nina and Everly on everything going on—that Jake is Sabrina's husband, that the four of them had dinner at Jake's mansion in Flynn Cove, that she cried in front of him on the Fourth of July. The fact that Molly's very normal, steady life had transformed overnight.

"What did he *say*?" Nina presses.

"I didn't pick up."

"Voicemail?"

"Nope. And now I'm spiraling. I can't stop thinking about him, Nina."

"Have you seen him? Since the fireworks?"

"No. Sabrina invited us over for dinner again last weekend, but I made something up to get out of it. I've seen *her*—we get together pretty regularly now, I mean, we're genuinely *friends*—but I just . . . I think I need to avoid Jake. It feels dangerous or something." Molly pauses. "Hence the reason I didn't call him back and called you instead."

"Oh, Moll." Nina sighs. "I can't imagine. Plus, Sabrina thinks you guys barely dated, and it's not like you can correct her."

"Exactly." Molly nods into the phone, appreciating how Nina just *gets* it. "That would open a very awkward can of worms."

"Right. And you certainly can't vent to Hunter."

"No way. Hunt will barely acknowledge what's going on."

"Classic guy behavior."

"I just . . ." Molly sighs. "I feel like I'm alone on an island."

"Well, I'm always here."

"I know you are." Molly feels a stitch of affection for her best friend. "And I love you for it."

"Wait, I'm such an asshole. I didn't even ask how the transfer went yesterday. How are you feeling?"

"Oh, you are the furthest thing from an asshole. I feel okay. Just kind of exhausted, honestly." Molly appreciates that Nina has become so familiar with the IVF process on her behalf. "I'm not getting my hopes up with this one, Neens. I try to be optimistic around Hunt, but you know this is our last embryo, and to be honest, if it fails, I'm not sure I can do it all again."

"Physically or emotionally?"

"Both. Not to mention financially. But starting all over again, *another* egg retrieval? The testing, the hormones, the shots, the anxiety? It's overwhelming and kind of all-consuming. Sometimes I worry it's taking over my identity. Like I've forgotten who I am outside of it."

Nina is quiet for a moment. "Maybe that's why this stuff with Jake is getting under your skin," she says. "Maybe being around him again is connecting you with that part of yourself you feel like you've lost. It doesn't mean you still love him or that you don't love Hunter."

Tears spring to Molly's eyes. A beat of silence passes before she speaks.

"That's exactly what I needed to hear, Neens. You're so wise."

"Tell that to my boss. And tell her to give me a raise along with the title promotion." Nina exhales, and Molly hears the clicking sound of the keyboard. "Shoot, I gotta run. I have a call in two."

"Okay. Thanks for chatting. Tell Michael I said hi."

"Same to Hunt. And give my goddaughter a kiss for me. I can't believe she's about to be six. I'll see you both on the *very* important occasion of August twentieth. *Frozen* piñata in hand."

"Do not even *think* about forgetting that *Frozen* piñata." Molly laughs. "Best godmama ever."

After they hang up, Molly pours herself a second cup of coffee—she's drinking decaf since the embryo transfer—and brings it out back to the patio. Their lot is small—not even a quarter of an acre—and she looks out at the manicured square of grass that Hunter takes pride in mowing himself. It's nothing compared to Sabrina and Jake's expansive, rolling lawn with its pool and pristine landscaping, but it still feels like an oasis after years of city living.

Molly sips her decaf and thinks about Nina, who is juggling wedding planning and new responsibilities at work. Nina waited a long time to find Michael, and Molly was so happy when they got engaged. But selfishly, it was more than that—she realizes how comforting it is to have their paths aligning. *Marriage is something you don't understand until you're in it,* Molly thinks. A circle, for lack of a better word. Everly gets it—she and Sage tied the knot last fall—but Nina is her very closest friend, and it'll be nice to have her on the inside.

Molly's mind drifts to Liz, then—God knows what's become of Liz. The last she heard from Everly, Liz was dating a fortysomething divorcé— some gazillionaire with a private jet whom she met through work. Molly still feels sad when she thinks about their friendship and how quickly it deteriorated. Right when she needed Liz the most.

Nina always reasons that Liz simply couldn't handle Molly getting engaged first, especially not after Zander dumped her. When Hunter proposed, Liz effectively disappeared. She didn't come wedding dress shopping or show up at the congratulatory drinks Nina had planned at the Spaniard, and in the end, she hadn't even come to the wedding.

Liz never called to say she was sorry or explain why. She didn't pick up the phone when Molly broke the news of her pregnancy, or visit her in the hospital with Nina and Everly after Stella was born. Every now and then, she'd ask for updates over text, but that was it. There was never an apology or a come-to-Jesus moment, the way Molly always expected there would be. With the exception of a perfunctory conversation at Everly and Sage's wedding last October, it had been years since they'd spoken.

It used to infuriate Molly, the way Liz had just disappeared from her life. But as time went on, losing Liz only made Molly more grateful for Nina and Everly. They are her forever sisters, the years have proven, as different as the past six have been for each of them. And even though they can't directly relate to what she's going through with IVF, Molly knows how much they care.

Besides, now she has Sabrina for that. Sabrina, the first close friend she's made in years, whose empathy restored her faith in the possibility of making true friends in your thirties. Sabrina, who she sees at least twice a week for yoga, who she strolls through the farmers' market with on Saturday mornings, or meets for early cocktails at Dune, the American bistro in town.

Sabrina, who is married to *Jake*.

Molly sinks back into the Adirondack chair. The late July sun is strong overhead, baking her skin. Suddenly her phone is vibrating on the arm of the chair. The 252 number appears on the screen again, this time a text message. Her heart picks up speed.

Moll. Can we meet? Please. I really want to see you.

Molly studies the message. She thinks of the power of letters, of words, of the meaning that—strung together—they form. The consequences they yield. A physical response that can't be controlled, like the electrifying prickle that dusts the back of her neck.

It's arrogant, of course, for Jake to assume she knows the 252 number is him, after all this time. But that's Jake. He can't help who he is.

Maybe Molly should see him, the defenseless part of her reasons. She can't avoid him, not when they live in the same town, not if she's going to continue a friendship with his wife. They'll have to clear the air at some point. If he needs closure, Molly can give him that. She can make it evident that there is nothing left between them—at least where she's concerned.

She taps out a text, hits Send before she can change her mind.

Why don't we go for a walk at Skipping Beach on Sunday? Hunter has
tennis. I'll bring Stella.

Molly feels a twinge of guilt. She's essentially using her daughter for
armor against the overwhelming chemistry she feels in the presence of
a man she used to love.

Molly walks back inside, the cool of the AC a welcome relief, and
sticks her phone in to charge on the counter. The kitchen is clean, but
the wood floors that extend into the rest of the downstairs look grubby,
littered with a week's accumulation of dust and dirt. Molly takes the vacuum from the front hall closet. Perhaps her life is a mess, but that doesn't
mean her house needs to be.

She vacuums the entire downstairs, relishing the satisfying crunch
of the Dyson sucking up crumbs and hair and filth, a spotless path in
its wake.

She's already at it, in a groove, so she runs the vacuum up the stairs
and into Stella's room, a haven of pale pink and *Frozen* memorabilia.
Then into the master bedroom and both upstairs bathrooms, her
thoughts suspended by the loud, churning sound of the machine. She
doesn't even need her music. Perhaps vacuuming is a form of meditation, Molly considers as she does a final sweep through the hallway.

Molly powers off the Dyson when she reaches a closed door—the
only door in the house that's almost always closed. Without really thinking, she pushes it open.

Inside is mostly empty except for a few plastic storage bins filled with
winter clothes and Christmas decorations. The room is small but cozy,
and well lit with north- and west-facing windows that fill two adjacent
walls. When they first moved in, Hunter had gotten excited and painted
it "Pale Powder," a gentle aqua from Farrow & Ball. The ideal color for a
gender-neutral nursery. They'd been trying for only a couple of months
then, and easy hope was something they'd taken for granted.

Then months flew away from them, and nothing happened. Then
years.

Molly knows she should turn the space into a guest room or a home
office for Hunter, make some use out of the extra square footage, but
she's never been able to bring herself to do it. No matter how many disappointments there have been over the past four years—all the negative
pregnancy tests, all the times her period came unwanted, the solemn

phone calls from Dr. Ricci bearing bad news—there is still a tiny flame of hope that flickers in a tiny corner of Molly's heart, refusing to be beaten. To turn this room into anything but a nursery for their second baby would feel like an admission of defeat, once and for all.

Molly leaves the vacuum in the doorway and walks toward the windows, brushing her hand along the sills, where dust has gathered. She looks out at their little backyard, at the hydrangea bush that frames the outside edge of the view. She remembers how she'd meant to put a glider in this corner of the room, how she'd pictured it to be the perfect spot to nurse while gazing out at the fat, purple blooms.

Molly sits down on the floor and hugs her knees into her chest. For a fleeting, dishonest moment, she wonders if she's even sad anymore. But no. She's devastated. For herself, of course, but overwhelmingly for Hunter and Stella. As much as she tries to talk herself out of it, she can't help but feel that they won't truly be a family until she gives her daughter a sibling.

But there's another chance, she reminds herself. She bows her head and closes her eyes, summoning the energy to imagine what might be happening inside her body at this very second, the life that could be brewing deep inside the parts that have failed her so many times before. With every fiber of optimism she can muster, she digs out that stubborn hope in her heart. And then Molly does something she hasn't in longer than she can remember. She is not a religious person, but she prays.

Chapter Twenty-five
Sabrina

You've never mentioned her by name, but I have the sense that the way things ended with Liz haunts you. You don't even know this woman anymore, not really, but the lack of closure makes you miss her. I know how these kinds of unresolved relationships fester.

The spring I first started frequenting Equinox, I would bump into Liz a few times a week. I'd smile and wave, and she'd do the same, though she never seemed eager to stop and chat. Liz is not exactly a *chatty* girl, is she, Molly?

I also made it a point to take Erin's Monday and Wednesday Pilates classes—on Liz's recommendation—and that's where I started to gain traction. One night, after a particularly sweaty and arduous hour, Liz turned to me while we were lacing up our sneakers outside the studio.

"That was fucking brutal." Her eyes were wide and coppery brown, flecks of hazel in the irises.

I nodded, wincing. "I won't be able to walk tomorrow."

"She'll change your body, though." Liz buttoned her jacket, a cream-colored trench. "My boyfriend can attest."

I grinned. "If only men knew what it took."

"Right?" Liz raised a dark eyebrow. "Zander literally lies on the couch eating Cheetos when he's not at work, and he still has a six-pack. It's annoying as shit."

I sensed it, then—an opportunity. "Hey." I glanced at my watch, hesitating. "You want to grab a drink? On me. I owe you for introducing me to Erin's class."

Liz checked the time on her phone. She looked at me and blinked, her expression indifferent. "Why not? There's a place around the corner, El Toro, that does amazing margs. They're not sweet."

"Perfect."

The upscale Mexican restaurant was candlelit and packed with corporate types in pressed suits, drowning their sorrows in happy hour. We grabbed two free stools at the bar. They were stylish but comfy, with high, padded backs.

"Two skinny margs," Liz told the bartender when he tried to hand us menus. She interlaced her fingers and fixed her gaze on me. "So . . . Caitlin, right? What do you do?"

The question caught me off guard—I hadn't adequately prepared for this moment with Liz. I'd nearly forgotten I'd first introduced myself as Caitlin and was grateful for the reminder.

"I . . . I work for my father," I lied. "He owns an accounting firm in Palm Beach. I'm his bookkeeper, basically. I work remotely."

Liz untied her ponytail and shook her head, her short, dark hair falling pin straight to either side of her face. I assessed her attractiveness; her features were small and sharp. She possessed a severe, unique sort of draw. I wasn't quite sure I'd call it beauty.

"Sounds boring, like my job." Liz sipped her margarita. "But hey, at least you don't have to go into an office. I wish I could work remotely."

Liz was right—the drinks were delicious. Strong and tart, not too sweet. We finished them quickly, and the conversation began to take less effort. Halfway through the second round, we'd fallen into a fluid banter. Except for the fact that my parents lived in Palm Beach, nothing I told her was true. But I wasn't worried. Though discerning, Liz didn't seem like the type who would go home and stalk me online. Besides, I hadn't even told her my last name.

I waited patiently for an opening—some perforation through which to redirect our conversation toward you and Jake—but none was presenting itself. I could tell by the way Liz kept an eye on her phone that she was getting antsy and that we probably wouldn't stay for a third drink. I had to act fast.

"So how long have you lived with your boyfriend?" I asked. I hadn't eaten since lunch—a healthy salad from Chopped—and I could feel the alcohol working its way through my system, wrapping itself around my senses. I was getting drunk.

Liz pointed her chin forward in thought. "Since the summer. Eight months."

"And before that you lived with the Danner Lane girl?"

"Yes." She laughed softly. "Danner Lane girl. A.k.a., the now-famous Molly of 'Molly's Song.'" Liz's lips curled into a sly smile, and her eyes looked a little unfocused. Perhaps she was tipsy, too.

"I've heard that song."

"Right. Who hasn't?" Liz cocked her head. "It's an overrated song, in my humble opinion."

"I assume that means they're back together?"

Liz stared at me, her dark brows knitting together. "Huh?"

"Didn't you say . . . before, you said . . . they broke up." I felt my face flush. "Maybe not."

"Oh." Liz shifted on her stool. "A couple of months ago, right. Yeah, that was short-lived. He cheated on her, I guess—she saw some picture of it. But he claimed he didn't and that someone set him up or something." Liz shrugged. "Molly kind of sugarcoated it when she told me the story. She knows, obviously, that I don't trust Jake."

"You don't?" I leaned forward on the bar, pressing my elbows into the stained wood.

"Hell no." Liz clinked the watery ice around in her glass. "He's a gorgeous fucking rock star, with an ego the size of Mount Everest. She hardly even knew him when they moved in together—it had barely been six months. And now he's cheated on her and she's in denial, and it's not the first time something sketchy like that happened, either. It's just kind of . . . pathetic. I always thought Molly had more self-worth than this."

I studied Liz's face, the slightest hint of jealousy etched into her expression. And of course she was jealous, Molly. *You* had Jake Danner on your arm—a gorgeous fucking rock star, like she said. I felt powerful, suddenly, knowing my little scheme had been so effective. You and Jake had reunited, okay, but even your *friends* thought you were pathetic to forgive him so easily.

"Well, do you think they'll last?"

"Who the fuck knows." Liz peered at me quizzically, scrunching her nose. "Why are you so curious?"

"I . . . I'm not." The bartender caught my eye, and though I wanted nothing more than to order another drink—to stay there at the sleek, comfortable bar prying Liz about you and Jake all night long—I sensed my time was up. "Sorry, I just . . . Jake looks so much like my ex. I'm kind of a fangirl."

"Ha. You and every other chick in the city, it seems." Liz held up her palm, waving for the check. She turned back to me. "Well, trust me when I say Molly and Jake are boring as hell these days. If she ever ditches him, I'll let you know."

The bill appeared in front of us. Liz dug out her wallet—black Chanel—but I swatted my hand. "I got it," I insisted, dropping four twenties on the bar. No way was I using my credit card—what if Liz happened to see my real name?

"Cool." She slipped on her trench coat. "I never carry cash. What're you, Caitlin, a drug dealer?"

We walked out onto the street, a chilly wind nipping our faces.

"It's going to be May next week, and it's fucking arctic." Liz frowned, pulling her jacket closer. "Spring in New York is so deceiving."

I nodded in agreement. "It's supposed to be nice this weekend, I think."

Liz stuck her arm out at an approaching cab. "Thanks for the drinks, Caitlin. I'll get the next round."

I smiled to myself as her cab pulled away. I watched it break at the light before hooking a left on East Forty-fifth Street, relief drenching my bones. I hadn't fucked it up. *I'll get the next round.* There would be a next round.

Liz would be my ally. She would be my inside source of all knowledge of you and Jake. And knowledge is power, Molly. The more I knew, the easier it would be for me to tear the two of you apart—for good this time.

Chapter Twenty-six
Molly

2015

That first day at the coffee shop, Molly and Hunter didn't get any work done. After ten minutes of sitting across from each other—half working, half chatting—Hunter closed his laptop and asked if he could buy her a cup of coffee.

She glanced down at her latte. "I've got one, but thanks." She closed her own computer. Molly was sick of picking apart her manuscript, endlessly searching for ways to make it worthy of a book deal, and the man in front of her was nice to look at. Not Jake attractive, but tall, dark, and handsome in a grown-up looking way that reminded her of the dads in kid movies who shaved every day and wore crisp, clean suits to work and always carried the newspaper. Molly thought he had to be at least thirty.

"Right." Hunter's smile was slightly crooked, but endearing. Like that cute actor, Molly couldn't remember his name. Rory's love interest on *Gilmore Girls*. "So what are you working on?"

"Editing a novel." Molly gave him a synopsis of the manuscript, explained that she'd been signed by a literary agent but that they were still trying to find the right editor for it. She noticed, as she was talking, how much confidence she'd acquired over the past two years. She used to hate discussing her writing with strangers—it had made her feel exposed, presumptuous. But then Jake—a successful "working" artist—had deemed her a writer, and it became a label she stopped questioning, one she started to wear with pride. Molly wondered, fleetingly, why she had needed Jake to believe in her before she believed in herself. It didn't feel romantic or fated, as it once had in the beginning. It felt wrong.

"That's huge that you have an agent," Hunter said when she'd finished speaking, his expression genuine. "My aunt is a writer, and she's never been able to find representation, not in thirty years. She's self-published three novels now, each of which have about seven Amazon reviews. All by family members, I'm fairly sure." Hunter smiled. "No, really, publishing is a tough business to crack. I don't think I've ever met anyone with a literary agent. Well done." He blinked. His eyes were the color of milk chocolate, and something in them was so familiar.

"Thank you." Molly knew he could be trying to flatter her, but his words felt authentic. "And what do you do?"

She listened to Hunter describe his job in sports marketing, a career that seemed to fit him entirely. The industry wasn't particularly interesting to Molly, but she could tell that he was genuinely passionate about his work, and she'd always found passion attractive.

When the waitress came by, Hunter ordered another coffee, and Molly followed suit. She didn't think too hard about it. It was *nice* talking with a man who wasn't Jake, someone who wasn't consumed by his own impenetrable self-torment, who hadn't thought to ask her once in the past two weeks how *she* was doing.

Their conversation flowed into the afternoon, the tables around them emptying and filling with new customers. Molly learned that Hunter had grown up in Connecticut, where his mother and older brother still lived. He'd gone to Dartmouth and, after graduating, had spent a year traveling through South America before moving to San Francisco for business school, then back to the East Coast. He'd recently moved out of the Murray Hill apartment he'd shared with friends and into his own place, a one-bedroom in a high-rise on Kent, overlooking the river. He played in a weeknight soccer league and loved sports, and woodworking was a longtime hobby. And, he confessed to Molly, he'd recently broken up with someone. They'd dated for a year and change, and he hadn't felt serious enough about her to keep it going.

Hunter interlaced his hands on the table, and Molly noticed the half-moons on his neatly trimmed fingernails—the opposite of Jake's, which were bitten down to the quick. She needed to stop doing this, stop comparing everything about this stranger to Jake.

"And what about you? Boyfriend?" The way Hunter asked the question wasn't creepy or intrusive. Slightly hopeful maybe, but nothing more.

Molly nodded. She felt an odd impulse to apologize, but knew it wasn't necessary. "We live together," she said.

"Ah." Hunter glanced down into his steaming mug, then back up. His eyes found hers. "Well, at least I didn't put myself through the humilia-tion of asking you out." He smiled softly, and Molly couldn't help but do the same. He had a sense of humor; he was nice. There was something so easy and familiar about talking to him, she couldn't help but feel like they'd known each other for years.

"What does your boyfriend do?" he asked.

"He's a musician. Have you heard of Danner Lane?"

Hunter chortled, sitting back into his chair. "Yes. My ex was obsessed. I've been to a couple of their shows." He paused. "'Molly's Song'—let me guess. You're *that* Molly."

"I'm that Molly." She flipped her palms up, felt Hunter's eyes on her. "Jake—he's the songwriter and lead vocalist—he's the one I date."

Hunter grinned, impressed. "That is very cool."

"Sometimes," she said, clipping her gaze to Hunter's. She almost added, *It doesn't feel as cool as it used to,* but thought better of it. There was something in the air between them that felt weighted, charged with a feeling she couldn't identify. "This is weird, but . . ." She paused. "I feel like I've seen you somewhere before. Is that possible?"

He tipped his chin forward, and there was something about his face that was so likable, so genuine. "I don't know," he said. "Maybe around the neighborhood?"

"Maybe." Molly blinked, unsatisfied. "Well, speaking of the neigh-borhood . . . you're new to Williamsburg, right?"

He nodded. "Yes, and it's a world away from Murray Hill, let me tell you."

"So maybe . . . maybe we could be friends." These words had formed as a thought in Molly's head; she wasn't entirely sure what prompted her to speak them out loud. It wasn't flirtation—despite the place they were in, her heart belonged to Jake. She was sure of that.

Hunter's mouth cracked into a small smile. "I could use a friend or two in Brooklyn."

"Good," Molly said, waving to the waitress for the check.

Hours later, she lay in bed with a book, feeling funny about the cof-feeshop interaction, and exchanging numbers with a man she hardly knew. A twinge of guilt. Jake continued to scribble frantically in the other room. He worked through dinner and didn't come to bed till long after Molly had turned out the light.

Molly didn't really expect Hunter to text her—what guy is stoked about making a female *friend*—but a couple of weeks later, he did. The sight of his name on her phone sent a jolt up her spine. She wished she'd forgotten all about this arbitrary man, but she hadn't.

Hey Molly, it's Hunter O'Neil. Was thinking of checking out the Brooklyn Flea on Saturday—in need of some artwork for my bachelor pad. Any interest in joining? Bring Jake, if he's free.

The text made Molly smile. It was just Brooklyn Flea—no *the*.

She didn't respond for twenty-four hours. She knew Jake would be wrapped up with the album all weekend—it was due to the record label by Sunday—and something about spending Saturday afternoon with another man felt wrong. But Molly was *allowed* to be friends with a guy, wasn't she? She didn't have any real male friends these days, but that was probably because she spent most of her time with Jake.

Molly's internal debate persisted through the three back-to-back yoga classes she subbed that Wednesday. Between the *exhale chataraungas* and the *inhale up-dogs* and the million other yogic cues she recited from memory—as ingrained in her as her own breath—Molly considered the text from Hunter, sitting unanswered in her phone.

She hurried back to the apartment after teaching, speed walking through the biting wind chill. Like most New Yorkers, Molly was ready for winter to end.

Jake was making a sandwich when she walked in the door. It was the first real meal she'd seen him prepare for himself in weeks.

"Hey, beautiful." There was a peppiness in his voice that told Molly he'd had a productive morning. She brushed a golden curl off his forehead, her body filling with lust at the sight of him.

Jake pulled her in for a kiss. "I love when your cheeks are all pink after you teach." He pressed his forehead against hers. "I love *you*, Molly Diamond."

"And I love you, Jake Danner." She nestled her face into his good-smelling neck and thought how much she meant it, and how the thing with Hunter truly *was* harmless, platonic. "Random thing I wanted to run by you."

"Yeah?" Jake went back to slicing an avocado. His knife skills were excellent. Molly was always impressed when she watched him in the kitchen.

"I met this guy at Devoción the other day—you know that coffee shop I like on Grand Street? Anyway, he sat at my table because the place was packed, and we ended up talking for a while and he was really . . . nice."

Jake looked up from the cutting board, his lips parted. "Nice?"

"I told him about you and everything—believe me, it wasn't like that. He's actually been to a couple of your shows. His ex was a fan." Molly smiled innocently. "Anyway, I sort of felt like we could be friends. He's new to Williamsburg and wanted to check out Brooklyn Flea Saturday. Would that be weird?"

"Would what be weird, Moll?" Jake cocked his head and gave her a funny look. "Are you asking me if you can go to Brooklyn Flea with this guy?"

"I guess." She shrugged. "You know I love Brooklyn Flea. He said to bring you, too, but I know you're on deadline. I don't really have any male friends, but I figure there's nothing wrong with it. Right?"

Jake laid the avocado slices over one end of his open sandwich—turkey, bacon, tomato, and provolone cheese. "Well, do you get the vibe that he likes you? As more than friends?"

"No." She shook her head. "It really wasn't like that." Molly knew she should probably tell Jake what Hunter had said after learning she had a boyfriend—*Well, at least I didn't put myself through the humiliation of asking you out*—but decided it would only prompt unnecessary concern.

"If you say it's harmless, it's harmless." Jake took a huge bite of sandwich.

"Totally harmless." Molly leaned against the laminate countertop and began riffling through the mail. "That looks good, Jake."

"He's single, though?" Jake's mouth was still full, and the question came out muffled.

"Apparently, he just broke up with someone."

"Last question." Jake swallowed his bite. "Is he good-looking?"

"He's not bad looking." Molly used her thumb to wipe a smear of mustard from the corner of Jake's mouth. "But trust me when I say he's nothing compared to you. I will never—as long as I live—be as attracted to anyone as I am to you, Jake Danner." She meant it then. She meant it always.

When Molly met Hunter at Brooklyn Flea on Saturday, she hoped she'd be able to recognize him—the details of his physical appearance were fuzzy in her memory. But he spotted her first, and once he called her name and she whipped around to the sight of him, she remembered. Floppy, dark hair, that crooked smile, wide-set brown eyes that still seemed familiar. Taller than Jake by an inch or two, maybe. He'd traded in his suit for a pair of worn jeans and a dark red Patagonia. They laughed because Molly was wearing a similar outfit—jeans and her crimson puffer jacket.

"You're cramping my style," Hunter deadpanned.

Molly grinned. "I don't think you're using that phrase correctly."

He shrugged. "You would know, writer."

They walked around all afternoon, browsing the dozens of vendors selling furniture, art, vintage clothing, funky jewelry, and antiques. Hunter found an oil painting of the ocean that he loved and a few old issues of *Life* magazine.

"I collect these," he explained, picking up an issue from 1965. On the cover, Frank Sinatra beamed in an orange sweater. "Well, my dad did. Now I do."

"Is your father . . ."

"He died when I was in grad school." Hunter blinked, staring at the magazine. "Brain tumor."

"God. I'm so sorry. Were you close?" A beat of silence passed, and Molly immediately regretted the question. "I'm sorry. I shouldn't have—"

"No, it's okay. We were very close. We did so much together—he got me and my brother into sailing and skiing when we were little. He always stayed so active, until he couldn't anymore." Hunter paused. "It's still hard. I miss him."

"I can't imagine." Molly studied him, the anguish in his expression. But there was pride there, too. And respect. And fondness. She wondered what it was like to feel that way about your father.

"What about you?" Hunter asks. "Your parents are still around, I hope?"

"My mom is. She's a nurse. Lives and works in New Jersey, where I grew up. My dad . . ." Molly blinked. "He left when I was young."

Hunter's eyes softened. "I'm sorry."

"It was a long time ago." Molly tapped Sinatra's face, eager to change the subject. "So. What are you going to do with all these *Life* covers? Why did your dad collect them?"

"You know, I think he just liked them, the history they captured.

He never really had a reason beyond that. But I do." Hunter paused, his eyes sparkling. "One day, when I have a house, I'm going to use them to wallpaper a bathroom."

"No way." Molly laughed. "I've always wanted to do the same thing, but with old issues of *The New Yorker*. I have a subscription and save them all."

"Great minds." Hunter winked, his soft brown gaze catching hers in a way that made her stomach flip. "Should we grab a beer?" Around them, the sky was beginning to darken. "Or you probably need to get back."

"I do, yeah." Molly stuffed her hands inside her pockets, chewed her bottom lip. Hunter was staring at her, and he was handsome. Had he been this handsome in the coffee shop? She was having trouble distinguishing the flipping feeling in her stomach. Was it butterflies or guilt? "Jake and I have dinner plans," she lied. "Rain check?"

"Sure." Hunter gave a gentle smile. "Thanks for keeping me company today."

After they parted ways, Molly practically sprinted back to the apartment, eager to fall into Jake's arms and alleviate the feeling of distance that had cropped up in her day with Hunter—a distance she hadn't totally minded. But when she arrived home just after six, he wasn't there. A note lay on the counter. *At the studio finishing a few things. Back by 8, then let's figure out dinner? Love you.*

This quirk of Jake's—leaving physical notes instead of shooting a quick text—was a trait that partially frustrated Molly, but also one she found old-fashioned and endearing.

She decided to open a bottle of wine—she needed to calm down—and was deliberating between Cab and Pinot Noir when her phone began to vibrate on the kitchen counter. Bella was calling her on FaceTime, which seemed odd. They never spoke over the weekend.

"Hey, Bella."

"*Girl.*" Bella's friendly face appeared on the screen of Molly's phone. She wore more makeup than usual behind her horn-rimmed glasses, her raven hair loose around her shoulders. "I have major news. Are you sitting down?"

"What is it?" Molly's heart began to race inside her chest. She slid onto a counter stool—one of the cheap steel ones Jake had ordered from IKEA. "I'm sitting."

"We got an *offer.*"

"Stop. Are you serious?"

"A *fantastic* editor—Alexis Rubio from Penguin—adores your brilliant manuscript. Now, she has a good amount of feedback, which she's going to send you in an email on Monday. But, Molly, she loves this book as much as I do. She wants to buy it."

"Oh my god, Bella."

"She's offering fifty grand for world English rights, which I know is probably le—"

"Fifty thousand dollars?"

"Yes." There was a note of apprehension in Bella's voice. "Tell me what you're thinking."

Molly laughed out loud, her heart light in her chest. "Bella, I teach yoga. Before that I was serving coffee. Fifty grand is a lot for me."

"Oh." Bella tilted her head, seeming to consider this. "Good. Well, for what it's worth, I see us tripling or even quadrupling your advance for book two when this one blows up. Which it *will*."

"Book two?"

"Hell yes. Book two, book three, book four. You're at the start of a big career, Molly Diamond, and this is only the beginning. I'm lucky I snagged you when I did." There was the sound of clinking glass in the background, and a man appeared at the edge of the frame beside Bella, whispering something in her ear. She turned back toward the screen, cleared her throat. "Sorry, Molly, I should run. I'm at drinks for a friend's birthday but just saw the email from Alexis—she works around the clock—and I *had* to FaceTime. I'll touch base Monday with the details."

"Thanks, Bella." Molly was smiling so wide, her mouth hurt. "I can't thank you enough. This is the best phone call I've ever received."

"Of course. I'll talk to you in a couple of days. And, Molly? I'm proud of you."

After they hung up, Molly slumped against the kitchen counter, face in her hands, and cried. With joy, but mostly with sweet relief. Her MFA, the student loans, every shift at Angelina's, every rude customer whose cappuccino she'd messed up, the late nights writing and revising and torturing herself with worry that she'd never get the manuscript exactly right—it had been worth it. All of it. Someone loved the words she'd written enough to publish them. Was there anything more she could want from this life?

Molly's instinct was to call someone—Nina or Everly or her mother—but instead, she decided to take the moment for herself. Bask in it a bit, before letting the rest of the world in on the most exciting news of her life. She nixed the red wine in favor of some champagne she found in the cabinet—it felt more celebratory. Molly popped the bottle and curled up on the couch, savoring the afterglow of Bella's phone call while she waited for Jake to come home.

He was back at quarter of ten, his hair a rumpled mess, his blue eyes red around the rims.

"We're done," he said, sinking down onto the couch beside her and tipping his head back. "We're *dooooone*."

"That's amazing, Jake." Molly rested her hand on his leg. Any other night, she would've been annoyed that he hadn't texted to say he was running this late, but she was too high on her own good news to care. Besides, Jake's album was done. Finally. It was a weight off both their chests. "You're not going back in tomorrow?"

"Nope. We sent everything to Jerry and Ron tonight. Now we wait."

"I know they're going to love it. What did you end up calling it?"

"*Precipice*." Jake made a face. It was the album title Sam and Hale had wanted. Jake had been outvoted.

"I don't mind that, really." Molly pressed her lips together. "It's intriguing."

"I hate it."

"Try to be positive, Jake. The album is off your hands. You did it." She paused, ready to redirect the conversation. "So, I got some crazy—"

"The thing is, Moll . . ." Jake pivoted his shoulders so he was facing her. His expression was wild, almost manic, his eyebrows climbing up his forehead. "I don't know how I *feel* about this album. *Precipice* doesn't feel as seamless as *The Narrows,* and Sam and Hale are still telling me the songs I wrote are 'too lovey-dovey and pop-y.'" He used air quotes around the words. "They think it's your fault, actually."

His tone was indignant. Molly sat up straighter on the couch. "Excuse me?"

"Well, not *your* fault, but you know what I mean. They think having a girlfriend has made me go all soft."

"Is that so?"

Jake shrugged.

Molly glared at him. "I hope you corrected them."

Jake said nothing. He leaned back into the couch, rubbed the inner corners of his eyes.

"Jesus, Jake." Molly felt shot through with anger. "I thought I was supposed to be your 'muse.'"

"You *are* my muse." He sighed. "I guess I just haven't felt very inspired lately."

"That isn't *my* fucking fault!" Molly stood, furious.

"I'm not saying it's your fault!"

"And you're not saying it isn't, either." Molly narrowed her eyes. She started toward the bedroom, though she was tempted to leave the apartment.

"Moll, I'm sorry," he called behind her. "I didn't mean—wait. What're you doing drinking champagne, anyway?" He gestured to the bottle of Veuve and the two flutes on the table, the one untouched meant for him.

"I got a book deal, Jake," Molly said flatly, wanting to spite him. "Bella sold *Needs*."

"Are you serious?" Jake jumped from the couch, running over to where she stood. He wrapped his arms around her, squeezing her tightly. "Jesus, I'm proud of you. We need to celebrate. I ate at the studio, but we could go for drinks?"

Molly wriggled out of his grasp. "You ate at the studio?" She didn't know why she was *this* angry, only that she was. "If *you* already ate, then I guess dinner is off the table. Drinks it is!"

He looked at her, mouth gaping, not getting it.

"What about *me*, Jake? Did it even occur to you that I haven't eaten yet because *you* said in your note that we'd figure out dinner when you got back? That you told me you'd be home two hours ago and I've been sitting here all night, waiting for you?" She was seething.

"Christ, Molly." Jake threw his head back, exasperated. "Why are you so *on* me right now? I'm sorry, okay? I had a long-ass day, cut me a break. Sorry my chivalrous manners aren't in tip-top shape at the moment."

"This isn't about *manners*. You're being an asshole."

"I'm an asshole? Because I had to work late and you're incapable of getting yourself food? If you want dinner, just say so! We'll go get something to eat right now!"

"Screw you. I'm not doing this." Molly turned away from him. "I'm going to read in bed."

"Molly, no." Jake reached for her arm, his combative expression softening. "Come on. Look, I'm sorry I was late. Let's just go out, cool off. It's Saturday."

She pulled away from him. "I'm really not in the mood."

He frowned. "We'll stay here, then. Finish the champers. I'll make you an omelet."

"I'm exhausted," she lied. "I'm just going to read in bed."

"What about dinner?"

"I had a late lunch. I'm not hungry." The second part was true, at least. She'd lost her appetite.

"Really?" Jake looked down at her, and his eyes were sorry. "Don't let me ruin tonight."

You already have, Molly wanted to say. But she felt too deflated to continue their argument. Her happy mood was gone—Jake had sucked it out—and she hated that he had the ability to do that. To suck the life out of her just by being who he was. Lately he saved all his charisma and charm for the stage—for his fans—and Molly was left to bear the brunt of his stress. His dark side.

"I really am tired," she told him with a shrug, desperate to be alone. "We'll celebrate another night."

"Tomorrow? I want to hear everything."

"Sure."

"I really am so crazy proud of you." Jake squeezed her shoulder. "I guess I'll watch a movie if you're going to sleep. Can you toss me a beer on your way to the bedroom?"

Molly took an IPA out of the fridge. She placed it on the coffee table, resisting the urge to chuck it at Jake's head.

As she brushed her teeth and washed her face, she realized he hadn't even asked about Brooklyn Flea. She'd harbored a pang of guilt all day, suspecting Jake might be anxious about her spending several hours with another man, but he hadn't even remembered.

Molly read the same page of her paperback four or five times before giving up—her mind was elsewhere. She turned out the light and nestled underneath the covers, her thoughts restless, churning. When Jake crawled into bed beside her a couple of hours later and whispered, "I love you," she pretended to be asleep. And she realized, with a pang of sadness, that it wasn't the first time that winter she'd done so.

Early feedback on *Precipice* came in a few weeks later. Jerry called Jake to say that Ron and his team at Dixon Entertainment liked it, though they agreed it was a departure from *The Narrows* in terms of sounding a bit more pop infused. By that point, Jake could read between the lines when it came to Jerry, and it was obvious his manager was painting a prettier picture than the real thing. Clearly Dixon wasn't going crazy over *Precipice,* but it had been a full year since "Molly's Song" released as a single, and a second album was overdue. They would have to make it work.

The album drop was slated for June, which meant the band would spend the spring recording and gearing up for the launch.

Jake was barely around, spending most waking hours at the fancy recording studio Ron had booked for them in Tribeca. Everly was crazed with work, Nina and Cash were off in their own world, and Liz hardly ever seemed to be available. Molly had the book deal keeping her busy— she and Alexis were deep in revisions—but still. Writing was often a solitary process, and as thrilled as she was to be doing it, Molly found that her days could be lonely. And so, she continued to see Hunter.

She wasn't entirely sure why or how their friendship blossomed, only that the connection they shared felt natural. *Romantic* wasn't the word for it. Hunter felt like someone she'd known all her life; there was something familiar in his smile that infused their meetings with a déjà vu–like quality.

They'd meet for coffee or a casual lunch, sometimes a walk along the waterfront. He told her about the dates he went on—some promising, some disastrous—and she gave him unfiltered advice. In turn, however, Molly never said much about Jake. They weren't in a great place, but somehow, discussing her and Jake's relationship with Hunter—as close as they'd become—felt like a betrayal. Whenever Hunter did inquire about Jake, Molly only said that he was busy recording the new album. Which was true.

"He's playing the long game with you," Nina insisted one night in April. They were at Charlie Bird in SoHo with Liz and Everly. The four of them hadn't had a meal together in ages, and Molly had roped everyone in to getting a dinner on the books. It was finally spring, and the mood in the city was happy and light.

"Hunter? No." Molly sipped her martini. She used the little plastic stick to spear an olive, then slurped it down. "He's my friend."

Liz raised an eyebrow. "How often do you see him?"

"Once a week, probably."

"Hmm." Everly flashed her a skeptical look that mirrored Liz's and Nina's.

"But that's because *you guys* are all too busy to hang out with me," Molly justified. "And Jake never leaves the studio. Plus, Hunter and I are practically neighbors." She didn't like sounding defensive. Especially because she wasn't *doing* anything wrong. Since when was it a crime to be friends with someone of the opposite sex?

Molly did wonder, a month later, why she felt a stab of envy when Hunter told her about a girl he'd hit it off with. Her name was Blair; she was an interior designer from Westchester and the first girl Hunter had felt excited about since his ex.

That night, Molly found Blair on Facebook and scrolled through her pictures. She looked preppy and manicured, too conservative for Hunter. Hunter was traditional, yes, but rough around the edges. He chopped wood for his mother in Connecticut; he built things with his hands. If he dressed like a prep, it was because he wore old Brooks Brothers sweaters of his father's from the seventies. There was no effort in his style. A man like Hunter was timeless.

Molly turned out the light and flopped onto her side, pulling the covers up around her shoulders. For what seemed like the millionth night in a row, Jake was still at the studio, and she was falling asleep alone. Again.

Molly closed her eyes and saw the Facebook images of Blair behind her lids, something small and sharp pricking her chest. She had no reason to be jealous. She was with *Jake,* who still made her stomach flip, even just waking up next to him. Who filled her with a love so consuming and complex it drove her to the brink of madness and back again in the span of ten minutes. Perhaps Hunter felt familiar to her because he was the type of man she'd once thought she'd marry: the tall, dark and handsome breed; a little dorky and straitlaced, a steady gentleman, who didn't take himself too seriously.

But that was before Jake, and it was why Molly never felt truly guilty for spending time with Hunter. Her feelings for Jake hadn't changed, and she knew in the depths of her soul that they never would. For better or worse, Jake Danner was the love of her life.

On the eve of *Precipice*'s launch in June, Jake was a basket of nerves. *Rolling Stone*'s review of the album would be live first thing in the morning.

Molly ordered them pizza from Roberta's—Jake's favorite—which he barely touched. His cerulean eyes were unfocused, far away, as he nursed a glass of whiskey. Even when Molly slid her hand under the waistband of his jeans and pressed her mouth against his neck, there was no reaction.

"I'm sorry, Moll," he mumbled. "Tonight's just . . . can we not?"

Jake was already up when Molly woke the next morning—she doubted if he'd slept at all. He was perched on the couch, elbows on his knees, cradling his face in his hands.

"Jake?"

He didn't answer. Then Molly noticed his laptop, which sat open on the kitchen counter, the *Rolling Stone* article up on the screen. The headline, in big, bold letters: DANNER LANE RETURNS, LACKING AND CONTRIVED.

Dread pooled in Molly's gut. She moved closer to the computer.

The whimsical, homegrown vibe that won our hearts in Danner Lane's debut album The Narrows *is, unfortunately, deficient in its follow-up. In* Precipice, *out today, the trio targets a more mainstream sound that deviates from its roots, and in doing so wholly misses the mark. The exception is "Molly's Song," which topped the charts when it released as a single last year, and stands to be the album's one-hit wonder. On guitar and lead vocals, Jake Danner edges for the spotlight. The comradeship of* The Narrows' *backup vocals has all but disappeared in* Precipice, *and the talent of bass guitarist Sam Lane and drummer Hale Lane fades into the backdrop.*

Molly stopped reading, unable to stomach another word of the scorching review. Her eyes flickered to Jake, whose golden head remained dropped between his knees, palms pressed to his face. This was bad. This was worse than she ever imagined.

Chapter Twenty-seven
Molly

July 2022

Sunday is overcast, the sky knotted with clouds. A tangible humidity hangs in the air. Molly doesn't lie to Hunter about her plans for the day.

"I told Jake I'd take a walk with him on the beach this morning," she tells him over breakfast. "I'm bringing Stella." Molly doesn't know if this strengthens or weakens her case. "She has a playdate with Jade at noon, so we won't be long."

Hunter says nothing, eyes glued to his phone. At the other end of the table, Stella is absorbed in a *Frozen* coloring book.

"Are you okay with that?" Molly hesitates, swallowing a piece of toast. "I just . . . I think it would be good for us to catch up. I mean, he lives here now, and if we're going to be friends . . ." She lowers her voice. "It's been a long time, Hunt. He was important to me."

"I know." Hunter presses his palms to the table and stands. He slips his phone into the back pocket of his tennis shorts. "Sometimes I just . . ." He shakes his head, his dark hair swaying lightly. "I can't believe he ended up here, in our town. I mean, what are the chances, Molly?"

"I get it." She nods sincerely. "I feel the same way."

"But it's fine. You do what you have to do. I trust you." His eyes clip hers. "It's just . . . it's been a weird summer."

"I know."

"It's almost August, and we haven't sailed together. Not once." He sighs. "You just seem distracted."

There's a pit in Molly's stomach. Hunter is right. She has been distracted, and the summer is slipping away from them.

"I'm not trying to make you feel guilty," he adds, squeezing her hand. "I know we've had a lot going on."

She knows he means the fertility stuff. She nods. "Well, why don't we go for a sail this afternoon? You, me, and Stell. We can take your mom's catboat."

"It's supposed to rain this afternoon."

"Oh." Molly never remembers to check the forecast. Hunter, on the other hand, always seems to know what the weather is doing. This is one of the myriad ways they balance each other out.

"We'll find a time."

She nods, pressing against him, leaning up for a kiss. "I love you, Hunt."

On the way to Skipping Beach, Molly lets Stella use her iPad in the back seat. She should be better about screen time—she knows this—but she needs the ten minutes to ready herself.

Her stomach is tangled with nerves as she pulls the Audi into the parking lot of Skipping Beach. She hasn't been here much this summer—she typically takes Stella to the beach at the yacht club or to swim at Becky's pool. The last time she was here was with Sabrina back in May, after the parade. The memory is a soft punch in her gut, and Molly feels a stab of guilt realizing she hasn't told Sabrina that she's meeting up with Jake today. The last thing she wants to do is be a shitty friend to the one woman in this town she actually likes. She'll call Sabrina later, she decides.

Molly spots Jake right away, standing down at the water, ankle deep. Stella follows Molly's gaze, breaking into a sprint when she sees him, too. He turns, raises a hand in greeting.

When she's close, he leans in to kiss her cheek. Molly isn't prepared for this—the slow drag of his stubble across her face combined with the familiar soap-and-pine scent of him unsteadies her. Her legs turn to putty.

Stella has already collected a handful of shells, which she proudly displays for Jake. He crouches to Stella's level, carefully examining each one.

"This is a beauty." He fingers a piece of turquoise sea glass. "See how smooth the edges are? This had to be in the ocean for a long, long time to get this soft."

"How long?" Stella asks, watching Jake closely. "Twenty years?"

He laughs. "Maybe twenty years."

"Oh." Stella cocks her hip. "I wasn't born then. Right, Mom?"

"That's right, baby."

Stella looks at Jake. "Did you bring your bathing suit? My mom didn't bring hers, but she said I could swim, so I'm wearing mine."

He gestures to his blue swim trunks, which match his eyes. "Duh." He stands, his shoulders rising in line with Molly's chin. He's wearing an old Bob Dylan T-shirt that Molly recognizes instantly—one he used to love to wear onstage. "Good thing we came when we did. Looks like rain later."

"Yeah. We need it, though. It's been such a dry summer." She only knows this because she's heard Hunter say it.

"Right." Jake tugs on the brim of his Panthers hat. "So how are you, Moll?"

"Fine. You know, fine." Molly hates that she stumbles over her words, but being so close to him, she feels physically unstable. "Should we walk? Stella has a playdate at noon, so we can't stay long."

"I'm going to my friend Jade's house," Stella announces, squinting up at Jake. "She has all the *Frozen* Barbies. And her name kinda sounds like yours."

"Off by one letter." Jake winks. To Molly, he whispers, "Should I know about *Frozen* Barbies?"

"You will soon enough. If you have a girl, at least."

Jake gives her a funny look. They start walking down the length of the beach, which is unusually empty for a Sunday. Perhaps the forecast has scared people off. Stella, in tow behind them, stops every few minutes to fill her yellow bucket with more shells.

"You look nice, Moll," he says, his knuckles inadvertently brushing the edge of her hand.

Molly thanks him, though she knows he's being generous. She wears jean cutoffs and a thin cotton tee splattered with grease from frying bacon that morning. She didn't change—mostly because she didn't want Hunter to think she was trying to look a certain way for Jake. Her wavy hair is pulled back into a low ponytail, the way she wears it when she's rushing, which is often.

She adjusts her billowy shirt, considering how her style has changed in the years since she and Jake were together. Back then, it was all crop tops and body-con dresses—she and Nina went to American Apparel almost every weekend. Now Molly wouldn't be caught dead in anything so formfitting.

"And you look . . . more like the Jake I remember." She grins, because in his worn tee and cap, he does.

He scrubs a hand through his untamed curls, a small, knowing smile playing over his mouth.

"How's Sabrina?" Molly asks. She can't help it. "Does she know you're meeting me? I mean—not that it's a secret. I forgot to mention it to her, is all."

"I didn't tell her yet, but I will. It's not a big deal." Jake hooks a hand around the nape of his neck. "She's fine, busy this weekend."

"With work?"

"And redecorating."

"Right. She mentioned wanting to redo your bedroom."

"And every room in the house, it seems." Jake shrugs.

Molly can't help but laugh. "Look at you, Jake Danner. Married to a woman with a passion for *décor*."

"Yeah. The house could look like my college dorm room and I probably wouldn't notice."

"I don't doubt it." Molly grins. "I guess I could've spruced up our place on Driggs a bit."

"Are you kidding? I loved that place."

Molly's heart clenches at the memory of their old apartment, of how it felt to walk in the door and into Jake's arms every single night. She remembers the tiny kitchen, the distinct smell of it. A blend of spices—the ones Jake cooked with—and those eucalyptus candles she used to buy.

"Don't sell yourself short," Jake continues. "You made it homey. You got those curtains. Remember the green flowered ones?"

"The ones I found at Brooklyn Flea. *Wow*, I haven't thought about those in a long time. They looked terrible, in retrospect. I don't even think they fit the windows."

"They were perfect, Moll." Jake smiles sadly. He lowers his voice. "We were perfect."

A breeze rolls off the ocean, with it the scent of salt and brine. Molly brushes a piece of hair off her face. Her throat is tight. "'Perfect' is a stretch, Jake."

"We were pretty damn close." He sighs. "Tell me how you really are, Moll."

She fidgets with her engagement ring, spinning it around the way she does when she's anxious. It's a three-stone diamond—an heirloom, Becky's late mother's—and Molly has barely taken it off since Hunter gave it to her six weeks before Stella was born. "I feel busy," she tells him. "Stella's had camp all summer, and I'm teaching four classes a week now, which I guess isn't *that* many, but still. The days are full."

"I'm glad you're still teaching," he says. "Your classes at Bhakti were always my favorite. Does it make you happy?"

"Teaching?" Molly considers this. It's a question she hasn't been asked in a long time. Maybe ever. "I'm not sure," she answers truthfully. "It used to. My first few years, I got so jazzed about sequencing my classes and building playlists and themes."

"I remember." Jake smiles.

"I never thought teaching yoga would be so permanent. But nearly a decade later, here I am." Molly pauses. "It's sort of a chore now, to be honest. I've been doing it for so long, I know I'm *good* at it, but I'm not sure I enjoy it."

"Hmm."

"When Stella started preschool, I thought about going for a steadier job—one where I'd be bringing in a real salary, but I don't know . . ." Molly's voice trails. She doesn't want to tell Jake that the real reason she's held off on going back to work full-time is because they've been trying to get pregnant again. It's the last thing she wants to discuss, especially with him. She shrugs. "Maybe in a few years."

Jake is quiet for a moment. "But what about writing? I need to know why you gave it up." He stops walking, pivots his shoulders so they're facing each other. Stella is still a ways behind them, hunting for shells. "I'm serious, Molly. You were really fucking great at it."

"Only if you tell me why you gave up music for a job in insurance that I can't imagine you actually care about." She studies his fingers, remembers the easy, expert way they used to strum his old acoustic guitar. "Because I think the whole world knows you were really fucking great at that."

"Well, I'm trying again to get it back, aren't I?" Jake's expression is tinged with remorse. "That's more than you can say." He lets out a breath. "Fine, I'll go first. To be clear, I didn't *give up* music. I'm sure you read about Danner Lane's split. It wasn't long after you and I . . ." His voice trails.

"I heard about it, Jake, yeah. I'm . . . I'm really so sorry. I couldn't believe Sam and Hale did that to you. I still can't."

He looks up at her, injured, and Molly can tell it's a wound that hasn't healed. "The fucking Lane Brothers." He shakes his head. "They thought they'd be better off without me, and look how right they were."

Molly remembers how hard Jake had always worked—his tireless grit, his late nights at the studio or agonizing over lyrics and chord progressions in their tiny living room—and his pain is palpable. She feels it for him. She's heard of the Lane Brothers, of course—they're popular—but she doesn't particularly enjoy the folksy, bluegrass style of the duo. In her opinion, they're nothing compared to what Danner Lane was at its best.

"Sam and Hale weren't right," she tells him. "You were the heart and soul of that band. You were its special sauce, and they knew it and resented you for it. You wrote the songs, Jake. Every last line of every last one."

He says nothing, gazing past her shoulder, out at the sea. Fat clouds fill the sky, more of them on the horizon.

"Not to toot my own horn," Molly starts, a smile at the corners her mouth, "but as far as I can tell, the Lane Brothers haven't had a hit that comes close to rivaling 'Molly's Song.'"

"I guess that's true."

"You could've done your own thing, like Sam and Hale did. Back then, I mean. You were the fan favorite, by leaps and bounds."

"It's not that simple, Molly." Jake blinks, and the way he's looking at her tells her that whatever he's about to say is the truth. "That was the year you left. You were just . . . gone. You left me with nothing but a note and a half-empty apartment. I was . . . broken." He rubs his forehead, closes his eyes. "Sam and Hale were done with me, you were done with me, Jerry and Ron went with Sam and Hale because they had a plan and I didn't. I can't explain it, I just . . . it all just seemed pointless without you."

Tears clog Molly's throat. She thinks of the last email Jake wrote her, remembering its bleak, desperate tone. She'd only skimmed it, truthfully—it was too painful to confront each of his carefully crafted, deliberate words. It had genuinely never occurred to her that leaving him could destroy his motivation, his potential. He was *Jake Danner*. An actual famous rock star, whose raw talent was just as breathtaking as his movie-star looks. His picture had started appearing in the tabloids of gossip magazines; flocks of girls desperate for his autograph swarmed him after every show. Molly knew he'd be crushed when she left, but she figured he'd wallow for a bit, then get on with the big life that awaited him. She'd banked on it. And after she became happy and settled with Hunter, she'd made it a point to stop googling Jake, even after learning of Danner Lane's split. She simply didn't want to know what he was up to—it was easier that way.

It *had* surprised her that she'd never heard Jake's name pop up over the years, the way she'd begun to hear of the Lane Brothers. Still, she'd assumed he was out there, doing *something* amazing, something behind the scenes but high powered, perhaps, and that his name would resurface in time.

"But you must've been approached by other managers, Jake?"

"A few." He sighs. "But I was in a terrible place. I didn't want to do it without Sam and Hale, but I literally *couldn't* do it without you." He studies her, wistful. "You were my muse. I always told you that."

Guilt wrenches Molly's insides, so intensely she can't speak.

"Then, finally, I got help." Jake blinks. "Well, what really happened is I bumped into Sisi." Light comes back into his eyes when he says this, and Molly feels a strange mix of relief and unwelcome spite.

She listens to him describe their reunion—how Sabrina got him to start seeing a therapist, how she convinced her father to give him the job at Randolph Group, insisting that a change of career—a fresh start— would do Jake good.

"I knew she wanted to get married," he continues. "Early on, she made that clear. It took me longer to get there, but eventually, of course, I did. And now, here we are."

The sheer irony of it hits Molly all over again. A fresh wave. "It's wild, Jake." She shakes her head. "I finally meet a woman in Flynn Cove who I actually connect with—who I actually *like*—and she turns out to be your wife." She pauses, tempted to mention the fertility issues they're both experiencing, but she doesn't want to betray Sabrina.

"If it's any consolation, she really likes you, too." Jake's gaze lands on Molly's, and she feels something sizzle inside her. Butter landing on a hot pan. "How could she not? Everyone likes you. You're kind and humble and good; you put people at ease. You're a treasure, Moll." His eyes are so blue they're piercing, hard to look at, and Molly can't stand the helpless surge of attraction she feels for him—still there, as powerful as ever after all these years. But it's more than just chemistry. It's unbearable, heartbreaking nostalgia.

"I'm sorry, Jake." She closes her eyes, feels the tears slip through. "I was a shit to you. I shouldn't have left the way I did—"

"No, Molly." He stops her. "*I* was the shit. I get that now. I had so many chances to be better to you, to quit prioritizing that stupid band—"

"But it *wasn't* a stupid band, Jake. It was your *dream.*" Molly feels a sort of turbulence churning through her veins, fogging her head. She is spitting out the words she needs to be true, a truth she's clung to for years now: *Jake was always going to put the band before me.*

"*You* were my dream, Moll." His voice is clear and impossibly sad. "Why did you really leave? It was for Hunter, wasn't it?"

A tear trickles down Molly's cheek. She draws in a shaky breath, unable to answer the question. So close to him, her body is a furnace.

"It's okay." He squints, and there are tears in his eyes, too. "Hunter is a good man—I knew it the first time I met him, all those years ago. You guys have built a beautiful life together, you have a beautiful daughter. You deserve all of your happiness."

Molly looks at Jake, and she sees the face she saw almost a decade earlier, in the back room of the Broken Mule; she feels the way his eyes latched onto hers while he sang that unforgettable rendition of "Mona Lisas and Mad Hatters" that lit up the stage. For a moment, she feels she's been flung nine and a half years back in time then pitched ahead again, her life playing out on a different track, the one that could've been if she'd never left, if she'd tried a little harder to hope for the best instead of preparing for the worst.

"You know what I think about sometimes?" She begins the question before she can stop herself, the desire to be honest a blazing force behind her collarbone. "I think about that picture I got emailed—you know, the one of you and that girl in Florida. Kissing in that club or whatever."

"Molly." Jake's face falls. "I know that was forever ago now, but I truly didn't even know that girl, I swear—"

"I know. That's not why I'm bringing it up. I'm not saying it's your fault, and it doesn't matter anymore, anyway." Molly pauses, presses her lips together. "I just think about that sometimes because I wonder, if that hadn't happened, if things might've been different. For us, I mean." She lets her shoulders drop.

Jake says nothing, his gaze falling toward the sand. When he finally looks up, his eyes are full of sorrow.

Suddenly, behind them, Stella lets out a sharp squeal.

"Mommy! Look!"

Molly turns to see a crab skittering across the sand near Stella's feet.

"He won't hurt you," Jake says, squatting. "He's just a little guy."

But Stella continues to screech as the crab scampers around her, whether in excitement or in fear, Molly isn't sure. With a five-year-old, it can be a fine line between the two emotions.

"He's gonna bite me, Jake!"

Jake hooks his hands under Stella's armpits and scoops her up in a flash. "All right, Stella. I saved you from the big bad crab!"

Stella shrieks in delight, wriggling her little body in Jake's strong arms. The sight of it is almost too much for Molly to take.

"Time for a swim, I think." Jake places Stella down for a moment. He peels off his shirt, then picks her up again, bounding into the water, Stella shrieking with laughter in his grasp.

Molly stands on the shore and watches them, a clamp around her heart. She watches as Stella, in her favorite pink bathing suit, jumps off Jake's bronzed shoulders and into the sea. She jumps over and over again, squealing with glee each time, Jake securing her ankles as she stands. Molly doesn't notice the tears in her eyes until Stella and Jake are out of the water, panting with exhaustion, and Stella wraps her arms around Molly's leg.

"Why are you crying, Mommy?"

It's the same question Stella asked her in the women's locker room on the Fourth of July. Molly glances down at her daughter—her perfect baby girl. She smooths her wet, salty hair, gently pinches her tiny earlobe. "I just thought of a memory and it made me sad. But happy sad. Tears can be happy, too."

Jake looks at Molly then, his irises the same glittering blue that she remembers, the curls she used to run her fingers through dark and damp. He reaches for her hand, and it's refreshingly cold from the ocean. The three of them stand there like that for a trancelike moment, the waves crashing at their feet. Time is frozen. It is bliss. She wants so badly to let herself bask it in, but something snaps inside her heart.

Molly yanks her hand from Jake's—she doesn't want Stella to see—and glances down at the Apple Watch Hunter gave her for her birthday. Pink. Stella picked the color.

"Shoot. It's quarter of twelve. We gotta go, Stell." Above them, the sky is filling with thicker clouds, rolling in from the east, a cloak of gray that obscures the sun.

"To Jade's?" Stella grabs her yellow bucket from where it lies on the sand. She turns to Jake. "You know Jade's dad makes her butter-and-sugar sandwiches?"

"Butter-and-sugar sandwiches?" Jake's eyes widen. "Hmm. Sounds nutritious."

"What's 'nutritious'?"

"It means healthy." Molly takes the bucket from Stella. It's heavy—full of rocks and shells. "But Jake is joking. Butter and sugar aren't healthy foods. They're okay to have once in a while, as a special treat. C'mon, Stell, say goodbye." She knows she's rushing, she knows she's done a terrible job "clearing the air" with Jake like she planned, but she doesn't care. There's been a tangible shift in the atmosphere—a riptide looming—and she needs to get out before it sucks her away.

"Bye, Jake." Stella places her hands on her hips and shifts her weight to one foot. "Are you coming to my birthday party on August twentieth?"

"Oh. I don't know." Jake gives a playful grin. "I didn't get an invitation."

"Oh. Well, there's gonna be a piñata there. Mom, can he come?" Stella looks up at Molly, her eyes wide and hopeful.

"That's fine," Molly answers, her voice strangled. What else is she supposed to say?

"Cool. I'll be there. I hope you like presents." Jake holds up his hand, and Stella gives him a high five with her tiny palm, a wide grin cracking across her face. "Bye, Stell," he calls. "Have fun at Jade's. Have a butter-and-sugar sandwich for me."

Molly forces a smile, averting her gaze. She's afraid if she looks at Jake, she'll burst into more tears.

She hands Stella a towel, and they walk back down the beach toward the car. Molly wants the shame of the emotions inside her to take over, but all she can feel now is the heavy, dizzying aftermath of being close to him again and the agony of the increasing space between them as she drives away from the beach.

She drops Stella at Jade's house on the west side of town. She's grateful that Jade's mother isn't home—she's too debilitated for small talk. She feels detached from her own voice and body as she explains the contents of Stella's tote bag to the Patels' nanny—raincoat, a change of clothes, her stuffed rabbit, Mr. Bunny, just in case.

Molly leaves her phone in the car, and when she climbs back in the front seat, she has a new text. The fact that it's from Jake makes complete sense. Of course. Who else could it be but the person currently occupying all the space in her mind?

The message is a single line. Come back to the beach.

Molly drives there without thinking. She knows she should think, but she doesn't want to. She is sick of thinking. Instead, she lets herself be pulled by the feelings ballooning inside of her, seeping into every inch of her. It's so easy.

A drop of rain splatters the windshield as she slows to a stop in the parking lot. The sky is marbled with dense, dark clouds. People are fleeing the beach, covering their heads with towels as they scramble toward the shelter of their cars.

Molly spots Jake in the distance. He's inside the gazebo, leaning against the rail, staring out over Long Island Sound. She runs to him, tears filling her eyes and spilling down her face. Light rain pricks Molly's bare arms, but it's still too humid to be cold. By the time she reaches the gazebo, the beach has cleared. There's no one left but the two of them.

Jake smiles when he sees her, the edges of his mouth breaking into a laugh. "Everybody is afraid of a little rain."

Molly stares at him, her heart in her throat. "I'm worried I'm still in love with you, Jake."

The rain begins to fall more steadily, drumming on the roof of the gazebo. He steps toward her.

"Moll." Jake's voice is old and familiar; a heartstring echoes in her chest. "I've loved you since the moment I saw you at that grungy bar in Brooklyn."

A roll of thunder cracks in the distance. His shoulders are square with hers now, and his body is close—too close—and there's something happening that she cannot stop. She thinks about the most mundane parts of her daily existence—opening Amazon boxes, folding up the cardboard. Sponging crumbs from the kitchen counter. Laundry. Hormone injections that make her feel like a dump truck. Blood tests. Cutting up another batch of chicken nuggets into bite-size pieces. Rinse and repeat. Then, suddenly, one summer Sunday—*this*. Jake. Him. *Them*.

Jake uses his thumbs to brush the tears from her cheeks, an electric current hissing in the space between their bodies. Molly's knees soften, the joints disintegrating. She feels heavy and light at the same time. She won't have the willpower to push him away, and it feels good to know this, to accept it.

Jake leans forward; the edge of his nose brushes hers, and she gives in to the heady combination of heart and loins against which her mind is defenseless.

"I never stopped loving you," he whispers, just before he kisses her.

It's a kiss that demolishes her, that relieves her. She feels as if she's falling, tumbling backward through the air while his mouth works hers open, his lips soft but firm and too familiar, a time capsule. She runs her fingers along the stubble of his jawline and through the curls at the back of his neck, locked in the present moment, deliciously free from the anxieties of the past, of the future.

Jake pushes her against the wall of the gazebo with the weight of his body as rain smacks the roof above them. He cups her face with his hands, rakes his fingers through her hair and down the length of her body. If he never stops, Molly thinks, that would be okay.

"My car," he whispers, and she nods into his neck.

They run through the rain to Jake's Jeep Wrangler, which is the only car left in the lot besides Molly's. In the back seat, Molly hooks her thighs around his waist, and it's pure muscle memory, the two of them being together like this. He works the T-shirt over her head, pressing his mouth to the silky fabric of her bra, over the hardness of her nipple, and it is then that the sensory momentum propelling Molly forward jerks to a halt.

She thinks of Hunter, suddenly: Hunter sitting beside her in the waiting room at every prenatal appointment with Stella, flipping through old issues of *Parents* magazine. Hunter building the IKEA crib in the nursery on a brutally hot summer day, before they moved into a place with air-conditioning. Hunter installing the car seat in their old green Subaru. Hunter squeezing Molly's sweat-slicked hand in those last wild moments before she pushed Stella out into the world. Hunter carrying their tiny blond bundle in the Babybjörn on walks, that first magical fall the three of them spent as a family. Hunter sending her Zillow links to homes in Flynn Cove, along with comprehensive notes on each: *Nice but needs new roof; kitchen just renovated—beautiful; TWO working fireplaces; might be too close to the highway; a full acre but some of it could be wetlands—will check town map.* More recent memories, too: Hunter's content smile on Becky's boat, tiller in hand, Molly and Stella sitting in the cockpit—his happy place, out for a sail with his girls. Hunter reading with Stella every night after her bath, the line of concentration that furrows his brow as he helps her sound out the words in *The Cat in the Hat*. Hunter bringing Molly her coffee in bed more mornings than not. Hunter mowing the lawn every weekend, the sweaty, earthy smell of his skin when he comes in from working outside. The hope that shimmered in Hunter's kind, grounding eyes after their latest embryo transfer, the heartening optimism in his voice: *This is going to happen for us, I know it, Moll.* Hunter. Her husband. Her daughter's father. Her whole life.

Molly pulls back, studying Jake, her head a tornado. Tears run down her cheeks. She loathes herself.

"I love you," Jake is whispering, his hands gripping her rib cage. "I love you. I love you. I love you."

He is there, ready, lips parted, and despite all that is at stake, there is a magnetic force that Molly cannot fight. She knows, then, as her body pitches forward, loses herself in his kiss, in his touch, that she isn't the woman she thought she was.

Who is she?

Chapter Twenty-eight
Sabrina

Jake has been distracted for the past few days—I have to ask him three times which fabric he prefers for the living room pillows before he even registers what I'm talking about.

He's started to look at his phone with the frequency of a teenage girl. This morning, when he takes the garbage out, I finally steal a glance at his texts.

You have plans to meet at Skipping Beach at eleven. You're bringing Stella, which I presume means you've told Hunter where you're going. You're using your daughter, no doubt, to make your husband feel more comfortable. To make it appear as though you're not really seeing Jake "alone." You have such an agenda, Molly.

Jake comes back inside, his hair still tousled from sleep. He rubs the inner corners of his eyes. He seems to notice me for the first time all morning, standing at the sink, doing his fucking dishes.

"Sees." He walks around the kitchen island and shuts off the faucet. He encircles my waist with his arms, clasping his fingers at my low back and pulling me in close. Heat zips up the length of my spine. As angry as I am with him, I will never take this for granted—this proximity to the man that I fought for so fiercely for so many years. "You look nice this morning."

He leans down and kisses me, his two-day stubble scratchy on my face. I pull away, blinking up at him. He tilts his head as if to say, *What's the matter?*

I wriggle out of his grasp, turning back to the sink. "Maybe you should brush your teeth," I say, willing the contempt out of my voice. He can't suspect that I know anything.

He leaves half an hour later, claiming there are errands to run. He pecks my cheek, and I notice his breath is minty. The overpowering scent of Listerine lingers in his wake.

Why Jake won't just man up and tell me the truth about his plans, I do not know. He's the love of my life, but he's a coward. You both are.

At quarter of eleven, my car pulls to a stop in the parking lot of the public tennis courts, a ten-minute walk from Skipping Beach. Despite the humid heat, I wear leggings and a rain slicker—an old gray one from the back of the mudroom closet that I doubt Jake has ever laid eyes on— and my most oversize sunglasses. The sky is overcast, and I grab my bag and an umbrella from the back seat, just in case. I pull the hood up over my head. I can't be seen.

The beach isn't crowded; I can't decide if this is good or bad. On the one hand, I have a slimmer chance of running into someone I know; on the other, there's not much of a crowd to blend in to. I take a seat at one of the empty picnic tables behind the gazebo and stare at my phone, pretending to be engrossed with something on the screen.

I don't have to wait long. I spot you almost right away, Molly, in your frayed denim shorts and white top, little Stella skipping at your side. Your hair is pulled back, and there's a beach towel slung over your shoulder. You head toward the water. I follow your path, and there, at the end of it, is Jake. My husband. The man who just told me in our kitchen that he had errands to run all morning.

Still, I don't hate him. It's you I despise. *You* are the one who damaged him, who left him with questions that rot inside his heart, that cause him to doubt his place in the world without you. You were the lost look in his eyes on our wedding day. You are the pain that contours the edges of his face when he's asked what happened with Danner Lane, when someone wants to know why he gave up music when the band fell apart. You are the darkness that festers inside of him, and it isn't fair to either of us, Molly. Jake doesn't know any better, but I do. We need you gone. We deserve a life without you infiltrating the understructure of our marriage. We deserve happiness. We deserve peace.

I watch the three of you walk down the beach, using my binoculars as discreetly as I can. The ones my father sent us for "bird-watching" out in the suburbs. They were a wedding gift and had never been removed from the box until this morning.

I guess I'm lucky there's no one around the picnic tables to notice me—Sabrina the spy. I watch Jake and Stella go for a swim. I see the girl laugh with delight each time she springs herself off his shoulders and into the ocean. How dear.

It's eighty-five degrees and I'm getting sticky in my rain jacket, but the clouds are growing thick and dark, and a downpour seems inevitable—my choice of attire was smart. I watch Jake and Stella clamber out of the ocean, dodging the mellow waves as they make their way back onto the beach. I don't know what is said—too bad binoculars don't work for hearing—but it must be something emotional, because you and Jake have a moment. I see the way he takes hold of your hand, his gaze fixed to yours, grave and unmoving, like a glass-eyed doll. Really, Molly? In front of Stella? Bold.

And then the two of you pull apart, and you're walking back down the beach with Stella at a brisker pace than before. There's something helpless in Jake's body language as he watches you go, arms hanging limply at his sides, palms open. It's unclear if there was any kind of formal goodbye.

You're getting closer now; I put down the binoculars and turn back to my phone. Out of the corner of my eye, I see you load Stella into your Audi—buckling her into her car seat like the responsible parent you pride yourself on being—and drive away.

Jake—poor, pathetic Jake—stares after your car like a sad child. He doesn't move for several minutes. When he finally does, he spins around and looks toward the picnic tables, so quickly and directly I almost fall off the bench. But my body relaxes when I see that he's heading for the gazebo, that he hasn't noticed me sitting here at all.

Thunder rumbles through the sky. The rain starts slowly, one droplet at a time. The few families that are still gathered on the beach start to pack up their belongings. Whining children covered in sand are dragged toward SUVs. I watch Jake typing on his phone, and I know—I just *know*, Molly—that he's texting you.

I'm not going anywhere until Jake leaves the beach, but I have to change my post. I'm too close to the gazebo. Dangerously close.

The umbrella was a good idea. I open it, using the canopy to shield my face as I walk to the right of the gazebo and head down the beach. I need to be careful, so I don't stop until I've gone at least a quarter mile, well out of Jake's sight. Then I sit down on the sand and take the binoculars back out of my bag. It isn't easy to use them and keep the umbrella propped over my head at the same time—it's started raining more steadily now—but I make it work. I study Jake. He leans against the railing of the gazebo, staring pensively out over the water. I don't know if he just needs a moment alone to collect his thoughts, or if he's waiting for you. I am praying, begging, pleading with the universe that it isn't the latter.

But the universe is not on my side today, Molly. Because there is your car, pulling back into the parking lot. A knife stabs my gut. A sharp, unfurling pain.

You run down the beach toward the gazebo, toward Jake, your ponytail a flash of yellow dancing behind you. I watch the two of you collide; I watch him wipe the rain—or tears?—off your face.

There's a loud crack of lightning, and the rain falls faster, slapping the umbrella at a steady pace. Water gathers in the lenses of the binoculars, and it's harder to see, but there are Jake's hands, running down the length of your body, pushing you against the rail of the gazebo. I want to die, Molly. I really want to fucking die.

It's pouring now. The bottom half of my leggings are soaked, and I can't see a thing. I stand and jog haphazardly toward the gazebo, and that's when I see the two of you heading toward Jake's Jeep, ducking your heads as you run through the rain. You climb into the back seat, and the knife inside me twists, burrowing deeper. I stop in my tracks. I can't risk getting any closer.

Time stands still. I drop the umbrella and stare at the car through thick silver sheets of rain. I am drenched and sick and helpless. I don't know how much time passes—ten minutes, or maybe it's hours. Eventually, the back door of the Jeep flings open. I watch you climb out and run across the parking lot to your own vehicle. I watch your engine rev; I watch you speed away from Skipping Beach, your taillights flashing red in the blur of wet, gray darkness.

You won't get away with this, Molly. Not on my watch.

Chapter Twenty-nine

Molly

2015

It was September, but the summer heat hadn't cooled. Despite the AC unit that hummed in their bedroom window on Driggs, Molly still woke up sticky with sweat. Beside her, Jake stirred. She was almost afraid for the moment when he'd open his eyes. She never knew what kind of mood he'd wake up in.

"Morning, Moll." His voice was scratchy. He reached for her underneath the covers, wrapping one arm around her bare abdomen and pulling her in close.

"I'm too hot, Jake." Molly wriggled free from his grasp and climbed out of bed. "I'm going to put on some coffee."

In the kitchen, she filled the percolator with water and loaded the basket with ground beans. Jake wandered in a moment later, rubbing his eyes. He wore the boxers printed with little guitars that she'd found for him at J.Crew. He'd been running lately, and his chest was toned and golden brown from the late summer sun.

"Why are you in a bad mood?" He slid onto a counter stool.

"I'm not," Molly lied, mainly because she couldn't pinpoint the source of her residual annoyance toward Jake. She'd simply grown weary of his erratic, volatile existence. The hot and cold of it. Since *Precipice*'s release, the music world had made it clear that Danner Lane's sophomore effort was a flop. The scorching *Rolling Stone* review had been followed by similar sentiments from *Billboard*, *The Times*' Jon Caramanica, and countless others. Jake, who'd poured his heart and soul into writing the album, let every word of criticism convince him that he was a failure. And the backlash was Molly's to endure.

She placed a mug of coffee in front of Jake—black with sugar, the way he liked it. They both drank it hot, even in the warm weather.

"Thanks." He took a slow sip.

"My student loan payment is overdue," Molly said, eyes on her phone. "I just got an email."

"Oh. Shit."

"Can you transfer money into my account? Remember I asked you last week?"

"Right," he muttered, hesitant.

"What?" Molly glanced up, scanning his face.

"I just—" Jake sighed. "Money's kind of tight right now."

"For real? I thought you got a big advance for *Precipice*."

"The album isn't doing well, Molly. And most of our advance is already gone."

"Are you serious?"

"Between the insane cost of recording and studio time, marketing, all the new equipment we invested in earlier this year . . . well, yeah." Jake stood, walked over to the windows that looked out over Driggs. "Besides, I thought my paying your loans was only supposed to be temporary? I thought we agreed that once you got a book deal, you'd start making the payments again."

"You're the one who wanted to pay my loans, Jake."

"Right." A beat of silence passed.

"Well, we should talk about this," Molly broached. "Because, frankly, my advance is chump change next to yours, and I only got a third of it up front. I don't get the next third until my manuscript is accepted, and the rest when it publishes. If you want me to start making the payments again, I need to get a waitressing job or something."

"This isn't about what I *want*, Molly. I don't *want* the album to be failing." Jake pressed his forehead against the window, exasperated. "Can we not do this right now? It's early."

"Whatever." She picked up her mug, her fingers trembling in frustration, in fear. This wasn't about money—or was it? No, it was that Jake had always had her back, her best interests at heart. It had always felt like they were on the same team. But lately, the two of them seemed to be opposing factions.

"What are you doing today?" he asked.

"Editing this morning. My revision is due to Alexis by the end of next week."

"Right. Are you guys still on track to pub next year?"

"Huh?" Molly looked at him, irritated. "We were never going to pub next year. Early 2017 is what I said."

Jake rubbed his temples. "Sorry. That's what I meant."

"So yeah, I'm working. Then I have lunch with Hunter, then teaching tonight. Bhakti switched me to the eight thirty candlelit on Wednesdays."

"You see this Hunter guy a lot, huh?"

"Jake, I've been hanging out with Hunter for months. We're friends. You know this."

"Okay, but why are you seeing him in the middle of a weekday? Doesn't he work?"

"You know that he works. His office is being renovated this week, so they're all working from home. He can take a lunch break."

"I see." Jake paused, staring into his coffee. "Does he still have a girl-friend?"

"Yes," Molly said, somewhat begrudgingly. "Blair." She opened the fridge and grabbed a vanilla Chobani.

"Well, maybe we should all get dinner soon. What do you think?" Jake brushed a hand through his hair, still rumpled from sleep.

Molly considered this. She couldn't really imagine the four of them having a meal together; at the same time, part of her felt relief that Jake was expressing an interest in meeting Hunter. He was finally showing a smidgen of curiosity—maybe even envy—like a boyfriend with a pulse.

"Okay." She peeled the top off the yogurt and stuck it in the trash. "I'll talk to Hunter and see if they're free this weekend."

That Friday, Molly put on a white dress with thin straps and her favorite gold hoops, and she and Jake headed to St. Anselm. It was a restaurant they'd been wanting to try for a while, a casual-but-trendy steak house on Metropolitan. Blair and Hunter were already at a table when they walked through the door, and Molly waved across the room.

"They're early," Jake mumbled under his breath, which smelled like the beer he'd been drinking earlier. He was in an awful mood. Danner Lane had played Bowery Ballroom the night before, and it was one of their most poorly attended shows of the summer.

"No," Molly whispered, annoyed. "We're ten minutes late."

"Well, they're weirdly on time."

"Well, this dinner was *your* idea, Jake, so why don't you cool it with the snark?"

She forced herself to smile as they approached the table. Hunter stood and kissed her on the cheek, then shook Jake's hand.

"The famous Jake Danner."

"Once upon a time," Jake replied dryly.

"This is my girlfriend, Blair." Hunter drew his arm in her direction.

Blair stood, her sleek strawberry-blond hair tumbling past her shoulders. She wore a flamingo-pink tunic and tailored white pants, her cobalt-blue eyes gleaming. She was startlingly pretty—prettier in person than in the Facebook photos Molly had stalked.

"I've heard so much about you." Molly pulled her in for a hug, because suddenly that was the kind of girl she wanted to be in front of Blair—the overly friendly breed who hugged strangers upon meeting them. She could feel Jake staring at her, confused.

When the waiter slid up to their table, they all ordered martinis, except for Jake, who stuck with his regular whiskey on the rocks.

"I've been hearing about you for months, Hunter," Jake started, cradling his drink, a derisive edge to his voice. "It's good to finally meet the man my girlfriend spends so much time with." He was wearing the same wrinkled Zeppelin T-shirt he'd worn the day before. He looked disheveled but good, obnoxiously good, better than Molly felt he deserved to look in that moment.

"I hope that's not accusatory." Hunter smiled uncomfortably. "I'm surprised we haven't met sooner. Molly was my first friend in Williamsburg."

Blair examined her nails—shellacked, bright coral.

"Not accusatory at all," Jake said with a sardonic grin that sent a bolt of anger through Molly's chest. She knew Jake wasn't legitimately jealous, but he was acting like a jealous asshole anyway, simply because he could. Because he was bitter with the world and it was something to do.

"My friend Louise was at your San Francisco show in July," Blair offered. "She loves the new album."

"Louise may be the only one, I'm afraid." Jake rubbed his jawline, which was scruffy. He hadn't bothered to shave.

"I wouldn't say that," Hunter tried warmly. "'Molly's Song' is a hit, obviously, but I also like 'Gut Feeling' and 'Lost in Bushwick.'"

"You're too kind." Jake knocked back another sip of whiskey. Molly wanted to grab the drink and throw it in his face.

"Jake is just coming off a tough show at Bowery Ballroom last night."

Molly touched his arm. She could feel her cheeks burning with embarrassment. Jake was normally so warm with people he'd just met, especially her friends. Things were tense between the two of them—yes—but this cold, passive character sitting next to her was someone she didn't recognize.

By the time the waitress came back to take their order, Jake's whiskey was empty, and he ordered another. The rest of them had barely made dents in their martinis.

"It can't be easy, your second album not being as well received as your first," Hunter said, loosening his tie. "All that pressure. But hey, there's always a third album, right?"

Molly smiled at him, grateful for his optimism, his kindness. Underneath the table, she pressed her heel down on the toe of Jake's foot, daring him to produce a snarky response.

"Right," he answered, smiling weakly. "So Moll says you're in sports marketing?"

Hunter nodded, proceeding to explain his job at Octagon.

Molly could tell Jake was bored and uninterested—he always said he'd rather work at a gas station than for a corporate conglomerate—but he nodded along politely, and she was thankful for that.

From there, Molly took the opening to ask Blair about her career, which she already knew some about from Hunter. She listened to Blair describe her job at the interior design firm.

"I love it. It's my calling," Blair hummed, finishing a bite of kale salad. Molly could see the bones of her sinewy clavicle protruding underneath the tunic and thought that she probably ate salad for every meal. "I just love it. I can't wait to decorate our place." Blair's eyes flickered to Hunter, and she beamed, the apples of her cheeks rosy.

Molly's stomach seesawed. She felt her jaw drop unwittingly. "Your place?" She studied Hunter.

"That's right," Blair crowed. "Hunter's moving in with me in the West Village once his lease is up in the winter. Brooklyn isn't really his vibe."

"Oh. Wow." Molly kept her eyes on Hunter, who stared at his steak.

"I know it'll only have been . . ." Blair glanced up at the ceiling, calculating. "Nine months by then. But when you know, you know."

"Nine months? Please." Jake let out a strange, feigned chuckle that Molly had never heard before. She had almost forgotten he was there. "I got this one to shack up with me after five." He leaned over and gave

Molly a playful kiss on the cheek. She could smell the booze, thick and pungent on his breath.

"Six," Molly countered.

Jake shrugged. "Anyway, cheers to you two. Being roommates is the best." He raised his empty glass, signaling to the waitress for another.

"Molly, sorry, I didn't even ask you about *your* job," Blair said peppily, her meticulously plucked eyebrows jumping. "Hunter says you're a writer and that you have a *book deal.* That's so amazing."

Molly gave an appreciative smile, trying not to think about the fact that Jake was on his third drink. "Thank you. I've been working on this novel for a while—since grad school—and yeah, it's just a dream come true to have sold it, really."

"And when will it be available?" Blair chirruped.

"Probably not for another year and a half, give or take. I'm in the middle of a heavy revision with my editor now. She's supposed to set the pub date soon."

"How's the revision going, by the way?" Jake turned to her, sipping his whiskey, and Molly was so stunned she couldn't speak. A wave of debilitating humiliation shrouded her.

Jake hadn't had the consideration to check in with her about the revision in weeks, and *now* he was asking? In front of Blair and Hunter? Was he completely unaware that he was making their relationship look like a trivial, immature joke? Molly inhaled sharply. She needed another martini. She needed this dinner to end.

"It's fine," she said, forcing the anger down, bottling it for later. "Alexis is easy to work with." She glanced at Blair and Hunter. "Alexis is my editor. But her notes were pretty extensive, so it's taking longer than I expected. Publishing is a deceivingly drawn-out process."

Hunter's warm eyes rested on hers, and Molly had the clear-cut feeling that he was the only person at the table who understood her. The thought depressed her more than she could stand. She was so mad at Jake she couldn't bring herself to look at him for the remainder of the dinner, and by the time they left St. Anselm, she was seething, on the brink of tears. She walked half a block ahead of him the whole way home.

"What the fuck is the matter with you?" she spat the second they were in the apartment, which felt hotter and more stifling than it had two hours earlier.

"What?" Jake stared at her, his gaze unfocused. Molly was used to this foggy look in his eyes. Despite the fact that he'd been working out to blow off steam, he'd also been drinking like a fish all summer. Drinking like his father, she wanted to tell him.

Molly burst into sudden, intractable tears. She didn't even know how to talk to Jake anymore. She was afraid she didn't know the person he'd become. Or perhaps this was who he'd been all along, and she'd simply been too blinded by the feeling of being "chosen" to see it. Regardless, she had no idea what had happened to them or was in the process of happening to them. Whatever was going on felt completely out of her control.

Jake opened the fridge and pulled out a longneck. He cracked off the cap and took a long sip.

"You really need another fucking drink, Jake?"

"Jesus, Molly." He slammed the beer down on the counter, so hard foam spit out the top and spilled down the sides. "It's been a *long* fucking summer."

"You know what?" Molly swiped the tears from her cheeks. "Just because *you're* having a shitty stretch doesn't mean you can act like a total dick in front of other people. You *humiliated* me tonight. In so many ways I can't even list them all. And you don't even give a shit that I'm upset."

"Oh, I'm sorry, Molly. I'm sorry I humiliated you in front of your boyfriend Hunter."

"Why are you suddenly pretending to be jealous of Hunter? I know you're not *actually*—you don't give a shit that I spend time with him. You don't *actually notice* a single thing that I do!" Molly was so angry, she was shaking. She steadied her hands on the counter.

"Did you ever think that maybe I do notice? That maybe I am jealous you've gotten so close with him and that you *clearly* care a whole fucking lot what he thinks about you?"

"Hunter is my friend, Jake. Don't make this about him. This is about us. This is about *you* acting like a bitter, entitled ass who doesn't care about anyone but himself."

"You think I don't care about you?" Jake's eyes narrowed, blazing blue. "How can you even imply that?"

"I think you used to care about me. Now, I'm not so sure. Now it seems like all you care about is the band. And if things aren't right with the band, things aren't right anywhere else, and *certainly* not with us.

Tonight was the first time in weeks you've asked me how editing is going and only because Blair brought it up."

Jake was silent for several moments, staring down the neck of his beer bottle. Finally, his gaze lifted, landing on hers. "I'm sorry." He sounded sincere for the first time all night. "I feel like I'm under so much pressure—it drives me mad. I love Danner Lane so much that sometimes I feel like I'm going out of my mind. Sam and Hale, they're my family. And this is our shot, and if we screw it up, if I lose them . . . I'll lose my whole foundation, the only solid thing I come from. But, Moll, what I'm trying to say is that as much as I love the band, I love you even more. Please, please know this. Even if I've been a shit lately. You're my heart." Tears pooled in the corners of his eyes, his bottom lip quivered. Molly saw it then, lucidly. How broken he was. Jake was broken and maybe he always had been, and it didn't have anything to do with her.

His phone rang then, buzzing in the back pocket of his jeans. He pulled it out, looked at the screen. "It's Sam. I should—"

"It's fine. Take it."

Molly filled a glass with tap water and brought it to the bedroom. She changed into boxers and an NYU T-shirt, and while she brushed her teeth and washed her face, she thought back to Danner Lane's cover of "Mona Lisas and Mad Hatters," the first night she ever saw Jake. It was such a beautiful, beautiful cover. Why didn't they play it anymore?

She popped in headphones and found the song on Spotify, nestling against the pillows.

And now I know
Spanish Harlem are not just pretty words to say

Molly played the track over and over again. She saw Jake's face with vivid clarity at the Broken Mule, the way he'd found her eyes in the crowd and held on to them through the entire show. There had been something so genuine in his expression, something that filled her heart with hope that night and had ever since. Maybe it was the hope of them that had always been enough, that had allowed them to come this far.

She listened to the song until her pillow was damp with tears, until Jake came into the room and pulled the headphones out of her ears and kissed her deeply. It was a kiss that almost made her forget they'd been fighting.

"What did Sam say?" she whispered in the dark.

"There's good news and bad news. Which do you want first?"

"I don't care, Jake. Just tell me."

He exhaled, sinking down onto the bed. "Jerry talked to Ron. *Precipice* is having more success in Europe, so they're extending our European tour. That's the good news. But . . . it's long. We'll be on the road for a while. A few months, maybe. And it could be more time overseas; if the tour goes well, they might have us play in a few of the top festivals over there this summer. We might even get to headline one."

"Jesus. That's huge, but . . . I'm guessing that's also the bad news."

"It's a crazy long time to be away, I know."

"When do you leave?"

Jake shook his head. "Not sure yet. They need to confirm dates. But it's looking like later this fall. Maybe November."

"Wow. That's kind of soon." Molly was suddenly bone weary—from dinner, from another blowout fight with Jake, from the constant strain on their relationship that didn't seem to be going away. Her eyelids drooped, and all she wanted was to close them.

"I know." Jake smoothed a lock of hair off her face, which was sticky with dried tears. "I'm gonna see if they'll fly you over for a bit. It's the tour manager I need to check with, not Dixon. But I really will ask this time. I promise."

"We'll figure it out," she mumbled sleepily.

"Moll?"

"Mm?"

"I'm sorry I was a jerk tonight. I really do love you."

"I know."

"Say you love me, too."

"I do love you, Jake. You know that." But for the first time since she'd made the decision to forgive him last spring, she let herself wonder: What if their love wasn't enough?

Chapter Thirty
Molly

"I can't believe any of this." Everly cups her hands to her face, staring at Molly in disbelief.

"I know." Molly nods. She's just finished telling them about what happened with Jake at Skipping Beach. "I'm going to hell."

"But, like . . . it's *Jake*." Nina stirs a packet of turbinado sugar into her latte.

The three of them are having coffee at Gwen's after Molly sent an urgent group text calling for an emergency meeting. Nina and Everly offered to drive out to Flynn Cove since they can both get away with being "remote" on Fridays. Plus, it's August. Half their colleagues are on vacation.

"Seriously, Molly." Nina eyes her. "How were you supposed to *not* kiss Jake?"

"Well, I'm *married,* for starters." Molly takes her nerves out on her napkin, which is shredded to bits.

"Yeah, and I'm engaged, and I love the shit out of Michael, but if Cash came running back into my life and told me he'd never stopped loving me and came on to me, well . . ." Nina sighs dramatically. "I'd be fucked."

Nina's empathy is one of the qualities Molly loves most in her. Everly isn't judgmental in the slightest, but she doesn't have a Jake or a Cash—Sage was her first love. Nina is the only person who actually understands the intensity—the *impossibility*—of Molly's situation.

"Do you still think about Cash?"

"Of course. Not as much as I used to, but I still think about what would've happened if he hadn't taken that job in LA. If all those miles hadn't pushed us apart. But then I think about Michael and how if *he'd* had to take a job in LA, we would've made it work, because he's Michael.

Because he doesn't have communication issues and he's the person I'm meant to be with. Doesn't mean I don't still have a weak spot for Cash. It's a chemical thing, really."

"Totally chemical." Molly sighs. "It's like I lose control of my body when Jake is around."

"I think it's normal."

"Is it, though? Hunter's baby could be in my uterus as we speak."

Everly gives Molly a hopeful smile, her slate-blue eyes filling with tenderness. "I have a good feeling about this time."

"Me, too," Nina concurs. "You find out next week?"

"Monday." Molly picks at her muffin. She has no appetite. "Ugh, I need to talk to Hunter about what happened. My guilt is making me sick."

"You do." Everly nods. "But wait until you get the pregnancy results back. You don't need the added stress."

"*Agreed.*" Nina holds up a crumbling piece of her blueberry scone. "Okay, side note, but please tell me how this pastry cost eight dollars? It's not even warm."

Molly rolls her eyes. "That's Flynn Cove for you." She glances around the café's refined interior—pale wood tables, shiny walnut floors, tasteful art on the bright white walls. A Maggie Rogers song plays through the built-in speakers, the sound quality pristine. Molly lowers her voice. "Couldn't you tell walking in here that you were about to get ripped off?"

"Seriously." Everly—ever the health nut—rakes a plastic fork through her quinoa salad. "Last time I pay fifteen bucks for a tiny container of grains."

Molly raises an eyebrow. "Please, Ev. Dumbo is the capital of over-priced salads."

"Yeah, and they actually taste good!"

"Ugh, you guys." Molly laughs, despite herself. "Thanks for coming all the way out here. You're saints."

"You act like we made some epic journey." Nina crosses her legs.

"Yeah, Flynn Cove is only an hour drive, Moll. That's basically as long as it takes me to get to Nina's, now that she and Michael live on the *Upper East Side.*" Everly makes a face, and Molly laughs again.

"Don't knock it, Ev. There's a gay bar around the corner from our apartment."

Everly rolls her eyes. "I would *love* to see the crowd that place draws. The closeted homosexuals of Park Avenue."

Nina giggles, conceding. "You're right. I totally miss Brooklyn."

"Not as much as *I* miss Brooklyn." Molly sighs wistfully. Over Everly's shoulder, she spots Betsy Worthington ordering at the counter. Betsy wears tennis whites, her limbs deeply tanned, her chestnut ponytail swinging. They make eye contact, and Molly gives a small wave. Betsy frowns, pretends not to see her, then turns back to the register.

"What's up her butt?" Nina whispers, observing the interaction.

Molly waits till Betsy retrieves her iced coffee and is headed toward the exit.

"That woman hasn't spoken to me since we showed up to the country club fireworks wearing the same dress."

Everly laughs so loud the barista looks over. "Sorry," she says, tucking a blond lock behind her ear. "I was momentarily transported back to seventh grade."

"God." An incredulous expression crosses Nina's face. "No wonder you want to stay friends with Jake's wife. The women in this town seem *brutal.* Sabrina actually sounds normal."

"Yeah, Sabrina really is so great." But all of a sudden, it hits Molly: she hasn't seen or heard from Sabrina in nearly ten days. They haven't spoken since before she met up with Jake at Skipping Beach. Her stomach flips. How is that possible?

Nina studies her. "You okay?"

"I just—hang on." Molly digs her phone out of her purse, scrolls through her messages. Her last text to Sabrina is outgoing, sent Sunday morning. Dinner at Dune next week? I'm craving their calamari.

Molly remembers sending the text. It was a few hours before her walk with Jake, and she'd been harboring guilt over the fact that she hadn't said anything to Sabrina about their plans. She didn't want to make a big *deal* of it. Molly had hoped they could have dinner in the next few days so that she could casually mention how she and Jake had caught up in person, emphasize how platonic it had been.

But, of course, it hadn't been platonic at all, and in the days that followed, Molly had been too absorbed in her own emotional shitstorm—Jake, Hunter, the embryo that may or may not have implanted inside her—to remember that Sabrina had never answered her text.

"That's weird." Molly placed her phone down on the table, glancing from Nina to Everly. "I just realized I haven't heard from Sabrina in a week and a half—which isn't like her. She comes to at least one of my weekly classes at Yoga Tree. And she didn't reply to my last text."

Nina tilts her head in thought. "When's the last you heard from her?"

"The day before the embryo transfer, she wished me good luck. So early last week."

"Well, don't jump to any conclusions. It doesn't mean she knows about you and Jake. There's no way he would've told her what happened."

"Agreed." Everly sips her matcha. "People just get busy in the summer, you know? Follow up with her."

"I guess." Molly shrugs. "God, living in this town has made me so self-conscious. I should really be worrying less about Sabrina and more about Hunter. And Stella. And the fact that I've fucked up my marriage."

"Molly." Nina squeezes her forearm. "Take a deep breath. Just slow it down, okay?"

Molly glances at her phone. "Shoot, it's eleven thirty. I gotta go." She groans. She wants nothing more than to stay in the comforting cocoon of her closest friends, but she has to be at Yoga Tree to teach the noon Vinyasa flow.

The three of them hug goodbye on the sidewalk outside Gwen's.

Nina's eyes brighten. "Maybe Sabrina will show up at your class?"

"I'm not counting on it." Molly sighs.

"*Don't* panic," Ev says. "It's great you're still teaching so much, by the way."

Molly gives a strained smile, thinking suddenly of Bella's voicemail, the one she still hasn't deleted from her phone. Molly has the sharp urge to mention this to her friends—she never told them Bella tried to get in touch; she never told anyone—but Nina is already opening the door to Everly's Lexus. Their time is up.

"We'll see you in two weeks," Ev calls with a wave.

Nina gives a little shimmy. "Can't wait to party with the six-year-olds!"

Fifteen minutes later, Molly sits behind the front desk at Yoga Tree, signing students in to class. After her heart-to-heart with Nina and Everly, she feels calmer, her confidence partially restored. It's amazing, the healing powers of best friends. And she knows they're right about Sabrina. People are busy, people forget to respond to texts all the time—Molly is overreacting.

Before she goes into the studio, where her students wait in child's pose, Molly takes out her phone.

She has one new text—Jake. I can't stop thinking about you . . .

Fuck. Molly breathes slowly, tries to ignore the heavy, buzzy feeling in her body. The electricity in her stomach, like she's a magnet being pulled.

She deletes his text. Then, she crafts a new message to Sabrina.

Hi, stranger! Missed you in class this week. How are you? Want to walk this weekend? Or grab lunch? Let me know!

Molly tries not to cringe at her own desperation, her hypocrisy. She hits Send before she has the chance to change her mind.

Chapter Thirty-one
Sabrina

You've been texting me, Molly. You kissed my husband on the beach—you probably fucked him in his car—and now you're texting me as if everything is normal. You'd like to know if I want to go on a walk with you. A fucking *stroll*. Well, the answer is no—I don't want to go on a walk with you, and I don't want to grab lunch. What I want is to *destroy* you.

And if you don't believe I have the power to do just that, listen to this. Listen to what happened the last time I saw your old pal Liz Esposito.

Throughout the remainder of my twenties in New York, Liz and I maintained a casual friendship. We were mainly just gym buddies, but every now and then—usually after one of Erin's Pilates classes—we went out for drinks and a bite.

Liz and I had a lot in common, actually, and I genuinely enjoyed her company. For starters, we both came from moneyed families and from parents who possessed little to no interest in monitoring their children. In turn, we'd adopted a similarly unfettered approach to many aspects of our lives.

I tried not to ask Liz about you and Jake *too* often, if I could help it. But she was under the impression that I was a Danner Lane fangirl, and so it was a subject I could afford to bring up semi-regularly during our get-togethers, though she never offered many specific updates.

"Jake's just so self-involved," she'd sometimes mutter in response to my questions, never really elaborating when I pressed her for the reason.

As the months passed, Jake's Instagram revealed that the two of you were fully back together. *Epic summer with the love of my life,* he captioned a September 2014 selfie of your sun-kissed faces on an unspecified beach. Meanwhile, I threw myself into work. I got promoted again—this time to senior merchandise planner—a role in which I managed a group of twenty. I was excellent at my job, Molly—I don't like to fail, and I'd gone the extra mile at Marc Jacobs since the moment I started there. My boss, a fortysomething divorcée named Portia, considered me her right-hand woman. She'd brought me to Paris and Milan for Fashion Week every year I'd been at the company, while many of my colleagues had never gotten to go. During my darkest days, the ones when I pined for Jake so badly I thought I might split in two, my career was the one place where I felt in control.

Debbie suggested I find a hobby, which made me laugh out loud. Did she expect me to take up knitting? Pottery? Do I seem like the kind of woman who has *hobbies,* Molly?

Elena pestered me about dating; she said I had to stop wallowing and get back out there. To prove her wrong, I let a guy buy me dinner once every couple of months. But none of them excited me—none of them were Jake—and I always left these bland, tedious dates freshly reminded of the person who was no longer mine.

But then, one day in 2016, everything changed. It was late March, the city still chilly but alive with the promise of spring—fat red buds sprouting on the branches of maple trees, the friendly sight of daffodils. Liz and I were splitting a bottle of wine after a particularly challenging Pilates session with Erin.

"Thank God Lent ended last weekend," she said, ordering an over-priced bottle of Sancerre. "I gave up booze this year."

"Oh, wow." I drummed my fingers on the stained wood surface of the table, excited for the wine. "Are you religious?"

"Meh. My grandmother is super Catholic. She always asks what I'm giving up for Lent, and I feel guilty lying. She's, like, ninety-three, but calls me more than either of my parents." The waitress poured us two large glasses and placed the bottle in the cooler on our table. Liz snatched hers up. "But I *really* need this drink, after the week I've had."

"Work issues?" I pinched the stem of my glass and took a generous sip.

"Nah. Work is fine." She pursed her lips as if considering something important. She seemed in a chattier mood than usual. "*You'll* find this interesting, actually, seeing how obsessed you are with Jake Danner."

My ears perked up. "I'm not *obsessed* with Jake Danner," I said, perhaps too defensively.

"Then why are you constantly asking about him and my friend

Molly?" The corners of Liz's mouth twitched—a small, knowing smile. She flicked her wrist. "Anyway, I have a juicy piece of gossip that I'm not even supposed to know, but it's too outrageous not to share with *some-one*. So it's your lucky day."

I took another sip of wine, every cell in my body brimming with anticipation.

Liz dug her elbows into the table, leaning forward. "So a few months ago—I guess it was New Year's Day, actually—Molly showed up at my apartment. She seemed upset, she'd been fighting with Jake, and she wanted to talk. But we got into this really awkward argument—she laid into me about my relationship with Zander and was just acting totally bizarre—and then she stormed out. And we haven't talked since."

"Really? That's weird."

"Right? So anyway, I kept asking our other friends what the hell was going on with Molly—like, was she even okay, I legit hadn't heard from her at all—and no one would give me a straight answer. And then *finally,* two nights ago, my friend Everly came over for dinner, and we were drinking, and I wrangled it out of her." Liz drew in a breath. "Turns out, Molly is *pregnant.*"

I nearly spat out the Sancerre. "Oh my god."

"No, Caitlin, it gets even more insane. Are you ready for this?" Liz rested her hands on the table, her dark eyes growing wide. "Jake isn't the father."

The room froze. My mind spun rapidly, a tornado gathering speed. It took me several seconds to process her words, several more to speak. *"What?"*

"That's right." Liz tipped the rest of the wine in her glass down her throat. "She and Jake broke up, apparently—I had no idea. I guess she dumped him when he got back from his big tour in Europe a few weeks ago. He'd been gone for months. And this other guy, the dude who knocked her up? Hunter something. Molly is *with him now.*"

"Holy shit. So wait—she was cheating on Jake?"

"Yup." Liz plucked the bottle of Sancerre from the wine cooler and refilled our glasses. A little sloshed over the rim of hers, dribbling down the outside of the bowl. "All those months Jake was away, and she never even told him there was someone else."

"Oh my god. So Jake doesn't even know about this other guy?"

"I doubt it." Liz cocked her head in thought. "From what I gather,

Molly doesn't plan on telling him. He *definitely* doesn't know she got pregnant. Everly swore me to secrecy, so even though part of me would love to throw Molly under the bus, I can't betray Ev. Plus, it's not like I actually want to get in the middle of *that* drama. I'm just pissed at Molly for being so judgmental about *my* relationship one minute, and then the next, being so sketchy and MIA and not even telling me what was going on with hers." A wounded expression darkened Liz's face, and I could tell that despite her tipsy bravado, she was genuinely hurting.

"I'm sorry. I'd be pissed, too." I nodded empathetically. "What was your fight about? Something to do with Zander, you said?"

Liz waved her hand. "It's not worth getting into the details." She stared past my shoulder, her eyes glazed over. "She's just changed, you know? Molly used to be so easygoing and really secure in herself. She's become kind of a hypocrite, honestly. She was so quick to judge my life, my relationship, even though her own has been *way* more fucked up."

"What do you mean?" I probed, trying to streamline the endless questions whirling around inside my head. "How is she a hypocrite?"

Liz's eyes narrowed. She studied me skeptically, and I knew I'd crossed a line. I'd made the mistake of sounding more interested in Molly than I was in her.

Liz said nothing for a moment, ripping the edge of her cocktail napkin. When she spoke, something in her voice had shifted. The gossipy air between us had turned. "I'm tipsy. I haven't eaten since lunch. I need to go pick up some dinner."

"Why don't we order food here?" I loathed myself for sounding so desperate.

Liz shook her head. "I told Zander I'd eat at home with him. Sorry." She stood, poking her arms into her Moncler jacket—the same silver puffer she'd worn the first day I laid eyes on her. "You should finish the wine, or bring the bottle home. You have Venmo? Charge me for half."

"Don't worry about it." I bit my bottom lip, overcome with an anxious, heavy feeling of helplessness. I couldn't afford to scare Liz off. Not now. Not with all that was still at stake. "Erin's class next week?"

"I'm traveling for work, actually." Liz slung her leather tote bag over her shoulder. "But I'll see you around the gym at some point. And, Caitlin? Don't mention what I just told you to anyone. Seriously."

"Of course! I mean, I would never." I swallowed the lump in my throat, filled with both annoyance and awe as I watched her leave the restaurant. Liz was someone who did as she pleased without weighing the consequences; she didn't worry about the implications of being brusque or dismissive. She was kind of a bitch, and she knew it and was fine with it. I admired that quality in her, Molly. I found it oddly inspiring. It's funny to think that the two of you were once such close friends. You really have nothing in common at all.

Over the next several months, whenever I ran into Liz at the gym, I made a point of not mentioning you or Jake. I didn't want to look like a weirdo. But what I didn't know—and what I desperately needed to find out—was whether or not you'd kept the baby. After all, the timeline as Liz had explained it was rather vague. It was unclear how far along you were in your pregnancy when Liz had gotten wind of the news. Perhaps you were only in your first trimester then; it was possible that you'd still been weighing your options.

I was all too familiar with the excruciating disappointment of believing you and Jake had split, only to discover you were back together and more in love than ever. If you *hadn't* gone through with the pregnancy, perhaps you'd decided to ditch this Hunter character and were already back in Jake's arms. Or perhaps you and Jake were really done, this time for good.

But Jake's Instagram revealed nothing. Except for concert and tour photos, he'd barely been updating it. He hadn't posted a photo of you since December (a black-and-white shot of you laughing at the camera, captioned: *Every time I sing #MollysSong, I sing it for her.* Gross, Jake).

Finally, one evening in June, post Pilates, when I could no longer stand the not knowing, I asked Liz if she wanted to grab a drink.

"It's been a while," I said casually as we gathered our gym bags and laced up our sneakers on the bench outside the studio. "And I'm dying for one of those skinny margs from El Toro."

One side of Liz's mouth curled. "Actually, same. And it's nice out. They have a sweet terrace."

I waited until we were on our second round of margaritas to bring up the subject that had been stuck in the center of my mind for months.

"By the way, what ever happened with your friend? The one who got pregnant?" I spoke tentatively, praying Liz would fail to detect the apprehension in my voice.

She laughed softly, sliding her finger along the rim of her glass to brush off the salt. "I'm surprised it took you so long to ask. If you're so in love with Jake Danner, maybe you should just go for it."

A layer of fizz prickled my skin, a warm current rising underneath. "So they're still broken up?"

"Apparently." Liz shrugged, sipping her drink.

"And she's still pregnant? They're definitely not together? Because you said that last time, and they hadn't actually broken up for good." These were the questions that had been circling for weeks in my mind, but I hadn't meant to actually say them out loud. My hand flew to my mouth.

A sour expression morphed Liz's face. "What do you mean 'last time'?" She scrunched her nose, peering at me suspiciously.

"Never mind." I shook my head, mortified, staring into my lap.

"Honestly, Caitlin, it's kind of creepy how obsessed you are with this whole situation." She emitted a dismissive sound—half chuckle, half scowl. I could feel her watching me. "I have to use the bathroom," she said. "If the waitress comes by, grab the check. I have to meet a friend downtown."

Liz grabbed her purse and disappeared inside the restaurant, and that's when I noticed she'd left her phone facedown on the table. I hesitated, weighing my options. I still had so many questions, and Liz was clearly done giving me answers. The way she'd just looked at me made me feel like a leper, a pariah, Tom Ripley in the eyes of Dickie Greenleaf. I knew I'd be wise to never broach the subject of you and Jake in her presence again. Looking through Liz's phone was a risk, but it might be my only chance to learn the truth.

Time was ticking. Before I could change my mind, I snatched the phone. I'd sat beside Liz at enough post-Pilates drinks to have had the chance to watch her enter her passcode—four sevens in a row—which thankfully she hadn't changed.

I quickly clicked the green messages icon, scrolling down, but there was nothing from you on Liz's phone. I stopped when I saw the name Everly—the friend who'd let it slip to Liz that you were pregnant. Their latest text exchange was from ten days earlier.

Everly: Moll is engaged, can't you just be supportive? Hunter is a really good guy. Nina is planning a drinks thing at the Spaniard later this month—just come. She's sending you the invite.
Liz: I'll think about it.

My breath slipped out of my throat. I exited the text exchange and put the phone back on the table, facedown the way I'd found it, my heart thrashing inside my chest.

You were engaged, Molly. You were engaged to the new guy, Hunter, the man with whom you'd cheated on Jake. Already? How was it possible?

Liz came back from the bathroom, sliding into the chair across from mine. She picked up her phone, checked the screen, and tossed it into her bag. "Did you ask for the check?"

"Huh?"

"Caitlin?" Liz raised a dark, thin eyebrow. "What's wrong? You look like you've seen a ghost."

"Oh." I blinked. "No, I . . . I think I just drank this last marg too quickly. Um, no, the waitress hasn't come by yet. If you need to go, that's fine. I've got it."

"Well, thanks." Liz stood, studying me strangely. I suddenly had the distinct feeling I would never see her again. "Get home safe."

But after she left, I ordered a third margarita. I needed to be drunk enough to do what I did next.

I needed to *know*, Molly. I needed to see it with my own eyes. Because the fact that you'd gotten engaged to a man you'd only been with for a few short months, after years with Jake—this narrative made me assume that you'd kept the baby. That you and Hunter had made the decision to tie the knot and raise your child as a real family.

But I'd made the mistake of *assuming* things about you before. There was only one way to be 100 percent certain.

I'd long since memorized your Bhakti Yoga schedule. You taught the 8:30 candlelit flow on Wednesday evenings, which gave me half an hour to get to Williamsburg. The timing was perfect. Three skinny margs deep, it felt especially meant to be. I left cash on the table and ordered an Uber.

I wasn't actually going to take the class. What if, somehow, via Jake, you knew what I looked like? What if you recognized me? It was too risky. Instead, I lingered on the sidewalk outside the studio, pretending to look at my phone while slyly glancing through the glass windows at the front desk, where you sat beside a dish of burning incense, checking students in.

I remember how you looked exactly, because how could I ever forget? Your wheat-blond hair pulled up into a topknot, a few loose strands sprinkling the back of your neck. Your wide, genuine smile as you handed students rolled-up yoga mats, swiped their credit cards. Your body, of course, is what I remember most. The cantaloupe-size bump protruding from your midsection, stretching the fabric of your white racer-back top. A baby growing inside of you. Visible proof of your infidelity.

A rail-thin guy sporting a man bun and a beaded necklace paused in the entryway to Bhakti. He grinned at me, holding the door open. "Coming in for Molly's eight thirty?"

I was in such a state of shock from seeing you in the flesh again—after years of you existing only in my mind—that several moments passed before I realized his question had been directed at me.

My breath was shallow, choppy. I shook my head. The hippie man shrugged and walked inside.

I roamed around Williamsburg aimlessly for the next hour, maybe longer. The June air was warm and soft, conducive to wandering, and I don't know how much time went by before I finally hailed a cab to take me home.

I didn't sleep that night. My thoughts spiraled—electric, hopeful, relieved. You were very much still pregnant. You were with Hunter and you were marrying him and you were having his baby. I couldn't imagine why you would've willingly deceived a man as beautiful and extraordinary as Jake, but it didn't matter.

And as I figured out how to reappear in Jake's life, I kept the memory of you at Bhakti Yoga—the sight of your cantaloupe belly—stashed in the back of my mind. A reminder that if I ever needed proof of your deception, it would always exist, and I'd never have to look very far.

Proof that lived, that breathed. Your child with Hunter.

Chapter Thirty-two
Molly

2015

Molly woke, a pang of panic striking her chest. The memory of the night before came violently rushing back, and for a fleeting moment, she thought it couldn't possibly be more than a terrifying dream. But then the edges of the memory began to reappear, giving it weight, substance, and no—it wasn't a dream. This was real. Too real.

Cold sweat dampened Molly's brow, at the same time her skull felt cracked open, like her brain was being stabbed by little knives. That was the price you paid for doing half a dozen shots of Fireball from an ice luge. *Ugh,* the ice luge. Nina and Cash's housewarming party at their new apartment. Molly recalled only snippets of the evening: drinking vodka sodas with Nina, Ev, and Liz in the kitchen before the other guests arrived; Cash clearing the floor so he could do the worm to a Kanye song; her intense conversation with Nina in the bathroom. Had they all gone out to a bar afterward? She had no recollection. But the end of the night—that she remembered clearly. For better or for worse.

God, she hadn't been that drunk in a *long* time. Which only made her guilt worse. She needed to call Jake, immediately. From bed, Molly flung her arm toward her nightstand, to the spot where her phone was normally plugged in to charge overnight. *Phew.* It was there. In the haze of her drunkenness, at least she'd kept track of her phone.

On the screen were several missed calls and texts. Most of them from Nina and Everly, asking where she'd gone, rows of question marks. And there was a message from Hunter. 3:52 a.m. Molly's stomach churned.

Hey, you were clearly wasted tonight. Call me in the morning, ok?? I want to make sure you're all right.

Fuck. She really had to get in touch with Jake. He was in Zurich until Tuesday, she was pretty sure—it was hard to keep track of his tour stops, and it had been a few days since they'd spoken. What time was it in Zurich? Six hours ahead, she was almost positive.

Molly tried him, but the call went straight to voicemail. Shit. She needed to talk to him, and not just about last night. She was supposed to be flying to Germany on Wednesday, but Jake still hadn't sent her the flight information. Molly was spending two weeks in Europe, traveling with Jake and the band from Munich to Amsterdam to Brussels and then finally to Paris, where they would spend Christmas and New Year's. Molly couldn't wait. She hated to miss Christmas at home with her mom and Andrew, but when Danner Lane's tour manager had offered to book her flights for this segment of the tour, Molly had been unable to say no. Christmas in *Paris* with Jake—what could be more romantic? She missed him desperately; plus, she'd never been to Europe. She'd never even been out of the country.

Molly rolled out of bed, trudging to the kitchen for water. Her mouth felt dry and rough, like it was made of sand, and she chugged two glasses of water at the sink. Her phone chimed on the counter, and she lunged for it, praying it was Jake. But Hunter's name appeared on the screen.

Are you all right? Just let me know you got home ok . . . worried.

Molly chewed her bottom lip, nerves coiling in her stomach. She typed out a response.

I'm fine, just hungover. I'm sorry about last night, hoping we can just forget it? I was way too drunk . . .

Hunter's reply arrived a few minutes later.

Of course, consider it forgotten. But if you need to talk, I'm here.

Molly groaned. She refilled her water glass, then closed all the curtains so the living room was a dark cave. She curled into a ball on the couch and called Jake again, a seed of panic unfurling in her gut, but he didn't answer. She stared at her phone, debated trying Nina next. Molly knew she should tell *someone* about last night. Her thumb hovered above the dial key for several moments before she changed her mind, tossing her phone to the other end of the couch. She just needed to be alone with her thoughts, at least for now.

Molly closed her eyes, the memory of the end of the night slamming her again. The air in the room hummed; even though her pounding head was a painful reminder that she was awake, she felt as if she were dreaming.

"Fuck," she said out loud to no one. "Fuck fuck fuck fuck fuck."

She must've drifted back to sleep, because when she woke to the sound of her ringtone, it felt much later. Only a smidgen of daylight peeked through the green flowered curtains.

Molly pounced for her phone, a fresh wave of disappointment crushing her when she saw that it wasn't Jake.

"Hey, Neens." Her voice was croaky.

"*Molly.* Jesus Christ. Did you see my texts? What happened to you last night? Are you okay?"

"Ugh." Molly sat up, her head still pounding. "I'm sorry I didn't call you earlier. I'm deathly hungover. I've been asleep. I'm okay, though. Why does everyone keep asking me that?"

"Because you were *really* drunk! I mean, we all were, but you especially. I just . . . I hadn't seen you like that in a while, I guess. And we were all at Freehold—"

"We were at *Freehold*? God, I don't even remember that, Nina."

"I'm not surprised. You ordered us those gross blue shots, but Everly didn't want hers, so you took two. We kept trying to get you to dance, but you wouldn't stop talking about Hunter. And then you just disappeared."

"Oh, Jesus. Who was I talking to about Hunter?"

"Just Ev and me. You were showing us pictures of his girlfriend on Instagram."

Molly groaned. "Great."

"And then you kept saying you were gonna call him and were talking about how wise and incredible he is—"

"Ugh." Molly felt like she was going to be sick.

"And *then* you disappeared. Did you actually call Hunter?"

"No." Molly hated to lie to Nina, but she couldn't deal with explaining everything, not in her current state. Besides, she needed to talk to Jake first.

"Did you go right home?"

"Yes." Another lie. "I passed out."

"Ah. Well, if it's any consolation, I feel like I got run over by a bus, too. Cash hasn't gotten out of bed all day, except for Gatorade and pizza."

"Mmm, pizza." Molly's stomach was grumbling. She should eat something.

"What a night, Moll. I can't party like that anymore. Please tell me how we did that in college, like, five nights a week?"

"I dunno, Neens." Molly sank back into the couch, pressed her palm to her throbbing forehead. "We're old now."

"Less than four years away from thirty. *Weird.*" Nina sighed. "You must be excited to see Jake so soon."

"Yeah, well, he's not picking up my calls. I'm flying to Munich on Wednesday morning, and he hasn't sent me my flight information or anything."

"Well, it's Sunday. You should probably figure that out. . . ."

"I *know.*" Molly picked at the cuticle of her thumbnail, her irritation building. "He does this whenever he goes away. It's, like, a *privilege* if I hear from him—from my own boyfriend—when he's on tour. It's like he doesn't know how to use his fucking phone, and he always says it's going to be different, and it never is." She felt tears gathering in her throat. Her whole body hurt from emotional and physical exhaustion, from drinking seven different types of liquor in the span of four hours. Her stomach growled again; she really was starving. "Neens, I need to go find some food. I'll call you later."

After they hung up, Molly foraged the fridge for leftovers. She dumped a pile of cold sesame noodles into a bowl and tried Jake again. Voicemail picked up instantly.

"Jake, where are you? *Please* call me back. We really need to talk— I'm serious, it's important. And you still need to forward me the travel itinerary for Wednesday. Just call me, okay? I love you."

Molly crawled into bed. She cradled her phone like a security blanket, willing Jake to call. But he didn't, and eventually, her worrying succumbed to exhaustion, and she fell asleep.

When she woke the next morning, she felt a little better—her headache was gone—but a fresh batch of dread pooled in her gut when she looked at her phone and didn't see Jake's name. Where *was* he?

Her anxiety was growing worse by the minute, but she willed herself into autopilot, pushing down thoughts of Saturday night. She made coffee and her usual cinnamon raisin toast with peanut butter and sat down at her desk, forcing herself to tackle some edits. She and Alexis were in a good place—*Needs* was slated to publish in January 2017, and they had roughly six months to finish revisions before the novel went into production. But the chapter she was currently adjusting—the part where Sebastian brings Grace to his coastal hometown in Georgia—felt so reminiscent of being at the Narrows with Jake the weekend they drove to North Carolina that Molly couldn't stand for it to be in the manuscript. She needed to turn her thoughts *away* from Jake, but in the book, he was everywhere.

By three, she'd barely made any progress at all and slapped her laptop shut in a fit of frustration. She had to be at Bhakti to sub the four o'clock class. How was she supposed to cue mindfulness and calm when her own brain was a tornado of panic?

Molly taught in a daze, as though she'd pressed Play on a tape recorder of her voice and was watching herself from above. Afterward, she wandered back to the apartment in the frosty cold and tried Jake three more times. But his phone was still off, and now, his voicemail was full. In the kitchen, she heated up some tomato soup—the kind that came in a box from Trader Joe's. She forced a few bites, but her appetite was extinguished.

She took a piping-hot shower, washed the day off. She lathered her hair with Jake's shampoo, and the smell pushed her over the edge. Molly began to sob, the tears sliding down her soapy body and into the drain. Afterward, she put on sweats and climbed into bed, staring at her phone like it might sprout wings and fly. Still nothing. Her flight to Munich was departing the day after tomorrow.

She knew she should try to get in touch with Sam or Hale or Jerry, but she didn't know their international cell numbers. In a fit of desperation, Molly opened her laptop and crafted an email to the three of them. She copied Jake, even though he was even worse on email than his phone.

> *Hi, all—I can't reach Jake. Is everything ok? I'm supposed to fly to Munich Weds and don't have any flight details. I need the airport, flight time and number, tickets, etc. Can one of you please send ASAP? Thanks, M*

Molly fell into a fitful, restless sleep, waking every few hours to check her phone and email. But there continued to be no word from anyone, and when she woke up on Tuesday and there was still nothing from Jake on her phone, she fought the urge to hurl the thing across the room.

She felt too sick to eat. She managed a few sips of coffee and water before heading to Bhakti, where she taught two back-to-back power flows in a trance. Molly was technically supposed to wait half an hour after class before leaving the studio, but Veronica found her slumped behind the front desk, her back against the watercooler.

"You look like shit." Veronica was never one to beat around the bush.

"Ugh." Molly rubbed her temples. "I don't feel so hot, V."

"Go home." The studio manager patted her shoulder. "You leave for your big trip tomorrow, anyway, right? You should go pack."

Back at the apartment, Molly didn't bother changing out of her sweaty yoga clothes before crawling into bed. She curled into a ball under the covers, seized by her own helplessness, her own visceral agony. Where *the fuck* was Jake? At first, she had felt guilty for getting so drunk on Saturday night, then angry when he didn't return any of her calls, but now, she was starting to grow genuinely concerned. Had something happened? She knew how hard the band partied on tour. Jake didn't do drugs often, but he experimented every now and then. Coke, mushrooms, even acid once or twice when Hale was involved. Maybe someone had overdosed. The thought turned her blood cold.

When he finally called just after six, Molly thought the sight of his name on her phone was an apparition.

"Jake?" Her voice was barely a whisper. She was a shred of herself.

"Moll." Jake sounded winded, like he'd been running. "I'm so sorry. Holy shit. Please listen to me. We just checked into our hotel in Munich and my charger *finally* works here. The fucking Swiss outlets! Did you know the outlets in Switzerland are different from every other country in Europe?"

Molly screwed her eyes shut, fighting back tears of relief, of devastated fury. Jake hadn't overdosed. He'd ignored her for five days, but he was perfectly fucking fine.

"Are you kidding me, Jake? Do you have any idea what I've been . . . what the *hell*?"

"Molly, it was out of my control—"

"Out of your control? You could've found an adapter. You could've borrowed a phone. You could have emailed. There's literally an endless number of things you could've done that you didn't do." How could she explain to him how terrible this feigned helplessness of his made her feel? A line that Veronica used in her classes popped into her head: *We accept the love we think we deserve.*

Was this the love she thought she deserved? A partner who was reliable and attentive some of the time, but not when he didn't feel like it? A man who heedlessly put his needs and dreams and desires before her own, time and time again? That was the problem with her love for Jake, Molly realized. Her feelings for him were so sheer and annihilating that she couldn't see him clearly at all.

"I'm so sorry, Moll. I just—it's been so insanely busy over here, I feel like I haven't had a minute to breathe." He paused, and Molly heard the sound of a keyboard clicking. "Check your email. I just forwarded you everything. You fly out of JFK tomorrow at ten thirty. American Airlines."

"I'm not coming, Jake." She hadn't meant to say it, but as soon as the words left her mouth, she knew they were true. She couldn't get on that plane.

"What?"

"I'm not coming."

"Molly, don't do this."

"*Me,* Jake? You're the one who did this. I can't be in a relationship that's completely on your terms."

"On my terms? What does that even mean? I fucked up, and I'm really sorry. But don't let this ruin the next two weeks for both of us. Please. Just get on the plane. Come to Munich, and we'll figure everything out."

"No." Molly shook her head into the phone. She closed her eyes, hot tears slipping through. They streamed down her cheeks.

"Think about Christmas in Paris," he pressed, his voice weak, pleading. "The Eiffel Tower, dinner in Montmartre, the Louvre. We said we'd see it all together."

"Jake, I haven't heard from you in almost a week. I've been desperately trying to contact you. Saturday night—" Molly's breath caught in her throat. There was a crack in her heart, but she couldn't say the words. What was the point in telling him? She knew, in her gut, the only way forward.

"What? What happened?"

She brushed it off. "It's nothing. I got really drunk at Nina's party. I was hungover and anxious on Sunday, and I kept trying to reach you."

"I'm so sorry. Look, I know I messed up, but please just cut me a break. You know me, you *know* I'm bad with my phone, especially on tour—"

"Just *stop,* Jake. Stop saying you're 'bad with your phone,' like that's an excuse for making me feel so shitty. I was seriously worried. I was freaking out. Did you ever stop to think that I was actually terrified something might've happened to you?"

"Like what, though? Don't you get that it's just chaos over here? That we're all swamped?"

Molly swallowed the lump in her throat. She was brimming with anger. "I know Maxine is there." She couldn't help herself.

"Yeah, because I *told* you Maxine is here. I never tried to hide that. And there's nothing going on between Maxine and me, so it really doesn't fucking matter!"

"But how do I know that for sure when I can't even get in touch with you?"

"I dunno, Moll, it's a little thing called trust? Last time I checked, a relationship doesn't work without it."

"Don't you *dare* be sarcastic right now, Jake. A relationship doesn't work without communication, either, but you've been more than willing to throw that right out the window. And you're delusional if you think there's a healthy amount of trust here, especially when you're impossible to reach on the phone!"

"But you *know* I'm shit with my phone!"

"So what? I just have to accept the fact that when you're out of town, I may or may not hear from you? How many times can we have this same fucking fight, Jake? You can't just drop off the face of the earth when you feel like it!" Molly was yelling now, the anger rising like a tide inside her chest. "How do you not realize how *selfish* that is?"

"Take it easy, Molly. What more can I do right now than apologize? It's gonna be a *long* life together if you lay into me this hard every time I make a mistake."

"What life together?" Normally, Molly was instantly soothed when Jake referenced their future, the idea that theirs was a forever love. But not this time.

"Ours, I thought! Christmas in Paris, you in a white dress someday, music, writing, kids. Happiness. Isn't that the plan?"

"*Kids?*" Molly spat. "You think you're in any kind of position to have *kids*? Mr. 'It's all out of my control, you know I'm bad with my phone'?" Molly could hear her tone turning ugly, but something in her had snapped and she couldn't stop now. "You'd be a *terrible* father, Jake, just like your own. You don't know how to care about anyone other than yourself." It was the cruelest thing she could say, but the words felt good flying out of her mouth; she felt them soar through the phone, across the Atlantic Ocean, landing bitterly in Jake's heart. Stinging there. She hoped they'd rot there. She was happy to hurt him, to inflict a semblance of the pain she felt.

He said nothing. Molly could only hear the sound of his shallow breathing on the other end of the phone. She pictured him perched on the edge of the hotel bed, the cotton of his T-shirt pulled taut between the span of his shoulder blades as he rubbed the nape of his neck with his free hand.

In her head, Molly heard her mother's voice the first time she'd brought Jake home to Denville, two Labor Day weekends ago. *Just keep your wits about you. People change, especially when they're young and have dreams.*

And Jake's own voice, the very next day. *Sometimes I feel like I don't know how to be a good man. No one ever showed me, you know? And that scares me.*

"What do we do now?" The words cracked as Jake spoke them; she could tell he was crying now, too.

"I'm not coming tomorrow," Molly said as evenly as she could muster. "Please just accept that. There isn't anything you can do to change my mind." She hung up, powered off her phone. She huddled underneath the covers as racking sobs seized her body. All these years, Molly had been so wrong about Jake. She'd always thought he was the one who extinguished her darkness, who infiltrated her most desolate corners with permanent light—but she'd been mistaken. Jake was like the sun, only shining on her when his conditions allowed it. And she was the earth, revolving around him, often in darkness.

Christmas came and went. Molly spent the holiday at home in Denville. She told her mother she'd canceled her trip to Europe because Alexis had given her a new deadline.

"She's making you work over the holidays?" Her mother had frowned.

"You must be so upset. You and Jake had this all planned out. And you've been talking about seeing Paris forever."

"Yeah." Molly had nodded glumly, looking as destroyed as she felt. "But Jake will be there for a while. I might try to go visit in February instead." She felt guilty, but she'd been unable to tell her mother the truth—about Jake, about the night of Nina's party, about any of it. Until she spoke the words out loud, none of it needed to be real.

Another lie slipped the day after Christmas when Molly explained to her family that she needed to get back to Brooklyn to teach.

"But I thought you got subs for all your classes?" her mom challenged. "Since you're supposed to be in Europe?"

"I did, but when I canceled the trip, I asked Veronica if I could pick up some extras. A lot of other teachers are away right now, and I need the money."

"I see." A skeptical expression had crossed her mother's face. "Well, we'll miss you in Naples. If you change your mind, I'd be happy to pay for your flight."

"That's nice of you, Mom, but I should probably just sequester myself in Brooklyn, anyway, so I can tackle this revision."

Of course, Molly *hadn't* picked up extra classes; like everyone else, Veronica thought she was drinking Gamay and eating buttery pastries in France. But Molly couldn't have put on a happy face and gone to Naples with her mom and Andrew, as much as she missed her grandmother. She needed the time in Williamsburg to wallow in the remnants of her own shattered heart, and to figure out what the hell she was going to do.

Molly spent the week after Christmas alone in the apartment, ordering takeout and binging all ten seasons of *Friends* and speaking to no one. Jake called so many times that she finally blocked his number. The sound of his voice would break her, and Molly couldn't afford to break. Not anymore.

On New Year's Day, it poured rain. Thick gray sheets smacked against the windows of the apartment, and Molly felt so miserable and lonely she almost wished she weren't alive. Nobody except for her family even knew she was in Brooklyn—she still hadn't told her friends she'd bailed on Jake, and none of them were in town, anyway. Nina was ringing in 2016 in Vermont with Cash, Everly and Sage were visiting Sage's sister in D.C., and Hunter was on some romantic vacation in the Bahamas with

Blair. Molly realized that she didn't actually know where Liz was, and without thinking twice, she called her.

"Hey, Molls." Liz answered on the second ring. Her voice was low, slightly husky.

"Hey. Happy New Year. Where are you?"

"At my apartment, debilitatingly hungover. Aren't you in Europe?"

"I didn't go, actually. I'm in the city."

"Oh." A beat of silence. "Is everything okay with Jake?"

"Not exactly. Can I come over? I'll explain. And there's something I need to tell you."

"Sure. Bring me ginger ale? I'll love you for the rest of eternity."

Molly hung up the phone, relieved. She hadn't seen Liz one-on-one in months, and they definitely weren't as close as they used to be, but right now, Liz was everything she needed. Molly suddenly felt ready to talk about what had happened the night of Nina and Cash's housewarming party. She needed to get it off her chest, needed someone else to bear the weight of it, too, and really, who better than Liz? An old friend, a dose of comfort and pragmatism. Someone who really knew her.

"You got it," Molly said. "Is Zander there?"

"Nah. He went back to Cleveland for the holidays."

"Okay. I'll leave here in a few. See you soon."

Forty minutes later, Molly rang the buzzer outside Liz's Greenwich Village apartment. Upstairs, she found Liz splayed on the couch in sweatpants, a bag of frozen peas pressed to her forehead.

"You look exactly like I did the day after Nina and Cash's housewarming, Lizzie." Molly removed her raincoat and sank down into the adjacent armchair. She placed a cold can of Canada Dry on the coffee table.

"*Lifesaver.*" Liz reached for the soda, cracking it open. "That was a dumb party. I still think Cash is such a loser. Don't tell Nina I said so." Her eyes lingered on Molly. "You don't look so good yourself. What'd you get into last night?"

"Nothing. I lay low."

Liz frowned. "You didn't go out on New Year's Eve?"

"No. I was . . . tired." Molly glanced out the double window, which had a partial view of Washington Square Park. The rain had mostly stopped.

"This weather is shit," Liz said, following her gaze.

"Yeah. I wish it would just snow."

"So what happened with Jake?" Liz sat up on the couch, tucking her knees underneath her. "Why'd you bail on him?"

"We had a fight. I got pissed and canceled my trip."

Liz eyed her inquiringly. "Must've been a pretty bad fight for you to give up a free vacation to Europe. You've been wanting to go to Paris for, like, forever, Molls."

Molly smiled, despite herself. "You sound like my mom." She sighed. "Jake is just . . . he's an *awful* communicator, Liz. He goes days without calling or texting. He didn't send my itinerary through until the eleventh hour, and I just . . . I can't keep putting up with this shit. Something has to change."

"Well, good for you for putting him in his place." Liz pushed her short, dark hair behind her ears, tilted her chin forward. "But yeah, Jake Danner isn't exactly the world's most dependable man."

Liz's hangover seemed to have vanished; she was suddenly alert and laser-focused, and Molly remembered that this was the way Liz liked things best—when Molly was unsure, afraid, in crisis. This was the state in which their friendship thrived. She'd been too young and ignorant to see it before, but now it was almost comically apparent.

"One sec, I gotta pee." Liz stood and stretched her arms overhead, revealing her taut, gym-bunny stomach.

As the bathroom door clicked shut, Liz's phone pinged on the coffee table. Without really thinking, Molly leaned over and checked the screen. It was a text from a number she didn't recognize—and one that was clearly not saved in Liz's phone—beginning with a New York City area code.

Last night was wild. Sorry I had to leave so early this am. When did u say ur boyfriend is back?

Molly froze, her heart picking up speed. She reread the message. Liz was cheating on Zander? It seemed impossible. She was always telling everyone how she and Zander would be engaged by her twenty-seventh birthday next summer. He knew what kind of ring she wanted and everything.

A minute later, Liz reappeared on the couch. She picked up the can of ginger ale and took a long, thirsty sip.

Then she gave Molly a curious smile. "You okay? You look frazzled."

"I just saw your phone." Molly couldn't help herself. How could she turn a blind eye to something this outrageous? She and Liz had been too close for that.

"What?"

"I wasn't snooping. It pinged, and I saw the text." Molly gestured to where the phone lay on the coffee table.

Liz's face darkened, and she snatched up her cell. Molly watched her read the message. The air in the room grew tense, uneasy.

Eventually, Liz looked up from the screen and shrugged. "You caught me."

"You cheated on Zander?" Molly's brow knitted together. "*Why?* With who?" She knew she sounded judgmental, but she didn't care.

"He's a guy from work. He's hot. Want to see a picture?"

"No, I don't." Molly shifted in her seat, a mix of anger and anxiety building inside her. "I thought you and Zander were looking at rings. I thought you were happy."

"Don't freak out, Molls." Liz waved a hand, as if swatting a fly. "This thing with Sean—the guy from work—it's nothing. It's just physical. I know I need to end it, and I will . . . eventually. He's just *so* fucking hot. But Zander—of course Zander is the real deal."

"Wait, so this has happened more than once? Like, you're having an affair?"

Liz seemed to consider this. "I think the term *affair* technically only applies when you're married."

"Jesus. And Zander doesn't know?"

Liz flashed her a look. "Obviously not."

"What the hell, Liz?" Molly stood. She was fuming. "How can you be so blasé about this? I thought you loved Zander."

"I *do* love him, Molly! The world is not black and white. Don't make this personal, just because Jake went behind your back—"

"That was *not* the same thing and you know it. Jake didn't knowingly deceive me the way you're deceiving Zander. Maxine came on to him, and that girl at the club was a setup—"

"Okay, Molly. If that's what you need to tell yourself to sleep at night. What do you think Jake's doing in Europe when he's not calling you for days on end?"

"Fuck you, Liz! You've had it out for Jake since the moment I met him. You've never liked him. You've never liked *me* being happy." Molly grabbed her raincoat from the back of the armchair and stormed toward the front door. She couldn't stand to be in Liz's apartment for another second.

"Wait!" Liz scrambled after her, grabbing her shoulder.

Molly spun around. "Don't touch me!"

"Molly, you're *freaking* out. You think I don't want you to be happy? That's insane. Just hang on a second before you go. You said on the phone that you needed to tell me something?"

Molly narrowed her eyes. "I have *nothing* to say to you." Tears gathered in her throat. Her hands trembled as she pulled open the door to the apartment and hurried out, letting it slam in Liz's face.

She rode the subway back to Brooklyn feeling sick in her soul. She couldn't believe she'd thought going to Liz's would make her feel better. Instead, she'd left with the gut-wrenching realization that one of her so-called best friends had become a stranger. Maybe Molly shouldn't have been so shocked; Liz had always had a dark side, a part of herself she thrived on keeping separate from the bubbly energy of their foursome. But this—this deliberate, apathetic infidelity—Molly couldn't just sit there and tolerate it.

She spent the rest of the afternoon in her apartment, eating saltines and peanut butter in a trance on the couch. When she finally got herself up, the digital clock on the cable box read quarter after eight. She hadn't moved in hours.

Molly couldn't go on like this, she decided. She *had* to talk to someone, and with sudden clarity, she knew exactly who that person needed to be. She had to talk to Hunter.

She'd been putting it off for too long now, but she couldn't any longer. If nothing else, she owed him a real explanation for her insane behavior the night of Nina and Cash's party weeks earlier.

Molly reached for her cell. She didn't love initiating contact with Hunter these days—it gave her a funny feeling knowing that Blair was likely around, noticing her name on his phone. But this was too important. She crafted a text.

Hey. I'm really sorry to bother you while you and Blair are on vacation, but I need to talk to you about what happened a few weeks ago. Whenever you have ten minutes, can you give me a call? I'm in Brooklyn, by the way. Long story.

After she sent the message, Molly took a long shower, letting the hot water pound her back. Then she put on clean pajamas and climbed into bed. When she plugged her phone in to charge on the nightstand, she saw that Hunter had replied.

Happy New Year, Moll. Just back from the Bahamas this afternoon. Yes, of course we can talk. How about tomorrow—walk the waterfront at noon? We'll grab lunch if it's too cold.

Molly wrote back instantly, something loosening in her chest.

Perfect. See you tomorrow.

She turned off the bedside light, then huddled underneath the covers and closed her eyes. Molly hated sleeping in the bed without Jake, but she pushed the thought out of her mind. She would get better and better at doing this—pushing the thoughts and feelings that threatened to strangle her away so that there was space for her to breathe, to release herself from the consequences of her choices.

Chapter Thirty-three

Molly

August 2022

Molly's mind has been so jumbled and preoccupied, she forgets about the blood test at Dr. Ricci's office until the morning of, when Hunter reminds her.

He hands her a mug of coffee. "So I'll go in late this morning and stay with Stell while you're out, yeah? You think you'll be back by nine?"

She stares at her husband blankly, coils of steam rising in front of her face.

"Moll? 'Cause if it's gonna be later, that's fine, but I may have to drop her at my mom's. I have a meeting at nine thirty."

Molly fights through the thick layer of muck in her brain to try to remember what Hunter is talking about. It's Monday. Where is she supposed to be on Monday morning?

Hunter sighs. "Just call me when you leave Dr. Ricci's, okay?"

Dr. Ricci's. The blood test. The pregnancy results. Today.

"Yes!" Molly exclaims, an octave too loudly. "No, that's fine. If I'm not back by nine, drop her at Becky's on your way to your meeting. But I'll call you when I'm done, regardless." She places her coffee on the counter and wraps her arms around Hunter's neck. "I love you." She kisses him, inhaling the minty aroma of his freshly shaven face.

The blood test is routine. A fast prick. Molly is all too familiar with the process by now.

Claudia, one of the nurses at the practice, removes the rubber band cinching Molly's arm and smiles kindly. "Dr. Ricci will call you in a few hours."

Molly's heart feels heavy as she leaves the doctor's office, the August sun beating down in sweltering rays. She is already dreading Dr. Ricci's call. She doesn't know how she and Hunter will bear another negative result.

She thinks of Sabrina, then, and wishes so badly that they could talk. But Sabrina *still* hasn't replied to any of her texts, and now it's been almost two weeks since Molly has heard from her. In her gut, Molly knows that something is up. She can't imagine Jake telling Sabrina what happened between them at Skipping Beach; then again, what else would explain her friend's silence? Besides, it wouldn't be the first time Molly has been wrong about Jake Danner. There is only one way to find out for sure.

She climbs into her car and switches the AC on full blast. She touches the tender spot on the inside of her elbow where the needle went in, then digs her phone out of her purse and crafts a text to Hunter.

> Just leaving doc, all went fine, they'll call later. Can you take S to Becky's after all? I'm going to stop by Sabrina's. I haven't seen her in a while and could use a friend right now.

Molly heads west, looping through the beautiful back roads of Flynn Cove. The lush green leaves of the trees envelop the streets, a majestic tunnel. There's an old John Mellencamp song on the radio that makes Molly nostalgic for something she can't quite identify. She cranks the volume, sings along.

She's about to turn onto Sabrina's road when she spots a familiar blond ponytail. It's Whitney, pushing a double stroller along the shoulder of the road in big, dark sunglasses.

Molly slows the car to a stop and rolls down her window. She turns down the music.

"Whit!"

"Molly! Hi!" Whitney smiles her wide, generous smile, pushing her sunglasses on top of her head. "Meet Bea and Chloe." She leans down and adjusts something in one of the bassinets.

"Oh, Whit. They're beautiful." The twins are burrito-wrapped in matching swaddles, sleeping peacefully. "They're just perfect."

"Three is a lot." Whitney sighs. "But exhaustion aside, it's been a pretty magical summer. Liam is so sweet with them."

"I bet he's the best big brother. I'm so happy for you guys."

Whitney adjusts the strap of her workout top. "It's great to see you, Moll. It's been forever. Though I've hardly seen anyone since the girls were born, I guess. What're you doing on this side of town?"

"I'm heading to my friend Sabrina's, actually. Sabrina Danner. She lives right around the corner on Woodson. I don't think you guys have met; she's newish to town. You'd like her."

"Ah." Whitney nods. "We actually met briefly at the club the other day. Meredith introduced us."

Molly's stomach sinks. She wonders if Meredith told Whitney what happened between them on the Fourth of July.

"Actually," Whitney starts, reading her, "Meredith mentioned that you and Hunter were at the fireworks with the Danners. I was bummed to miss it. That's always such a fun night."

"Yeah." Molly manages a smile. "We missed you."

"Meredith told me what Hunter said to her," Whitney continues, and Molly's stomach plummets even lower. "Well, she told me *her* version." Whitney's eyes narrow. "Between you and me, that woman needs to watch herself. I know she's my friend, but she has no business bullying you guys into joining the club, especially in front of Stella. Hunter was right to give her a piece of his mind. Meredith's just insecure at the root of it. That's why she acts the way she does."

Molly nods, the knot in her belly slackening. Relief. "Thanks for saying that, Whit. Seriously."

"Of course. But anyway, yes, Sabrina seemed nice when we met. Although it's funny, she doesn't seem like the type who would want to be involved somewhere like the FCCC. I don't mean to sound snooty—" Whitney pauses, clearly embarrassed.

"No, I know what you mean," Molly says sincerely, because she does, and because that's the last thing she thinks about Whitney. She's unlike Meredith and Edie and Betsy in that way. "Supposedly, they only joined because Sabrina's grandparents were very involved at the club. They used to live in Flynn Cove."

"Is that what Sabrina said?"

Molly nods.

"That doesn't make any sense." The lines between Whitney's eyebrows sharpen in confusion.

"What do you mean?"

"Well, George and I are on the board, so I see every application that comes through." Whitney's fingers are clenched around the stroller's handlebar, gently pushing it back and forth. "If Sabrina's grandparents had been members, that definitely would've been noted on her application."

"Seriously?" Molly leans her forearm against the base of the open window. "Her grandparents weren't members?"

Whitney shakes her head. "No. I mean, if they had been, the Danners wouldn't have needed a letter of recommendation, let alone one from Meredith."

"*Meredith* wrote them a letter of recommendation?"

"Yeah. Apparently, they have a mutual friend—a former colleague of Sabrina's from the city who introduced her to Meredith when they moved out here."

"Huh. But why would she . . ." Molly's voice trails. She is thoroughly baffled. Why didn't Sabrina mention having a mutual friend with Meredith? And why would she lie about her grandparents having been members? "That's so weird."

Whitney frowns. "Look, maybe there was some misunderstanding between you guys, but if Sabrina's grandparents had belonged to the club, trust me, I would know."

Despite the August heat, Molly's arms suddenly prickle with goose bumps.

One of the twins fusses in the stroller, and Whitney reaches into the bassinet. "Shh, Chlo, it's okay." She looks up at Molly. "I should get these babes home; they're due for a feeding. God knows I've got to keep them on some semblance of a schedule if there's any hope for my own sleep!"

Molly smiles passively, her mind elsewhere. "Of course. Well, it was great to see you, Whit. You look great. And the girls are precious."

"*So* great to see you, Moll. Let's get a walk on the books soon, have a real catch-up. Or you and Hunter come over for a drink. I'll text you."

"I would love that. Say hi to George."

Molly waves goodbye to her friend and puts the car in drive. An eerie feeling wobbles through her as she turns onto Woodson Road and into the Danners' driveway. She could turn around, but she doesn't. Despite what Whitney has told her, Molly still feels an unshakable urge to see Sabrina.

Thankfully, there's no sign of Jake's Jeep, as she hoped would be the case on a weekday morning. She parks her car and strides up the slate walk, past the immaculately trimmed hedges and garden beds toward the front of the house before she can change her mind. She rings the bell, and Sabrina opens the door moments later. When she sees Molly, her face falls.

"Molly." She wears jean shorts and a sleeveless embroidered blouse, her dark hair pulled back into a low pony. "I was just heading out."

"Can I come in? Just for a sec?" Molly brushes past her and into the foyer. She feels brazen and—even though she's technically the guilty one—annoyed. "Sabrina." Molly folds her arms. "Did I do something to piss you off?"

Sabrina stares at the floor. Her toes are perfectly pedicured, the color of rubies. "No," she says eventually, lifting her head.

"You haven't replied to any of my texts."

"I've just been busy. Sorry."

"With what?" Molly studies Sabrina's face. Her eyes are naked, free of the heavy mascara and liquid liner she usually wears. Without makeup, she looks tired and much younger.

"Life. House projects. Fertility stuff, mostly." Sabrina latches her gaze to Molly's—a shock of green that betrays nothing. "Summers are always crazy. I'm sorry we haven't gotten together. We're overdue."

Molly feels unsettled in Sabrina's presence, almost sick to her stomach. The woman standing in front of her isn't the same person she knew two weeks earlier, the fast friend she bonded with like they'd known each other forever.

Whitney's words play in her mind. *If Sabrina's grandparents had belonged to the club, trust me, I would know.*

"We're heading to Martha's Vineyard tomorrow," Sabrina says. "We aren't back until the following Friday. Maybe dinner the weekend of the twentieth?"

"You're gone two whole weeks?" Molly fails to mask her surprise, but she's caught off guard. It seems strange that Jake never mentioned they were going out of town for a while. But maybe it isn't strange at all. God, why does she even care?

"Ten days." Sabrina eyes her curiously. Her voice is thin, clipped. "Jake and I have rented a house on the Vineyard every summer for the past few years."

"Oh. Fun. Well, the twentieth is actually Stella's birthday. She'll be six."

"How exciting."

"We're having a party at Hunter's mom's house. I told—" Molly swallows. "I was going to invite you guys. Stella, specifically, asked if you'd come."

"Great." One edge of Sabrina's mouth curls into a mysterious grin. Molly can't figure out what's going on. "Count us in."

"Are you . . . are you *sure* everything is okay, Sabrina?" Molly chews her bottom lip, anxiety gathering behind her rib cage.

"Of course." Sabrina reaches for her bag—a black Celine—which sits on a cream upholstered bench. "I *am* running out to do errands, though." She roots through her purse. "Crap, my wallet is in the other bag. Hang on a sec. Then I'll walk you out."

Sabrina turns and trots up the staircase. Molly takes a slow, deep breath. Maybe she's overreacting. She tends to get too in her head about this kind of stuff, especially lately. If Sabrina says everything is fine, it probably is. She probably *has* been busy. There probably *is* some misunderstanding about her grandparents belonging to the club. Molly will just be normal and ask her about it up front. Give her the benefit of the doubt. Besides, *Molly* is the one who's been a shitty friend, a disgraceful wife. She's the one who isn't to be trusted.

While she waits for Sabrina, Molly looks around the foyer and admires the lavish details: intricate crown moldings, sleek oak floors, the thick glass pendant overhanging the round lacquered table, centered on a zebra hide. It looks like something out of *Architectural Digest*. Sabrina really does have beautiful taste.

To the side of the entrance, there's a smaller table, waxed wood. A glass bowl filled with fake moss spheres sits on top, along with several framed photographs. There are Jake and Sabrina on their wedding day, recessing down the aisle at an outdoor beach ceremony, giant smiles plastered to their faces. There they are on a ski vacation, beaming in front of a dramatic, snow-covered peak. Molly stares at the photo, hit with the reality of how much has changed. The Jake she used to know had never been on skis.

A third picture catches Molly's eye. It's a black-and-white image of a young Sabrina—age ten or eleven, by the looks of it—standing beside a chicly dressed woman with a dark bob.

They're on what appears to be a terrace of some sort, and Sabrina's arms are wrapped around the woman's middle in a big bear hug, their smiles broad. Could it be Sabrina's mother? Molly doubts it. What little

Sabrina has shared of her mother makes it clear that theirs has never been a loving relationship. And whatever is happening in this picture, it was obviously a moment of genuine love.

Curious, Molly picks up the photo and examines it more closely. Unlike the others on the table, the frame isn't fancy. It's a four-by-six made of cheap plastic, the kind that doubles as a sign holder. Molly flips the frame around and sees the small, handwritten inscription on the back of the picture: *Sisi and Lenore, June 2001.*

The words are written in faded pencil—barely legible, but there. An icy sliver of dread slinks itself behind Molly's sternum. Lenore. It's not a common name, and she knows exactly where she's heard it before.

She hears Sabrina bounding down the stairs, and rushes to replace the picture on the side table.

"Sorry about that." Sabrina smiles, sounding cheerier as she slings a different leather purse over her sculpted shoulder, this one butter yellow with an intricate weave. "My wallet wasn't in the bag I thought it was. But I found it. Ready?" She skips out the front door, Molly numb and speechless in her wake.

"Fuck, it's hot." Sabrina climbs into her Range Rover. She starts the engine and rolls down the window. "I'm glad you stopped by. We'll definitely see you on the twentieth for Stella's party—it's a good thing we'll be back in time. Let me know what I can bring."

Molly nods absently, forcing a stiff smile and a wave goodbye. As she gets into her own car, she is shaking, her hands sweaty and trembling as she turns the keys in the ignition.

lenore.smith@gmail.com. She will never forget, as long as she lives, the name of the person who emailed her the photo of Jake cheating in West Palm Beach all those years ago. More than Maxine, that photo was the catalyst for her trust issues with Jake, the issues that eventually caused their foundation to crumble. Lenore Smith must be Sabrina. Sabrina must be the one who set Jake up. Sabrina—*Sisi*—must have sent Molly that picture to drive her away from Jake.

The world freezes on its axis. Molly feels the presence of something toxic, like poison—ominous, looming. She is so distracted she forgets she's supposed to pick Stella up at Becky's. Instead, she drives straight home, runs upstairs to her bedroom, and lies facedown on the duvet, questioning every decision she's made since that email from Lenore Smith landed in her inbox nearly nine years earlier.

At some point, her phone rings. *Stella,* she thinks, lunging for it.

"Hi, Molly, it's Lisa Ricci." The doctor's familiar voice sends a searing jolt to the base of Molly's spine. Her pulse quickens. This morning's blood test. The results. How could she have forgotten?

"Molly?" Dr. Ricci continues. "I have some very good news to share with you and Hunter. Congratulations. You're pregnant."

Chapter Thirty-four

Jake

2016–2021

Jake arrived back from Europe on a gray, slushy Sunday in March. He wasn't completely surprised to find that Molly wasn't home—she'd made it clear on the phone two months earlier that she needed space from their relationship, and they'd hardly talked since. But he wasn't prepared for the sight of the apartment when he walked through the door.

There was no sign of Molly anywhere. Every trace of her had vanished. All her books, her framed Warhol prints that had lived above the flat-screen, the stack of *New Yorkers* she'd kept in an old milk crate beside the couch. Her blender. Her mugs. Her toiletries. Her entire dresser was missing, her portion of their small closet cleared out. Molly was gone. Jake understood, with a clarity that immobilized him—that drilled straight into his heart—that she'd left him.

There was a folded note on the kitchen counter, and as Jake picked it up, he was flooded with a series of memories of the two of them there in that very spot: Jake extending a wooden spoon of warm pasta sauce for Molly to taste; Molly topping off their glasses with more wine, an intrigued smile on her face as she sat watching him cook; her spine arched against the laminate as he pressed his mouth to her neck while the sauce simmered; the sound of her laugh, wild and deep.

The note, in Molly's signature looped handwriting, said what he already knew. She was not here. She was not coming back.

He called again and again, but she wouldn't answer. He got desperate enough to try Nina, who picked up only to say that if Molly didn't want to talk to him, he should respect that.

Night after night, Jake sat on the couch and drank whiskey until he wept, then more until he'd numbed himself, immobile, his heart barely beating.

In the spring, Jake called Octagon—he remembered the name of the sports marketing firm—and tracked down Hunter's email address.

Hey—Sorry if this is weird, but I'm really worried about Molly. She probably told you we broke up, but I haven't been able to reach her in months and I have no idea where she is. Do you know if she's okay? Hope to hear from you.

Days went by, and Hunter didn't respond. Then weeks. Then months.

The band fell apart at the end of the summer. The European tour had been a moderate success, but not enough of one to secure Danner Lane spots in several of the continent's biggest summer festivals like Jerry had hoped. By June, Jake was barely showing up to the studio. Sam and Hale were eager to get going on a third album—they were ready to create something bold, something that would resurrect them from the *Precipice* flop—but Jake was a wreck, and he needed a break. He told them as much. Sam said they couldn't afford a break. Hale said to quit wallowing, to channel his pain into the music.

So Jake started dragging himself to the studio. But no matter how hard he tried, he couldn't find a way to be productive with his pain; the despair inside of him wasn't making him feel motivated, just stuck. It wasn't just hard to write music without Molly; it felt legitimately impossible to access the creative part of himself that required remembering the person he was trying to forget. Molly had been the one who read his lyrics and knew what worked and what didn't, what needed to be shifted or omitted, which lines felt cheesy or contrived. She just got it. Their minds had been in sync that way.

Jake showed the few songs he did wrangle out of himself to Sam and Hale—knowing they were terrible—and in retrospect, it was probably the expressions on their faces in that moment when Jake knew the end had come. The Lanes didn't look angry the way they had when Jake had showed them the first batch of *Precipice* tracks nearly two years earlier. Instead, their eyes were full of pity. The next day, they told him they'd decided to make a go of it as a duo on their own and that Jerry was sticking with them.

"We love you, Danner, but we can't just put our careers on hold while you figure out how to get your shit together," Sam had said, his eyes sorry but certain. "The momentum is too important right now.

This just isn't working. There's strength in knowing when it's time to say goodbye."

The agony of losing Sam and Hale—his brothers; the closest thing he'd had to family—hit slowly. Jake was so consumed by the pain of being without Molly that the loss of the band came in gradual waves, until one day he realized he had nothing and no one left that mattered to him. No Sam and Hale, no Danner Lane, no Molly.

One Saturday early in the fall, Jake rode the subway over to the East Village. The Lanes had decided to give up their studio lease after Jerry had found them some super-high-tech space uptown, and Jake was required to drop off his keys.

No one was there when he entered the room, the three hundred square feet where he'd spent so much of the past five years. Jake drank in the sight of the studio for the last time: the black walls, the worn red carpet, the drum kit and amp in the corner, the cracked leather couch where the three of them used to sit and unwind with beers after endless hours of practice. He inhaled its slightly musty scent—like dried paint mixed with Heineken—before walking out the door, his heart a shriveled muscle inside his chest.

Out on the street, the October sun was strong overhead. Jake rubbed his eyes—he was in desperate need of coffee, and there was a good spot a few blocks north. He walked up Avenue A, turning left on East Twelfth Street and crossing First Avenue, where he popped into the little corner café. At the counter, Jake ordered a large black coffee and a ham-and-cheese croissant. He wasn't hungry—he almost never was lately—but his jeans were loose. He had to eat.

Jake was the only customer in the tiny shop, so when the bells chimed and a brunette breezed through the swinging door, he turned his head. His jaw dropped as his eyes landed on the woman's, a bolt of recognition piercing his gut.

It had been more than two and a half years since they'd seen each other, that strange night at the club in West Palm Beach when she'd come on to him.

"Sisi?"

"Jake." She pressed a palm to her chest, clearly as shocked as he was. He took in the sight of her: she wore fitted black jeans and a slouchy gray sweater, her long brown locks swept back. Her green eyes were clear and bright. She looked rested. And better than he remembered. He looked down at his sweatpants and threadbare T-shirt, realizing how exhausted and grubby he appeared in comparison.

"What are you doing here?" he asked.

"My ex lives a couple of blocks away," Sisi explained. "I had a bunch of stuff there and finally went and picked it all up." She gestured to the tote bag slung through her elbow.

"That's always a joy." Jake gave a tight smile.

The barista cleared her throat, annoyed at the holdup. "Sir? Anything else with your coffee and croissant?"

"Oh. Umm." Jake turned back to Sisi, remembering his manners. "What can I get you?"

"Small skim latte," she told the barista, stepping closer to him. He could smell her perfume, something floral and sharp. "Thanks, Jake."

"Busy now?" he asked her, handing over his credit card. "Tompkins Square Park is just around the corner. It's nice out. We could drink these. Catch up." He wasn't fully sure what he was doing; he only knew he'd rather die than go back to his apartment, where he could barely stand to exist without Molly. The whole place smelled sour and damp, like dirty laundry and two weeks' worth of food-crusted dishes piled in the sink. Jake couldn't spend another day there, cooped up with his thoughts.

"Sure," she said. "Why not?"

They grabbed their coffees from the counter and walked back toward the park. Sisi smiled beside him, and it lit up her whole face. For the first time in months, Jake felt his loneliness subside.

His rekindling with Sisi wasn't completely conscious—there wasn't one particular moment when he *decided* he wanted her back. It happened naturally, a gradual descent into togetherness. What had occurred in West Palm Beach all those years earlier felt like a distant memory, an immature, drunken slip on her part that no longer seemed to weigh as much. Sisi was a breath of fresh air, and he was grateful to have her in his life again.

One Sunday morning, over a lazy brunch of bagels and mimosas at her apartment, she said something that caught him off guard.

"So this Molly girl," she started, pouring more champagne into her glass. "Should we talk about it?"

The light, airy mood in the room shifted, and Jake felt a wave of darkness pass through him. Anguish. Regret. A pastiche of unsettled emotions. "There's not much to say."

"Come on, Jake." Sisi twisted the glass stem of her flute. "'Molly's Song' was like, *the* song of 2014. I know this girl was important to you. I'm no idiot."

He dropped his shoulders slightly, leaning back into his chair. "Fine." He sighed, knowing this was a topic he'd have to address with Sisi eventually. "Molly was important to me. But it's over now."

"How did it end?"

Jake frowned. He didn't want to think of this part, let alone discuss it. "I don't really know. I got back from tour to find she'd moved out of our apartment. She left me a note, and that was it."

"That's awful, Jake." Sisi's face fell. "Where is she now?"

"I have no idea. I haven't heard from her since we broke up." He glanced down at the half-eaten bagel on his plate, his appetite suddenly extinguished. "My relationship with Molly wasn't always . . . healthy. A lot of it was my fault. I wasn't a good partner to her." He glanced up at Sisi, reaching across the table for her hand. "Let's not talk about Molly anymore, okay? I've been really happy with you these last few weeks, Sees. The past is in the past. Let's just focus on us."

She smiled, seemingly pleased with his declaration. Jake hadn't been lying, either—he *was* happy being back with Sisi. On their best days, it felt like destiny that they'd both ended up in that tiny East Village coffee shop on the same October morning. As the months passed, the fog of Jake's depression continued to lift, until life grew clear again.

And still, there were lingering traces of Molly that Jake couldn't shake from his system. He thought of her constantly, wondering how she was doing and if she was okay and why she'd left without saying goodbye. Every time he walked by a bookstore, he went inside, scouring the shelves for *Needs*. He asked countless booksellers when the novel was slated for publication, but strangely, none of them had heard of it.

Jake was hit with the urge to call Molly countless times, but he knew in his gut she wouldn't answer, the same way she hadn't answered when they'd first broken up. In March, a year after their split, he sent her an email he'd been drafting in the notes section of his phone for months. He wrote about the band breaking up and how much he missed her. He said that if she was ever ready to talk, he'd drop everything and run to where she was.

Months passed by, and she didn't write back. Jake had gotten in the habit of checking her Facebook page somewhat frequently, and though there were never updates, he remained hopeful that at some point there'd be *something* there—some nugget of information to shed light on her existence.

That summer, Jake checked her profile to find that she'd *finally* updated her page for the first time in half a decade. His heart turned to stone when he saw that she'd changed her name—Molly Diamond had become Molly Diamond O'Neil. She had a new picture, too. The photo was a black-and-white portrait of Molly and a dark-haired man whom Jake recognized immediately. It was Hunter.

Jake studied the photo in disbelief, his breath knocked out of his chest. Molly and Hunter posed on a dock in front of the ocean, their smiles wide and jubilant. She wore a long, strapless column of a gown, a delicate veil floating behind her, caught in a gust of wind. Beside her, Hunter stood tall and proud, his thick hair neatly combed, his left hand supporting the small of her back.

Not a year and a half after their breakup, and Molly was *married*? And to *Hunter*? Jake was pissed—no, he was *indignant*—but more than that, the news smashed his heart all over again. And there was nothing he could do about it, except try to hide his feelings from Sisi.

In August, when Jake had been unemployed for nearly a year, he received a phone call from someone in HR at the Manhattan branch of Randolph Group, the insurance company founded by Sisi's father. They were offering Jake a job.

That afternoon, he texted Sisi and asked her to meet him at the Standard after she got off work.

"I don't need you doing me any favors," Jake told her, signaling to their waitress for another beer. He'd quickly drained the first one. "And I've never expressed any interest in working in insurance." He frowned.

She took a sip of her vodka soda. "I thought you'd be excited," she said. "You've been wallowing, Jake. You're clearly depressed. You have to move on with your life; you can't just sit at home all day and feel sad about Danner Lane—"

"I'm not sad about Danner Lane."

"Then what are you sad about?" Her emerald eyes locked on his, the question a challenge.

"Nothing," he answered quickly. "But I told you, I've been approached by a few managers. A solo album isn't off the table—"

"But do you really want to go through all that? Just to try to prove to Sam and Hale that you're better?"

"It's not about them." He stared into his empty glass, not sure if he believed his own words.

"Really? They've got a good thing going, Jake. You know it's true. *The Times* called them the next Allman Brothers."

"*Avett* Brothers, Sisi." Jake grunted. "There's a big difference."

"Whatever. They're not as good as you guys were, but everyone in my office has heard of the Lane Brothers."

Jake shrugged, dipping a piece of soft pretzel into a plastic container of cheese sauce. "I guess they've found their niche."

"Look." She placed her hand over his, interlacing their fingers. The volume of chattering voices began to rise around them as more of the after-work crowd packed into the Standard's outdoor biergarten. "I'm giving you tough love because I want you to be happy, Jake. What happens when Sam and Hale are killing it as this new folk duo and you're just yesterday's gravy?"

He glanced up at Sisi. Her expression was full of care, of genuine concern. He was lucky, he knew more than ever, to have a smart, strong, beautiful woman in his life who looked at him this way. Who loved him this deeply.

"The position at Randolph Group pays well," she pressed, though they both knew the money didn't matter. If they ended up together, whatever he made would be a drop in the ocean of her trust fund. "You need a change. A fresh start. We both do. We need to start looking forward, not back." Sisi was always making them a *we*. He'd grown to love this about her, the way she made them feel like a team.

"You're right, Sees." Jake sighed, touching his forehead to hers. As impossible as it was for him to imagine his life without music, it seemed even more unthinkable to start playing again. Revisiting that part of his psyche would be like picking off a giant scab, reopening a raw wound and watching the blood pool. "I know you're right."

Jake started at Randolph Group in September, the same month he and Sisi moved into a spacious two-bedroom on the Upper East Side. They were happy, for the most part, as they fell into a steady routine. Sisi worked her butt off at Marc Jacobs—she always had—and this was a character trait that Jake found inspiring. A job wasn't always a vocation, he was learning. For the majority of people, a job meant setting an early alarm and putting in the hours and harboring a sense of purpose when the ACH deposit hit biweekly, even if you weren't fully clear on what that purpose was. You worked, you came home to your person, and this was life. It was predictable, and steady, and—Jake was discovering—not so bad.

And yet, there were moments that set him back, moments when he found himself reaching for the past instead of rooting his feet in the present. There was the night that Sisi was at a work dinner and he passed out on the couch, ice cubes melting in his whiskey, "Molly's Song" blaring from the Sonos speakers. He'd drunk too much, and hadn't remembered queueing the song on repeat when he woke to it playing at 3:00 a.m. Sisi was home from her dinner, asleep in bed. She didn't mention what had happened in the morning, but they both knew. She stepped around the elephant in the room, her eyes cold.

Then there was the evening Jake came home from work to find Sisi on the floor of his closet, rummaging through an orange Nike shoebox he recognized instantly. It was his collection of Molly memories: old photographs, his tattered song notebook, ticket stubs from concerts and movies and Broadway plays, matchbooks from various New York restaurants, her pink scrunchie—the one he'd found in the bathroom of their apartment after she left. It was stretched out and ratty, but he hadn't mustered the strength to throw it away.

Jake's heart clenched, shrouded in guilt. He knew how bad this looked.

"What is this, Jake?"

"Sees." He removed his navy coat, the shoulders dusted with snow. "I didn't think your flight landed until nine." Sisi had been in Milan for Fashion Week; she'd been gone ten days. "I . . . I found that box in the back of my closet last night. I was just bored without you, so I started looking through it. I don't even know why. And I guess I forgot to clean it up before I left this morning." He set his briefcase down.

"What *is* it?" Her eyes narrowed, green slits.

"A bunch of stuff I saved after Molly and I broke up." He rubbed the back of his neck. "Honestly, I'd forgotten it even existed. I'm obviously going to toss it."

But he didn't. He couldn't bring himself to trash what little he had left of Molly, even if their story was ancient history.

It wasn't until four years into their relationship that Jake and Sisi began to talk seriously about marriage. Her nudges in this direction were not as subtle as he could tell she intended, but by that point, Jake loved her enough to find this endearing. He couldn't imagine losing Sisi, the way he'd lost everyone else. And so, one early spring day among the cherry blossoms in Central Park, he dropped to one knee. She squealed, elated, like he'd known she would be. Sisi had been wanting the proposal for a while, but Jake had taken longer to be ready. And still, at the sight of her wearing the ring—a brilliant-cut diamond flanked by tapered baguettes—he couldn't help imagining what it would've felt like to slip an engagement ring over Molly's finger. The thought filled him with shame, and he pushed it away.

They scheduled the wedding for January in Miami, at a luxury resort in South Beach. It surprised Jake that Sisi wanted to get married so close to where her parents lived, but she countered that it had nothing to do with them at all, that she'd been close with relatives in Miami growing up and loved the city, and the idea of a winter ceremony on the ocean.

A month before the wedding, Jake got a call from a music manager named Clay Berenson. Jake had continued to be approached by a number of managers in the years since he'd started working for Randolph Group, but never anyone he'd considered seriously. The few he'd agreed to have coffee with were all focused on "Molly's Song" and how to re-create this same kind of superhit. Jake could practically see the dollar signs in their eyes.

But Clay Berenson was different. He didn't even mention "Molly's Song" at first. Instead, he gushed about the lesser-hyped tracks from Danner Lane, his favorites from *The Narrows* and *Precipice*, songs no one had mentioned to Jake in years. "January Girl," "Gut Feeling," "Bayside," "Give it Love, Give it Time."

"But if you're actually serious about a solo album, we'd have to do *something* with 'Molly's Song,'" Clay told him candidly. "For better or for worse, it's what everyone still remembers about you. It's your hook—the way you get people to listen. Otherwise, no one will give a shit."

Jake knew Clay was right, and appreciated his straightforward approach. And though a significant part of Jake was so still hesitant to face the music—no pun intended—he craved it in his heart. He missed the weight of the guitar in his hands, the freeing way it felt to sing from the very bottom of his soul.

"This guy Clay actually *gets* it," he'd gushed to Sisi after their lunch meeting. "He truly believes in my work—my old songs from back in the day that nobody else even remembers. He thinks a solo album has real potential." Jake smiled pensively, a dreamy sheen in his eyes. He felt light and buzzy. Maybe he was simply worn out from spending every day of the last four years behind a computer screen, his fingers glued to the keyboard, crunching numbers for the kind of conglomerate his younger self never would've entertained selling out to. Maybe the appeal of a reliable job was wearing off; maybe it had always only been a matter of time. "I think I'm going to give him a shot."

"Wow. Babe." Sisi grinned, but she looked worried. "That's great, but what about work? You've been at Randolph Group for a while now, and my dad got you that job."

"It's not like I'm gonna quit, Sees. This solo album—if it even happens—would just be a side gig, at least for now. I've really missed music. You have to know that."

"Not really. You never say that to me."

"Well, I'm sorry. I should." He reached for her hand, which was smooth and steady. His love. His future wife. "Since the band split, something in my life has just been . . . missing. I mean, I started playing guitar with the Lanes when I was a little kid."

"Do you miss them?"

Jake nodded wistfully. "Of course." He rarely listened to the Lane Brothers—it was too hard—though he thought of Sam and Hale often. Jerry as well. He wasn't even sure he was angry with them anymore, for leaving him in the dust. In retrospect, he saw where they were coming from, though he didn't think he deserved the way they treated him. But he wasn't sure what good it did, holding on to anger like that. Still, the Lanes were the closest thing to brothers Jake had ever had. "It's not about them, though, Sees. Making music is part of who I am. Despite what I've said before, I don't think I'm ready to walk away for good."

As Jake spoke the words, he knew they were true. And perhaps the fact that he still wanted to try meant that he was an artist at heart. With or without Molly.

Chapter Thirty-five

Sabrina

Jake signed with Clay quickly, and they immediately started the acoustic cover of "Molly's Song." Yup, that's right. Weeks before our wedding, and I was listening to my future husband sing about his ex in our living room.

Enough was enough. *Something* had to be done. I'd worked tirelessly to get Jake to myself for years—I'd followed him into the coffee shop on East Twelfth Street that morning to orchestrate our rekindling—and I hadn't come this far just to settle for half his heart. I deserved the whole damn thing, on a silver fucking platter.

And here was the thing I kept coming back to: your child existed in the world. I'd seen you visibly pregnant through the window at Bhakti Yoga. I didn't know precisely when the baby had been born, but I *did* know that once I figured it out, the math would speak for itself. Once Jake discovered you'd gone behind his back with Hunter during Danner Lane's Euro tour all those years ago, your pedestal would vanish. The irony of my task was this: I needed to find a way to bring you back into Jake's world in order to push you out for good.

This had to be done organically, in a way that would prompt Jake to wake up and smell the coffee on his own. *The girl you think you still love—the so-called one that got away—is actually a lying, duplicitous cheater.* A quick Google search pulled up your bio on the website of Yoga Tree, a small, privately owned studio in Flynn Cove, Connecticut. *Molly Diamond O'Neil has been teaching Vinyasa yoga for nearly a decade. Her classes integrate creative sequences with meditation, music, and spiritual philosophy. She lives here in town with her husband and daughter.*

It was easier to convince Jake to move out of the city than I'd imagined it might be. Plus, the timing worked in my favor.

I raised the topic one night on our honeymoon in Maui, during a romantic dinner on the beach arranged by the hotel staff. Everything was perfect—the air was soft and warm, the food and cocktails delectable. Palm trees stretched above our heads as the sun dipped below the horizon, the sky lighting up into an idyllic Hawaiian sunset. The gentle surf lapped against the shore just feet from our table. Jake and I were finally relaxed and rested after our whirlwind wedding weekend, just able to enjoy each other.

"Babe," I started, caressing his sun-kissed forearm. "I'm going out on a limb here, but what do you think about moving out of the city? Nothing permanent, but just while you're working on the solo album. Could be nice to have a bit more room. Some peace and quiet so you can really focus. New York just gets so claustrophobic."

A slow smile crept across Jake's face, and the shimmer in his eyes told me he liked the idea.

When we got back from Maui, I didn't waste any time before looking at real estate.

"How about this place?" I passed Jake my laptop, opened to a Zillow listing. It was a wintry Saturday morning, and we were drinking coffee, cozy in our bed. "There's an open house tomorrow."

"Flynn Cove?" Jake squinted at the screen. "Too WASPy for me, Sees."

"It's a beautiful town, Jake. An hour from Manhattan, easy commute."

"I dunno." He sipped his coffee. "Too preppy. Expensive."

"Didn't I tell you my grandparents used to live there?" The lie slid out easily. "I have memories of visiting them as a child. It's right on the water. Besides, you know the money isn't a problem."

Jake didn't care about wealth, not actually. But he wasn't threatened by the fact that I had money; on the contrary, he respected it. He prided himself on never standing in my way.

He sighed. "Let's look at it."

I put in my notice at Marc Jacobs three weeks before we left New York. I didn't exactly *want* to leave my job—I'd been there since graduating from FIT and had really climbed up the ranks and made a name for myself—but we didn't need the money, and though Jake would be making the daily commute into Manhattan on the train, I had no interest in doing the same. I decided I'd consult for a few brands, but nothing full-time. The truth was, I'd worked like crazy for many years—first as a distraction, and then later, to prove to myself how independent I could be. Besides, I had a new priority now: you.

My plan was straightforward. The first step was to get close to you, worm my way into your circle of trust. It's the reason I landed in Dr. Ricci's office that morning back in May. I couldn't merely pretend to like yoga and assume that would be enough to fuse a genuine bond between us. No, I needed to discover the root of your most potent pain. I needed to meet you there. *That* would be what solidified our connection.

Believe it or not, it was Meredith Duffy who clued me in on your prolonged struggle to conceive baby number two. My ex-colleague Amber, a senior buyer at Marc Jacobs, e-introduced me to Meredith when I announced to the office that Jake and I had closed on a house in the suburbs.

"*Omigosh,* you're moving to Flynn Cove? I *have* to connect you with my sorority sister Meredith Duffy," Amber had gushed. "She's, like, Mrs. Flynn Cove. Runs that town. I'll set it up on email."

I knew I wasn't likely to hit it off with a sorority sister. Nonetheless, I took Amber up on her offer and arranged a lunch with Meredith a few weeks before our move. If she actually did *run that town* like Amber insisted, perhaps she knew things about its residents.

So over Cobb salads at the FCCC—hers sans blue cheese, dressing on the side—I happened to mention that my husband's ex lived in town.

"To be honest, he doesn't know that I know," I'd confessed. I watched her eyes bloom with curiosity. Meredith, too, is a woman who does her fair share of snooping.

When I told her your name, she'd nodded with recognition, pursing her lips. She explained, with blatant distaste, that you weren't a club member but that your daughters were in the same class.

"I don't know much about Molly, except that she teaches yoga at the little studio in town," Meredith had shared. "And she's married to a guy who grew up here. He's an O'Neil—big sailing family. *Also* . . ." She'd lowered her voice, which hummed with excitement—this woman clearly thrived on gossip. She moved her face across the table, closer to mine. "Between you and me, I hear through the grapevine that the O'Neils are having a *very* hard time getting pregnant again. Their only child is five. Apparently, they've been doing IVF for years with Dr. Ricci—that woman could get a cactus pregnant—and it isn't working. There's been at least one miscarriage."

I nearly buckled at the word. *Miscarriage.* I'd never spoken it out loud, given a label to my own haunting experience. But that evening, when I was back in the city packing boxes, I did. Jake was still at the office, working late.

"Miscarriage." I repeated the word several times, the three syllables reverberating in our near-empty apartment. The sound caused me to shudder, to screw my eyes shut until tears spilled out and ran down my cheeks. I sat down on the floor and hugged my knees to my chest and cried. I'd still never told Jake.

When he got home, he found me on the floor, my face wet.

"Sisi?" He crouched down beside me, wiping the tears from my face. "Jesus. Are you okay?"

I blinked. I didn't want to lie. "I want to have a baby, and you don't." This was the truth, part of it at least.

He sighed, rubbing the bridge of his perfect nose. It wasn't the first time I'd brought up the topic of children—we'd started discussing it shortly after getting back from our honeymoon. I'd been ovulating; I'd suggested we start trying.

"Sees, we just got married," he'd said. "I told you, I'm not sure I'm cut out to be a dad."

"But that's not what you said before." *Jake-and-Sisi babies.* Did he not remember his own words? "Besides, you'd be an incredible father. I know we both have scars from our own parents, but I promise you'll be nothing like your—"

"Look." His voice was hard, clipped. "Let's just take it slow. Marriage is a big step."

I would've mentioned the miscarriage then if I'd thought it might change his mind. But the look in his eyes at the mention of fatherhood— pure, unalloyed fear—told me it would only make him run further in the other direction.

So you see, Molly, I know what it feels like to yearn for a baby that might never be. And I know miscarriage. After all my deception, it's ironic that I didn't even need to fake the empathy. Mine was the real thing.

Meredith had already given me Dr. Ricci's name, and so one afternoon in April, I called her office. I pretended to be you, explaining to the receptionist that I couldn't remember the date of my next visit. Would they mind checking?

Contrary to popular belief, you don't need an appointment to sit in the waiting room of a doctor's office. I worried about looking suspicious, but when I arrived at the clinic on the morning of your appointment, there were so many women waiting to see Dr. Ricci that I was easily able to slink in unnoticed. I found one of the few vacant seats and opened an ancient issue of *People*.

You arrived at four on the dot—right on time—and that's when I went in for the kill. I'd already attended your yoga class—I made sure to sign up using my maiden name—but that moment in Dr. Ricci's waiting room was really the point from which our friendship took flight. Don't you agree?

I'll admit that seeing you and Jake together again was worse than I'd imagined. During that first foursome dinner at our house, his eyes practically dropped out of his head at the sight of you. It was maddening to witness, but what could I do? The groundwork had to be laid.

I figured Jake would put two and two together when he learned Stella's age—it's the reason I brought it up at dinner. But he was oblivious. On the Fourth of July, Jake even *asked* Stella her age himself, completely unprompted. But when she responded that she was five and three quarters, he didn't bat an eye.

I began losing patience, especially after seeing Jake so clearly smitten in your presence. When I watched the two of you share that passionate kiss under the gazebo at Skipping Beach, then climb into Jake's car together, the resentment that already coursed through my bloodstream exploded in my veins.

Clearly, time is running out. But you were kind to invite us to Stella's birthday party in a couple of weeks. We'll be there. I, for one, wouldn't miss it for the world.

Chapter Thirty-six

Molly

August 2022

On Stella's birthday, she jumps into bed with Molly and Hunter at the crack of dawn.

"Mom." She jostles Molly's shoulder. "I'm six."

Molly blinks her eyes open to the sight of Stella's precious face, her blond curls tousled, her eyes still swollen from sleep. Her beautiful baby girl is six. How? She opens her arms to her daughter, who nestles in close.

"Happy birthday, Stell." Molly kisses her temple. "I love you."

They lie like that for a while, Hunter still passed out beside them, and Molly is delirious with joy. She can feel Stella's little heart beating through her chest, she feels the new life inside of her, and it's the most complete Molly has ever felt in her life.

An hour later, downstairs, Hunter brews coffee and makes chocolate-chip pancakes on the griddle. He places his hand over Molly's stomach, his eyes brightening.

"How are you two feeling this morning?" he whispers, handing her a cup of decaf. Dr. Ricci says a little caffeine won't hurt, but it's still early, and she doesn't want to chance it. Not after everything she's been through.

"We're great." Molly leans in to kiss her husband, letting her lips linger on his for several moments. She inhales his smell—coffee grounds and warm skin and aftershave. She knows she needs to tell Hunter about Jake, but he's just been so happy since finding out about the pregnancy. It's still early—only five and a half weeks—but Molly's HCG levels have been rising steadily, and yesterday, Dr. Ricci was able to find the fetal pole during an ultrasound. *Finally,* they are pregnant. Stella is going to have a sibling. The last thing Molly wants to do is to ruin it all with the news of her fuckup.

When they break apart, Stella is watching. She sits on one of the island stools, twirling a piece of pancake into a puddle of maple syrup.

"Mommy and Daddy," she announces, a knowing smile playing over her mouth. "We are a very happy family."

It's a perfect day, sunny but less sweltering than earlier in the month. Becky is hosting Stella's party in her spacious backyard, up by the pool.

While they're setting up, Becky comes over to Molly and squeezes her shoulder. "Hunt told me the news," she says, a smile bursting from the corners of her lips. Her eyes glitter with excitement, but there is something else in them, too. Relief. "I hope you don't mind. Oh, Moll. I'm so happy for you guys. For all of us." Tears prick Molly's eyes as her mother-in-law pulls her in for a hug.

The guests begin to arrive at noon. Molly's mom is one of the first, accompanied by Andrew and his girlfriend, Sydney. Molly told her mother the news the day she found out, and her elated expression mirrors Becky's.

There is Hunter's brother, Clark, with his wife, Tara, and their two boys, who live an hour up the coast in Old Lyme. There's a flock of Stella's classmates and friends from sailing, along with their parents, several with whom Molly has become friendly over the years. Unfortunately, Meredith is among them, and she bypasses Molly without a greeting. Meredith may have felt insulted after Hunter's sharp rebuke on the Fourth of July, but she wouldn't dare miss a social gathering in Flynn Cove. Even one hosted by plebian non–club members like the O'Neils.

Finally, Molly spots the two people she's most eager to see. Nina and Everly cross the lawn, waving in her direction, Michael and Sage a few steps behind them. Michael carries the coveted *Frozen* piñata, a sight that fills Molly with relief. She never doubted Nina, but still. Stella has been talking about this piñata nonstop for months.

A steep rise of stone steps leads up to the pool area, and Molly waits eagerly while her friends climb to meet her. When they reach the top, she sees that there is someone else behind Michael and Sage, a fifth in their group. The woman has sleek, dark hair, chopped halfway down her neck, and a small, distinct face that Molly would recognize anywhere. It's Liz.

"Don't be mad." It's Nina's voice in Molly's ear. She's rushed ahead of the others. "We were with her last night, we drank all this wine at dinner, and she was saying how much she misses you, so we . . . invited her. We hadn't seen her in ages, but she . . . she really seems like she's in a better place now. She ditched the divorced guy. I'm sorry, I . . . I should've told you." Nina sighs. "Life is short, Moll. I think you guys should talk."

Molly doesn't have time to react before Liz is in front of her. She's wearing a black sundress and a panama hat, a Mansur Gavriel bucket bag slung over her shoulder.

"Hey, Molls." Liz smiles cautiously, and regardless of what has happened between them, it's so good to see her old friend that Molly can't contain the smile spreading across her face, can't help but pull her in for a long, fierce hug.

Then Nina and Everly join in, and the four women are pouncing on one another, and for a fleeting moment Molly is overcome with a heavy mix of nostalgia and déjà vu. They are back in college at a keg party, on the precipice of getting drunk. Then they're in Nina's apartment in Williamsburg, listening to Vampire Weekend and drinking wine and talking about a future that isn't close enough to really matter.

"It's so, *so* good to see you guys, you have no idea," Molly says when they finally break apart. "And you two!" She moves past her friends to hug Michael, then Sage. "You're a true hero for bringing that piñata," she tells Michael. "The only thing my daughter might possibly love more than *Frozen* is sugar."

Michael laughs. "I have a four-year-old niece. I'm well aware of the *Frozen* phenomenon."

"As you can see, you're now in *Frozen* land." Molly gestures to the setup around them. Dozens of blue, white, and silver balloons are secured all around the fence, Pin the Nose on Olaf is set up against the side of the pool house, and several children already swarm the *Frozen*-inspired cookie decorating station. Becky has even secured a pair of felt antlers to Bodie, turning him into Sven for the afternoon. "The theme is 'Frozen in August.' Hunter thought that was cute."

"I'm impressed, Molly," Sage observes, glancing around.

"Oh my god!" Nina exclaims, staring across the pool. "*Look* at our girl." She's watching Stella, who is dressed in a glittery blue ball gown and cape, her pale blond hair pulled back into a single braid. "Where did that perfect little Elsa costume come from?"

"Fifteen bucks at Party City." Molly grins. "And I'm amazed you know who Elsa is."

"No, Michael's niece is actually obsessed. We spent a week with her on the Jersey Shore, and I had no choice but to learn the entire cast of characters."

"Holy shit," Liz gasps, her gaze fixed to the driveway. "Is that *Jake Danner*?"

In the chaos of everything that's unfolded over the past few weeks—the embryo transfer, kissing Jake at Skipping Beach, the discovery of Lenore Smith, the positive pregnancy test, prepping for Stella's birthday—Molly has nearly forgotten that she'd invited Jake and Sabrina to the party.

Everly's jaw drops to the ground, followed by Nina's. "Wait. You invited him?"

The brief window of time Molly has to explain is closing too quickly as Sabrina and Jake ascend the steps in their direction. Jake wears khaki shorts and a blue button-down that matches his eyes. Beside him, Sabrina looks irritatingly perfect in a white smocked maxi dress that flaunts her figure and tanned supermodel arms. A saccharine smile breaks across her face, revealing those straight, bleached teeth. She carries an oversized present wrapped in glossy white paper and a pink ribbon.

"Molly, you look stunning. As *always*." Sabrina leans forward to peck Molly's cheek, her voice oozing with an insincerity that perhaps only Molly can detect. "What a beautiful day. Here. A little something for the birthday girl."

Molly accepts the gift, forcing a grin. "You're so nice to come. These are my friends from New York, Everly, Nina, and Liz. And Ev's wife, Sage, and Nina's fiancé, Michael. All, this is Sabrina Danner. And you know her husband, Jake. Small world."

Molly can feel Jake staring at her, and she wishes so badly that he'd stop doing that in public. They haven't spoken since the beach, since Molly pulled away from the warmth of his body and leaped out of his car in a confused, guilt-ridden frenzy. She hasn't replied to any of the texts he sent afterward.

Nina flashes a wide grin, her trademark enthusiasm working its magic. "Wow! Jake Danner, blast from the past."

Liz's smile drops. She points at Sabrina. "Wait. I know you."

No one speaks. Sabrina's face turns pale, her cheery disposition vanishing.

"Caroline . . . no . . . Katie. No. Caitlin!" Liz exclaims. "Caitlin, that's it."

She emits a sound that's more a scoff than a laugh. "You're married to Jake now? You've got to be kidding me."

"What's going on?" Jake's eyes dart to Liz. "How do you know Sabrina?"

"You mean Caitlin?"

"Huh?" He folds his arms.

"She told me her name was Caitlin. When she was your groupie."

"My groupie?"

Liz cocks her head, studying Sabrina intensely, her lips parted in bewilderment. "What the actual fuck?"

Sabrina shrugs, but she looks tense, her gaze growing cold. "You must be confusing me with someone else."

"No, don't play that game. I know exactly who you are. You used to follow me around Equinox and ask me about Molly and Jake."

Sabrina's eyes narrow. "I have no idea what you're talking about." She scowls, glancing toward the bar. "Jake and I are going to get a drink. Excuse me. It was nice to meet you all."

Jake rubs the back of his neck, staring after his wife, then back at Liz. He looks thoroughly baffled. He gives an uncomfortable shrug, then follows Sabrina.

Molly watches them walk away, then whips her head around. "Liz. What the hell?"

"Molly." Liz turns to her. She looks like she's been socked in the stomach. "I know this sounds crazy, especially because we haven't seen each other in a million years, and I owe you a thousand apologies, but I'm not making this up. That woman—Jake's wife—she . . . how do I explain this?" Liz gives her a head a little shake. "She used to go to my gym. We would take Pilates together and sometimes get drinks after, and she said her name was Caitlin. She was, like, a Danner Lane fangirl. Obsessed with Jake. I mentioned the fact that one of my best friends was his girlfriend, and she used to ask me about your relationship."

"Are you serious, Lizzie?" Nina brings a hand to her mouth.

"No. Wait, Liz." Molly chews her bottom lip, her mind spinning. "Sabrina wasn't a Danner Lane fangirl. She dated Jake before I did. Remember Jake's ex, Sisi?"

"Yeah?"

"Same girl. 'Sisi' was an old nickname. She goes by Sabrina now."

"*What?*" Liz's jaw drops even lower, and Molly is caught off guard.

The Liz she used to know was hardly fazed by anything. She's never seen her this flustered.

Everly adjusts her round John Lennon sunglasses on the bridge of her nose. "I'm very confused."

"Same," says Nina. "Is she Sabrina, or Sisi, or Caitlin?"

Molly draws in a breath, studying the shock that lingers on Liz's face. "Are you sure it's the same person, Lizzie?"

"I'm positive. I would bet my life on it." She swallows. "I remember because . . . she gave me weird vibes. Really weird. I was glad when she stopped coming to the gym."

A sinister feeling wobbles through Molly, pooling in her gut. Regardless of the way Liz has treated her and how far apart they've drifted, she knows her old friend wouldn't lie to her about this. Liz is telling the truth. Molly hears it in her voice.

"And I'll never forget . . ." Liz pauses. She swallows and locks her eyes on Molly's. "The last time I ever saw Caitlin, or whatever her name is, I . . . told her you were pregnant. And that you and Jake were over."

The sinister feeling in her gut churns as Molly lets these words land, her mind reaching for their implication.

"It's still so crazy to me that you're friends with Jake's wife," Everly says.

"Wait. You're *friends* with her?" Liz's eyes grow even wider.

"Moll!" a voice calls, and Molly turns to see Becky striding toward her. She's holding a platter of chicken fingers. "Can you go get the rest of the food from the kitchen? It's in the oven. We need to make sure these kids eat."

Molly nods, then looks back at her friends. "Let's talk about all this later, okay? After everyone leaves." She gestures toward the makeshift bar. "Go get a drink. Becky made rum punch—it's strong."

Molly trots down the wide slate steps and into the house, her mind a tornado. She can't possibly process what Liz has just told her about Sabrina—not now, not with how perfect she needs to make this day for Stella.

Still, it's only half an hour into the party, and she's already dying for it to be over. She considers mixing herself a stiff gin and tonic, but smiles when she remembers why she can't. A warm glow spreads through the base of her belly. Molly thinks of the budding life there—her *baby*—and feels the tension drain from her shoulders. Nothing else matters, not actually.

She switches off the oven, sliding the array of crispy mozzarella sticks and pizza bagels onto a platter.

Back up at the pool, Hunter helps her serve the lunch onto *Frozen*-themed paper plates, arranging them all on the long, folding banquet table that Becky rented for the party. The children eat, lured from the pool by fried food, while the grown-ups drink and mingle in the sun.

After lunch, Hunter initiates Pin the Nose on Olaf—Jade Patel wins by a landslide—followed by cookie decorating and, finally, the piñata. When Emma Duffy is the one to knock out the biggest surge of candy, Stella's face crumples, reddening, her bottom lip quivering. From across the pool, Molly sees what's about to happen. She rushes to her daughter, opening her arms just as the tears begin to fall. She smooths the back of her long, blond braid.

"It's okay, Stell," she soothes. "You'll have another turn."

"There . . . are . . . no . . . more . . . turns," Stella sobs, the coarse material of her costume scratchy against Molly's neck.

Molly glances at the piñata and sees that her daughter is right—it's been thoroughly smashed. A dozen five- and six-year-olds scavenge its contents on the grass below.

Guests are beginning to stare, and Molly can sense that Stella, convulsing in her arms, is on the verge of a full-blown meltdown. She scans the scene for Hunter, but he's over by the bar chatting with the Patels, oblivious.

"Hey, Stell." Molly uses her thumbs to swipe the tears from her daughter's cheeks. "How about opening a present?"

At this, Stella stops crying. The trembling subsides. "A present?" Her tearstained, ocean eyes bloom. "I thought I had to wait till everyone goes home."

"How about you pick just one to open right now?"

Stella sniffles and nods, and Molly helps her to her feet, triumphant. It's already one thirty; the party ends in half an hour. She's almost to the finish line.

Stella runs to the pile of presents and, of course, selects the biggest. The one Sabrina brought. Or Caitlin. Or whoever the hell she is.

"All right, guys." Molly stands, clearing her throat. "The birthday girl is going to open *one* present. Then we'll have cake!"

The kids begin to gather around Stella, whose expression is now happy and buoyant. A passing storm. *Phew,* Molly thinks.

"This is from Sabrina and Jake," Molly announces as Stella tears into the paper with the ferocity of a wild animal. Or a six-year-old.

"Whoa, cool!" Stella's smile widens as she flings away the last of the wrapping. "Look, Mommy, it's the *Frozen* karaoke machine! Jade has this!"

Molly didn't know that a *Frozen* karaoke machine existed.

"All Jake," Sabrina calls out, tipping her head in his direction.

He winks, and Molly feels a squeeze around her heart.

"I *love* it," Stella chirps. "Thank you, Sabrina and Jake!" She turns to Molly. "Mommy, can I try it now?"

"Not now, baby. Later we can."

"Just one song? Just 'Let It Go'? *Please?*" Stella's expression is desperate, borderline unhinged. Molly doesn't typically indulge Stella's tantrums, but she knows that the threat of a public meltdown is still very much present in her child's exhausted, overstimulated state. Twenty more minutes until everyone goes home.

"You don't even need a plug, Mrs. O'Neil," Jade chimes brightly. "It's battery operated, and it comes with the batteries."

Molly's mother appears, squatting beside her granddaughter. "I think the birthday girl is allowed to perform *one* song on her birthday."

"Yay!" Stella claps her hands. "Mommy, Nana says I can."

"Wait, Stell, the machine has to be attached to a TV so you can see the lyrics on the screen. There's no TV up here. Later, okay?"

Stella scrunches her nose. "What are lyrics?"

"They're the words to the song," says Jade, the brightest six-year-old Molly has ever encountered. "But you already know them, Stella."

"I already know them," Stella repeats.

"Are you sure?" Molly studies her daughter's face for signs of apprehension, but she just nods excitedly.

Molly's mother unpacks the karaoke machine from its box and proceeds to set it up. "Moo." She lowers her voice. "I've been trying to find a moment with you all afternoon. Is Jake Danner at this party, or am I officially losing it in my advanced age?"

Molly glances to where Jake stands by the pool—she's been subconsciously tracking his whereabouts for the entire duration of the party—then back to her mother, whom she has yet to update on Jake's reemergence in her life.

"It's a long story, but yes. Jake lives in Flynn Cove now."

"*What?*" Her mother sputters. "Since when? How does he *live* here?"

Stella, fiddling with the plastic microphone, observes them curiously.

"Shhh. I'll explain later, Mom. Let's just—" Molly gestures toward the karaoke machine. "Let's get this show on the road."

"All right!" Molly stands, clapping her palms together. The steady hum of conversation around the pool subsides as all eyes land on her. She feels Jake's gaze most acutely, her stomach tensing into a familiar grinding knot. "Thank you all *so* much for coming to Stella's party. Stella, little miss Elsa that she is, has a special song she'd like to perform with her new karaoke machine—a smash-hit present from the Danners." There are a few laughs. The sun is strong overhead, and beads of sweat prick Molly's chest. She looks at her daughter. "Stell, take it away."

Jade hits Play on the music, and Stella steps forward in her blue ball gown and rhinestone tiara. At Stella's age—or at any age, really—Molly would've been immobilized with stage fright in such a moment, and she half expects her daughter to drop the microphone and come running into her arms. But Stella's expression is brazen, her little chin pointed forward as she waits for the lyrics to begin. Molly is filled with awe, and relief that her daughter seems to have evaded the self-consciousness that she herself has always battled. Though it doesn't come as a total surprise. After all, an entire half of Stella's genetic makeup has nothing to do with Molly.

"The snow glows white on the mountain tonight . . ." Stella's voice is smooth and melodious, and so stunning it catches Molly off guard.

Molly has heard her daughter sing before, of course. Stella has belted out the words to "Let It Go" countless times, and her singing voice has always been solid and sweet. But this—this is different. It's the microphone, perhaps, that reveals the exceptionality of her six-year-old's voice, and that what she's doing is so much more than singing. Stella is *performing,* captivating the crowd around her without an ounce of fear or hesitation in her being. She's a star.

Molly is speechless. She looks around at her guests, each of them watching her daughter intently, thirty pairs of eyes filled with wonder. Even Meredith Duffy looks impressed, her Restylane-filled lips parted.

"Let it go, let it go, can't hold it back anymore!"

Stella's voice hits the high notes triumphantly, perfectly, and it's too exquisite, and in Molly's head all she can hear is the sound of his voice, the same air of graceful confidence with which he sang the opening lines to "Mona Lisas and Mad Hatters" that first night in East Williamsburg at the Broken Mule, a million years ago.

And now I know
Spanish Harlem are not just pretty words to say

Molly is crying then, and she doesn't even try to stop because she knows it's pointless; the tears are involuntary, the by-product of an emotion that is too powerful to be ruled by her own will. She hears someone wonder aloud, *Where'd Stella learn to sing like that?* and she feels more tears fall because she knows, in her heart, that that kind of talent—that kind of presence in front of an audience—can't be taught. It's something that's in you, that's in your blood.

People are beginning to stare, but Molly cries, anyway, because she can't not, and because she's so angry with herself for so many reasons, and then there's Nina placing a hand on her shoulder and whispering, "Moll, let's go inside."

The song is over, and underneath every emotion that is ripping her open, Molly is so unthinkably proud of her daughter, and then Stella is there, her little face looking up at Molly's in confusion or maybe fear.

"Mommy, why are you crying?"

It's the third time this summer that Stella has asked her mother this question, and part of the answer, of course, is always Jake.

Molly drops to her knees, cupping Stella's face in her hands. Her daughter's eyes are wide and stunningly blue, blue like the richness of the sky on a cloudless day. Suddenly, Jake is there, too, crouching beside Stella, then staring at Molly with the same blue eyes—interchangeable eyes—and she cannot bear it.

"Molly." He blinks, and she knows him well enough to know that he knows, that he's figured it out for himself; she sees the discovery and astonishment and pride and pain all over his face. "Stella . . . her eyes."

Jake's voice is barely a whisper, but Sabrina hears. She approaches them, teetering a little. "What d'you mean, Jake? What about Stella's eyes?"

He turns to her. "I . . . it's nothing."

Sabrina's gaze moves to Stella. Then back to Jake again. She looks between the two of them several more times, the color draining from her face as it hits her. "Holy fuck." She whips her head in Molly's direction, her emerald eyes narrowing. "You psycho bitch."

"Sabrina—"

"What's going on, Mommy?" Stella is still holding the microphone in her hand. She looks scared. "Your friend is saying bad words."

"I can tell you exactly what's going on, sweetie." Sabrina's expression grows livid, almost manic, as she turns to Stella.

"Sabrina, don't—"

"Your mom almost had me fooled, just like everyone else. But, Stella, look at Jake here. Have you ever wondered why you look *so* much like him, but really nothing like your daddy?"

Molly freezes. Her heart is in her throat. Something primal hitches inside of her, taking over. "Shut up, Sabrina." Blood pounds in Molly's ears, so hard it feels like she's gone deaf. She hears Stella begin to cry, and out of the corner of her eye, she sees Hunter pick her up and carry her toward the house. Thank God.

"Wow, you really are a piece of work, Molly. And all this time, I'd just thought you cheated on Jake. But this is even worse." Sabrina laughs darkly. "I really can't believe I didn't see it for myself sooner. You're so right, Jake. It's the big blue eyes that give it away."

"Sabrina, please stop." Molly feels dizzy, her heart racing. She feels thirty pairs of eyes glued to them. "This isn't the time."

"Oh, I'm sorry. Is there a more convenient time for you to explain to all of your friends and family here that Hunter isn't Stella's real father? That she's really your ex-boyfriend—my *husband's*—kid?"

"Hunter knows," Molly says through clenched teeth, praying with every fiber of desperation in her body that Stella is already out of earshot.

"Really?" Sabrina purses her lips, the vein on her temple bulging. "Does he also know you've been screwing around with Jake behind his back this entire summer?"

Sabrina's voice is just loud enough. Halfway across the lawn, Hunter stops. He turns, stares at Molly. Stella squirms in his arms, breaking loose from his grasp and running back to the scene. Molly can't find her breath; it's stuck in her lungs. Sabrina knows about Skipping Beach. That's why she's been ignoring her. And now Hunter knows, too. This can't be happening.

Several people gasp, including Molly's mother. Most of the adults have begun to assemble their children, gathering towels and backpacks.

"Sabrina, that's enough." Jake grabs her arm. "You're drunk. We're leaving."

"I don't think so, Jake," she spits. "Not until I finish confronting the woman who's been fucking my husband. What, you also thought I was clueless?"

"We didn't—" Jake stammers. "We only kissed."

Hunter studies them, his face expressionless. Stella is crying harder now, her arms wrapped around Molly's legs.

Jake yanks Sabrina's arm again, more forcibly this time. "We're leaving. Now."

"I'm not going anywhere until she looks me in the eye and admits it." Sabrina pulls away from Jake, moving toward Molly. "My so-called *friend*. No wonder nobody in this town likes you."

Molly looks around for someone—anyone—to take her daughter inside. Both Becky and her mother are gaping at her, dumbstruck, but Nina reads her mind. She rushes over and untangles Stella from Molly's knees.

"Admit it." Sabrina steps closer, lowers her voice to a whisper. "Backstabbing whore."

Molly doesn't know how Nina lures Stella away from the commotion, but she breathes relief at the sight of them walking down the steps, toward Becky's house. A few guests still linger, but Molly is suddenly too angry to be embarrassed. The anger is a sheer, blinding force.

"You're calling *me* backstabbing?" Molly's eyes narrow. "Why don't you tell me—and Jake—about Lenore Smith?"

Sabrina's face darkens. Her gaze turns icy, brittle. "Excuse me?"

"Lenore-dot-smith at Gmail dot com. *You* were the one who sent me that email with the picture. You're the one who set Jake up. You wanted me to believe that he was cheating on me."

Jake looks like he's been socked in the stomach. "Is that true, Sabrina?" His voice is hoarse, barely audible.

"Of course not," she spits. "We know she's a fucking liar."

"So I'm a liar, and Liz is a liar, too?" Molly glowers. "What do you want from me? What did you want from Liz? Who *are* you?"

Sabrina moves toward Molly again. Her fists are clenched, and Molly takes a step back. "You're the one who lied." Sabrina speaks slowly, dragging each syllable. A muscle in her jaw twitches. "You lied to me. You lied to Jake. You lied to your husband. You lied to your own daughter about who her *father* is. Now it makes sense, why you can't get pregnant. Maybe you should man up and tell Stella the real reason you can't give her a sibling. Explain that her fake daddy's swimmers aren't up to the task."

The current of Molly's blood quickens into white-hot rage, at the same time a swell of tears gathers in her throat, pressing behind her eyes. She can feel her fury on the verge of boiling over. She takes another step back, away from the pool, outside the fence now. Sabrina paces forward, her green eyes demonic and wild, and presses her hands against Molly's shoulders, shoving her farther back.

Molly nearly trips, fighting to catch her footing in her leather sandals—the slippery ones she dislikes but told herself looked good with her outfit. She nearly topples toward Sabrina, who is ready for her. In one quick motion, she shoves her whole body into Molly's, springing her backward with surprising force. What happens next seems to pass in slow motion.

Molly feels herself slipping, feels her heels teeter at the edge of the top stone step—she hadn't realized they'd gotten so close to the stairs—and then her arms are circling instinctively, though she knows it's no use, she knows already she is going to fall, and in the moment before she does she takes stock of the scene around her—the colorful remains of the piñata hanging from Becky's oak tree, the unicorn float bobbing along the glassy surface of the pool, the bright sun sitting high in the cloudless sky, the petrified faces of the people who watch her, helpless. Molly has the fleeting, useless thought that Hunter had always been right to pester his mother about installing a gate at the top of the stone steps. But it's a moot point, of course, because Molly is already falling, and she's aware that she's falling and then there is pain—fast, rough, unstoppable pain she isn't ready for—and she's terrified at the same time she's grateful Stella isn't there to see it, and when it's over there is nothing, only darkness.

Chapter Thirty-seven

Molly

2016

Hunter leaned against the side of the railing, gazing over the East River. It was the second day of 2016—cold but bright, with little traffic on the pier. The sun hung low in the sky, casting a tangerine shimmer onto the surface of the water. Molly had just finished explaining everything to Hunter—the news of her pregnancy, canceling the Europe trip, her fight with Jake, and her plans to move out.

Spilling her heart to Hunter was everything she needed. Though she'd barely known him a year, it felt safe, comfortable. Molly didn't need to brace herself for opinionated feedback. Hunter knew just to listen.

"Wow," he said after several moments of silence. The expression on his face was indiscernible. "I'm glad you told me. I knew something was up the night you called me a couple of weeks ago."

"Yeah. I'm sorry again about that. I was a disaster that night." Molly pressed her forearms to the railing. "I was so *drunk,* first of all. And in the middle of being wasted, I decided it was a good time to take a pregnancy test and . . . well, yeah. It was bad."

"You don't have to apologize." Hunter studied her with those kind, wide-set brown eyes—eyes that had never stopped being familiar to Molly. "Are you feeling okay?"

"Physically? I've been so nauseous. I can only eat really simple foods, easy carbs like crackers and buttered noodles. Teaching yoga has been rough in my current state."

"I can only imagine. Maybe you should talk to your boss."

"I know. I think I'll have to sooner rather than later."

"But how are you feeling otherwise? Emotionally, I mean."

"I'm . . . hanging in." Molly studied Hunter's face. His smooth brow, his strong jaw that was covered in a layer of dark stubble he'd need to shave before returning to work. He was just back from the Bahamas, and a sunburn reddened the bridge of his nose. Molly knew Hunter had the kind of skin that didn't tan easily, that only darkened after an extended period of time in the sun.

"It's easy to doubt myself," Molly went on. "But I've played out the situation so many times in my head, and I . . ." She paused. "This is how it has to be. I want this baby—as crazy as it sounds, I can't imagine giving up this baby—but Jake can't be a dad right now."

"I understand." Hunter nodded. "It's a completely personal decision. No one can make it but you."

"But can I ask you something, Hunt? And you'll be honest with me?"

"Of course."

A gust of wind blew over the river. Molly tugged her wool hat down so it covered her ears. "Do you think it's unfair of me not to tell Jake?"

Hunter exhaled, his breath a white cloud. He pointed his chin toward the clear sky, then dropped it to her level. "I think, if I were Jake, I would want to know. He loves you."

"But he loves Danner Lane more." Molly swallowed. "Even if he doesn't realize it. His whole life has been working toward the opportunity he has right now. If the tour in Europe goes well, there's a chance they might get to play in a few big festivals over there this summer, maybe even as the headliner, which would be major. If I tell him I'm pregnant, that I want to have this kid . . . I'll be taking all that away from him. And eventually, he'll resent me for it, and I'll resent myself. I saw it happen with my dad. He had two kids by the time he was twenty-seven, and he had to put writing on the back burner because he wasn't making any money. My mom made him get a 'real' job, so he sold cars for a while until he couldn't stand it anymore. Then shit started to hit the fan, and eventually, she kicked him out."

Hunter's gaze softened. "I didn't realize that was the reason things fell apart with your parents. I'm sorry."

"I think it's part of the reason, though my mom has never admitted it. I just know my dad felt like he was wasting his life with us, and she knew it, too, and that weighed on her." Molly swallowed a hard lump down her throat. "Anyway, I couldn't stand it if I had to watch Jake give up on his biggest, wildest dream because of me."

"But what if Jake is different from your dad? What if he doesn't have to give it up? What if he can have both?"

"That's the thing." Molly squinted into the sunlight. "Jake can't do both. When his focus is the band, there's nothing else in the world. That's what's become clear to me since he left for this tour. I can't spend my life nagging him to put me first when I know that's never going to happen. It wouldn't be fair. To either of us."

Molly thought of her father's green station wagon pulling out of the driveway the morning he left, the way that simple but haunting image had defined her childhood. And then Jake's words were reverberating in her mind again, a slow drip: *Sometimes I feel like I don't know how to be a good man.*

She wasn't going to wait around for another tortured soul to leave her, for Jake's departure to become something else that defined her, or worse, that defined her child. This time, Molly would be the one doing the leaving. She was taking her life and the fledgling one inside her into her own hands.

Hunter's gaze fell to the river. "For what it's worth, Moll, I would never, ever judge you."

"I know you wouldn't. That's part of the reason I wanted to tell you." Through her mittens, she tightened her grip on the railing. "Anyway. Enough about me. Tell me about the Bahamas. How's Blair?" Molly asked, though she didn't really want to know. She'd spent enough time picturing it in her head, imagining the two of them drinking daiquiris and rubbing up against each other on the beach and lounging in their big hotel bed till noon. Molly still couldn't pinpoint exactly what it was about Blair that bothered her so much.

"It was nice to get out of the city, be somewhere warm." Hunter shrugged. "Blair is fine. I move in to her place pretty soon. My lease here is up in February."

"That's right." Molly gave a rueful smile. "I can't believe you only lasted a year in Williamsburg."

"I like it here. Truthfully, I wish I could stay. But Blair doesn't love Brooklyn, so . . ." Hunter stared at Molly, at the golden-blond wisps of hair that spun around her face, which was pink from the cold. "She wants to get married."

Molly's stomach pitched. "Wow. She said that?"

"Blair is a girl who likes to make plans." Hunter smiled tightly. "I'm not ready for marriage yet. But we'll move in together. We'll see how that goes."

Molly didn't know what that meant, but she nodded supportively.

"The wind is about to pick up." Hunter glanced toward the water again.

"How do you know?"

"See the whitecaps?" He moved closer to her, pointing out over the river, and Molly could smell the menthol in his aftershave. "Way out there, toward the mouth? That's how you can tell where the wind is. It's heading toward us, see?"

Molly nodded. She'd always been impressed with Hunter's knowledge of the water. He knew more about things like wind patterns, currents, and tides than anyone she'd ever met.

"The nerdy facts you learn being raised in a family of sailors." He grinned. "It's cold. Are you hungry? Let's get you some buttered noodles."

Molly felt better after spending the afternoon with Hunter, but when she got back to her apartment after lunch, she was hit with a debilitating wave of sorrow. Jake was gone, but he was everywhere—his favorite hoodie tossed over the arm of the couch; his old Crosley record player on the table in the corner; the spices he cooked with that he'd organized alphabetically in the pantry; the little white desk he'd found and painted for Molly just after they'd moved in together.

She picked up Jake's hoodie and held it to her face, inhaling the scent of him that lingered on the fabric. Something essential, a spring that fed them, had dried up. It felt final, the decision that she would leave him, and Molly was sadder than she'd been all her life. And how was she supposed to keep living in this apartment without him, knowing they were over? It was torture.

Molly reached for her phone, desperate, suddenly, to talk to Nina. She didn't really expect her to pick up—it was Saturday, and she was still in Vermont with Cash and his family—but she answered on the first ring.

Molly told her everything, and afterward, her friend was silent for so long, she thought the call had dropped.

"Holy shit," Nina said, when she finally spoke. "Well, I can't say I'm entirely surprised. I knew something was up."

"Really? Are you mad?"

"Do you remember our conversation in the bathroom the night of the housewarming party? You'd just realized your period was over a week late, and you were *freaking* out."

"Right . . . I only half remember that."

"And I kept telling you to wait until the next day to take a test—you were *hammered*—but obviously, you didn't listen . . ."

"Ugh. I should have. I mean, what kind of psychopath finds out she's pregnant in the middle of being blackout drunk?"

"Uh, my best friend?" Nina laughed. "And no, I'm not mad. I mean, of course I wish I knew about all this earlier—and I can't believe I thought you were in Europe this whole time—but I get it. You've been processing."

"Yeah. It's been . . . the weirdest two weeks of my life? I just . . . I completely shut down, Nina. I haven't been able to talk to anyone." Molly took a sip of her coffee, then instantly wondered if she should be drinking caffeine at all.

"So how exactly did you find out?" Nina asked. "You stopped at Duane Reade on your way home at, like, three in the morning? And bought a bunch of tests?"

"The details are fuzzy, but that sounds about right." Molly smiled despite herself. It felt so good to finally share everything with Nina. "Jesus, Neens. Can you imagine the cashier?"

"Oh, this is New York. People have seen it all."

"Truth. So anyway, I got home, peed on a few sticks, and they were all positive. Then I called Hunter—"

"So you *did* call Hunter. You kept saying you were going to earlier in the night."

"Oh yeah. Woke him *and* Blair up, of course. He said I was just mumbling a bunch of gibberish, but he was obviously worried."

"Obviously worried because he *loves* you."

Warmth spread in Molly's chest. "He doesn't love me."

"Sure. Keep telling yourself that."

"He has a girlfriend. They're moving in together."

"I'm not debating this with you right now. But I know I'm right." Nina pauses, and Molly hears the muffled sound of voices in the background. "I should go, Moll. I snuck off for a sec, but we're all at the lodge doing après."

"Fancy. Have a blast. And, Neens?"

"Yeah?"

"You *can't* tell Cash, okay? Promise me? If this ever got back to Jake—"

"I won't, I swear." Nina paused. "Wait, one last thing. Have you been to the doctor?"

"Not yet."

"You have to, Moll. Especially since you're leaning toward keeping the baby."

"I know. But the gyno I usually see is in New Jersey, and I figure I should find someone in the city."

"My sister loved the OB she saw through both her pregnancies," Nina said. "She's at Lenox Hill, I think. Want me to ask Sofi for her info?"

"That would be amazing."

"Your mom might have some recs, too. Being a labor and delivery nurse and all."

"Yeah. I haven't told her."

"Oh, Moll. You have to." Nina sighed. "Sorry, it's not my place—you tell her when you're ready. I just know she'd be supportive, that's all. And it would probably feel really good to talk to her about it."

Nina was right, Molly knew. After they hung up, she typed out a text.

Hey Mom. You and Andy get back from Naples today, right? I was thinking of taking the train out tomorrow morning and staying the night? I miss you guys! Let me know.

Her mother replied several hours later.

Hi Moo! We miss you SO much. Grams says she's proud of you for working so hard and can't wait to read your book soon. Yes, A and I just landed in Newark. Would love you to come out tomorrow! Let me know what train you get and I'll pick you up at the station ☺

Molly put her phone down, crippled with guilt. Her *book*. She hadn't touched the manuscript since before Christmas.

But she couldn't think about *Needs,* not right now. At least not until she'd gotten a bit more emotional distance from Jake. Besides, Bella and Alexis still thought she was on vacation in Europe for another whole week. This bought her a little time.

Molly woke early on Sunday morning, nausea shriveling her insides. She never felt sick enough to puke, which almost made it worse. All she could do was ride out the queasiness, nibbling saltines until the gut-churning waves finally subsided, leaving her in a hungover-like oblivion for the rest of the day.

But this morning, Molly was catching the 10:11 train to Denville out of Penn Station, and she didn't have the luxury of wallowing in bed. She tossed an array of toiletries and comfy sweats into her bag—she never cared what she wore at home—and tried not to think about how her mother would react when Molly told her that she was carrying Jake's baby. Christ.

Molly slid on a pair of black leggings and her favorite oversize cashmere sweater. She'd just requested an Uber—she didn't want to lug her big canvas tote on the subway—when the buzzer rang.

Her stomach flipped. Could it be Jake? Had he come back from Europe early as a romantic gesture to save their relationship? Molly shook her head, dismissing the thought. No, that was impossible, and besides, Jake had a key.

She pressed the intercom button. "Who is it?"

"It's Hunter. Can I come up?"

Molly's stomach flipped again, twisting into a hard knot. What was Hunter doing at her apartment at nine thirty on a Sunday morning?

"I'm coming down," she called into the intercom. "I just called a car to Penn Station. I'm heading to New Jersey, and my train leaves in forty minutes."

Molly's phone vibrated—a text that her Uber had arrived. She heaved the canvas bag over one shoulder and left the apartment.

Hunter was waiting on the sidewalk, hands stuffed in the pockets of his black overcoat, which he wore over dark jeans. His face was freshly shaven, but he looked exhausted, his eyes puffy. Behind him, Molly's Uber—a white Toyota Camry—slowed to a stop at the curb.

"I'm sorry to show up like this." Hunter stepped toward her, and somehow he seemed taller and bigger today, the span of his shoulders stretching his wool coat. "I really need to talk to you."

"Hunter." Molly sighed, her muscles aching from the weight of the bag. "I have to get this train. That's my Uber behind you."

"Let me ride with you? We can talk on the way there."

Molly couldn't argue. She let Hunter take her bag and climb inside the Camry, then slid into the seat beside him. The car began to move.

"You look tired," she told him. "No offense."

"I didn't sleep all night." He jiggled his knee, and Molly realized she'd never seen him so anxious. He was normally cool as a cucumber. "I'm sorry to bombard you like this."

"What's going on, Hunt?"

"I just . . . look." He paused, turning to face her, his brown eyes piercing. "I feel like I have this momentum going right now . . . maybe it's from lack of sleep, but if I don't say this to you now, I'm afraid I never will."

"Say what?" Molly's heart sped. She was nervous, suddenly.

"I broke up with Blair. We're not moving in together." Hunter paused. The relief that flooded Molly's chest was shocking and expected at once. "We were up all night talking. She didn't take it well. But I don't love her, Molly."

The Uber merged onto the Williamsburg Bridge. Outside, the sky was white and dense with cloud cover. As the car sped across the river, Manhattan's buildings sharpened into focus.

"I'm sorry," Molly said. "I guess it's better you realize that sooner—"

"Wait, just let me finish. There's more." He swallowed. "My ex, Lauren—the girl I dated before Blair—do you remember how I told you she was a huge Danner Lane fan? And how we'd been to a few of their shows together?"

Molly searched Hunter's face for some clue as to where he was going with this. "Yeah. I remember."

"Well, there was a show I saw with Lauren at Irving Plaza. It was ages ago now, but anyway, I saw you there."

"You saw me?"

Hunter nodded. "Because Jake pulled you up onstage. It was after the encore—they played 'Molly's Song'—and then he pulled you up from the front row."

Molly said nothing, a collection of memories floating back to her. The flashing lights of a thousand phone cameras, the way Jake had squeezed her hand while he shouted into the microphone: *Everyone, this is my Molly*. Then, the way he'd leaned down to kiss her, in front of all the screaming fans. Jake and Molly had done this bit many times after the encore performance of "Molly's Song"; she can't remember Irving Plaza distinctly, but she knows what Hunter saw.

"Wow, Hunt. That's crazy that you were there."

"There's more." Hunter paused, something hesitant in his expression. "Do you remember Danner Lane's show at Brooklyn Bowl? When they were opening for alt-J?"

Molly's heart stalled, turned to stone. She nodded slowly. "I'll never forget that show. It was one of the worst nights of my life. I caught Jake making out with his manager's assistant at the bar."

"I know." Hunter locked her gaze.

Molly studied him curiously. "What?"

"I was at that show, too. It was Lauren's birthday—there was a big group of us. We were hanging by the bar before the opening act, and I saw Jake Danner there, making out with some girl. I knew it wasn't you because I remembered you, from Irving Plaza. I remembered you exactly. Your hair, your face. Everything." Hunter drew in a shallow breath. "I watched it unfold. You came in, searching for Jake. Then you caught him with the girl and ran out. He chased after you, but you were already gone." He blinked. "Jake played a terrible show after that."

Molly remembered every excruciating detail of that night. She could still hear Jake's pleading voice in the doorway of her apartment the next morning, the words he spoke verbatim.

Maxine—she came on to me. She kissed me, Moll. She kissed me for half a second, and I pushed her off of me. I swear.

"God, Hunter." Molly shook her head. The cab was basically stopped now, in traffic on the bridge. "I can't believe you saw that. Can I . . . ask you something?"

"Of course."

Molly swallowed the lump down her throat. She had to know the truth, and she knew in her gut that Hunter wouldn't lie to her. Not about this. "You said you saw Jake making out with a girl. Were they . . . really making out? Because he told me . . . he told me Maxine—that girl—kissed him, but that he stopped it right away."

Hunter's expression grew tender, contrite. "They were really making out. At least for the few minutes that I saw them."

Molly nodded, surprised at how unaltered she is by this revelation. Perhaps deep down she'd always known it was a stretch to believe the things Jake pledged when he was trying to save himself. She knew him well enough to know that he didn't want to lie, but he did. He couldn't help himself. Jake wanted to be a better man than he was—this had always been true—but this struggle of his wasn't her problem anymore.

Molly closed her eyes, and another memory from that night sprang forward. Her twenty-three-year-old self, tipsy after graduation drinks with her friends, pushing through the crowded bar at Brooklyn Bowl to find Jake before the show. An elbow bumping her, one that belonged to a man in tailored work clothes. His dark floppy hair, kind eyes, quick apology.

"Oh my god. You *were* there," she told Hunter, astonished. "I bumped into you."

He smiled. "You remember. And I thought I bumped into you."

"I *knew* you looked familiar that day at the coffee shop."

"Yeah." Hunter rested his hands in his lap. "Which brings me to my last confession. That day at the coffee shop, I wasn't just looking for an open seat. I mean I was, but there were tables available—I think you were too in the zone writing to notice." He exhaled. "The truth is, I recognized you again. I couldn't believe it was you. I just . . . I know it sounds crazy, but I'd always remembered you from those two concerts. I thought about you sometimes—I remembered seeing you so upset over Jake at the Bowl and I . . . well, I just knew then and there that you were too good for him, that someone like you deserved more than what it seemed he was giving. It wasn't only because you're beautiful—which you are—but something else, too. Something about you that I've never been able to put my finger on. We'd never talked before, obviously, but I just had this feeling like . . . I needed to know you."

The driver glanced at them in the rearview mirror as he hooked a left on East Houston, raising a pair of bushy eyebrows as they inched into the clogged traffic.

Molly couldn't speak, her eyes pinned to Hunter's face. All she felt was the leap of her heart, the beat of her blood in her ears.

"I'm sorry I never said anything before," he went on. "I don't know, I felt weird, and you were with Jake." Hunter rubbed his forehead. "But the reason I'm telling you all of this now is because the *reason* I knew I didn't love Blair is because of you." His gaze softened. "I'm in love with you, Molly. I think I have been for a while now. Maybe the whole time I've known you. And I tried to stop it—I thought being with Blair would make it go away—but it didn't. And when you told me about the baby a few days ago, when you said you were leaving Jake, well, fuck. All I've been able to think about is telling you that I love you and that I want to be with you. I know it sounds insane, Moll. It *is* insane. But I realized it wasn't fair to Blair to keep going on the way we were. If I can't be with you, I want to be with someone I love the way I love you. That's all I know."

Molly said nothing for an eternal moment. Then her eyes filled suddenly—unexpectedly—and she blinked out a few heavy tears.

"Nina was right," Molly said, mostly to herself.

"What?"

"Sorry—Nina, my friend, said that you loved me. And she was right."

A smile played over his mouth. "Nina was right."

"But . . . but what about the baby, Hunt?"

He shrugged. "I want all of you, Moll. Whatever that means. And look, I would never want to be the guy trying to steal you from someone else. I meant what I said the other day—if you can make this work with Jake, you should. It's your baby together. I just . . . I had to be honest with you, for my own sanity. I'm sorry, I know it's probably selfish—"

"It's not selfish, Hunter." A tear slid down Molly's cheek. "It's the furthest thing from selfish." She reached for his hand, which was smooth and warm. For the first time since she'd taken the pregnancy test, she felt calm. She felt safe in whatever uncertainty the future would bring, at the same time her cells pulsed with a longing that threatened to shatter her.

"God, I think . . . I think I love you, too, Hunt." As the words escaped her lips, Molly knew they were true. "I hadn't been able to admit it to myself, but I think I realized it when the four of us had dinner at St. Anselm last summer. When I met Blair, I felt . . . *jealous.* Like I wanted you to belong to me, not her. Which wasn't fair, obviously. Because I had Jake. But that's the thing, Hunt—" Molly paused. She glanced out the window at the sea of traffic, overwhelmed by a thousand clashing emotions.

"What's the thing?" He squeezed her hand and she looked back at him. His thick, dark hair was ruffled, his face so classically handsome. Like an old-time movie star—Cary Grant, maybe. And who would Jake be? Someone scrappier. Paul Newman, she thought, an ache in her heart.

"The thing is, I still love Jake, too." Molly let her words sit in the space between them. They were the truth. A part of her feared they always would be.

"I know you do."

"But you need to understand—it's part of the reason I'm having this baby," she went on, her mind running. "*Because* I love Jake, and I can't imagine not having the baby that came from that kind of love, even if Jake isn't in the picture. Even though I don't *want* him to be in the picture. I know that sounds completely deranged—and probably selfish, too—but it's just . . . it's the only answer for me."

Hunter shook his head. "It's not deranged. And it's *not* selfish. This baby—whoever they are—will be so loved."

The driver swerved right onto Sixth Avenue, blaring his horn as a teenage couple jaywalked across the street. "Fucking idiots," he muttered in a thick New York accent.

Molly glanced at the time on her phone; she had fourteen minutes until her train.

"You'll make it," Hunter said, reading her. "Traffic's easing up."

Five minutes later, the Uber slowed to a stop in front of Penn Station.

"Good luck, you two." The driver winked in the rearview mirror as Molly and Hunter climbed out of the car, and they couldn't help but break into laughter.

Weekend crowds flocked the street—tourists in for Broadway matinees, families with children still on holiday break who'd come to catch a glimpse of the Rockefeller tree.

"Oh, New York." Molly slung her bag over her shoulder and gazed north toward the Empire State Building, its spire piercing the overcast sky. "I would hate to leave."

"Why would you leave?"

"I don't know." She shrugged. "I don't think I can afford my own place right now. If I move back to Jersey and live at my mom's for a while, we could still see each other."

"Don't be ridiculous." Hunter stepped toward her, reached for her hands again.

She thought she might drown in the warm, minty smell of his skin.

"Live with me, Molly."

She searched his face, her eyes filling again. "Live with you? I'm pregnant."

"So?"

"So, what? I should just live with you and have this baby with you? And it's just supposed to be that easy?"

Hunter smiled. "Yes, maybe it is."

She laughed as tears spilled over, dripping down her face, and Hunter used his thumbs to wipe them away. A simple yet profound notion landed in the center of her mind: *Maybe happiness is what you surrender to, not what you fight for.*

Molly smiled up at Hunter, feeling a wave of love. "Okay." She nodded, wrapping her arms around his neck and hoping she'd never have to let go. When he leaned down to kiss her, his lips felt perfect, like the lips she'd always been meant to kiss. Something true and right clicked within, and it was just as exhilarating as she'd always subconsciously imagined kissing Hunter would be. No drama, no ego, no volatility. Only love.

Chapter Thirty-eight

Jake

August 2022

On the way home from Stella's birthday party, Jake is silent behind the wheel. He can feel Sabrina's eyes on him from the passenger seat.

When they pull into the driveway, Jake turns off the ignition. He stares straight ahead. He doesn't blink.

"Jake." Sabrina rests her hand on his arm. He says nothing. "Jake, I'm so sorry. You must be devastated. And so confused."

He can't bring himself to speak.

"What a terrible person she is," she continues. "We can't let her get away with this."

At this, he finally turns to her, his eyes narrowing. "What?"

"I can't imagine how upset you are, baby." Sabrina moves her hand up his arm and gives his biceps a gentle squeeze. "She lied to you all these years."

Jake pulls away from her, unbuckles his seat belt. "What are you talking about, Sabrina?"

Her face darkens. "You never call me Sabrina."

Jake climbs out of the car. He storms down the driveway, away from Sabrina. She isn't Sisi right now. He can't envision a world where she'll ever be Sisi again. Behind him, he hears her sandals crunch over the gravel as she scrambles after him.

"I'm trying to help you, Jake!" she calls. "You cheated on me—you haven't even *mentioned* that—and I'm still here, trying to help you."

He stops, whips around so that they're facing each other. A few beats of silence pass. "I kissed Molly once," he says finally. "I'm sorry. It was wrong."

"You didn't just kiss her. You fucked her."

"I actually didn't." He can see how angry his apathy is making her—

the way the vein running through her temple bulges—but he doesn't care.

"Don't you even want to know how I found out?" Sabrina is practically trembling. A cloud parks itself over the sun, shadowing the driveway.

He shrugs. "Not really."

"What the fuck is *wrong* with you, Jake?"

"Wrong with me?" Anger rises in his chest. He stabs his pointer finger against his chest, then flips it around. "*You* just pushed a pregnant woman down a flight of stairs!"

"I didn't know she was pregnant!"

"It doesn't matter, Sabrina. Those things you said—in front of Stella, in front of Hunter, in front of *all* of Molly's family and friends—they were . . . they were evil." He glares at her in disbelief. His own wife is a stranger.

"Okay, maybe I took it a step too far because I'm upset, but *seriously,* Jake? How are you defending her? You *cheated* on me with her, not to mention the fact that she's been lying to you for years about your own child! I mean, really? Grow a pair."

His jaw clenches. "You don't know everything about Molly and me, Sabrina." He hisses the words, watching them slide into her veins like poison. He hopes they hurt.

"Stop calling me *Sabrina,*" she says, her voice catching.

"What should I call you, then?" he spits. "Caitlin? Lenore?"

She scowls. "Molly and her friend are both deranged."

"Are they? That's convenient." He throws his hands up. "I'm going for a walk. I need some time to think."

"When will you be back?" she calls behind him, but he ignores her, already halfway down the driveway.

At the mailbox, Jake turns right, his head fogged with a mix of devastation and regret and sheer, staggering confusion. He is Stella's father. Molly's beautiful, talented, curious, perfect girl is his daughter. Six and a half years ago, Molly was pregnant. That's why she left him so abruptly. That's the reason she moved out without saying goodbye.

He wants to be mad—he's almost willing himself toward anger—but he can't get there. Jake has done enough soul-searching in the years since he lost Molly to understand who he was back then, how incapable he'd been of putting anyone before himself, even when he wanted to. It's a painful pill, but one he has to swallow.

Jake walks all the way down Woodson Road, past joggers and flocks of women in sunglasses pushing fancy strollers. He thinks of Molly's mother, the horror that filled her eyes after Sabrina pushed her daughter, the hysteria rocking her voice: *She's pregnant, you bitch!* He thinks of the ambulance pulling into the driveway just as they were leaving, its lights flashing red like shiny jewels.

The memory feels like a nightmare. In this moment, nothing matters except for Molly and her baby. Jake just wants them to be okay. It doesn't matter that he has a thousand questions, like how Hunter wound up with Molly so quickly after she left him, and what kind of father Hunter is to Stella, and if this has all been hard for him, and if Jake will be able to see Stella again, and what inside of his own soul is so permanently broken that he ended up married to someone like Sabrina.

Jake walks in a trance until he's ended up all the way in town, standing between Gwen's and the post office. He blinks in surprise. He's walked more than five miles. By the time he gets back to the house, it's nearly dark out, the sky a rich, inky blue, the last of the light a dim thread of orange along the horizon.

He finds Sabrina in the kitchen, curled in the fetal position on the window seat overlooking the driveway. A smoky, charred scent permeates the room.

Jake flicks on the pendant lights above the center island. "Is something burning?" He goes over to the oven and removes a ceramic baking dish. Whatever meal it contains—lasagna, he guesses—is black and bubbling, inedible.

"Jesus, Sisi." He places the dish on the stove as smoke fills the kitchen. He opens the double windows above the sink and waves at the air until the smoke subsides.

"Where the hell have you been?" Sabrina sits up slowly, rubbing her eyes. "I called you a dozen times." Her voice is low and croaky; Jake can tell she's had more to drink since Stella's party. His eyes find a near-empty bottle of wine on the counter, a stemless glass smudged with her lip gloss.

"I turned off my phone." He plucks a tumbler from the dish drainer and fills it with tap water, then hands it to Sabrina, averting his gaze. He doesn't want to look at her. He can't. "You should drink this."

She takes a small sip. "Where the hell have you been?" she repeats.

"I told you I was going for a walk."

"For four hours?"

"I lost track of time." He sighs. "Molly is in the hospital right now. Because of you."

"I'm sorry," she mutters, not sounding sorry at all. "Think she's okay?"

"This is over, Sisi."

"Huh?"

"*We* are over. I'm leaving you."

The water glass slips from her fingers. There's a high-pitched clanging as the pieces shatter on the floor. "What are you talking about?" She studies him, her green eyes swimming with panic.

Jake rests a hand on the counter. "I'm packing a bag tonight, and I'm leaving. We'll figure out the rest later."

"Because of Molly?"

"No. Because of us. Because I don't love you." The words emerge as resolutely as he feels them inside.

Sabrina says nothing. She looks gutted, the color draining from her face. Jake goes over to the pantry and retrieves the dustpan. He sweeps up the broken glass and dumps the shards, then uses a dish towel to dry the water on the floor.

He disappears upstairs and packs his duffel bag. A few changes of clothes, toiletries, guitar, song notebook. He doesn't need much, and when Jake looks around their bedroom, he realizes that most of the stuff in the house is Sabrina's, anyway. He grabs his work briefcase, too, and goes back downstairs.

Sabrina is waiting for him, and he finally looks at her—really looks at her—for the first time since the party. Her eyes are red-rimmed and smeared with makeup, her dark hair flattened on one side from where she must've fallen asleep on the window seat. She appears hollow, afraid, a shell of herself.

"Jake, don't do this." Sabrina stands. She runs to him, wrapping her arms around his neck and pressing her face to his chest. "Please. We're married—we've only been married seven months. We're just building our life together. Our family."

Jake pulls back, the pity he feels for her morphing into a fresh wave of anger. "Are you delusional? Our marriage is built on lies." His eyes narrow. "Who is Lenore Smith? Tell me. Because I *know* you're the one who sent that email to Molly."

"Lenore was my—" She chokes on a sob as it emerges. "My great-aunt. I'm sorry, Jake—"

"How could you? You broke us apart. And you've been dishonest with me, all this time."

"So has Molly!"

"Molly isn't my wife!"

Sabrina screws her eyes shut, crumpling to Jake's feet. Tears spill down her face, and she doesn't bother to wipe them away. Neither of them speak. An eternity passes.

Finally, she lifts her head. "You know, when we were first together—before you left me for her—I got pregnant." Her voice is raspy, sadder than he's ever heard it.

"What?" Jake sets his bags on the ground. "Are you fucking with me?"

She shakes her head, sniffling. "It was wintertime, right before we broke up. I didn't tell you because I knew you were going to break up with me, and then—" She pauses. "Then I lost the baby."

"Jesus, Sisi." Jake stares at her, his lips parted in shock. "You should've . . . I'm sorry."

"It was awful. It still haunts me. I thought you wanted a family. And I thought when the time was right, we would try for one." Her eyes fill again. "I want another chance for our baby, Jake. I want that more than anything."

"Oh, Sisi."

"*Please,* Jake." Sabrina stands, her chest heaving, her gaze desperate. "We were supposed to be parents together. We were supposed to create the family neither of us ever had. Without you, I'm—" Her voice catches. "*Please.* Don't walk away from this."

He finds it in himself to open his arms to her, one last time. He holds the back of her head while she sobs into his chest. They stand like that for a minute or so, before he pulls away. He picks his duffel and briefcase up from the floor, then finally his guitar. "I have to go." His blue eyes are desolate, but certain.

"Wait," she pleads, sniffling. "There's something I need to know."

He's halfway out the door. "What is it?"

"What does it mean that you never wrote a song about me?"

Jake sighs, his shoulders aching under the weight of his bags. "It means that we're over."

He trudges out to the driveway, feels her watching him from under the portico. There's a nip in the August night that wasn't around a week earlier, a dispiriting chill that says fall isn't far off. From the walkway, Jake looks back over his shoulder to where Sabrina stands on the front stoop, her hands knotted together at her chest.

"If you want a family, Sisi, you should have one." His gaze softens. "Don't let me be the one to stop you."

He tosses his bags in the back seat of the Jeep, then climbs into the front and turns on the ignition. Part of him wishes he could travel back in time and do it all over. But what would he have done differently? Forsaken Danner Lane? He might've, if he'd known Molly was pregnant. More likely, he would've chosen all three of them—the band and Molly and Stella—and then what? Would a different breaking point have come for Molly eventually? Would she have left him, anyway? He doesn't know. There are a million ways their story could've played out, but this is the only way that it did. One thing Jake knows for sure is that he could have been a better partner back then, but he wasn't. He was twenty-six years old.

All there is now, is now. It's a dark evening, and he doesn't have answers as he pulls the Jeep out of the driveway. With the headlights on, he can only see a few feet ahead, but maybe that's the way it should be. Jake knows, at least, where he's going tonight.

Chapter Thirty-nine

Molly

August 2022

Molly blinks her eyes open. She's in bed in a dimly lit room, a single beam of sunlight slipping through the drapes and reaching across the tiled floor. She sees her mother's familiar face—soft cheeks, wide hazel eyes—above her. Pain sears the whole left side of her head.

"Moo." Her mother's voice is smooth and soft. "Can you hear me?"

She nods. The pain spreads lower, down through her abdomen and pelvis. Everything hurts. She wrestles her way through the cloudiness, fighting to remember. And suddenly, it comes back, all of it, rushing into her consciousness like the memory of a nightmare. Except that it was real.

"How long was I out?" Molly's voice is slow, creaky. She sees Andrew, perched in a chair behind her mother. He smiles and scoots forward.

"Just a few hours," her mom says. "You're in the hospital, honey. Oh, Moo, I'm so relieved you're awake. They said you'd wake up soon, but we've been so worried. It was a bad fall you had."

"Hey, Molls." Andrew reaches over, squeezes her hand.

"Hey, Andy." Molly gives a small smile. "Is Stella—" Her voice cracks. She has so many questions, she doesn't know where to start. "Are Stella and Hunter—"

"They're fine. They're at home." Her mother blinks. "Hunter was here for a while. He left about an hour ago to get Stella from Becky's."

"Hunter was here?" Molly can't believe it. She remembers the look on his face at the party, the way he'd stopped mid-step when Sabrina revealed what Molly had done. The unforgivable crime she's committed against their marriage, the vows she has broken. Molly feels heavy with shame.

"And Stella? Was she here, too? Does she know what happened? Did she . . . did she hear the things Sabrina said?"

Molly's mother shakes her head. "Stella has been at Becky's through all this." She pauses. "And no, she didn't register what Sabrina said about . . . her father. All she knows is that you and Sabrina had a fight and that you bumped your head and had to see a doctor."

"Oh, Mom. I'm so sorry. You must think—"

"Shh. Let's not worry about all that now. I don't think anything except I love you and I'm so glad you're all right."

Molly exhales, relieved, at least, that Stella doesn't know about her and Jake. "My head is killing me, Mom. But I'm all right? They said I'm all right?"

Her mother is quiet for several moments. "The doctors said it could have been much worse. You've got a concussion and a few bruised ribs. But, Moo . . ." She hesitates. "Hunter should be the one to tell you, but I . . ." Her mother's voice cracks. Her eyes are glossy.

"What—no—what is it?" Molly's breath slips from her throat. Panic takes over, edging toward hysteria. "Tell me. Please, tell me!"

Her mother's eyes are suddenly full of tears. "I'm so sorry, Moo. The doctors said *you* were very lucky not to be in worse condition, but the baby . . ."

Molly doesn't hear the rest. She feels as though she's falling all over again—her body pitching forward, scraping rock and gathering speed as the steepness of the steps increases—except at the bottom there isn't the soft relief of grass but a dark, vacuous pit of nothingness that swallows her whole. She will fall forever. Her heart has stopped, she knows. There isn't air to breathe.

Her mother's arms are around her, cradling her head as she shakes uncontrollably. She cries so hard she can't see. She thinks of Hunter. Their baby. Their tiny, miracle baby. Their last embryo. And Molly knows it's true. She feels it. Searing emptiness where the soft weight of a promise had been.

Molly cries until her throat is raw, until her eyes are swollen slits. Her heart feels dead. She thinks of the fall. She thinks of how different things would be, if only she hadn't invited Sabrina to Stella's party. If she'd never gone over there for dinner back in May. If Sabrina hadn't walked into her yoga class. Molly knows pain, she knows regret, but not like this.

She isn't aware that she's fallen asleep until she wakes up and her mother and Andrew are gone. In their place is the shadowy form of someone else. A man. She blinks into the dimness of the room, willing it to be Hunter, but as her eyes adjust to the light, she sees that it's Jake. He sits in the chair by her bed, hands resting in his lap. It must be nighttime; there isn't any light left through the curtains.

Jake looks as demolished as she feels. His curls are tousled, untamed. The sight of him fills Molly with a clashing mix of emotions. Buried in there, a tinge of relief. She manages a sad smile.

"Moll." His voice is husky and weak. "I'm so sorry."

The space above her left eye throbs with pain, but it's nothing compared to her heart. She reaches for the glass on her bedside table, takes a small sip of water. "I'm sorry, too."

"I heard what happened. God, Molly. I don't have the right words."

She sits up a little, leaning back into the stiff hospital pillows. "Neither do I. I feel empty, Jake."

"Moll." He slides his hand forward, resting his fingers on her open palm. "I can't believe . . ." His eyes search hers. "Stella is my kid."

She meets his gaze, nodding gently. "I should have told you. I'm sure you're furious."

"I don't know what I am." He gives his head a small shake. "But I don't feel angry."

She studies his face—Stella's bright blue eyes, Stella's berry-brown skin, Stella's bow-shaped mouth. Stella's father. "It was so long ago, Jake. I made so many mistakes."

"We both did."

"She's beautiful, isn't she?"

"The most beautiful thing I've ever seen." Jake's eyes fill, and he watches Molly's do the same. He can't believe they're sharing this, the knowledge that they've created a human life together, a little being that is half of each of them. Could anything feel more intimate?

"I couldn't have not had her." A tear rolls down Molly's cheek. "I loved you too much. And I didn't tell you because . . . I didn't want you to give up music. I worried you'd resent us—I saw the way my own father resented not having the time or space to pursue his dreams in a real way, and . . . I guess part of me was afraid of history repeating itself."

Jake shakes his head. "I would never have walked out like your dad did." He smooths a loose lock of hair away from her face. "I'd have stayed with the two of you forever, Moll."

"Don't say that," she whispers. "Please don't say that."

"I'm sorry, but it's true." His face falls. "But I have to take responsibility for who I was back then. I was self-centered, obviously."

"It wasn't just that."

"It was the picture, wasn't it? Of that girl kissing me in West Palm Beach? You never really trusted me after that."

"I tried to trust you." Molly swallows. "I thought I could. I wanted to." She sighs. "I can't believe it was Sabrina all along."

"I know." Jake feels the anger rising in his body, a powerful current that makes him feel physically unsteady. "It all adds up now. She was there that night in West Palm, you know. She came on to me. I turned her down, obviously. And I never told you because I didn't want you to feel threatened or worried. But truthfully, a part of me always suspected she had something to do with that picture."

"Jesus, Jake."

"How did you figure it out? That it was Sabrina, I mean?"

Molly explains about the photograph she saw in their foyer, the name written in faded pencil on the back, how it matched the email address. "I couldn't forget the name Lenore Smith if I tried."

"I'm an idiot, I guess." His leans forward, propping his forearms on his knees. "I never even knew her great-aunt was called Lenore. I don't think Sabrina ever mentioned it. If she did, I certainly never put two and two together."

"And then you heard what Liz said yesterday? About how Sabrina used a fake name to become friends with her? She was using Liz to get information about us, Jake."

"I know." Jake closes his eyes, wincing. "I can't believe I married someone like that, Molly. I feel so fucking stupid."

"It's not your fault. You couldn't have known." Molly is quiet for a moment. "I hate her."

He stares into his lap. "I know. Me, too."

"I really thought she was my friend, Jake. I *liked* her, more than I liked any woman I'd met in Flynn Cove. She just seemed so down to earth, so honest. Maybe it was because we were both going through fertility stuff . . ." Molly's heart sinks. She feels a kind of longing, tinged with remorse. "I just felt like she really *got* me."

Jake's eyebrows knit together, the line between them sharpening. "Fertility stuff?"

Molly nods. "She told me everything, how you guys have been trying for a baby since before your wedding, because of her eating disorder. The second time we met was at Dr. Ricci's office."

Jake groans, dropping his head in his hands. "I don't know who Dr. Ricci is, Molly." His tone is somber. He sounds more defeated than surprised. "She never had an eating disorder. Not that I know of, anyway. Sabrina and I weren't trying to get pregnant." Jake watches the shock register on Molly's face. "She *wanted* to be trying, but I . . ." He sighs. "Well, the truth is, I don't think I'm cut out to be anyone's father. I think I'd be pretty terrible at it."

"Oh, Jake. That isn't true."

"Well, you said it yourself."

"What?"

"It was years ago. We were on the phone when I was on tour in Munich, and you were back in Brooklyn. You'd just told me you weren't coming to Europe. We were fighting." His eyes are impossibly sad.

"Oh Jake, I . . . I was angry. I was *pregnant.* I didn't think you were ready to be a dad back then, but I didn't mean to say that you never would be. God, I'm sorry."

"Stop, Moll, you don't need to apologize. I was such a jerk back then. You were right to know that you deserved better."

"You weren't a jerk, Jake."

"I was arrogant."

"Not arrogant. You were selfish. There's a difference."

"Is there?" He smiles dryly.

"Yes. But a lot of people are selfish in their twenties when they're young and the whole world is up for grabs."

"Not you." Jake grins at the memory of Molly back then. "Somehow you managed to be so good to everyone in your life, *and* you followed your dreams."

"Not exactly." Regret flashes in her hazel eyes. "My dreams changed." Several moments of silence pass. "I really can't believe Sabrina lied about seeing Dr. Ricci. I feel like . . . such a pawn."

"So do I. Fuck, what else has she lied about, then? There's got to be more."

"The fact that her grandparents belonged to the country club, apparently. My friend Whitney is on the board—she's the one who reviewed your application—and she said there's no record of anyone related to Sabrina ever belonging to the club."

Jake says nothing.

"Do you know if her grandparents even lived in Flynn Cove, Jake?"

He shakes his head. "It's clear my wife is a pathological liar, so at this point, I can only assume they didn't. I think—" Jake pauses. "Sabrina was the one who suggested we move out of the city last winter. She pushed for Flynn Cove specifically."

"But *why*? What did she want from me?"

"I don't know. I think maybe she just wanted to hurt you. Maybe she knew . . ." Jake's eyes land on Molly's. "She knew I still loved you."

Molly says nothing. Her feelings orbit above her, a collection of sensations that won't land. She is suddenly overcome with exhaustion, her eyelids heavy and aching.

"I'm leaving her, Moll." Jake gives a sad smile. "Actually, I already left."

Molly swallows. "I'm not going to leave Hunter."

"I know that." Jake nods. Something profound and unspoken passes between them. She knows what he's going to say before the words leave his lips.

"I'll always love you, Moll."

"I'll always love you, too." Tears drip down her face.

"I'm so sorry again about . . . your baby. I can't imagine the pain you're in. You and Hunter. My heart is broken for you. But you're stronger than you know, all right? Don't ever forget that."

The way Jake is looking at her, Molly's heart trembles. She tastes her own tears. "I'll be okay."

"Look, can I ask you something?" Jake shifts in the chair, tilting his chin forward in a way that reminds Molly of Stella. "Something I have to know."

"Of course."

"Why didn't *Needs* ever publish? I loved that book so much—I kept looking for it in stores. What happened?"

Molly thinks back to that time in her life—the long days spent writing furiously in their apartment on Driggs—and it feels like a distant dream.

She takes a deep breath. "The truth is, you were such a huge part of the novel, Jake. I mean, before I met you, I'd never even told anyone I wanted to be a writer. And you know that Sebastian was largely based on . . ." Molly's voice trails. It's surreal, speaking the name of her character out loud after so long. "I just didn't realize how impossible it would be to keep working on *Needs* without you in my life. It broke my heart every time I opened the manuscript, so I stopped. It didn't even feel like a choice, really. I was pregnant, my life was changing . . ." She sighs. "Alexis was furious, but Bella was nice about it, all things considered. I'm pretty sure she thought I'd lost my mind, but when I finally told her what was going on, I think she could see how rattled I was. I asked her not to let it get back to you or the Lanes. And I had to pay back the signing portion of my advance. It was all horrible, honestly, but giving up the book just felt like what I needed to do in order to survive without you."

Jake reaches for her hand, resting on the bedspread. "I understand. That's what it was like for me with music for a while. Without you there, I just couldn't do it."

"But then you decided to try again." She smiles softly. "I'm proud of you for doing this solo album, Jake. You belong on a stage, standing in front of a microphone with your hands on a guitar. You saw Stella earlier. You saw what she did. She got that from *you*."

"I know." Jake's eyes fill. "I thought—when I first saw her—I saw her eyes and they felt so familiar. I just assumed it was because she was your daughter and that this crazy love I felt for her, like, instantaneously, was because I still loved you. But I didn't actually realize she was mine until I saw her sing." He closes his lids, lets the tears spill through. "It's such a miracle, Molly. That she's ours."

She squeezes his hand, too full of feeling to produce words. Silence fills the room; they sit in it, letting it absorb the things they cannot say.

Finally, Jake speaks. "You could try again, you know."

Molly understands that he means writing. "I know." She blinks. "I miss it, much more than I let myself acknowledge. I feel like a coward for walking away."

"You're not a coward, Moll. And it's never too late to chase your dreams. Even the ones you abandoned."

Molly lets this sink in. She considers what they have both lost.

"Bella called me a few months ago," she admits.

"She did?"

"Yeah. She left me a voicemail, wanting to talk. I never called her back."

"You should."

"I know." She blinks. "I will."

"I still don't think you've ever understood how talented you are. Even after you sold your book, you still spent so much time doubting your-self."

"Isn't that part of what it means to be an artist?"

"To be in a constant state of self-doubt except for the odd five minutes when you sit back and let yourself appreciate hard-earned success?" Jake smiles knowingly. "Sounds par for the course."

"And you hate golf." They both laugh.

There's a spark in Molly's heart, then, in the dark, dense grief that pools there. A flicker of something like hope, or maybe clarity. He isn't the love of her life—not anymore—but Jake Danner has always been the one to inspire her most. Molly thinks of what Nina said to her on the phone a few weeks earlier. *Maybe being around him again is connecting you with that part of yourself you feel like you've lost.* She understands, suddenly, that her pull to Jake this summer has been more about coming to terms with the life she abandoned, reclaiming the identity she lost, than it has been about him. Thanks to Stella, a piece of her will always love Jake, but she doesn't yearn for him. It isn't really about him at all.

He stands, giving a wistful smile. He leans down to touch her fore-head, tracing his fingers above the bandage on her left brow, along her scar, the one she got falling out of the apple tree when she was seven.

He kisses her forehead, then moves his lips lower, until they touch hers. She lets the kiss last a few beats longer than it should, knowing it will be the last time.

"I'll get your mom and Andy," Jake says on his way out. "They're grabbing a bite in the cafeteria."

"Thanks. Hey, Jake?"

"Yeah?" In the doorway, he turns back, his figure haloed by the fluo-rescent hallway lights.

"I'll find a way to tell Stella. She deserves to know the truth. And she deserves to have you in her life. In whatever capacity that can be. You . . . both deserve that."

Jake smiles, his eyes shining. "I'd love that, Moll. I really would love nothing more. Whenever you're ready, you know I'll be there."

He holds up a hand, and Molly absorbs the parting sight of him—Jake Danner, the man she's loved for so much of her life, who will always be a part of her. And then he is gone.

Chapter Forty
Molly

The morning after her fall, Molly is discharged from the hospital. The doctor tells her to rest and to call if the concussion seems to be worsening. Her mother, who stayed the night, drops Molly at home on her way back to New Jersey.

"Are you sure you don't want me to stay, Moo?" Her mom's voice—tender, brimming with concern—reminds Molly of being little.

"I'm sure." She leans over the center console and wraps her arms around her mother, comforted by the familiar smell of her Lancôme. She remembers the day she came home to Denville, newly pregnant, filled with equal parts conviction and fear as she sat her mother down at the kitchen table and explained that she was carrying Jake's baby. "I'm keeping it," she'd said, her voice trembling. "But I'm leaving him, Mom. I'm going to do this without him, and he can't know. Promise me you'll never tell him."

And her mother hadn't questioned or argued with her. She'd listened. She'd accepted. She'd provided gentle guidance, but she hadn't inserted her own opinions or tried to change her daughter's mind. Molly feels a burst of love. She knows how lucky she is to have a mother like that.

"Call if you need *anything*, okay?"

"I will. Thanks, Mom." Molly stretches her neck toward the window. Pain still blunts the left side of her head. "Is Andrew . . . ?"

"Back in the city. Took the train last night."

"Gosh. Sydney must think—"

"Shh. No one thinks a thing, Moo." Her mother tilts her head toward the house. "Now get in there and talk to Hunter."

Molly nods. "I love you so much. Safe drive back."

She watches the old blue Honda Civic pull away—the one her mother has driven since Molly was in college—her eyes glued to its tail until it hooks left at the end of the street, love and grief clenching her heart.

Molly walks around the house to the back door. Inside is quiet and cool, the air-conditioning a welcome relief. The kitchen counters are wiped clean, the chrome sink polished and empty.

Hunter sits at the round table with his mug of coffee. He wears boxers and an old Dartmouth T-shirt, his dark hair tousled from sleep. *The Times* is splayed out in front of him, but Molly can tell he's not really reading it.

He glances up, his eyes singed with fatigue. "You're home."

Tears gather in her throat at the sight of him, a sight that fills her with shame and love and the fresh, ferocious pain of their loss. He stands, catching her as she lets her body go limp in his strong arms. He leads her to the den off the kitchen, lowers them both down onto the couch.

She sobs into his chest. She doesn't know how much time passes, only that she's relieved just to be there in Hunter's arms, sharing the burden of this pain. When she finally picks her head up, Hunter is staring straight ahead, his gaze impenetrable.

"Where's Stella?" she asks, rubbing her eyes.

"Asleep in our bed."

"Really? She hasn't taken a morning nap since . . . I can't even remember."

"I know. Yesterday completely exhausted her, I think. She's wiped. I let her watch *Frozen* after breakfast, and she passed out five minutes in."

"You'd think she'd be sick of *Frozen* by now." Molly gives a tentative smile.

"You would think."

She wishes Hunter would look at her, but he stares into his lap.

"I'm so sorry, Hunt. I don't even know where to start."

He exhales—a deep, tired sigh. "Are you okay, Molly?"

"I will be," she says, remembering Jake's words. *But you're stronger than you know, all right? Don't ever forget that.* "Are you?"

"I'm angry."

"I know."

"I'm just . . . I'm wrecked."

"I'm so sorry," she repeats, though the words feel flimsy, futile against the weight of her actions.

"Do you love Jake?" Hunter finally looks at her, his eyes pained.

"Yes," Molly answers truthfully. She doesn't want to lie to him; she promises herself she never will again. "A small part of me probably always will. But I'm *in* love with you, Hunt. *You're* the love of my life. It's a completely different thing."

He says nothing. Closes his eyes for a long moment.

"I didn't sleep with him. I swear."

"But you kissed him."

Molly nods. "I slipped." She draws in a breath. "Honestly, when we found out Sabrina's husband was Jake, when he was all of a sudden in our lives, you and I never really . . . we didn't talk about it, Hunter. It was this huge, earth-shattering thing, and you barely acknowledged what was happening. It's made me feel completely isolated."

He frowns. "So, what, you turned to Jake?"

"No, that's not what I—"

"Because it's been isolating for me, too, Molly. Do you have any idea how hard it's been for me to watch the way the two of you are around each other? All hot and bothered?" Hunter shifts forward, pressing his forehead to his hands. "But you're right. I just . . . I shut down, I guess."

She reaches for the back of his head, runs her fingers through the neatly trimmed hairs at the nape of his neck. "I understand. I can't imagine how insanely weird and hard this has been for you, Hunt."

"But it's been hard for you, too. We should've been talking."

"From now on, we talk."

"Deal." They sit in silence for a few moments. Then Hunter's eyes lift, finding Molly's. "Did the kiss mean anything?"

She blinks. "I could say it meant nothing, but that wouldn't be true. It meant something for the person I left behind when I got pregnant with Stella . . . when I stopped writing . . . when I moved out here with you. That was wonderful, but it happened so fast—I became a mom, then a wife, and all in one second. Jake and I—" She swallows. "We had unfinished business. And even though I used to think he could've tried harder to get in touch—after some time had gone by, I mean—it was my fault for leaving it unfinished."

Hunter's mouth forms a thin line. He shifts forward, resting his forearms on his knees. "There's something I never told you."

Molly's eyebrows draw together. "What is it?"

"Jake emailed me, a couple of months after you guys broke up. He sounded really desperate and worried. He said he hadn't heard from you and wanted to know if you were okay. I never replied. I should've mentioned it, but I didn't. I just . . . I loved you so much, I didn't want to risk you going back to him."

Molly says nothing, absorbing this.

Hunter turns to her, his eyes growing serious. "Would it have mattered if I had told you?"

She shakes her head. The answer comes so easily. "No, Hunt. I chose you then. I choose you still. You're my husband."

His expression softens, but there's still worry there. Molly hates that she's done this to him, that she's the cause of this deep, anxious pain in the person she loves most.

"Is it finished now?" he asks. "Your business with Jake?"

"Yes. I promise it is." She reaches for his warm, steady hand. "I love you. You're the one I want, but I—" She hesitates.

"What is it?"

She blinks up at him. "That person I left behind, Hunt? I miss her. It's not about Jake, it's truly not, but I . . . I haven't really felt like myself here. In Flynn Cove, I mean."

"I know." Hunter sighs, rubbing his temples. "And I've been selfish."

"That's not what I—"

"No, listen. It doesn't matter where we live, okay? We can go somewhere else. I just want you to be happy."

"I'm not saying Flynn Cove is the problem." Molly pauses. "I don't know that it is. I mean, yes, there are some insufferable women in this town, but when I stop being so negative, I realize that there are also some really great ones. I think the problem is just . . . me."

Hunter is silent for several long beats. Finally, he turns to her and stands. "I want to show you something."

He leads Molly through the den and the kitchen, past the powder room they've wallpapered with old covers of *The New Yorker* and *Life*— half of each, their dreams combined. A literal dream come true, their life together. When did Molly stop remembering this? Or is it inevitable to forget how lucky you are, to eventually take the miraculous for granted when it's no longer shiny and new?

Hunter stops when he gets to the alcove off the dining room, the space he uses as a home office. It's where he pays the bills and keeps old trophies from sailing regattas, along with important documents like their tax returns and Social Security cards. But the secretary desk is gone, and so are his black file cabinets. In their place is a smaller desk that Molly recognizes instantly. It's her desk from Brooklyn, from her old apartment on Driggs. The desk Jake got her their first year together, the one he'd found at the secondhand store. He'd painted the grubby wood white.

Molly looks at Hunter, her heart in her throat. "My desk. How did you . . . ?"

"You're a writer, Molly. You should be writing. And I've been terrible about reminding you of that. Truthfully, I think . . . I've been scared." He rakes a hand through his dark flop of hair. "I know your creative side is so reminiscent of your life with Jake that I think a part of me has been afraid, that if you got back into writing . . . I could lose you to that. To him, even. I know that isn't fair."

"But you're my husband, Hunter. You're Stella's father—"

"But Stella is *his,* Molly. I mean, I know she's mine, but Jake is her *blood.* It doesn't change the way I love her, but I can't ever unknow that, and it's hard as hell sometimes."

Molly nods. There's a tightness in her chest. "I can't even imagine how hard it is, Hunt. I think—out of the *million* reasons why I want another baby—that's the biggest one of all."

"What do you mean?"

"I mean that I want you to know I'm never going to walk away from us. That this marriage is where I want to be, forever. And sometimes I feel like until we have a baby who's biologically ours, you won't ever feel completely safe with me. And that breaks my heart, and it eats away at me. Because even though I haven't acted like it lately, I'm the luckiest woman in the world to be your wife."

"Thank you for saying that." Hunter gives a small smile. "I know it's not fair of me to project those fears onto you. But I can also see that maybe you've been hesitant to ask for the things you really need from me, Moll. Because of how we started. Because subconsciously, you feel like I rearranged my whole life for you."

Molly nods. Hunter is articulating what has for so long been unspoken in their marriage, the thing she says to herself when she feels *something* isn't quite right. "But that isn't your fault."

"It's been my fault not to realize how much you need this. And I'm sorry." He smooths his palm over the surface of the desk, where the paint has begun to chip. "I may want to punch Jake Danner's head through a wall, but he is right about some things."

"Jake—" Molly's breath catches in her throat. "Jake was here?"

"Early this morning."

Molly drinks in the sight of her old desk. It was the one piece of furniture she'd wanted so badly to take with her when she left their apartment, but she'd been too rushed and disorganized to pack more than a few bags with her toiletries and clothes. She can't believe Jake kept it, after all this time.

"He said he could never bring himself to get rid of it," Hunter adds, reading her. "He wanted you to have it back. Thought it might . . . spark something."

"But where's all your stuff?"

"I moved it to the basement. This is your space now. I can help you make it nicer." He pauses, staring at the desk. "Jake really . . . knows you."

"Hunter." She turns to face him, reaches for his hands. "Look at me. Do you remember that day we went to Brooklyn Flea? Just after we first met?"

He nods. "Of course."

"I've never told you this, but I couldn't *believe* you texted me to hang out after I told you I had a boyfriend. It's just . . . most guys wouldn't have been interested, if sex was off the table. But you were so happy and willing to just be my friend, all that time, while I figured out my life. Do you have any idea how romantic that is? That you loved me like that? That you *valued* me like that? Because I promise you, it's much more romantic than being Molly of 'Molly's Song,' and it's a lot realer than getting pulled up on stage in a packed arena." She steps closer to him. "Jake knows me, but not the way you do."

His deep brown eyes clip hers.

"No matter what anyone says, you're Stella's father, Hunt. You know that, don't you? We need you."

A tear slides down Hunter's cheek. Molly has only seen him cry once before, at the hospital when Stella was born. "It's a girl!" he'd exclaimed, his eyes wet, his smile reaching his ears as Molly caught her breath, in sheer awe of what had just occurred, of the tiny human that had just emerged from her own body. A miracle.

"I need you guys, too." Hunter screws his eyes shut, more tears leaking through. "I can't believe we lost the baby."

"I can't, either." Molly's voice breaks. She wraps her arms around his neck, staining his shirt with her own tears. She feels hopelessly sad, swallowed whole by her sadness, but she knows, as impossible as it seems, that this is harder for Hunter. She wipes the corners of his eyes, smooths the hair back from his forehead.

"What do you want to do?" he whispers.

He could mean any number of things, but they are husband and wife, and Molly knows right away what he's asking. Above them is the sudden pitter-patter of little feet on the floor. Their daughter is awake from her nap.

Molly looks at Hunter, and his face is her home.

"We keep trying," she tells him. "We try again."

Epilogue
Sabrina

The worst part is finding a comfortable sleeping position. I toss and turn, wrap myself around an overpriced pregnancy pillow, but at this point, nothing helps. Oh well. I'll sleep when I'm dead.

Other than lack of shut-eye, being pregnant has been nothing short of a dream. My hair is thick and glossy, my skin dewy, and feeling his tiny elbows and knees poke around inside of me is the stuff of miracles.

His father, Hans, is six foot five and was a Division I swimmer in college—I kid you not. The sperm bank didn't specify which college, but they did divulge that Hans graduated summa cum laude with a degree in biochemistry. An athlete and a genius—what more could you desire from a stranger's genetic material?

When people learn that I'm having this baby on my own, they always ask me if it's strange, not knowing the father of my child, the person who will be half of my son. A few nosy bitches have even gone so far as to ask *why* I went and bought sperm on the internet when I'm only thirty-two years old.

"You have plenty of time to find someone else," they comment, inserting their own unsolicited judgment. "You can still remarry, start a family the right way."

I resist the urge to tell them that it's none of their damn business what I decide to do with my body or my love life; that this is the twenty-first century and there's more than one "right way" to start a family.

It was Jake who first put the idea in my head, the night we broke up last summer. I still remember the way the anger in his eyes softened into compassion when he spoke the words.

If you want a family, Sisi, you should have one. Don't let me be the one to stop you.

He was right, I realized. It wasn't Jake that I needed, not actually, not the way I'd thought for so long. What I truly yearned for was to fill the hole that had punctured my heart all those years ago, the night I lost our baby. The night I miscarried. *That* is what Jake had begun to represent to me. I let myself believe that if I could get him back, we could eventually replicate the child we had lost.

But Jake hadn't lost anything—the loss was mine alone. I didn't understand that until I finally told Jake about the miscarriage. He looked shocked and sorry, but not broken. I was the only one who'd been broken by it.

My love for Jake may have been real, but that didn't make him a life-line. He was a vessel. And there were other vessels. Like Hans.

Maybe I'll find a partner someday, but for now, it's not my concern. My priority is my son, who is due in just six weeks. I'm back in our old apartment on the Upper East Side—thank God we only subleased it during our time in Flynn Cove—and I've spent the past few months turning the second bedroom into a nursery. I like to drink my coffee in here in the mornings, admiring the way I've decorated the space: white vintage-style crib, sheepskin rug, a custom upholstered glider in my favorite blue ticking fabric. There's a tall bookcase full of children's classics in the corner and an airplane mobile floating above the navy rattan dresser–turned–changing table. A set of framed safari animal watercolors is spaced evenly across the wall above the crib. It's a little boy's dream.

It feels a bit excessive, the amount of effort I've put in to decorating the nursery, given we'll be leaving soon. New York will always have a place in my heart, but for the long term, it isn't for me. I'm still freelancing—which suits me, I've decided—so I can really work from anywhere. Once the baby is a little older and we're in a good rhythm, we'll head west. Malibu or Santa Barbara, probably. A house with a view of the ocean. A fresh start for our little family. The two of us.

I saw Jake several months ago, the afternoon we met in Flynn Cove to clear the last of the stuff from the house. It sold quickly once we finally put it on the market, after the divorce was finalized. I hadn't told Jake about the sperm donor, and when he saw me, my bump just big enough that it was starting to show through clothes, his eyes practically popped out of his head.

"Wow, Sisi . . ." His jaw hung open.

"The father's name is Hans." I didn't owe Jake an explanation of the details. It had been nearly ten months since our split.

"Good for you."

"How've you been?" I'd asked. "Seeing anyone?" I couldn't help myself.

Jake gave a soft chuckle. "You know, this is the first time I've been single in a decade, and it's pretty much exactly what I need."

I smiled, relieved, whether or not I wanted to be. "Still subletting that place in Greenpoint?"

He shook his head. "I bought a place, actually. It's a loft in Gowanus. I love Brooklyn. I can't really imagine going anywhere else."

"That's good," I told him. "You seem happy." I took in the sight of Jake, and it was true. His eyes were clear and bright, his shoulders relaxed. He seemed more comfortable in his own skin than when we'd been together. I hadn't been surprised to learn—through a passive-aggressive email from my father—that Jake had left Randolph Group to pursue music full-time again.

"Your solo album comes out soon, right?"

Jake nodded, pride blooming all over his face. "It drops October third. Look for it on Spotify."

"I will. That's just before the baby is due."

"Good." He'd grinned. "I hear listening to music in utero helps with brain development."

Jake had gestured to the box at my feet in the empty foyer, the last of my belongings from the house. Overlooked items, like the Sonos speakers from the pool cabana and a few forgotten toiletries from the medicine cabinet in our bathroom. Everything else had been packed up and taken on the moving truck the week before.

He picked up the crate of stuff. "Let me carry this to your car."

From the driveway, we turned to face the house together, one final time. Neither of us spoke. There was nothing to say.

I climbed into the driver's seat of my Range Rover. I turned on the ignition and rolled down the window, searching Jake's face.

My mouth opened instinctively—I wanted so badly to ask, to pose the question he must've known was on my mind. But I closed my lips. It had to be over, my sleuthing, my relentless interest in you. Why did I still care, anyway?

"Good luck to you and Hans." He held up his hand, a parting wave, as I began to reverse the car. "Sisi." He rapped the base of the window with his knuckles.

"Yeah?" I pressed down on the brake.

Jake found my eyes and studied them. I saw the pulse at his neck, the golden-brown stubble creeping up his jawline. "I know I deserved better." He sighed. "But so did you."

I watched him get smaller and smaller in the rearview mirror until I turned out of the driveway, and then he was gone. I sped back down I-95 toward Manhattan, leaving Flynn Cove in my wake. I doubted I'd ever go back there again.

That was back in the late spring. I'd be lying if I said you didn't still pop into my mind on occasion. Mostly I think about you and Hunter and the baby you lost. I lie in bed at night and feel the roundness of my growing belly, the thumping of a little foot or fist, and I hope you'll be able to feel this again, too. Because you deserve that, Molly—you do.

The first week in October, when I'm about ready to pop, I get a notification on my phone that Jake's new album—titled *Jake Danner*—is available to stream on Spotify. I'm out for a walk in Central Park—I've been walking daily after lunch to try to get things moving in the right direction. It's sunny and pleasant, but there's a crisp quality to the air that's a welcome relief after a hot summer, particularly for a nine-months'-pregnant-woman waddling through Strawberry Fields.

I pop my headphones in and click on Jake's album. The first song is the acoustic version of "Molly's Song"—hard pass—but I tap the second track and let the rest of the album play chronologically. I read the names of each song as a new one begins. "Wild Start," "This Time," "Night Drives," "The Music in Me," "Flipping Out," "Back in Brooklyn," "Tell Me Your Lies"—woof, I'm almost positive that one is about me. I guess I finally got my song after all. There are several others with ubiquitous names, all equally catchy and solid tunes. I can tell, by the time I'm nearly finished listening to the album, that it's going to be a hit. It's good—even better than *The Narrows*—and in spite of myself, I'm proud of him.

A new track begins to play—it's the last one, I think—and when I glance down at its title, "Stella's Song," I lose my breath. My heart sinks, but I keep listening because I can't not. The melody floods my ears, Jake's voice as clear and smooth as honey.

Yellow hair, sunny face
Beautiful like your mom
Stella; oh, sweet Stella
You deserve a song

Half of me hates it, of course, but it's the best song on the album, hands down, and the other half of me really fucking digs it. I play it again, exiting the park and crossing over to Lexington, back up toward my apartment. And then something funny happens. As I'm trudging up the street, out of breath and ready to park myself on the couch with my laptop for the rest of the afternoon, I see something, out of the corner of my eye.

It's you. You're sitting outside at a busy restaurant with a woman I don't recognize. She has thick raven hair—almost jet-black—pulled up into a messy-but-chic bun. She wears horn-rimmed eyeglasses and a starchy button-down shirt. I can only see your profile, but it's you without a doubt. That wavy curtain of sandy-blond hair, wide smile, sharp cheekbones. On one side of the table between the two of you sits a stack of papers, unbound. You're deep in conversation, your salads untouched. I notice something else, too. The woman you're with is drinking wine, but you're not. There's only a glass of tap water next to your plate, a wheel of lemon secured to the rim.

I feel something flicker inside me—call it instinct, call it affinity. I just have a *feeling*. You're wearing an oversize jean jacket, and the table next to yours blocks me from being able to see your figure. I linger at the street corner, watching you for a few minutes. But it's impossible to know for sure.

I secure my sunglasses more tightly as I pass by the restaurant. I don't want you to see me, but my apartment is just up the block, and I'm too damn uncomfortable to cross the street and take the long way home. I keep my head down as I get closer to your table, my heart beating fast and strong. Without really meaning to, I peel my eyes up from the ground, and that's when I see your head turn in my direction. It's slight, just an inch or two, but from behind the protection of my sunglasses, my gaze locks with yours. Those bright hazel eyes. My heart jumps. I feel naked as I sense you watching me, even when I turn my face straight ahead and keep walking. Maybe you recognize me. Maybe not.

When I've passed the restaurant, part of me expects to hear your voice at my back, calling my name. But I hear nothing except the bustling song of the city—cabs honking, people on lunch breaks gabbing into their cell phones, their voices absorbed into the rumble of the subway underground. Another day unfolding around you and me.

Acknowledgments

Writing is often a solitary endeavor, but it takes a village to morph a flawed first draft into a finished novel and to send that novel into the hands of readers. I am grateful to so many people. Thank you:

To my editor, Sarah Cantin, and my agent, Allison Hunter, I can't imagine a world where I don't list the two of you first. Thank you for your generous, insightful guidance and unwavering support. How lucky I am to be on this team, with two of the most brilliant women I know. I've said it before, but I'll say it again: I'd follow you both anywhere.

To the wildly talented and diligent team at St. Martin's Press, especially: Sallie Lotz, Katie Bassel, Marissa Sangiacomo, Jennifer Enderlin, Lisa Senz, Olga Grlic, Kejana Ayala, Sara LaCotti, Sara Ensey, Chrisinda Lynch, Kerry Nordling, Kim Ludlam, Tom Thompson, Anne Marie Tallberg, and Gisela Ramos.

To Natalie Edwards and the teams at Trellis and Janklow & Nesbit.

To Jason Richman, Addison Duffy, and the team at UTA.

To Karah Preiss, Emma Roberts, Matt Matruski, Meaghan Oppenheimer, Shannon Gibson, Laura Lewis, Stephanie Noonan, Sam Schlaifer, and the teams at Belletrist, Rebelle Media, Refinery29, and Hulu. You've helped my work reach many more readers, and you've made my wildest dream come true.

To Anna Faris, and to Abby Wike and the team at A&E.

To Crystal Patriarche and the team at BookSparks.

To everyone at Book of the Month.

To Joycie Hunter, for providing early feedback, and for reading my work so willingly (and quickly!) every single time. Your encouragement of my writing over the years has meant the world. I love you big.

To my mom, for being an early, devoted reader—I can't tell you how much I value your opinion and your notes. You are my best friend. White wine should always be chilled.

To Ben Cronin, for going above and beyond to answer my (many) questions about the music industry. This book is better thanks to your thoughtful and comprehensive feedback. Danner Lane has nothing on Gilligan Moss.

To Martha McAndrews, for your extremely helpful feedback. I value our friendship so much.

To my readers. You are the reason I'm able to keep writing.

To all the booksellers and librarians.

To my incredible friends—time has shown me who the true ones are. Thank you for being there with loyalty and love.

To my family, for absolutely everything. You're my heart.

To Rob—my sun rises and sets on you and James. Thank you for being such an extraordinary partner and father and for loving me exactly as I am. I'm endlessly proud of the life we're building together. How did we get so lucky?

To my James—you were a tiny speck when I started writing this book at the beginning of 2020, growing bigger and bigger in my belly as I raced to finish it before your arrival. Safe to say, I think this one was a team effort. Thank you for being there to give me strength and persistence during a year when it was not always easy to write. You are pure magic, baby. The greatest gift of my life is being your mama.